MARTIAN GHOST CENTAUR

ONI PRESS
AN ONI PRESS PUBLICATION

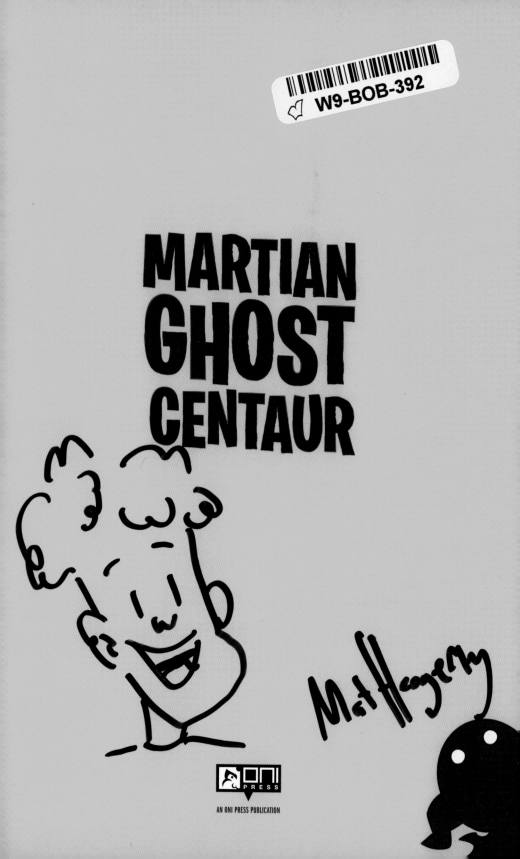

MARTIAN
GHOST
CENTAUR

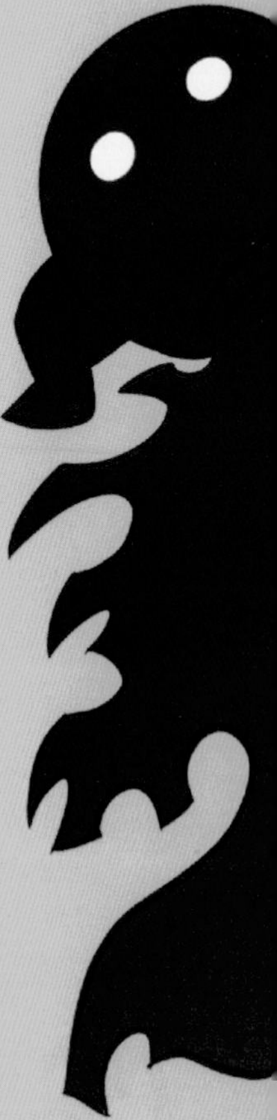

Written by MAT HEAGERTY
Illustrated by STEPH MIDED
Lettered by HASSAN OTSMANE-ELHAOU

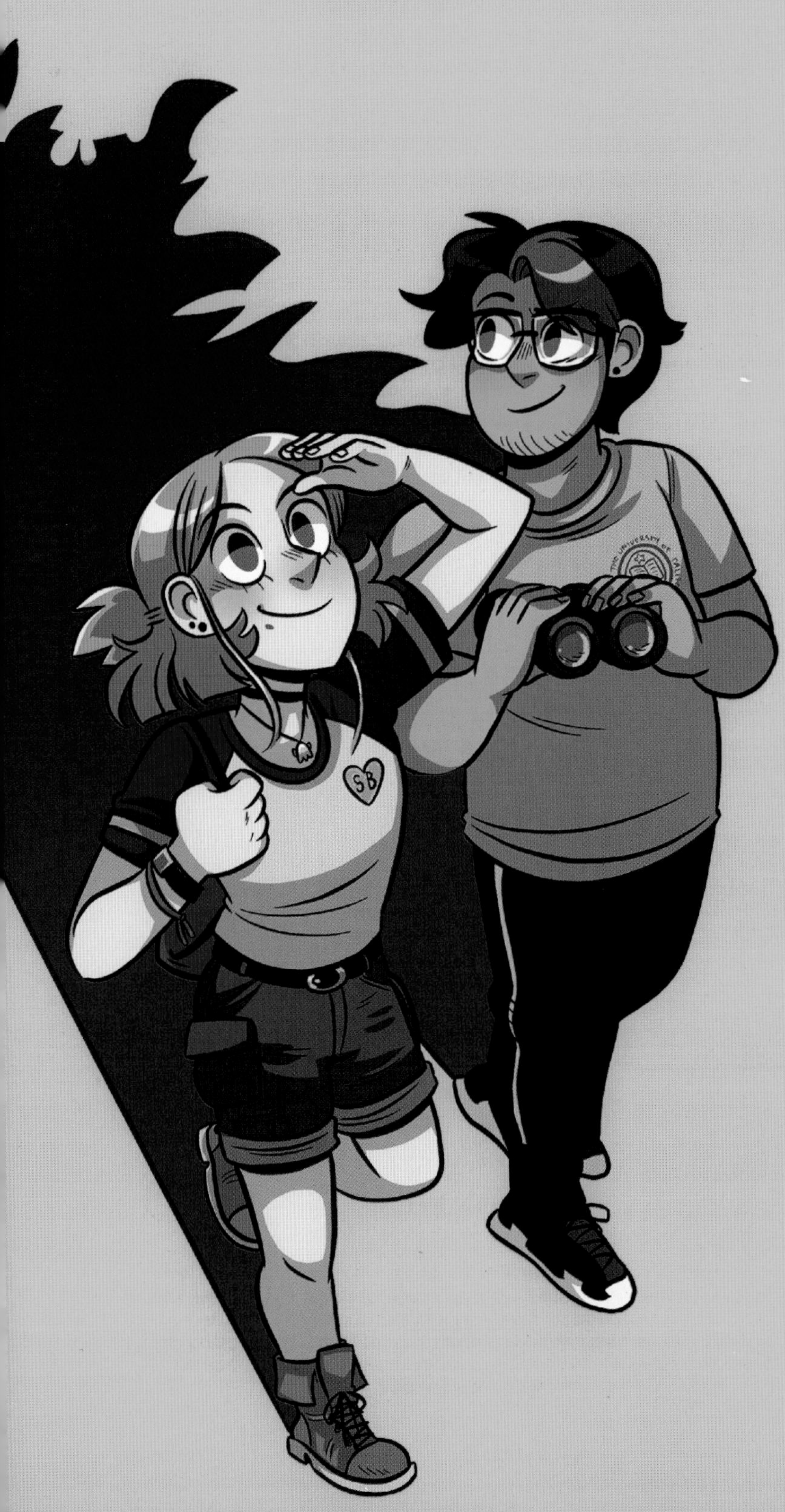
SB

Title logo design by SHAWN LEE
Designed by SONJA SYNAK
Edited by GRACE SCHEIPETER

PUBLISHED BY ONI-LION FORGE PUBLISHING GROUP, LLC

JAMES LUCAS JONES, PRESIDENT & PUBLISHER · SARAH GAYDOS, EDITOR IN CHIEF · CHARLIE CHU, E.V.P. OF CREATIVE & BUSINESS DEVELOPMENT · BRAD ROOKS, DIRECTOR OF OPERATIONS · AMBER O'NEILL, SPECIAL PROJECTS MANAGER · MARGOT WOOD, DIRECTOR OF MARKETING & SALES DEVIN FUNCHES, SALES & MARKETING MANAGER · KATIE SAINZ, MARKETING MANAGER · TARA LEHMANN, PUBLICIST · TROY LOOK, DIRECTOR OF DESIGN & PRODUCTION · KATE Z. STONE, SENIOR GRAPHIC DESIGNER · SONJA SYNAK, GRAPHIC DESIGNER · HILARY THOMPSON, GRAPHIC DESIGNER · SARAH ROCKWELL, GRAPHIC DESIGNER · ANGIE KNOWLES, DIGITAL PREPRESS LEAD · VINCENT KUKUA, DIGITAL PREPRESS TECHNICIAN · JASMINE AMIRI, SENIOR EDITOR · SHAWNA GORE, SENIOR EDITOR · AMANDA MEADOWS, SENIOR EDITOR · ROBERT MEYERS, SENIOR EDITOR, LICENSING · DESIREE RODRIGUEZ, EDITOR · GRACE SCHEIPETER, EDITOR · ZACK SOTO, EDITOR CHRIS CERASI, EDITORIAL COORDINATOR · STEVE ELLIS, VICE PRESIDENT OF GAMES · BEN EISNER, GAME DEVELOPER · MICHELLE NGUYEN, EXECUTIVE ASSISTANT · JUNG LEE, LOGISTICS COORDINATOR

JOE NOZEMACK, PUBLISHER EMERITUS

ONIPRESS.COM 🅕 · 🅨 · 🅘 LIONFORGE.COM

MATHEAGERTY.COM
STEPHMIDED.COM
HASSANOE.CO.UK

FIRST EDITION: MARCH 2021
ISBN: 978-1-62010-849-9
EISBN: 978-1-62010-850-5

1 2 3 4 5 6 7 8 9 10

LIBRARY OF CONGRESS CONTROL NUMBER: 2020939447

To my heartbeats: Blair, Ollie, and Wilder.

–Mat Heagerty

To my family and friends, but mostly to
my cats Mooshie and Dipper, who don't
understand the concept of books,
but deserve it anyways.

–Steph Mided

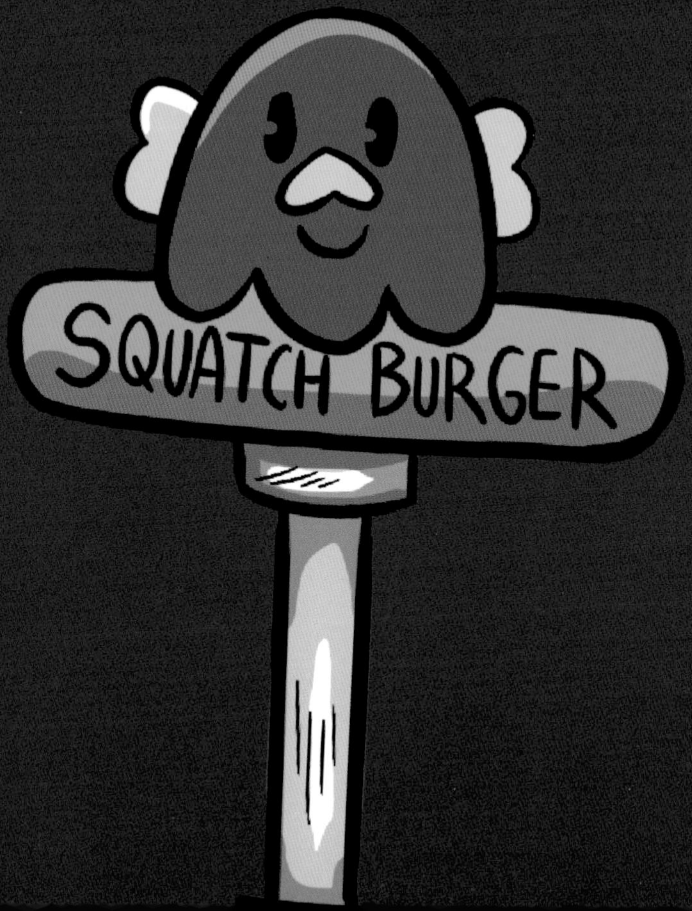
SQUATCH BURGER

CHAPTER 1

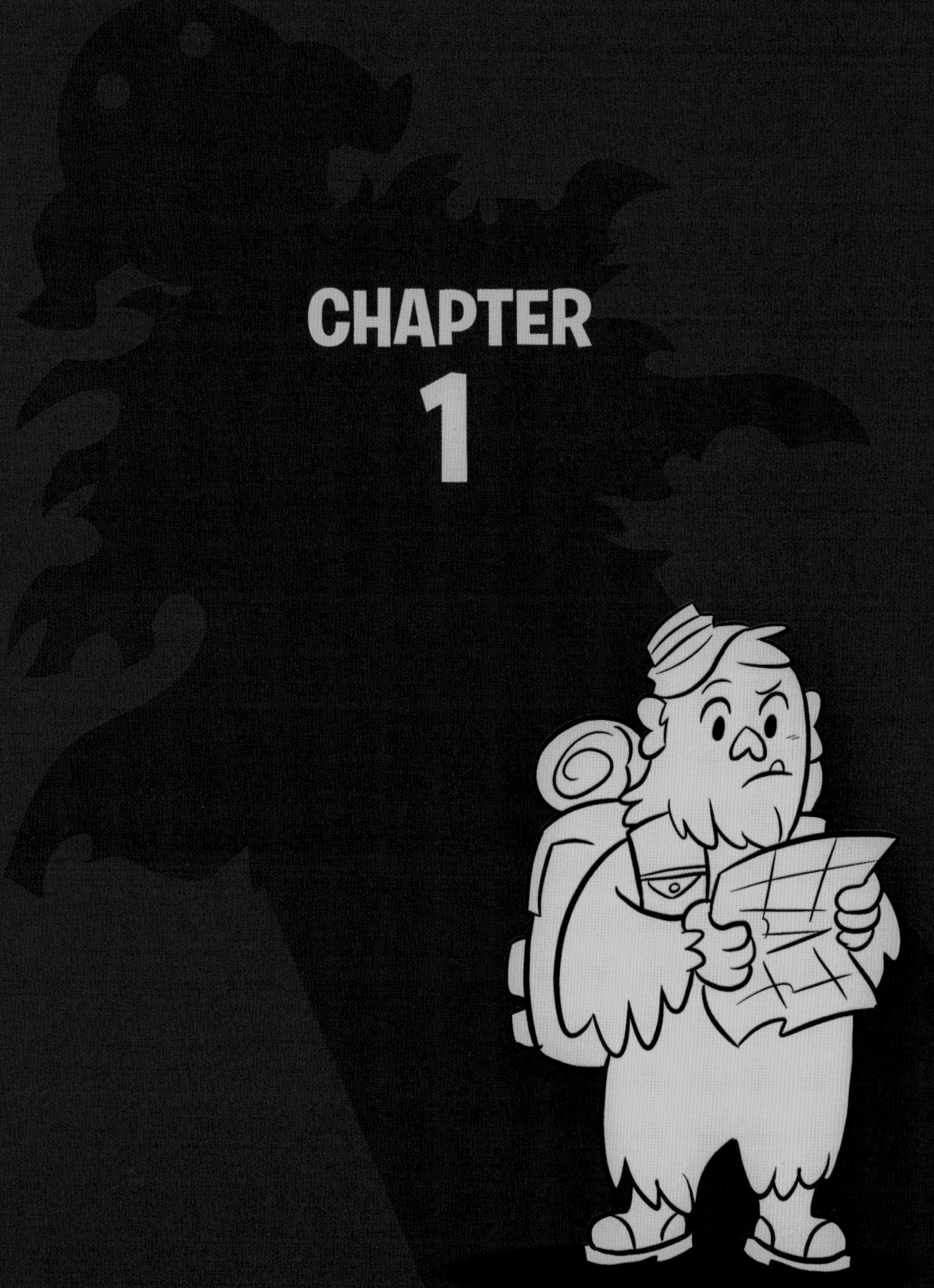

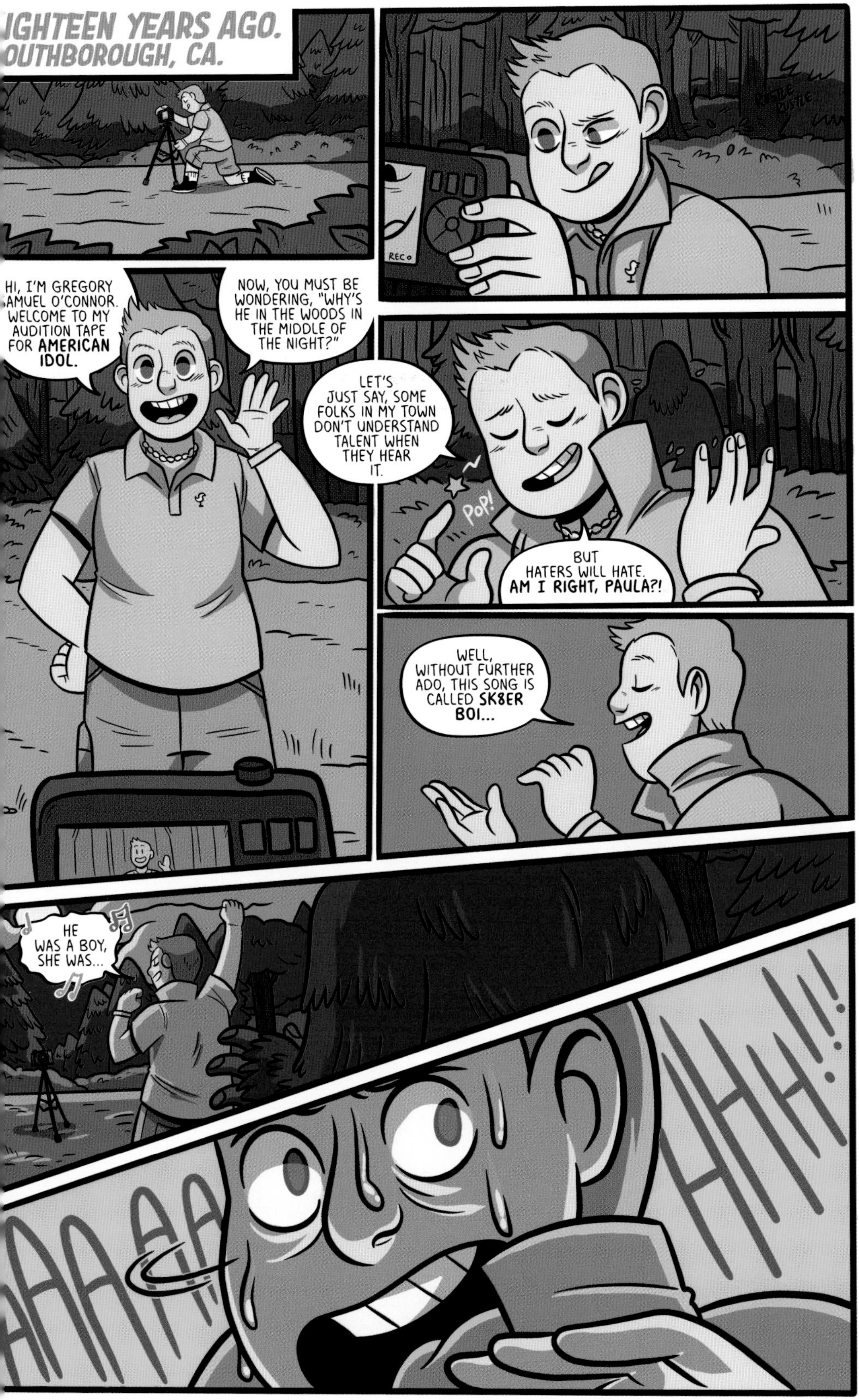
IGHTEEN YEARS AGO.
OUTHBOROUGH, CA.
RUSTLE RUSTLE
REC
HI, I'M GREGORY SAMUEL O'CONNOR. WELCOME TO MY AUDITION TAPE FOR **AMERICAN IDOL.**
NOW, YOU MUST BE WONDERING, "WHY'S HE IN THE WOODS IN THE MIDDLE OF THE NIGHT?"
LET'S JUST SAY, SOME FOLKS IN MY TOWN DON'T UNDERSTAND TALENT WHEN THEY HEAR IT.
POP!
BUT HATERS WILL HATE. **AM I RIGHT, PAULA?!**
WELL, WITHOUT FURTHER ADO, THIS SONG IS CALLED **SK8ER BOI...**
HE WAS A BOY, SHE WAS...
AAAAAHHH!!!

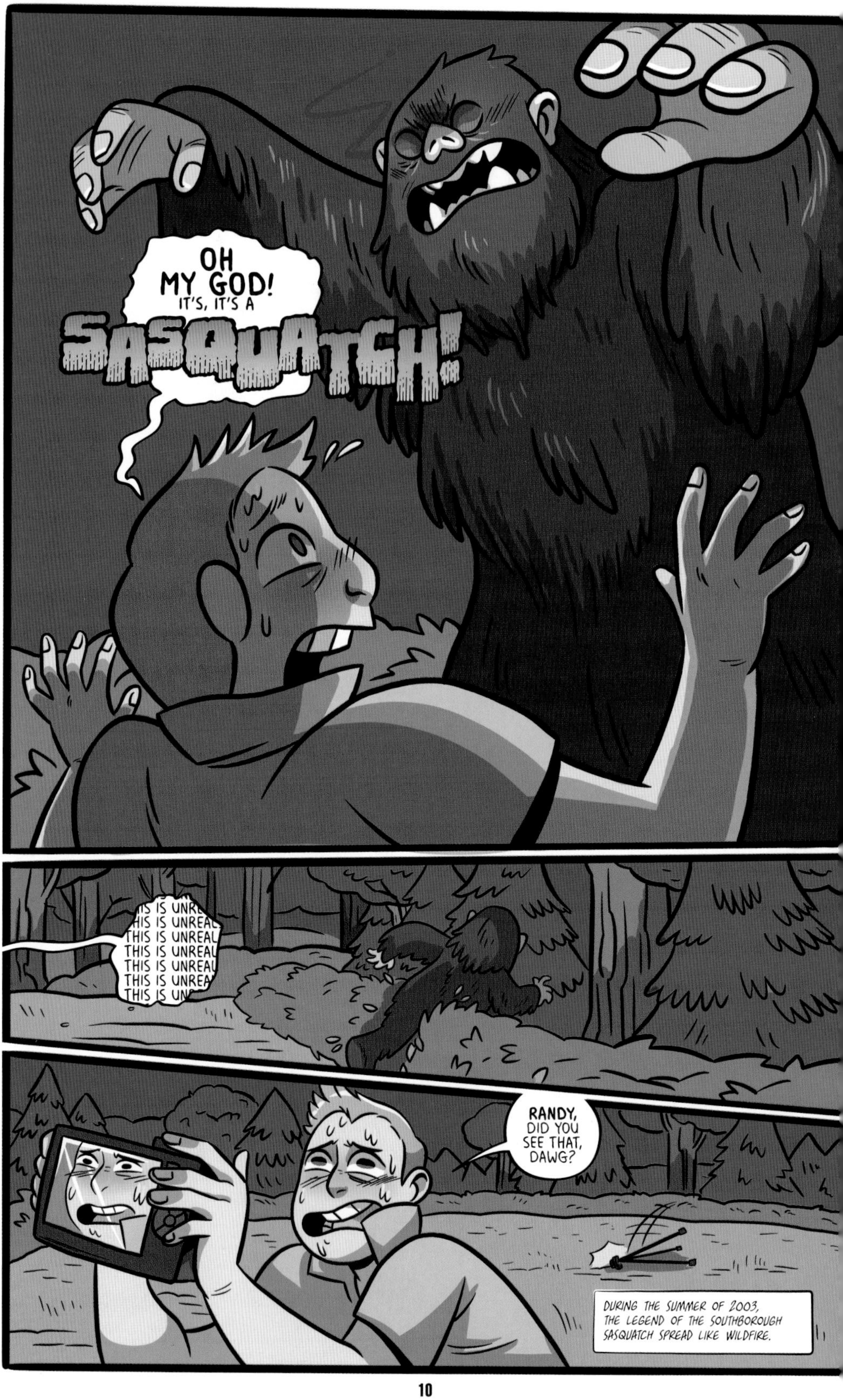
OH MY GOD! IT'S, IT'S A SASQUATCH!
THIS IS UNREAL THIS IS UNREAL THIS IS UNREAL THIS IS UNREAL THIS IS UNREAL THIS IS UNREAL
RANDY, DID YOU SEE THAT, DAWG?
DURING THE SUMMER OF 2003, THE LEGEND OF THE SOUTHBOROUGH SASQUATCH SPREAD LIKE WILDFIRE.

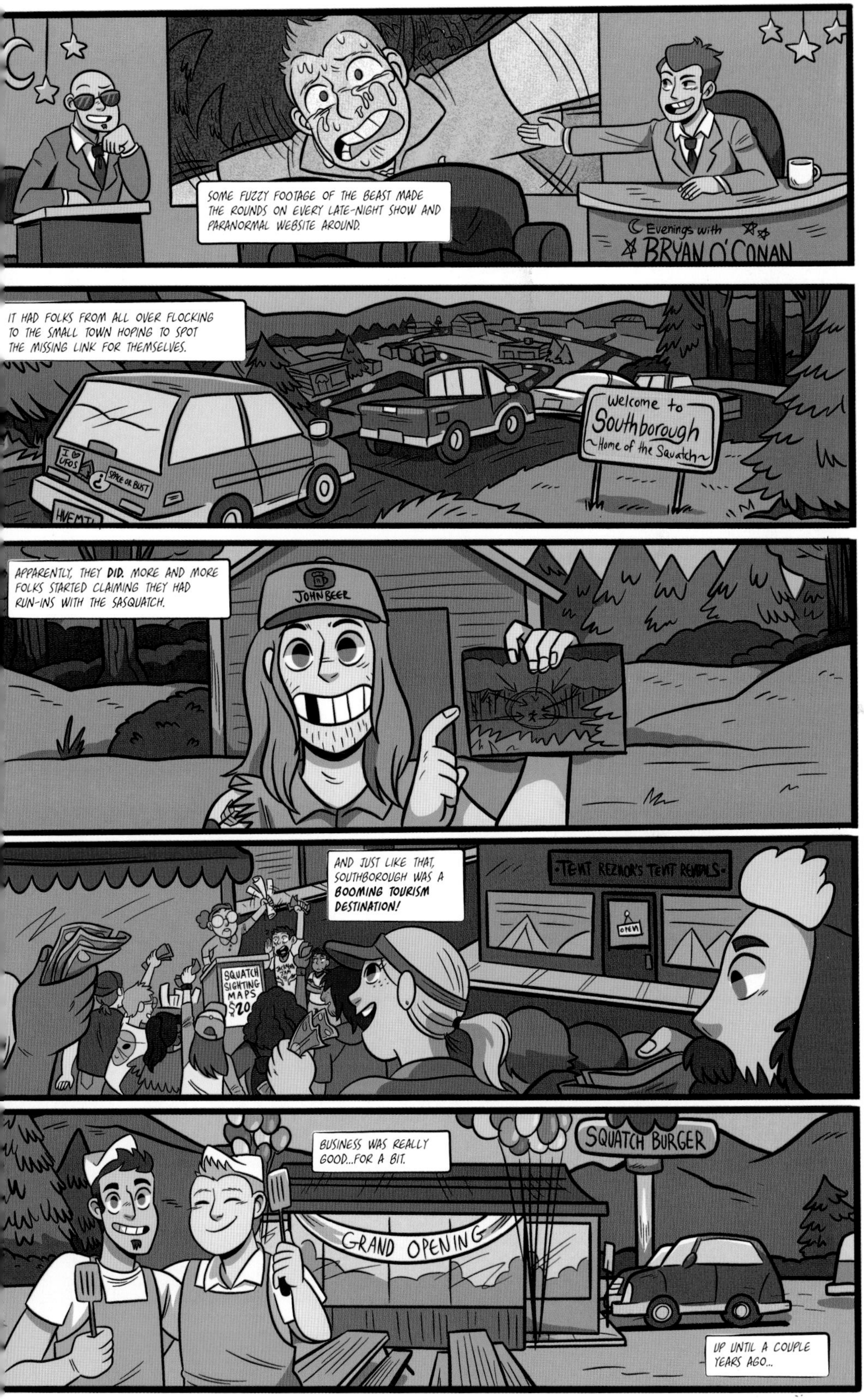
SOME FUZZY FOOTAGE OF THE BEAST MADE THE ROUNDS ON EVERY LATE-NIGHT SHOW AND PARANORMAL WEBSITE AROUND.
Evenings with
BRYAN O'CONAN
IT HAD FOLKS FROM ALL OVER FLOCKING TO THE SMALL TOWN HOPING TO SPOT THE MISSING LINK FOR THEMSELVES.
Welcome to
Southborough
Home of the Squatch
I ♥ UFOS
SPACE OR BUST
APPARENTLY, THEY **DID.** MORE AND MORE FOLKS STARTED CLAIMING THEY HAD RUN-INS WITH THE SASQUATCH.
JOHN BEER
AND JUST LIKE THAT, SOUTHBOROUGH WAS A **BOOMING TOURISM DESTINATION!**
TENT REZNOR'S TENT RENTALS
OPEN
SQUATCH SIGHTING MAPS $20
BUSINESS WAS REALLY GOOD...FOR A BIT.
SQUATCH BURGER
GRAND OPENING
UP UNTIL A COUPLE YEARS AGO...

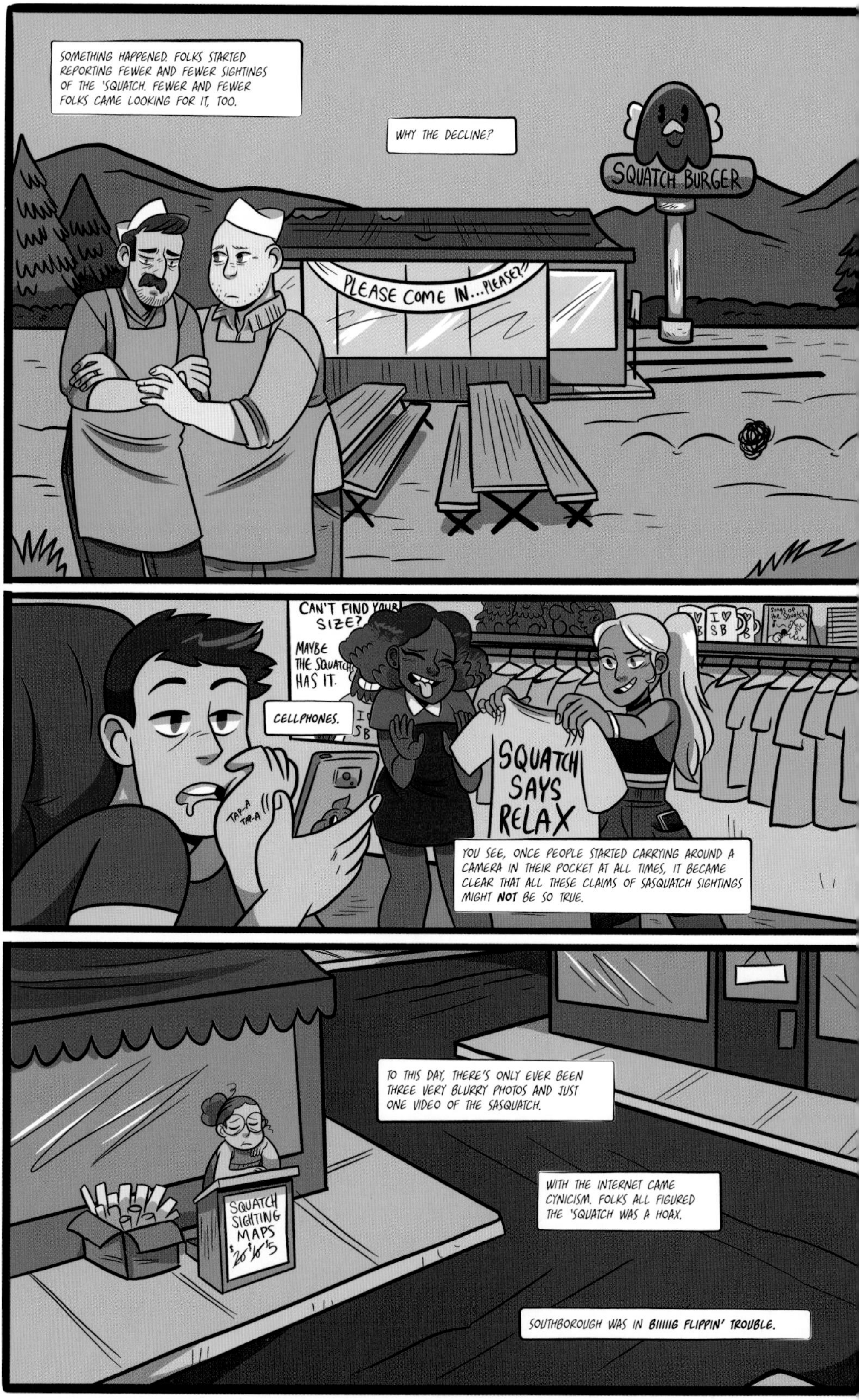
SOMETHING HAPPENED. FOLKS STARTED REPORTING FEWER AND FEWER SIGHTINGS OF THE 'SQUATCH. FEWER AND FEWER FOLKS CAME LOOKING FOR IT, TOO.
WHY THE DECLINE?
SQUATCH BURGER
PLEASE COME IN...PLEASE?
CAN'T FIND YOUR SIZE?
MAYBE THE SQUATCH HAS IT.
CELLPHONES.
TAP-A TAP-A
SQUATCH SAYS RELAX
YOU SEE, ONCE PEOPLE STARTED CARRYING AROUND A CAMERA IN THEIR POCKET AT ALL TIMES, IT BECAME CLEAR THAT ALL THESE CLAIMS OF SASQUATCH SIGHTINGS MIGHT **NOT** BE SO TRUE.
TO THIS DAY, THERE'S ONLY EVER BEEN THREE VERY BLURRY PHOTOS AND JUST ONE VIDEO OF THE SASQUATCH.
SQUATCH SIGHTING MAPS
WITH THE INTERNET CAME CYNICISM. FOLKS ALL FIGURED THE 'SQUATCH WAS A HOAX.
SOUTHBOROUGH WAS IN **BIIIIIG FLIPPIN' TROUBLE.**

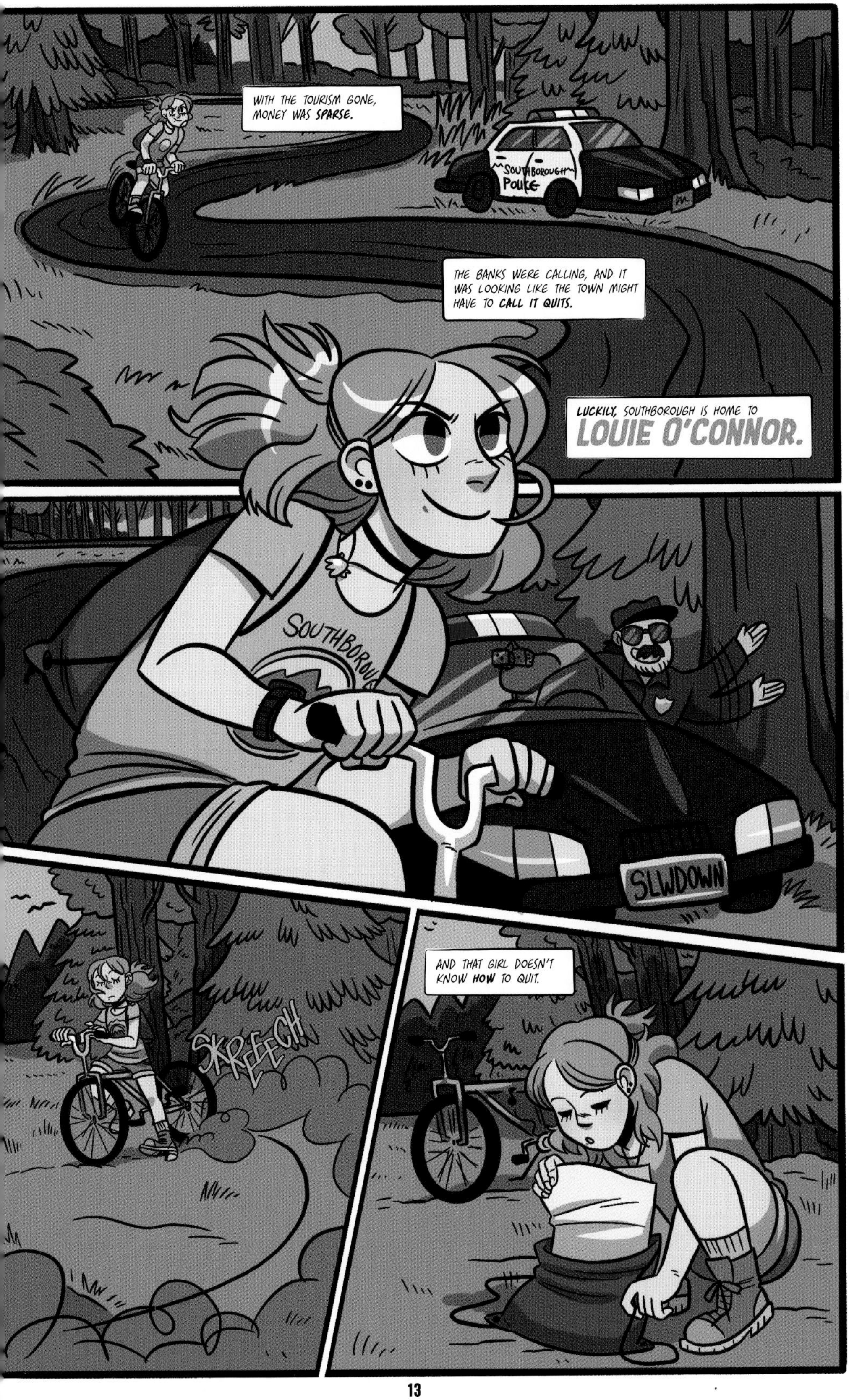
WITH THE TOURISM GONE, MONEY WAS SPARSE.
SOUTHBOROUGH POLICE
THE BANKS WERE CALLING, AND IT WAS LOOKING LIKE THE TOWN MIGHT HAVE TO CALL IT QUITS.
LUCKILY, SOUTHBOROUGH IS HOME TO LOUIE O'CONNOR.
SOUTHBOROU
SLWDOWN
SKREEECH!
AND THAT GIRL DOESN'T KNOW HOW TO QUIT.

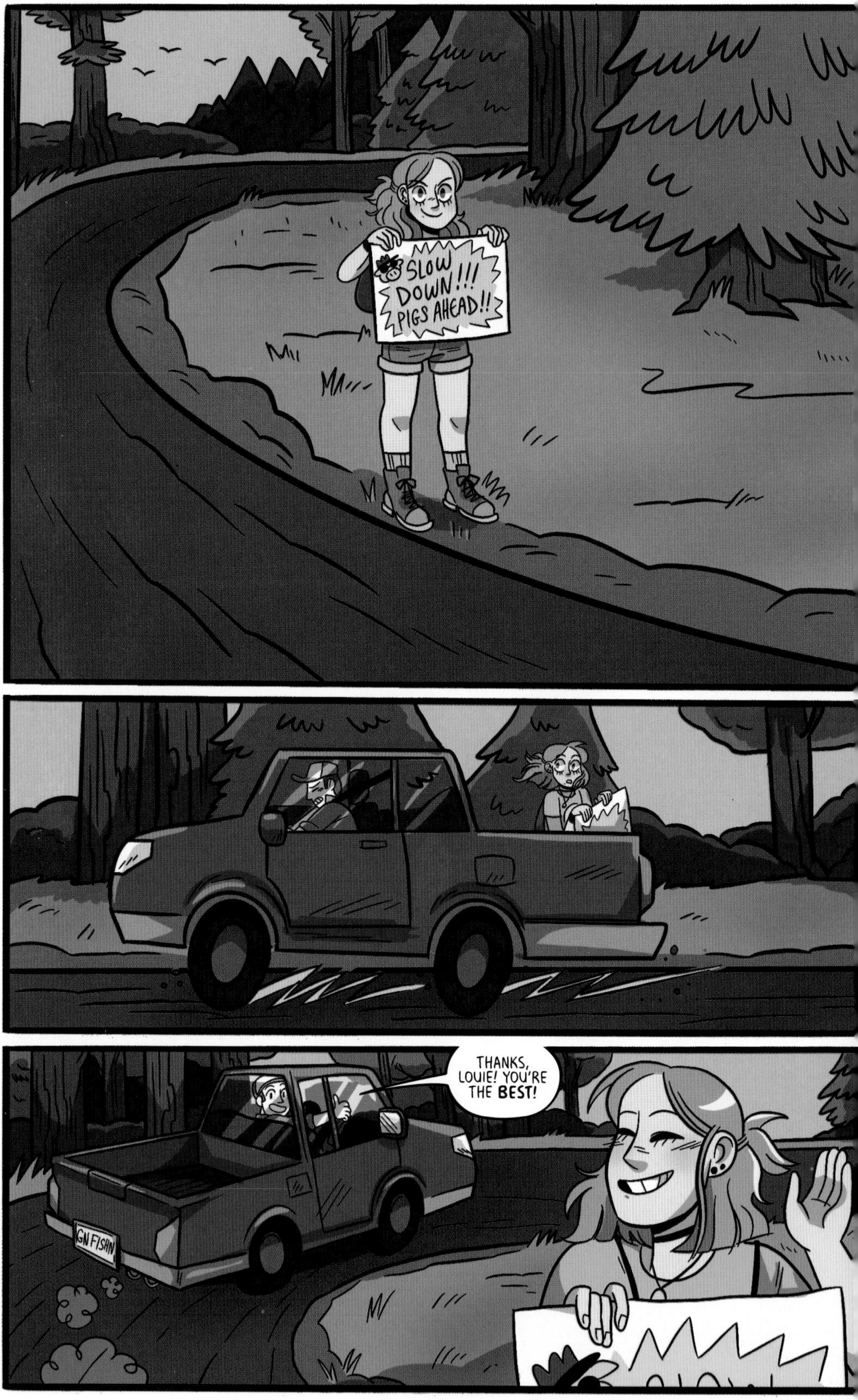

SLOW DOWN!!! PIGS AHEAD!!
THANKS, LOUIE! YOU'RE THE **BEST!**
GN FISHN

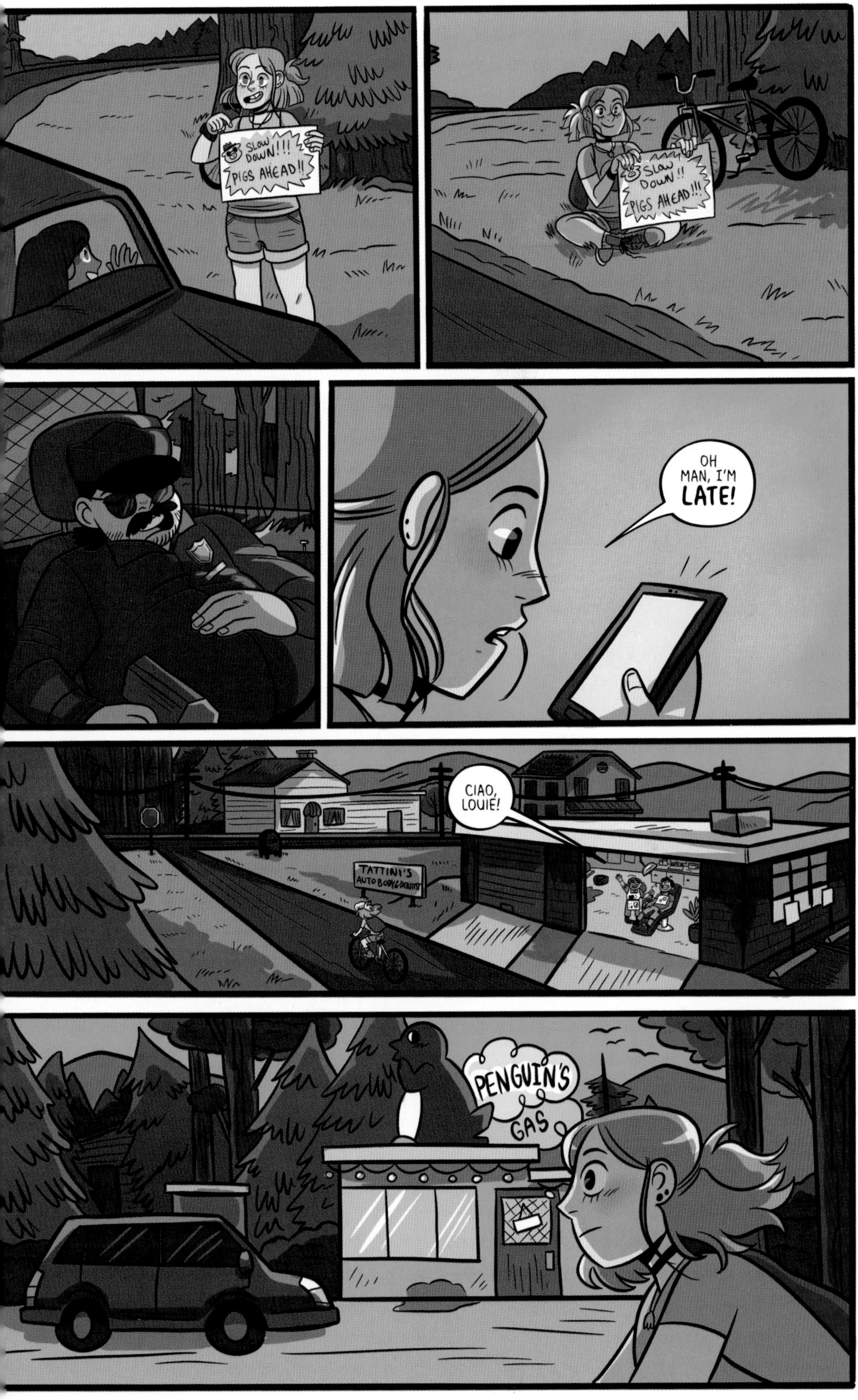
SLOW DOWN!!! PIGS AHEAD!!
SLOW DOWN!! PIGS AHEAD!!!
OH MAN, I'M LATE!
TATTINI'S AUTO BODY & DENTIST
CIAO, LOUIE!
PENGUIN'S GAS

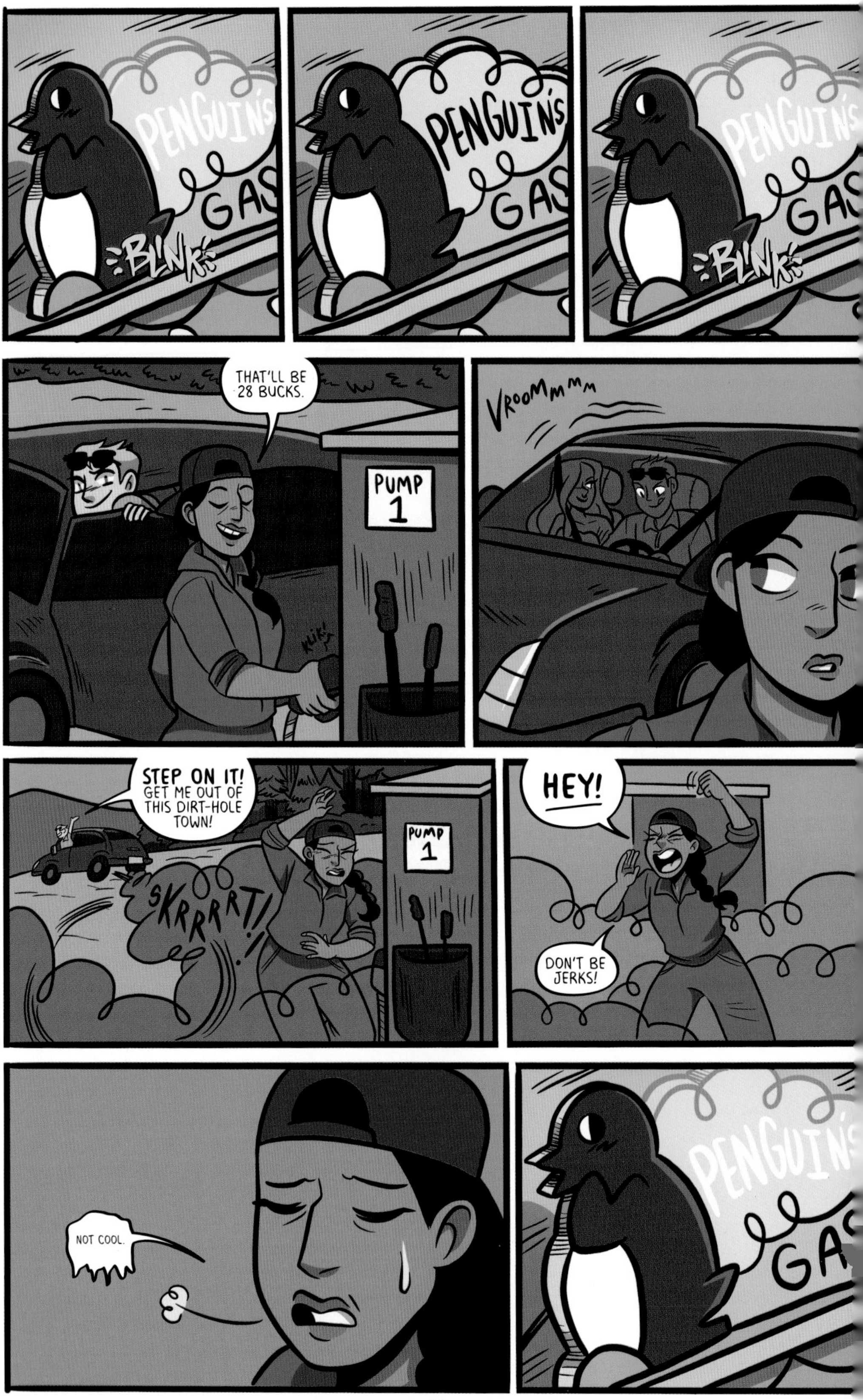
PENGUIN'S
GAS
BLINK
PENGUIN'S
GAS
PENGUIN'S
GAS
BLINK
THAT'LL BE 28 BUCKS.
PUMP 1
KLIK
VROOMMMM
STEP ON IT! GET ME OUT OF THIS DIRT-HOLE TOWN!
SKRRRRT!
PUMP 1
HEY!
DON'T BE JERKS!
NOT COOL.
PENGUIN'S
GAS

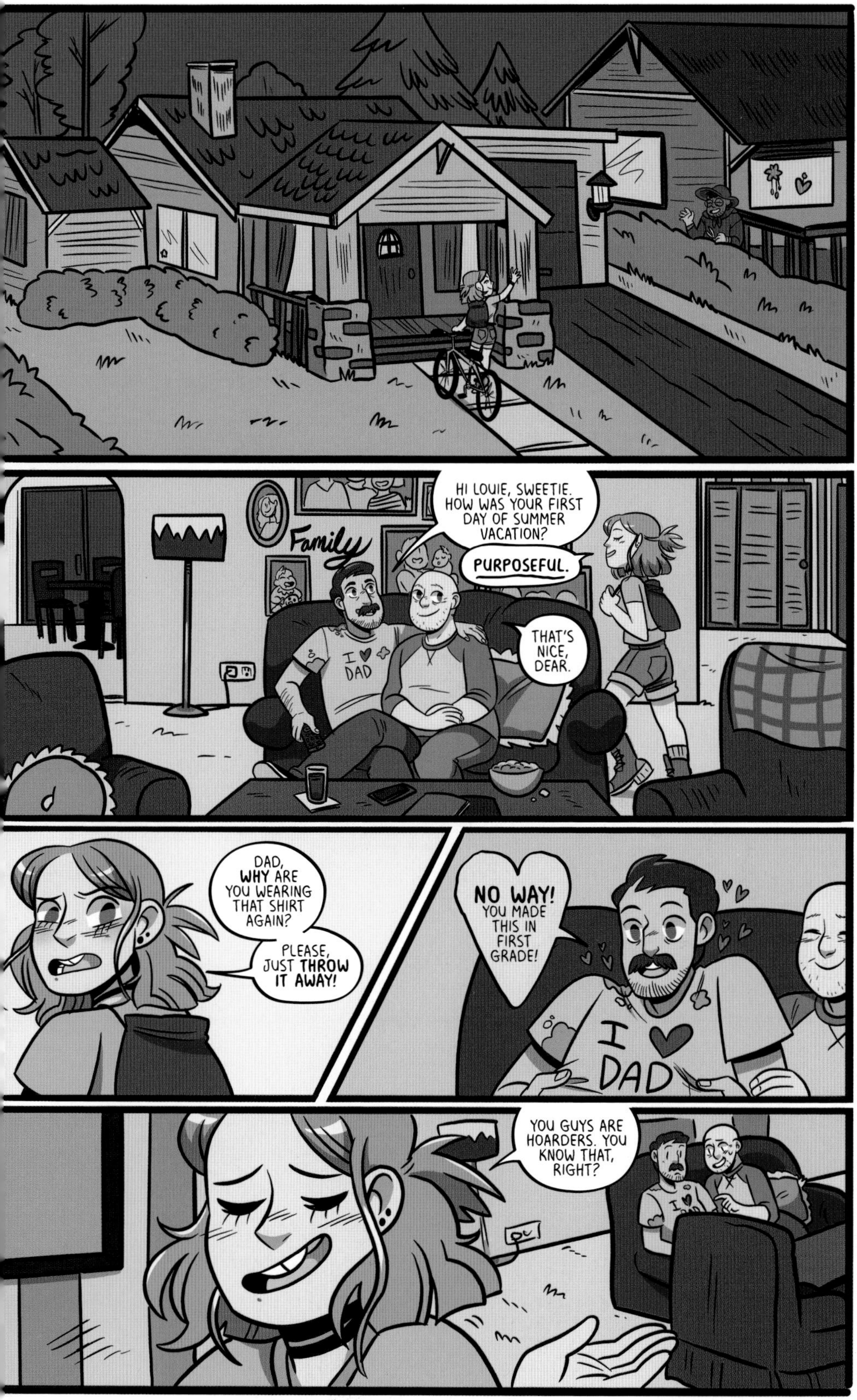

HI LOUIE, SWEETIE. HOW WAS YOUR FIRST DAY OF SUMMER VACATION?
PURPOSEFUL.
THAT'S NICE, DEAR.
Family
DAD, WHY ARE YOU WEARING THAT SHIRT AGAIN?
PLEASE, JUST THROW IT AWAY!
NO WAY! YOU MADE THIS IN FIRST GRADE!
I ♥ DAD
YOU GUYS ARE HOARDERS. YOU KNOW THAT, RIGHT?

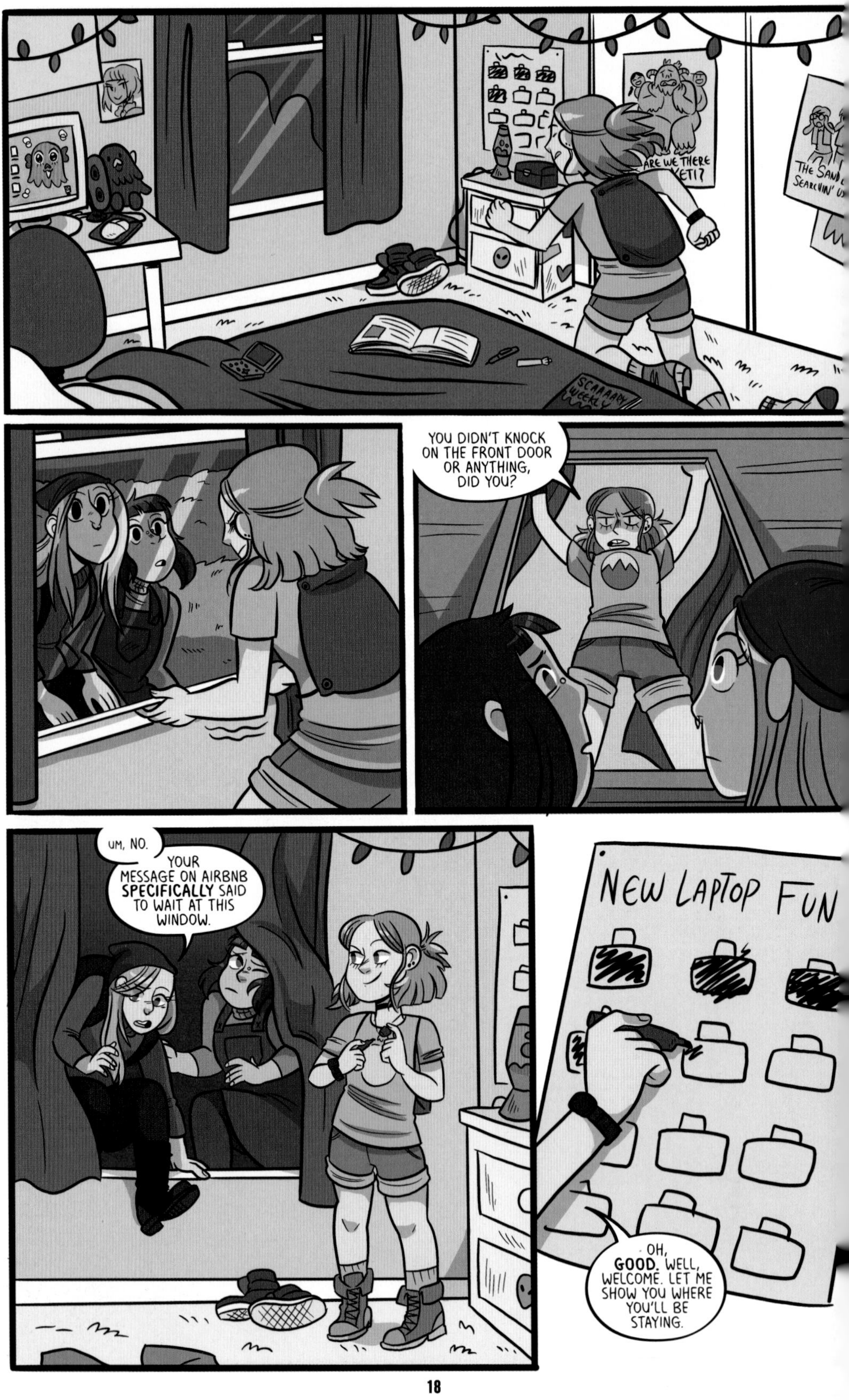

ARE WE THERE YETI?
THE SAND... SEARCHIN' ...
SCAAAARY WEEKLY
YOU DIDN'T KNOCK ON THE FRONT DOOR OR ANYTHING, DID YOU?
UM, NO.
YOUR MESSAGE ON AIRBNB SPECIFICALLY SAID TO WAIT AT THIS WINDOW.
NEW LAPTOP FUN
OH, GOOD. WELL, WELCOME. LET ME SHOW YOU WHERE YOU'LL BE STAYING.

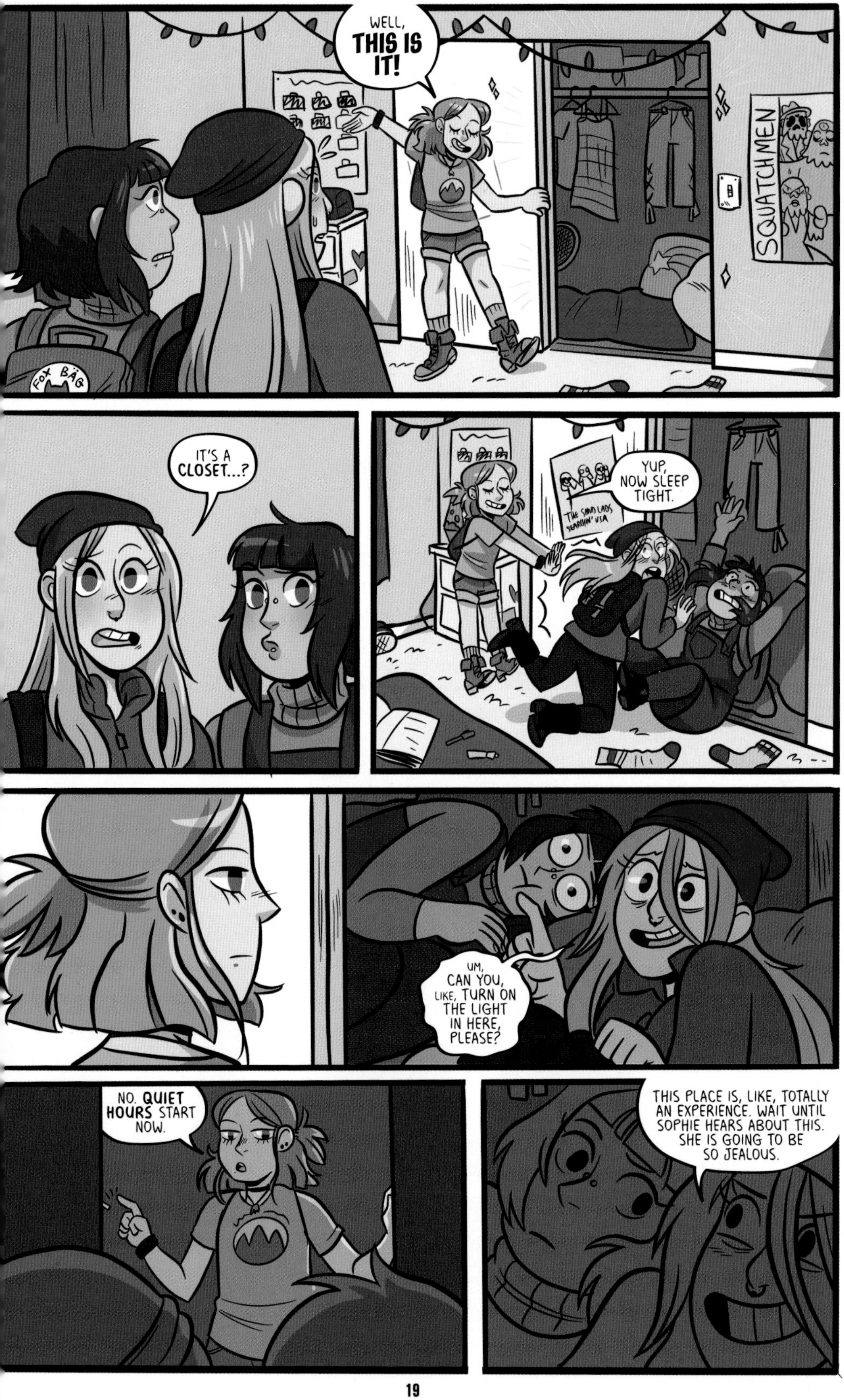

WELL, THIS IS IT!
SQUATCHMEN
FOX BÄG
IT'S A CLOSET...?
YUP, NOW SLEEP TIGHT.
UM, CAN YOU, LIKE, TURN ON THE LIGHT IN HERE, PLEASE?
NO. QUIET HOURS START NOW.
THIS PLACE IS, LIKE, TOTALLY AN EXPERIENCE. WAIT UNTIL SOPHIE HEARS ABOUT THIS. SHE IS GOING TO BE SO JEALOUS.

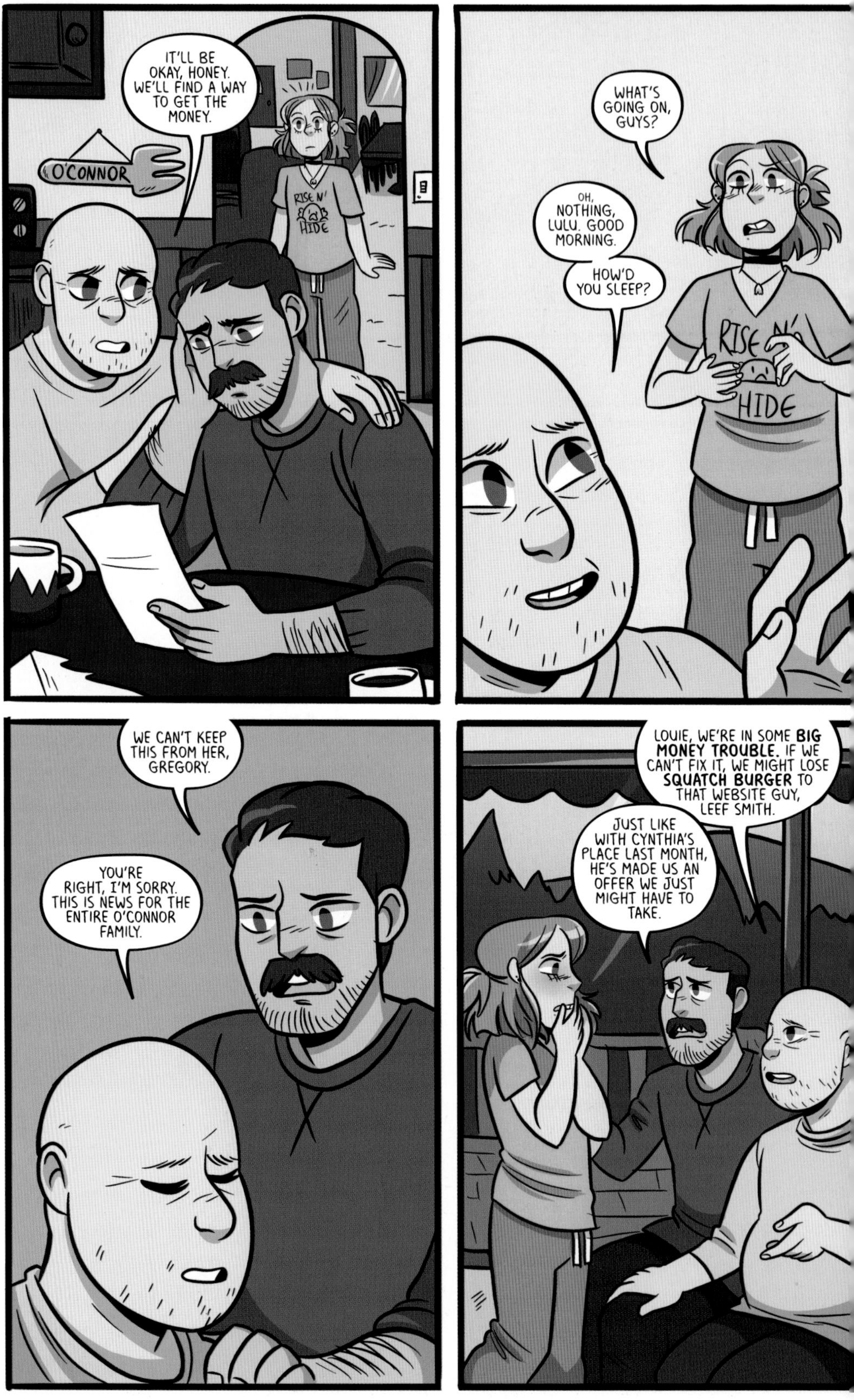
IT'LL BE OKAY, HONEY. WE'LL FIND A WAY TO GET THE MONEY.
O'CONNOR
RISE N' HIDE
WHAT'S GOING ON, GUYS?
OH, NOTHING, LULU. GOOD MORNING.
HOW'D YOU SLEEP?
WE CAN'T KEEP THIS FROM HER, GREGORY.
YOU'RE RIGHT, I'M SORRY. THIS IS NEWS FOR THE ENTIRE O'CONNOR FAMILY.
LOUIE, WE'RE IN SOME BIG MONEY TROUBLE. IF WE CAN'T FIX IT, WE MIGHT LOSE SQUATCH BURGER TO THAT WEBSITE GUY, LEEF SMITH.
JUST LIKE WITH CYNTHIA'S PLACE LAST MONTH, HE'S MADE US AN OFFER WE JUST MIGHT HAVE TO TAKE.

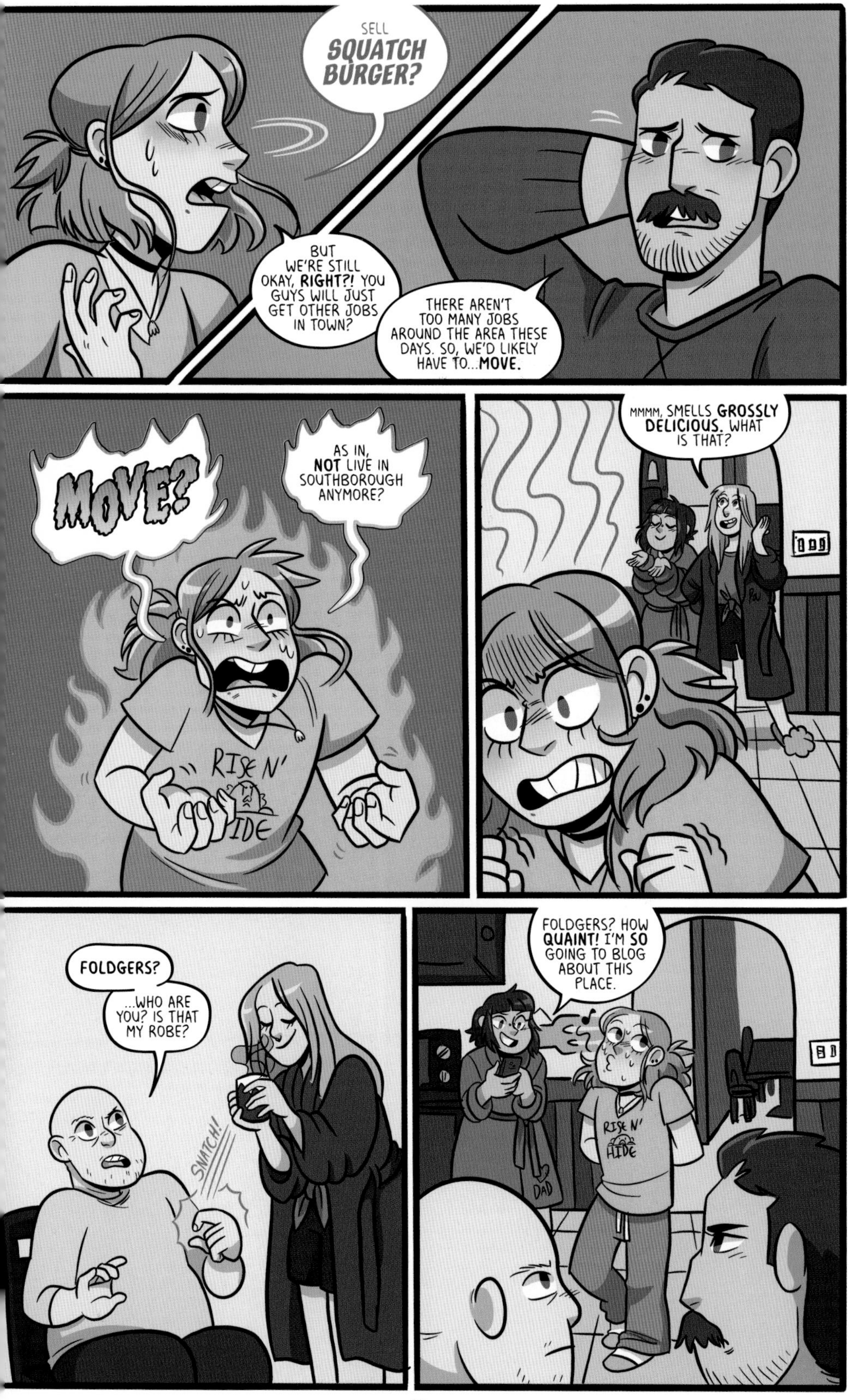
SELL SQUATCH BURGER?
BUT WE'RE STILL OKAY, RIGHT?! YOU GUYS WILL JUST GET OTHER JOBS IN TOWN?
THERE AREN'T TOO MANY JOBS AROUND THE AREA THESE DAYS. SO, WE'D LIKELY HAVE TO...MOVE.
MOVE?
AS IN, NOT LIVE IN SOUTHBOROUGH ANYMORE?
RISE N' HIDE
MMMM, SMELLS GROSSLY DELICIOUS. WHAT IS THAT?
FOLDGERS?
...WHO ARE YOU? IS THAT MY ROBE?
SNATCH!
FOLDGERS? HOW QUAINT! I'M SO GOING TO BLOG ABOUT THIS PLACE.
RISE N' HIDE
DAD

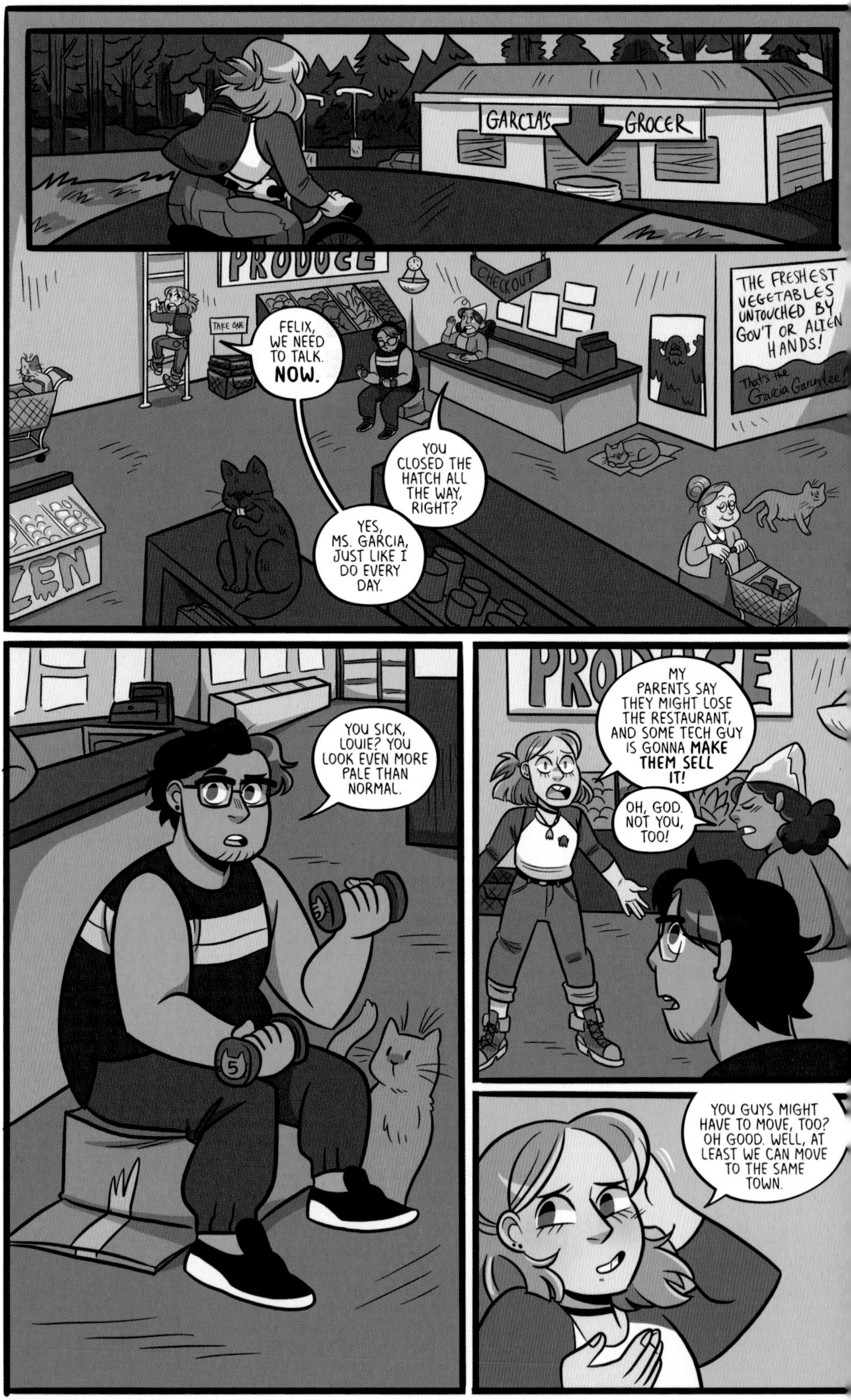
GARCIA'S GROCER
PRODUCE
TAKE ONE
CHECKOUT
THE FRESHEST VEGETABLES UNTOUCHED BY GOV'T OR ALIEN HANDS!
That's the Garcia Garuntee!
FELIX, WE NEED TO TALK. **NOW.**
YOU CLOSED THE HATCH ALL THE WAY, RIGHT?
YES, MS. GARCIA, JUST LIKE I DO EVERY DAY.
PRODUCE
YOU SICK, LOUIE? YOU LOOK EVEN MORE PALE THAN NORMAL.
5
PRODUCE
MY PARENTS SAY THEY MIGHT LOSE THE RESTAURANT, AND SOME TECH GUY IS GONNA **MAKE THEM SELL IT!**
OH, GOD. NOT YOU, TOO!
YOU GUYS MIGHT HAVE TO MOVE, TOO? OH GOOD. WELL, AT LEAST WE CAN MOVE TO THE SAME TOWN.

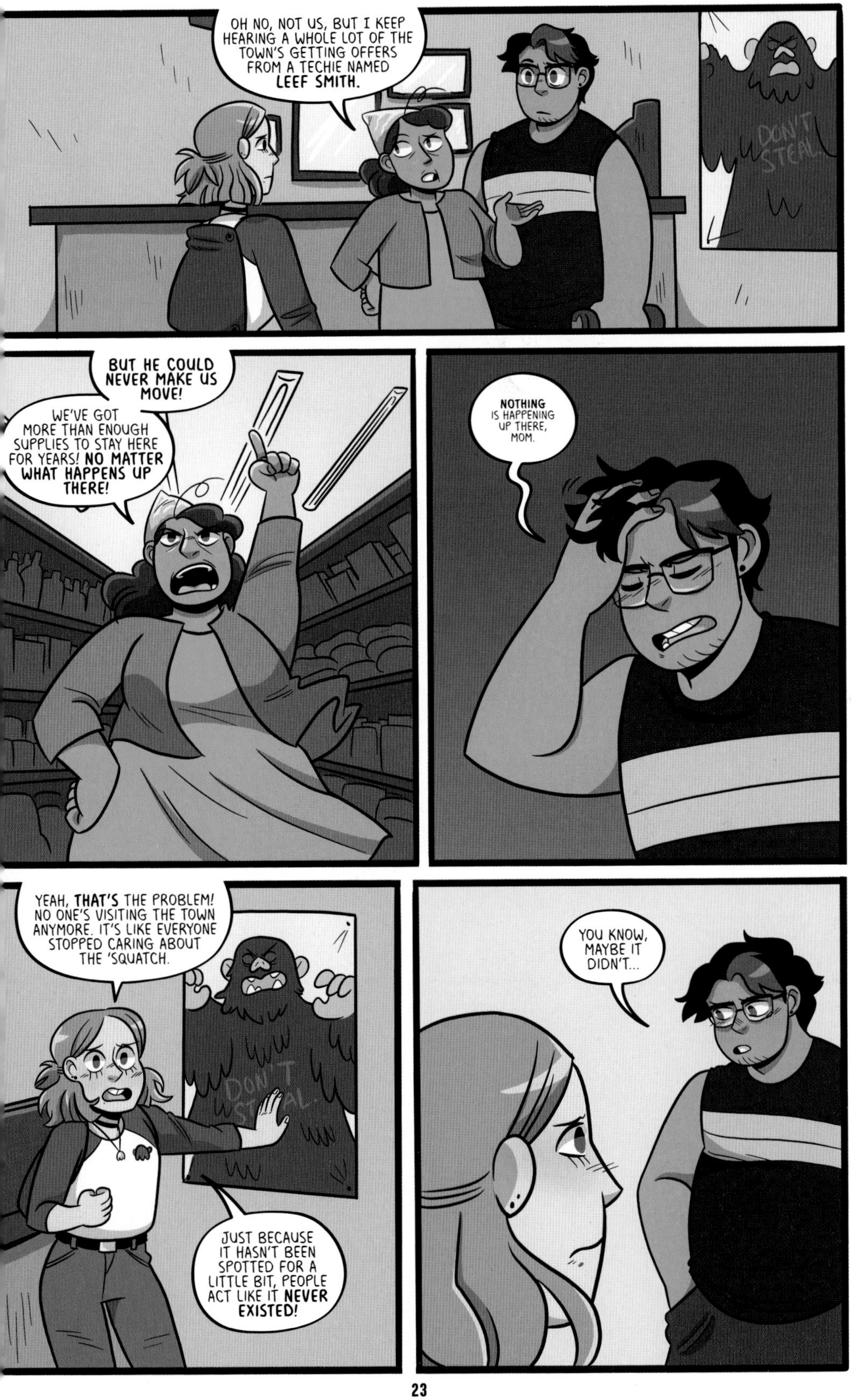

OH NO, NOT US, BUT I KEEP HEARING A WHOLE LOT OF THE TOWN'S GETTING OFFERS FROM A TECHIE NAMED **LEEF SMITH.**
DON'T STEAL.
BUT HE COULD NEVER MAKE US MOVE!
WE'VE GOT MORE THAN ENOUGH SUPPLIES TO STAY HERE FOR YEARS! **NO MATTER WHAT HAPPENS UP THERE!**
NOTHING IS HAPPENING UP THERE, MOM.
YEAH, **THAT'S** THE PROBLEM! NO ONE'S VISITING THE TOWN ANYMORE. IT'S LIKE EVERYONE STOPPED CARING ABOUT THE 'SQUATCH.
DON'T STEAL.
JUST BECAUSE IT HASN'T BEEN SPOTTED FOR A LITTLE BIT, PEOPLE ACT LIKE IT **NEVER EXISTED!**
YOU KNOW, MAYBE IT DIDN'T...

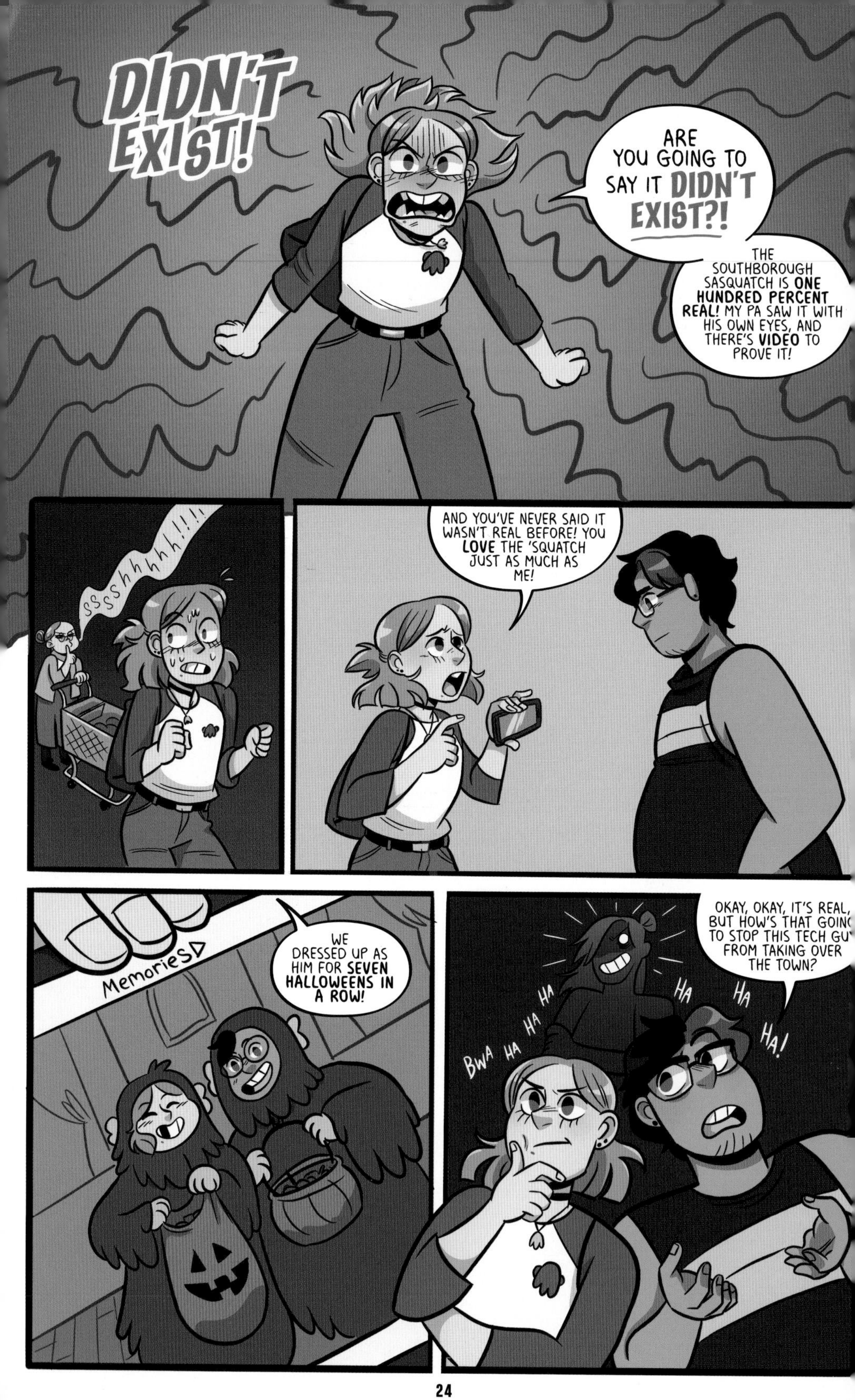
DIDN'T EXIST!
ARE YOU GOING TO SAY IT DIDN'T EXIST?!
THE SOUTHBOROUGH SASQUATCH IS ONE HUNDRED PERCENT REAL! MY PA SAW IT WITH HIS OWN EYES, AND THERE'S VIDEO TO PROVE IT!
SSSSHHHHHH!!!!
AND YOU'VE NEVER SAID IT WASN'T REAL BEFORE! YOU LOVE THE 'SQUATCH JUST AS MUCH AS ME!
Memories
WE DRESSED UP AS HIM FOR SEVEN HALLOWEENS IN A ROW!
OKAY, OKAY, IT'S REAL, BUT HOW'S THAT GOIN TO STOP THIS TECH GU FROM TAKING OVER THE TOWN?
BWA HA HA HA HA HA HA!

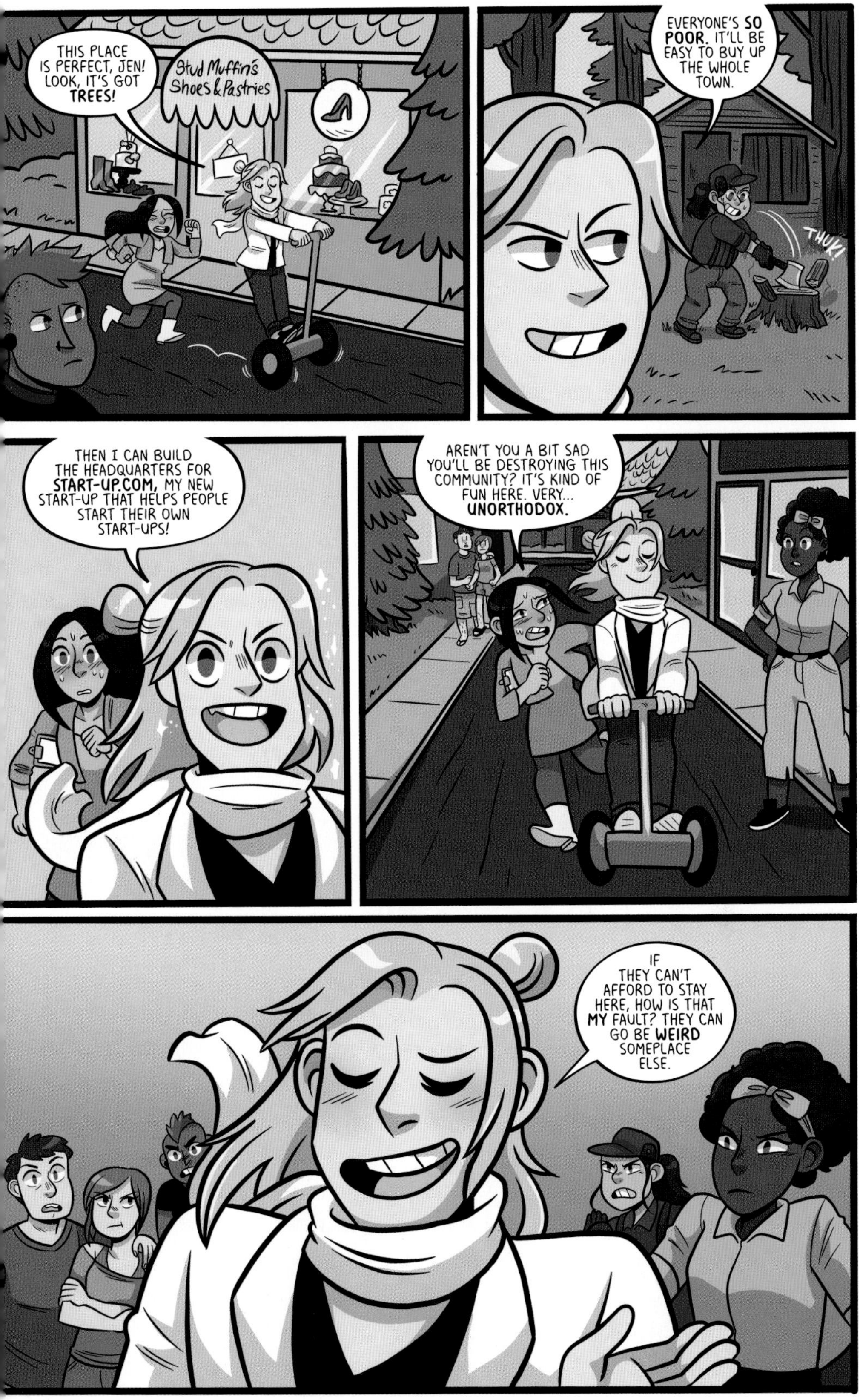
THIS PLACE IS PERFECT, JEN! LOOK, IT'S GOT TREES!
Stud Muffin's Shoes & Pastries
EVERYONE'S SO POOR. IT'LL BE EASY TO BUY UP THE WHOLE TOWN.
THUK!
THEN I CAN BUILD THE HEADQUARTERS FOR START-UP.COM, MY NEW START-UP THAT HELPS PEOPLE START THEIR OWN START-UPS!
AREN'T YOU A BIT SAD YOU'LL BE DESTROYING THIS COMMUNITY? IT'S KIND OF FUN HERE. VERY... UNORTHODOX.
IF THEY CAN'T AFFORD TO STAY HERE, HOW IS THAT MY FAULT? THEY CAN GO BE WEIRD SOMEPLACE ELSE.

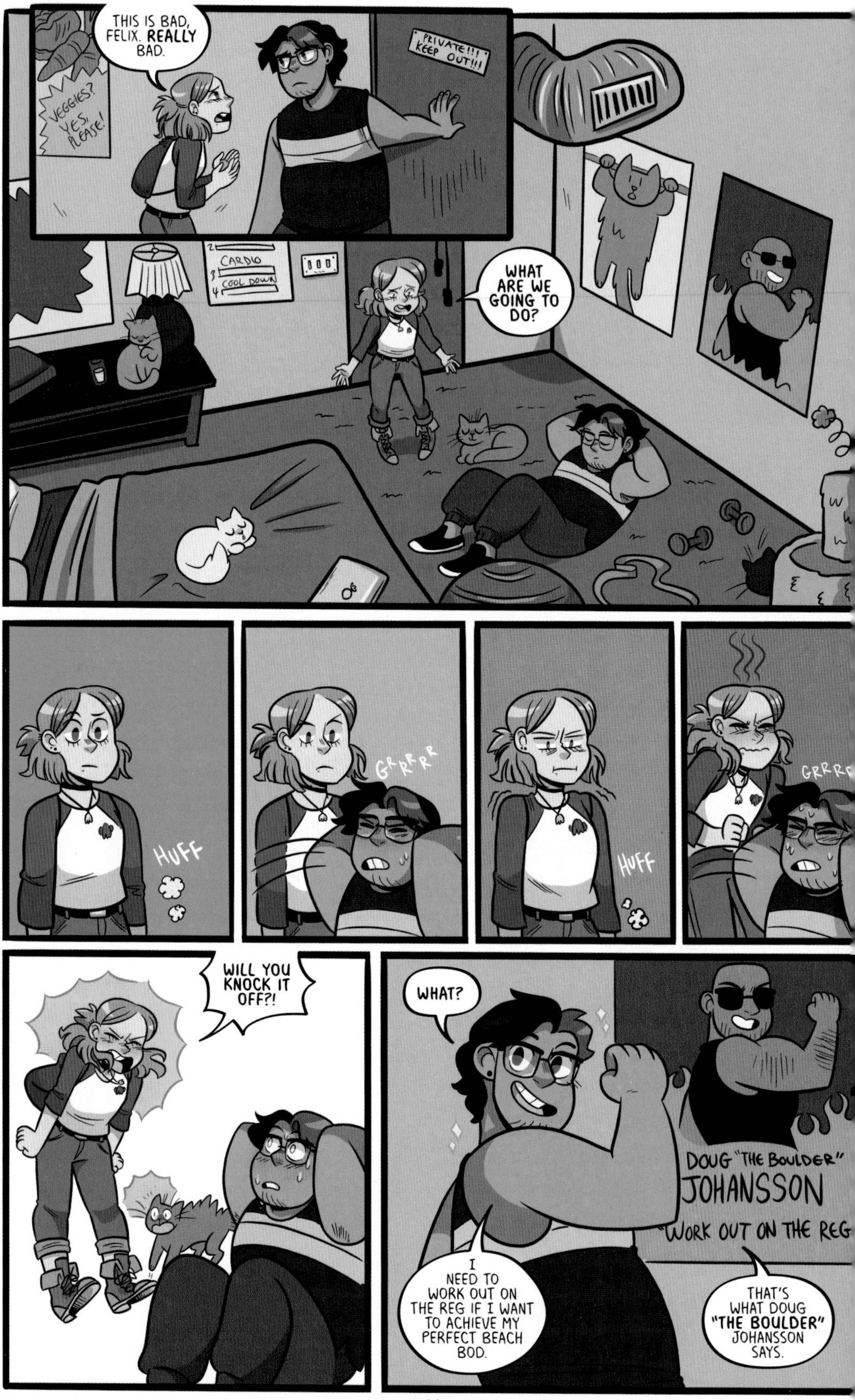
THIS IS BAD, FELIX. REALLY BAD.
PRIVATE!!! KEEP OUT!!!
VEGGIES? YES, PLEASE!
CARDIO
COOL DOWN
WHAT ARE WE GOING TO DO?
HUFF
GRRRRR
HUFF
GRRR
WILL YOU KNOCK IT OFF?!
WHAT?
DOUG "THE BOULDER" JOHANSSON
"WORK OUT ON THE REG
I NEED TO WORK OUT ON THE REG IF I WANT TO ACHIEVE MY PERFECT BEACH BOD.
THAT'S WHAT DOUG "THE BOULDER" JOHANSSON SAYS.

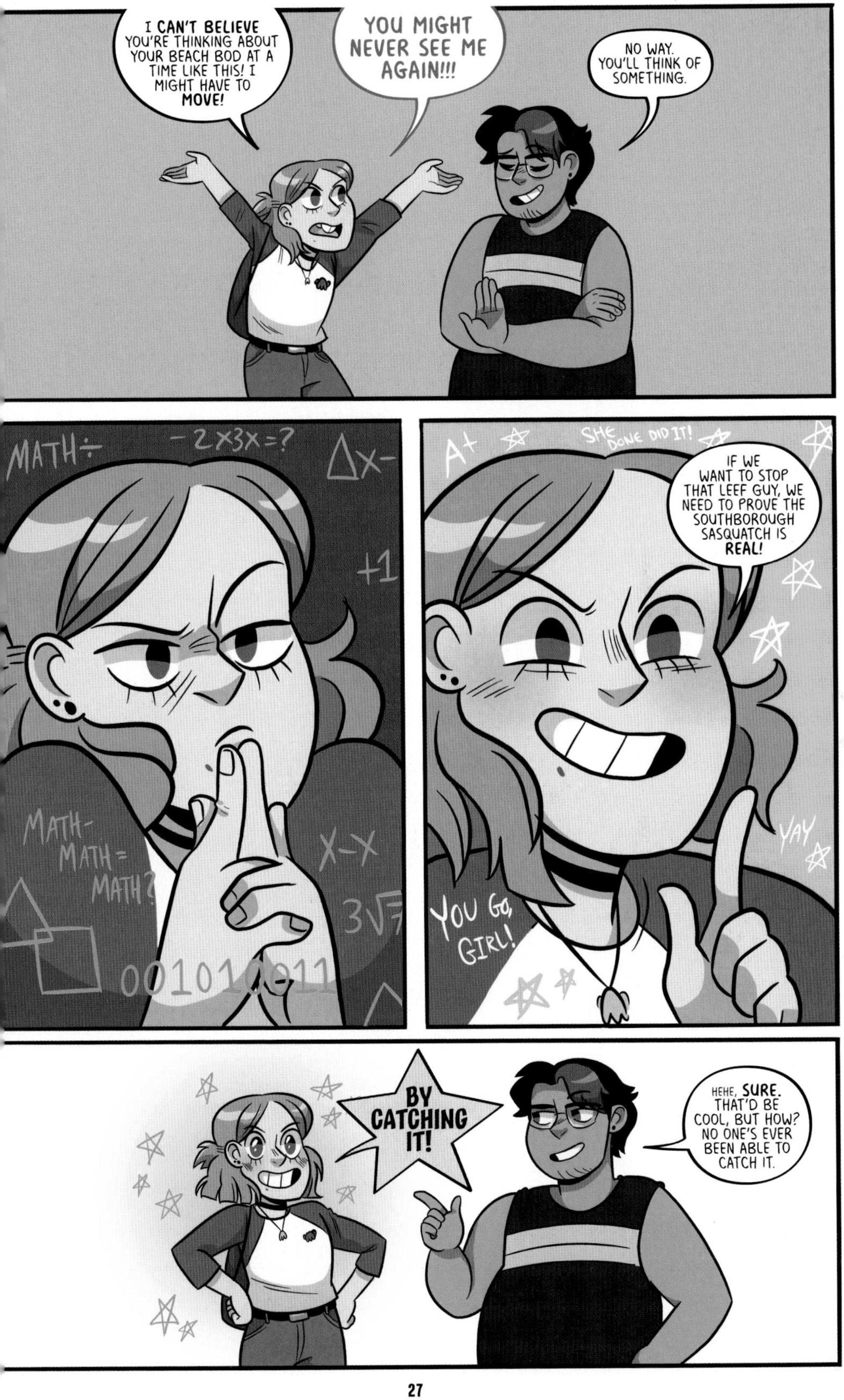

I **CAN'T BELIEVE** YOU'RE THINKING ABOUT YOUR BEACH BOD AT A TIME LIKE THIS! I MIGHT HAVE TO **MOVE!**
YOU MIGHT NEVER SEE ME AGAIN!!!
NO WAY. YOU'LL THINK OF SOMETHING.
MATH ÷
-2×3X=?
X-
+1
MATH-MATH= MATH?
X-X
0010100011
A+
SHE DONE DID IT!
IF WE WANT TO STOP THAT LEEF GUY, WE NEED TO PROVE THE SOUTHBOROUGH SASQUATCH IS **REAL!**
YAY
YOU GO, GIRL!
BY CATCHING IT!
HEHE, **SURE.** THAT'D BE COOL, BUT HOW? NO ONE'S EVER BEEN ABLE TO CATCH IT.

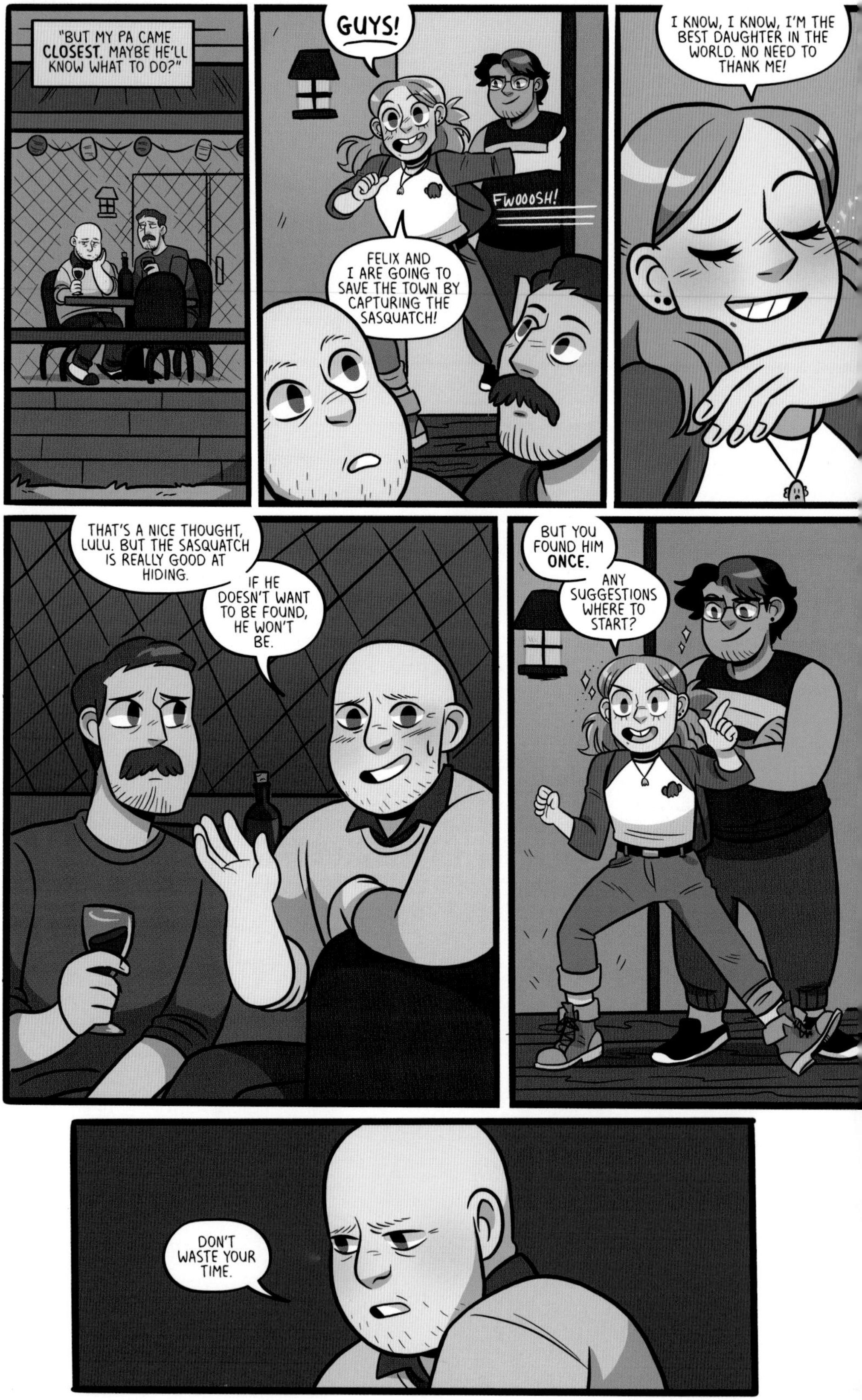
"BUT MY PA CAME **CLOSEST.** MAYBE HE'LL KNOW WHAT TO DO?"
GUYS!
FWOOOSH!
FELIX AND I ARE GOING TO SAVE THE TOWN BY CAPTURING THE SASQUATCH!
I KNOW, I KNOW, I'M THE BEST DAUGHTER IN THE WORLD. NO NEED TO THANK ME!
THAT'S A NICE THOUGHT, LULU. BUT THE SASQUATCH IS REALLY GOOD AT HIDING.
IF HE DOESN'T WANT TO BE FOUND, HE WON'T BE.
BUT YOU FOUND HIM **ONCE.**
ANY SUGGESTIONS WHERE TO START?
DON'T WASTE YOUR TIME.

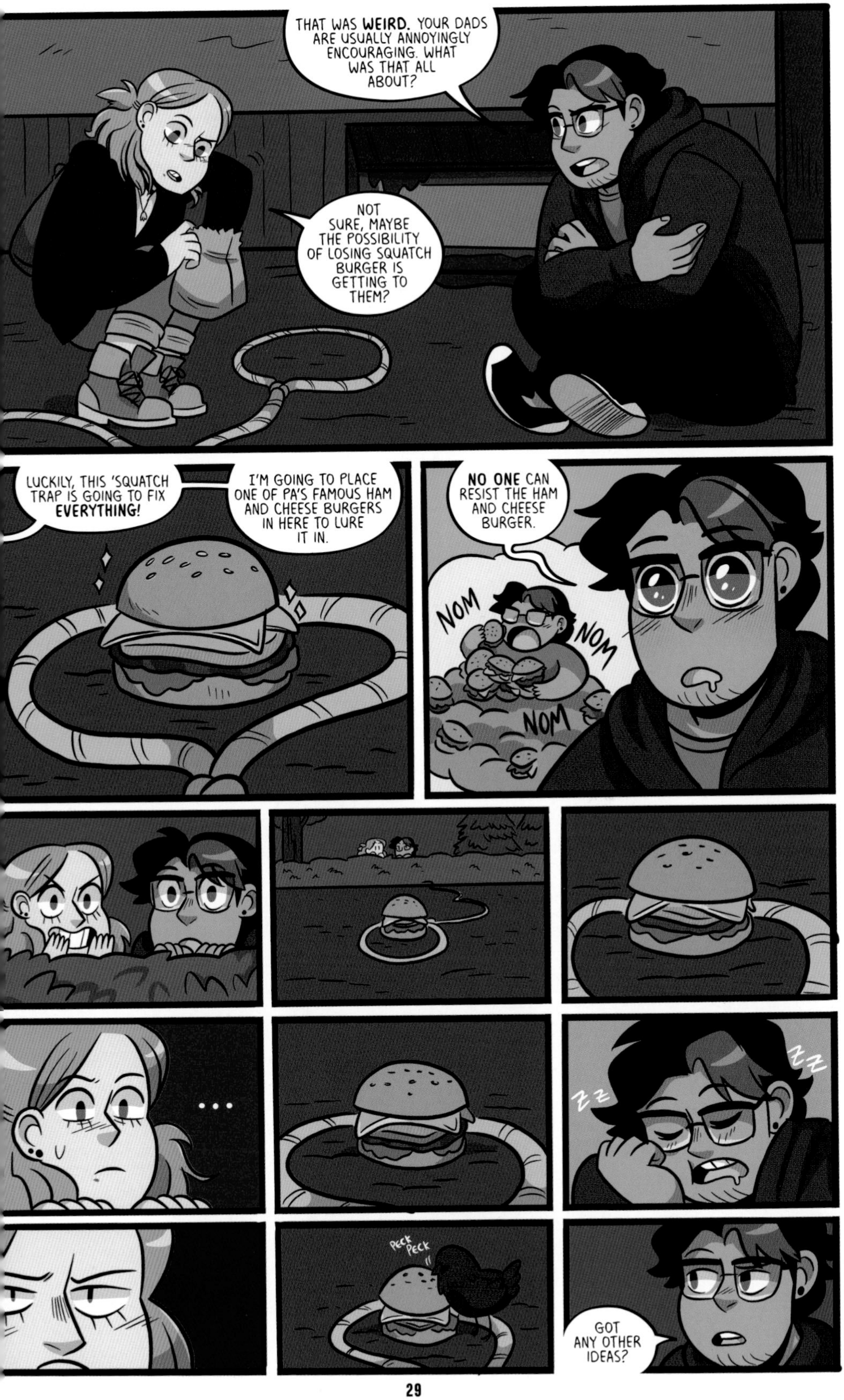

THAT WAS WEIRD. YOUR DADS ARE USUALLY ANNOYINGLY ENCOURAGING. WHAT WAS THAT ALL ABOUT?
NOT SURE, MAYBE THE POSSIBILITY OF LOSING SQUATCH BURGER IS GETTING TO THEM?
LUCKILY, THIS 'SQUATCH TRAP IS GOING TO FIX EVERYTHING!
I'M GOING TO PLACE ONE OF PA'S FAMOUS HAM AND CHEESE BURGERS IN HERE TO LURE IT IN.
NO ONE CAN RESIST THE HAM AND CHEESE BURGER.
NOM
NOM
NOM
...
Z Z
Z Z
PECK PECK
GOT ANY OTHER IDEAS?

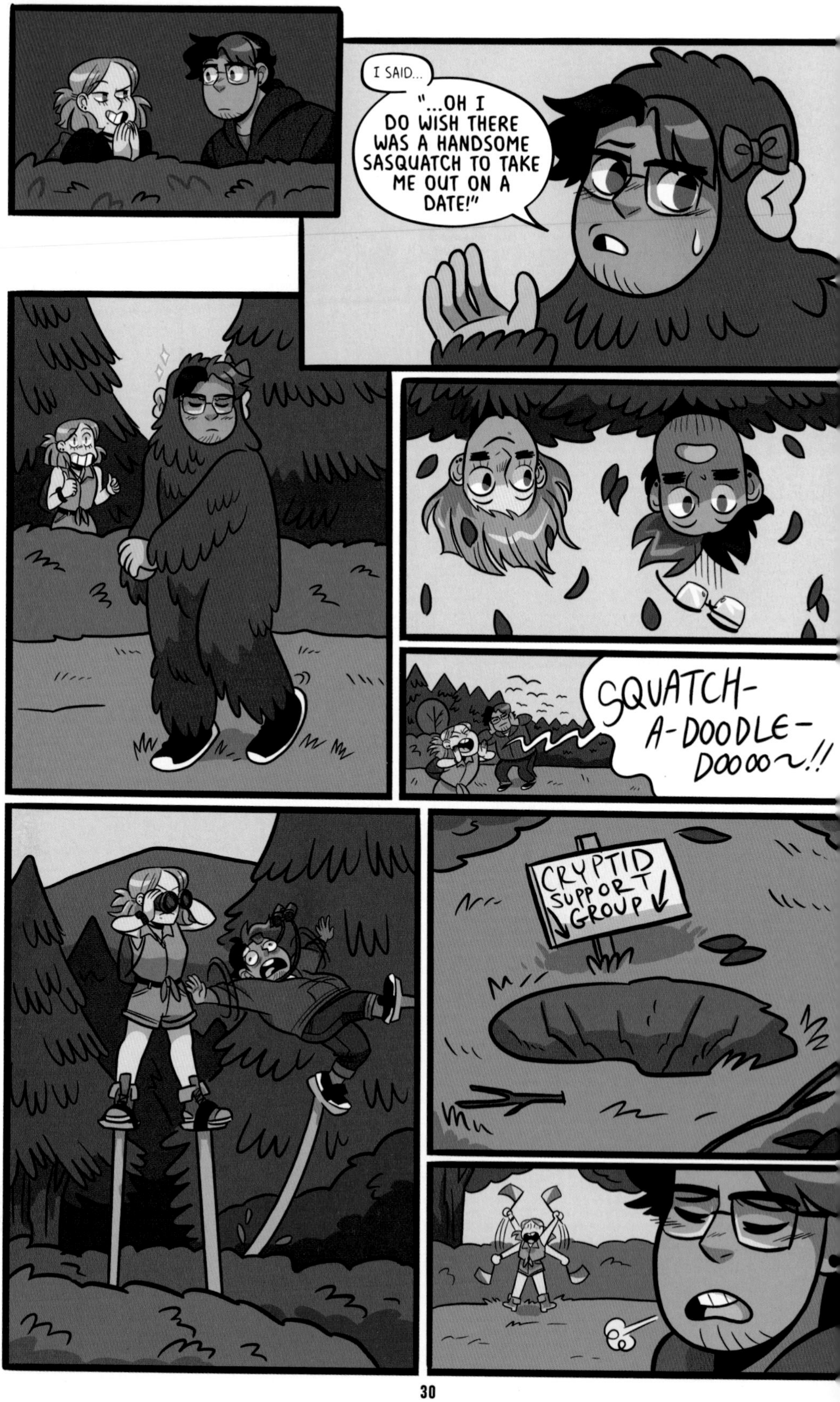

I SAID...
"...OH I DO WISH THERE WAS A HANDSOME SASQUATCH TO TAKE ME OUT ON A DATE!"
SQUATCH-A-DOODLE-DOOOO~!!
CRYPTID SUPPORT GROUP

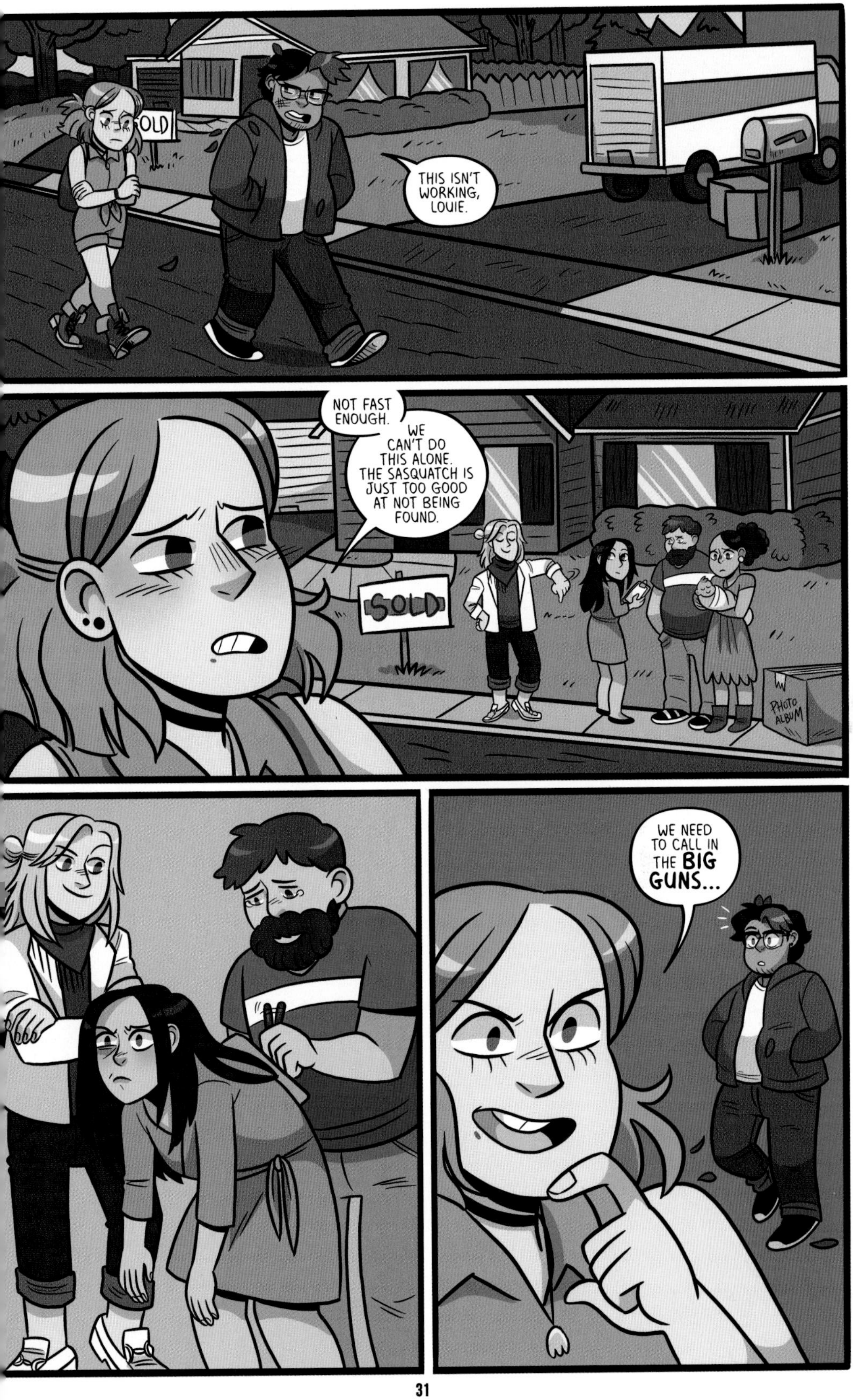

OLD
THIS ISN'T WORKING, LOUIE.
NOT FAST ENOUGH.
WE CAN'T DO THIS ALONE. THE SASQUATCH IS JUST TOO GOOD AT NOT BEING FOUND.
SOLD
PHOTO ALBUM
WE NEED TO CALL IN THE BIG GUNS...

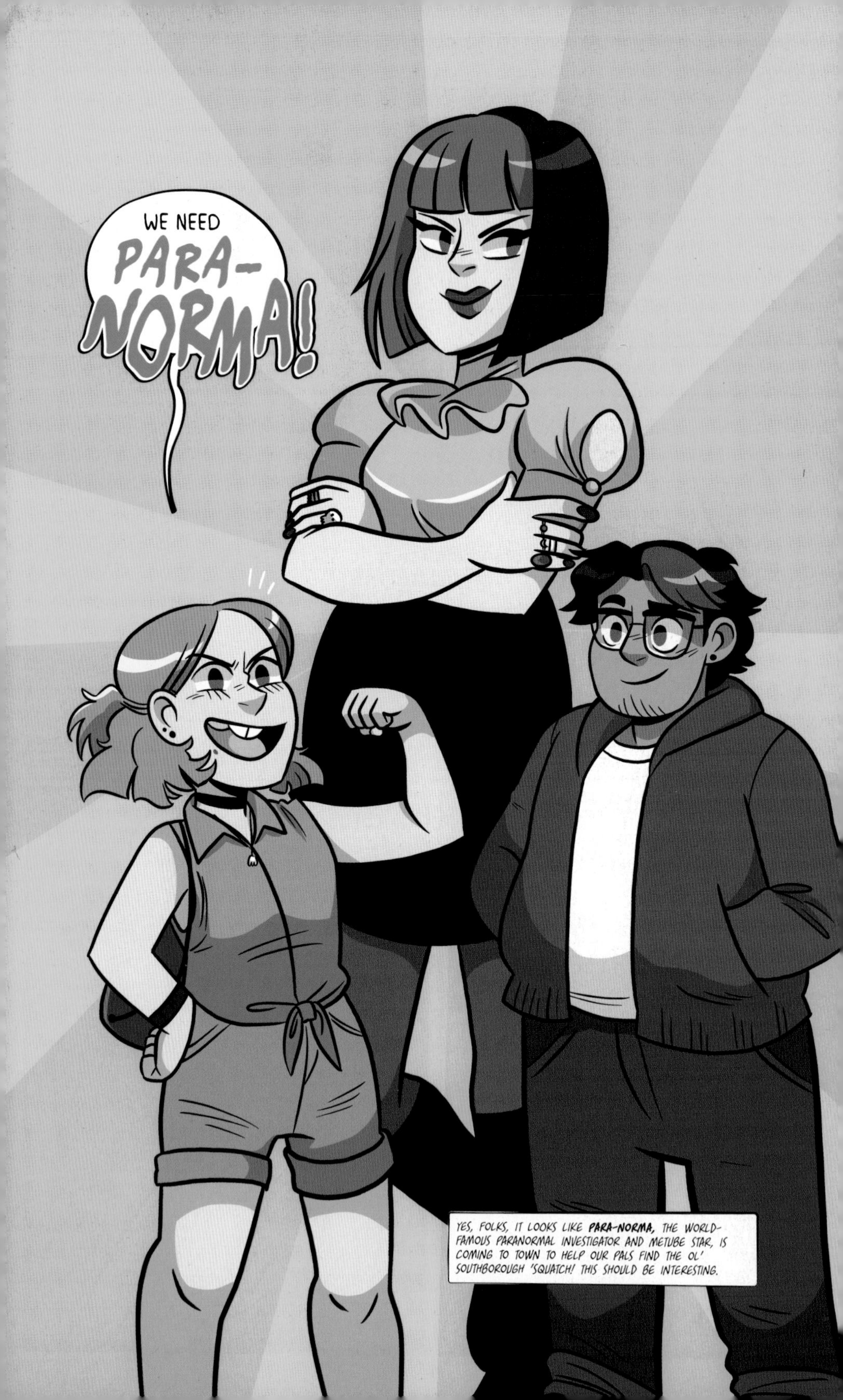
WE NEED PARA-NORMA!
YES, FOLKS, IT LOOKS LIKE **PARA-NORMA,** THE WORLD-FAMOUS PARANORMAL INVESTIGATOR AND METUBE STAR, IS COMING TO TOWN TO HELP OUR PALS FIND THE OL' SOUTHBOROUGH 'SQUATCH! THIS SHOULD BE INTERESTING.

CHAPTER 2

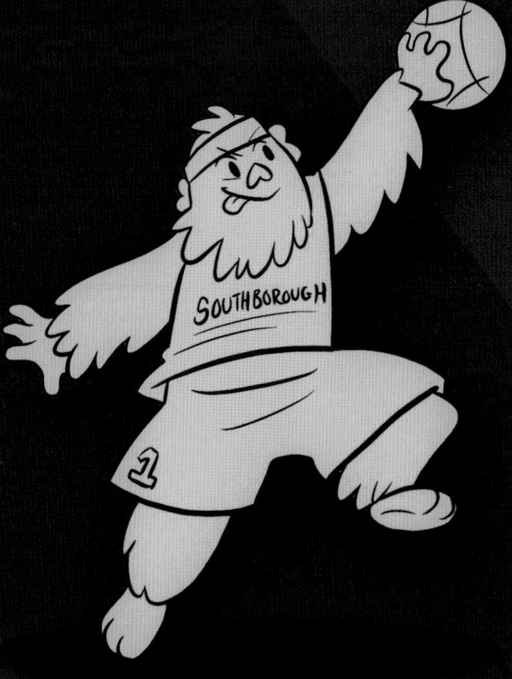
SOUTHBOROUGH

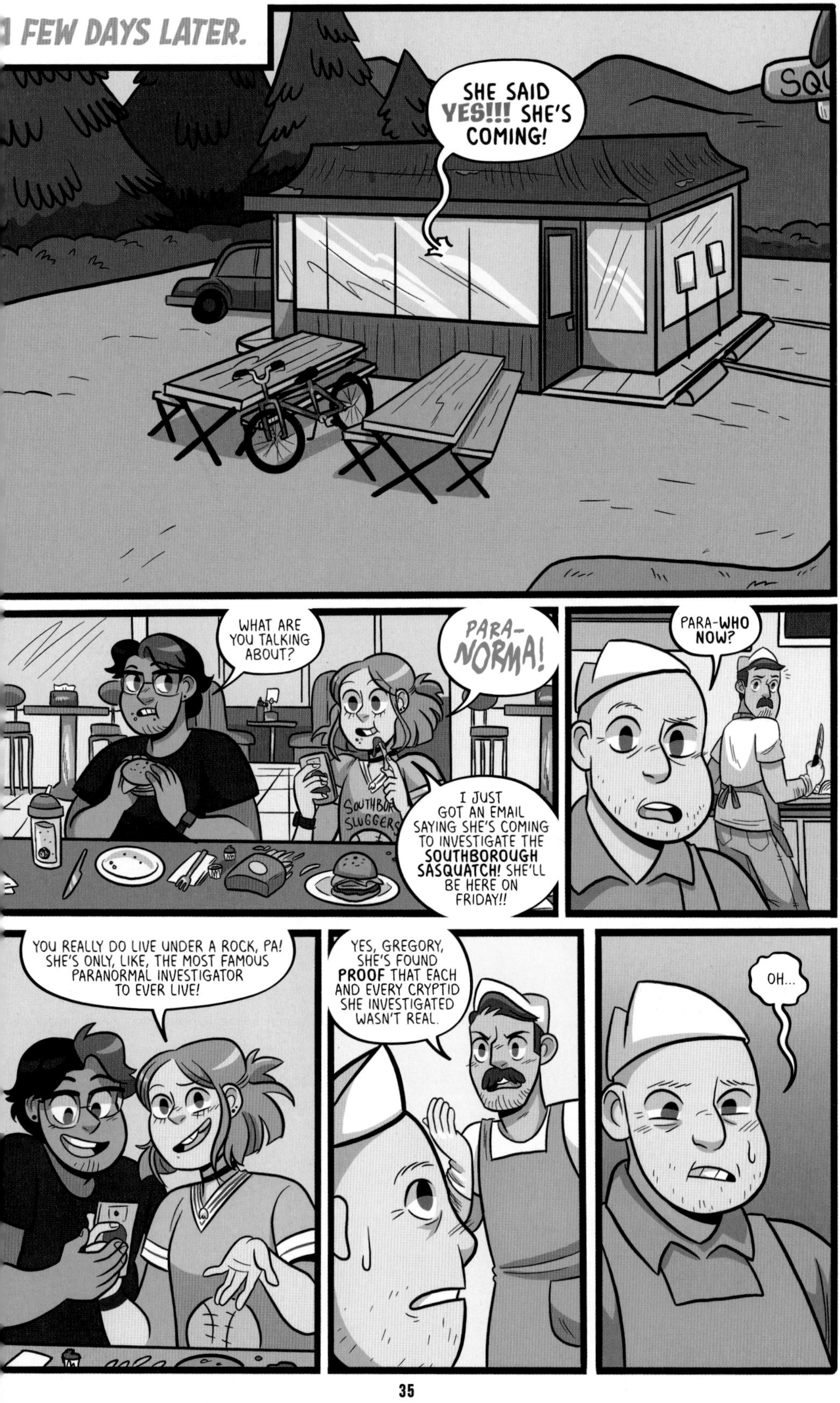
A FEW DAYS LATER.
SQU
SHE SAID YES!!! SHE'S COMING!
WHAT ARE YOU TALKING ABOUT?
PARA-NORMA!
I JUST GOT AN EMAIL SAYING SHE'S COMING TO INVESTIGATE THE SOUTHBOROUGH SASQUATCH! SHE'LL BE HERE ON FRIDAY!!
PARA-WHO NOW?
YOU REALLY DO LIVE UNDER A ROCK, PA! SHE'S ONLY, LIKE, THE MOST FAMOUS PARANORMAL INVESTIGATOR TO EVER LIVE!
YES, GREGORY, SHE'S FOUND PROOF THAT EACH AND EVERY CRYPTID SHE INVESTIGATED WASN'T REAL.
OH...

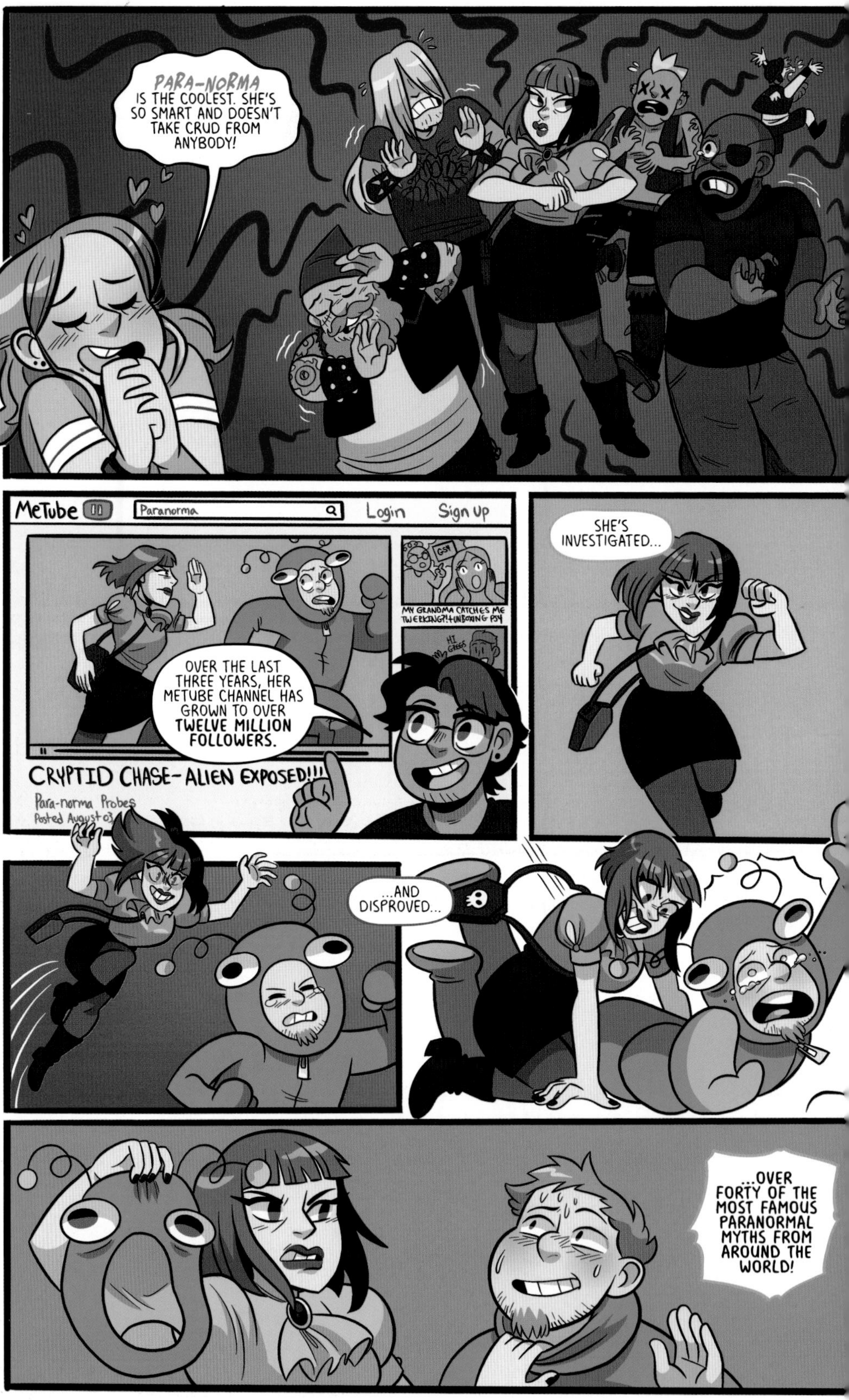
PARA-NORMA IS THE COOLEST. SHE'S SO SMART AND DOESN'T TAKE CRUD FROM ANYBODY!
MeTube
Paranorma
Login
Sign up
GS4
MY GRANDMA CATCHES ME TWERKING?! + UNBOXING PS4
HI GREGS
OVER THE LAST THREE YEARS, HER METUBE CHANNEL HAS GROWN TO OVER **TWELVE MILLION FOLLOWERS.**
CRYPTID CHASE- ALIEN EXPOSED!!!
Para-norma Probes
Posted August 03
SHE'S INVESTIGATED...
...AND DISPROVED...
...OVER FORTY OF THE MOST FAMOUS PARANORMAL MYTHS FROM AROUND THE WORLD!

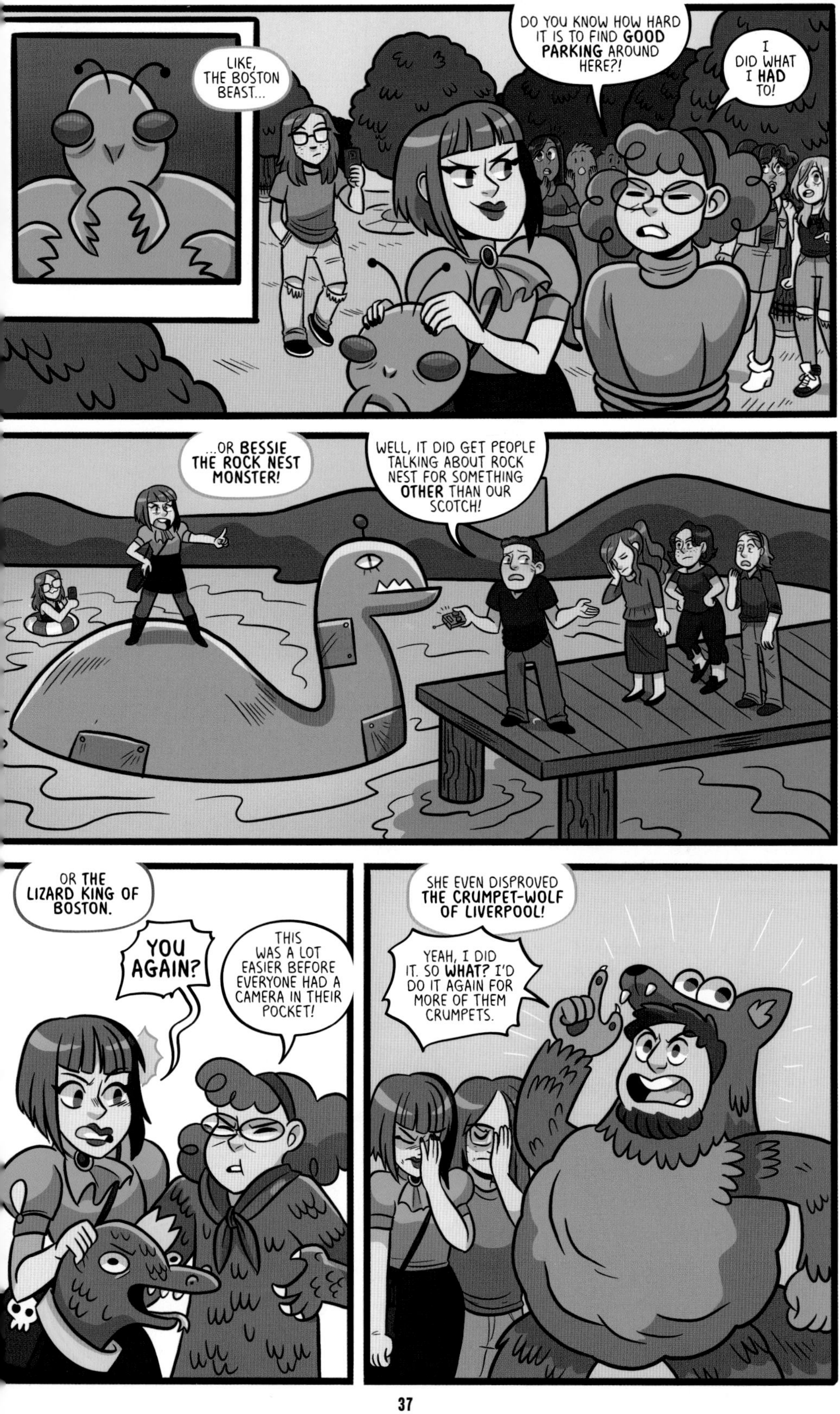

LIKE, THE BOSTON BEAST...
DO YOU KNOW HOW HARD IT IS TO FIND GOOD PARKING AROUND HERE?!
I DID WHAT I HAD TO!
...OR BESSIE THE ROCK NEST MONSTER!
WELL, IT DID GET PEOPLE TALKING ABOUT ROCK NEST FOR SOMETHING OTHER THAN OUR SCOTCH!
OR THE LIZARD KING OF BOSTON.
YOU AGAIN?
THIS WAS A LOT EASIER BEFORE EVERYONE HAD A CAMERA IN THEIR POCKET!
SHE EVEN DISPROVED THE CRUMPET-WOLF OF LIVERPOOL!
YEAH, I DID IT. SO WHAT? I'D DO IT AGAIN FOR MORE OF THEM CRUMPETS.

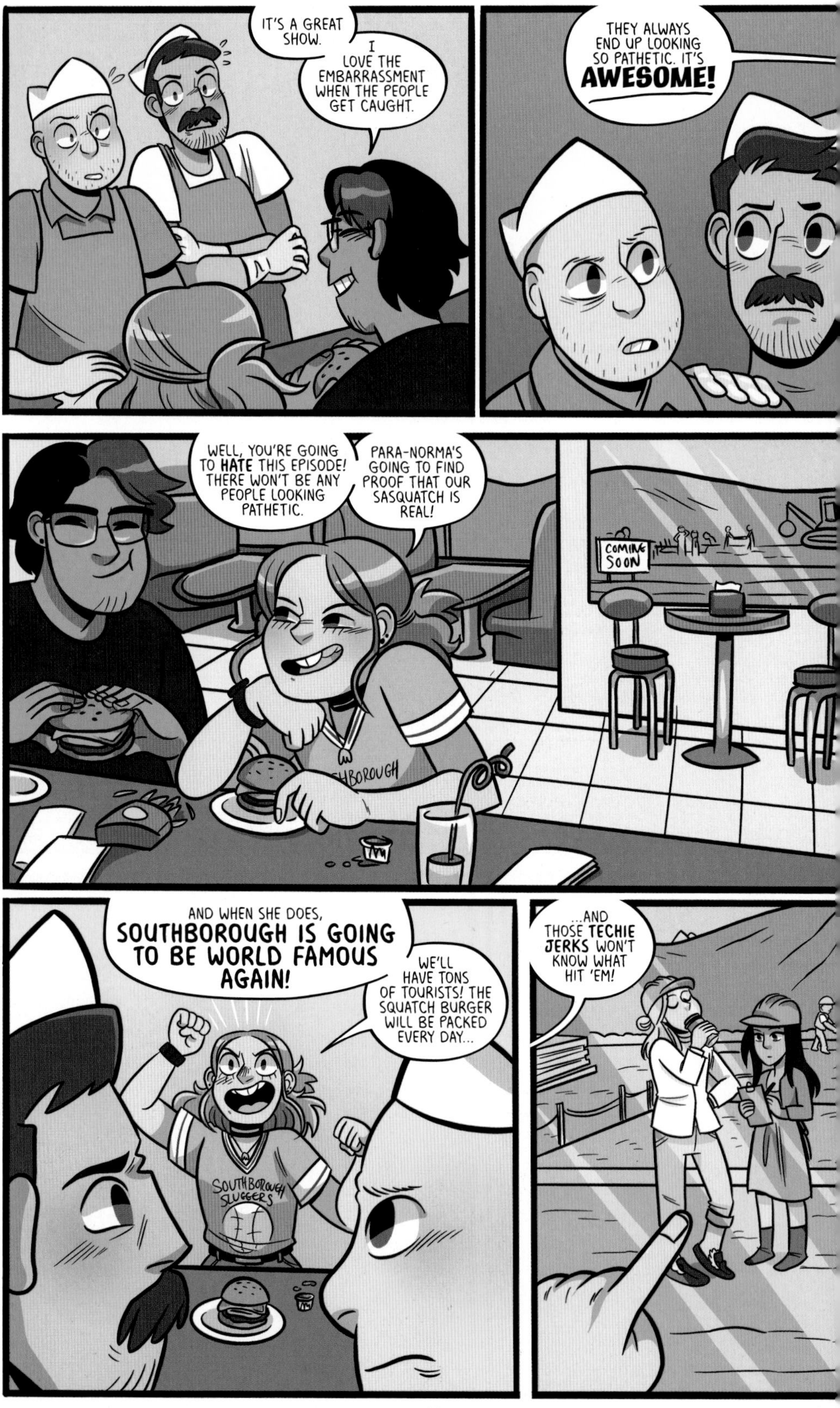
IT'S A GREAT SHOW.
I LOVE THE EMBARRASSMENT WHEN THE PEOPLE GET CAUGHT.
THEY ALWAYS END UP LOOKING SO PATHETIC. IT'S AWESOME!
WELL, YOU'RE GOING TO HATE THIS EPISODE! THERE WON'T BE ANY PEOPLE LOOKING PATHETIC.
PARA-NORMA'S GOING TO FIND PROOF THAT OUR SASQUATCH IS REAL!
COMING SOON
AND WHEN SHE DOES, SOUTHBOROUGH IS GOING TO BE WORLD FAMOUS AGAIN!
WE'LL HAVE TONS OF TOURISTS! THE SQUATCH BURGER WILL BE PACKED EVERY DAY...
SOUTHBOROUGH SLUGGERS
...AND THOSE TECHIE JERKS WON'T KNOW WHAT HIT 'EM!

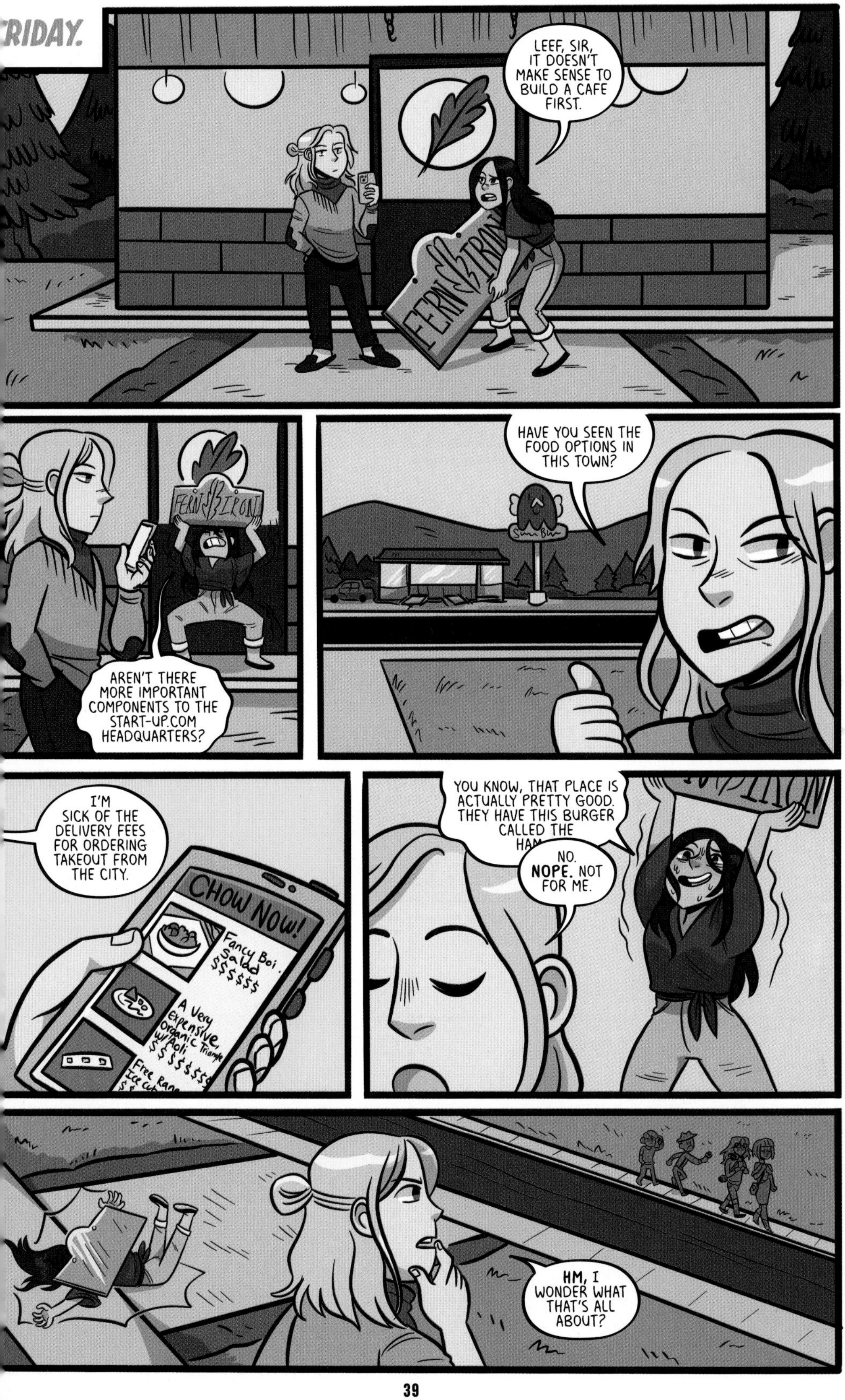
FRIDAY.
LEEF, SIR, IT DOESN'T MAKE SENSE TO BUILD A CAFE FIRST.
FERN IRON
AREN'T THERE MORE IMPORTANT COMPONENTS TO THE START-UP.COM HEADQUARTERS?
HAVE YOU SEEN THE FOOD OPTIONS IN THIS TOWN?
I'M SICK OF THE DELIVERY FEES FOR ORDERING TAKEOUT FROM THE CITY.
CHOW NOW!
Fancy Boi Salad $$$$$$
A Very Expensive, organic Triangle w/Aoli $$$$$$$
YOU KNOW, THAT PLACE IS ACTUALLY PRETTY GOOD. THEY HAVE THIS BURGER CALLED THE HAM
NO. **NOPE.** NOT FOR ME.
HM, I WONDER WHAT THAT'S ALL ABOUT?

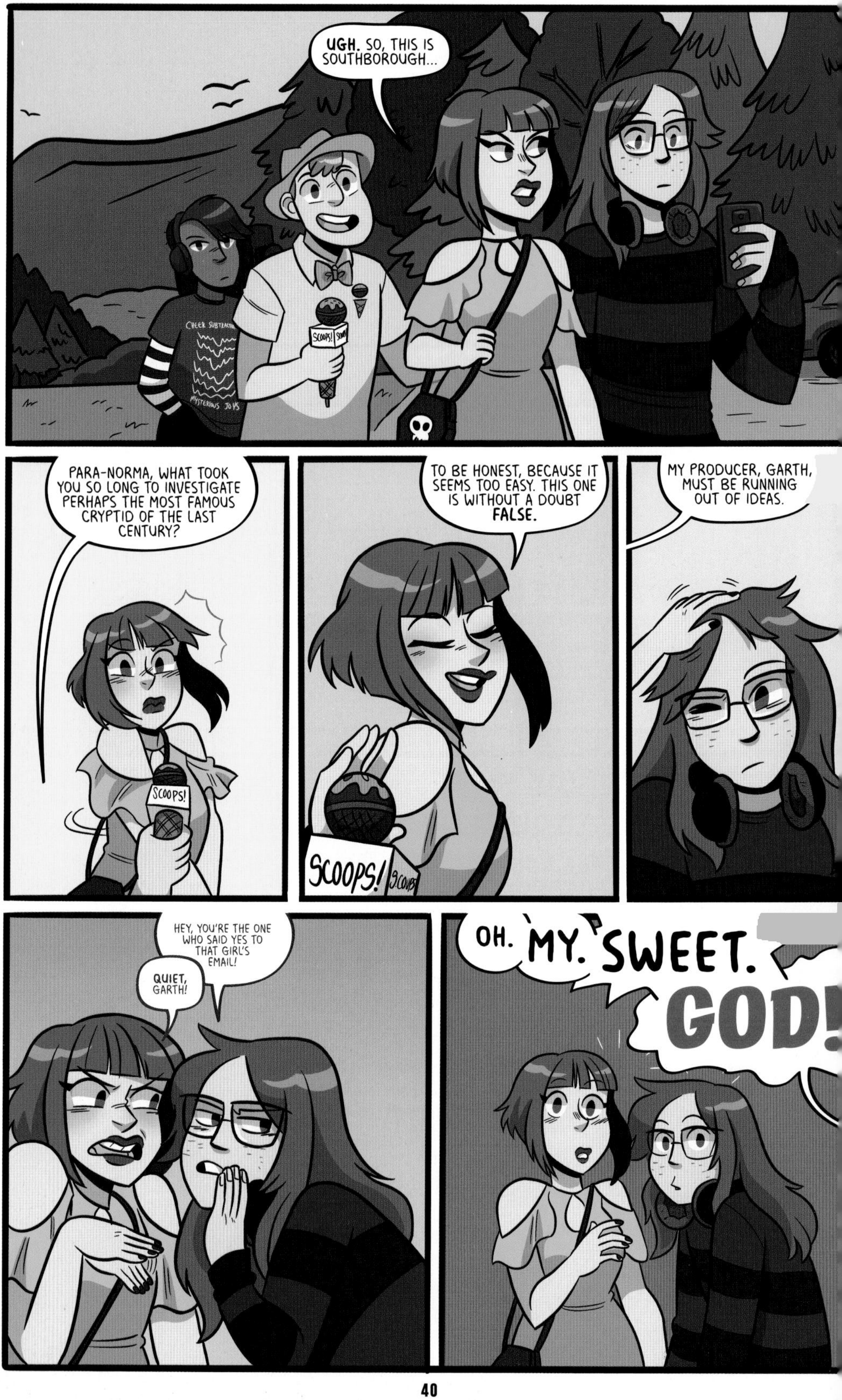

UGH. SO, THIS IS SOUTHBOROUGH...
CHEER SUBTRACTION
MYSTERIOUS JOYS
SCOOPS!
PARA-NORMA, WHAT TOOK YOU SO LONG TO INVESTIGATE PERHAPS THE MOST FAMOUS CRYPTID OF THE LAST CENTURY?
SCOOPS!
TO BE HONEST, BECAUSE IT SEEMS TOO EASY. THIS ONE IS WITHOUT A DOUBT FALSE.
SCOOPS!
MY PRODUCER, GARTH, MUST BE RUNNING OUT OF IDEAS.
HEY, YOU'RE THE ONE WHO SAID YES TO THAT GIRL'S EMAIL!
QUIET, GARTH!
OH. MY. SWEET. GOD!

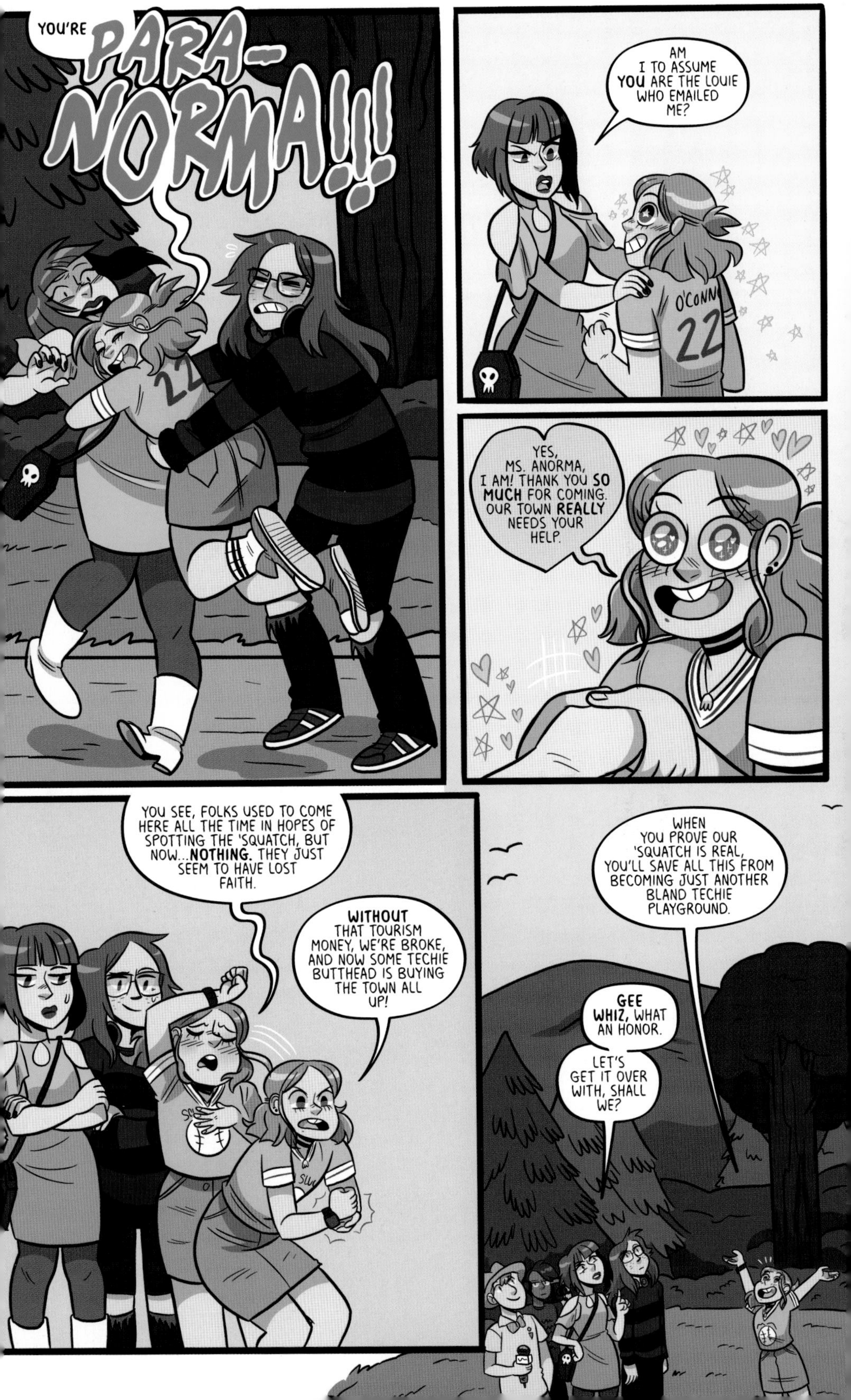

YOU'RE PARA-NORMA!!!
AM I TO ASSUME YOU ARE THE LOUIE WHO EMAILED ME?
O'CONN 22
YES, MS. ANORMA, I AM! THANK YOU SO MUCH FOR COMING. OUR TOWN REALLY NEEDS YOUR HELP.
YOU SEE, FOLKS USED TO COME HERE ALL THE TIME IN HOPES OF SPOTTING THE 'SQUATCH, BUT NOW...NOTHING. THEY JUST SEEM TO HAVE LOST FAITH.
WITHOUT THAT TOURISM MONEY, WE'RE BROKE, AND NOW SOME TECHIE BUTTHEAD IS BUYING THE TOWN ALL UP!
WHEN YOU PROVE OUR 'SQUATCH IS REAL, YOU'LL SAVE ALL THIS FROM BECOMING JUST ANOTHER BLAND TECHIE PLAYGROUND.
GEE WHIZ, WHAT AN HONOR.
LET'S GET IT OVER WITH, SHALL WE?

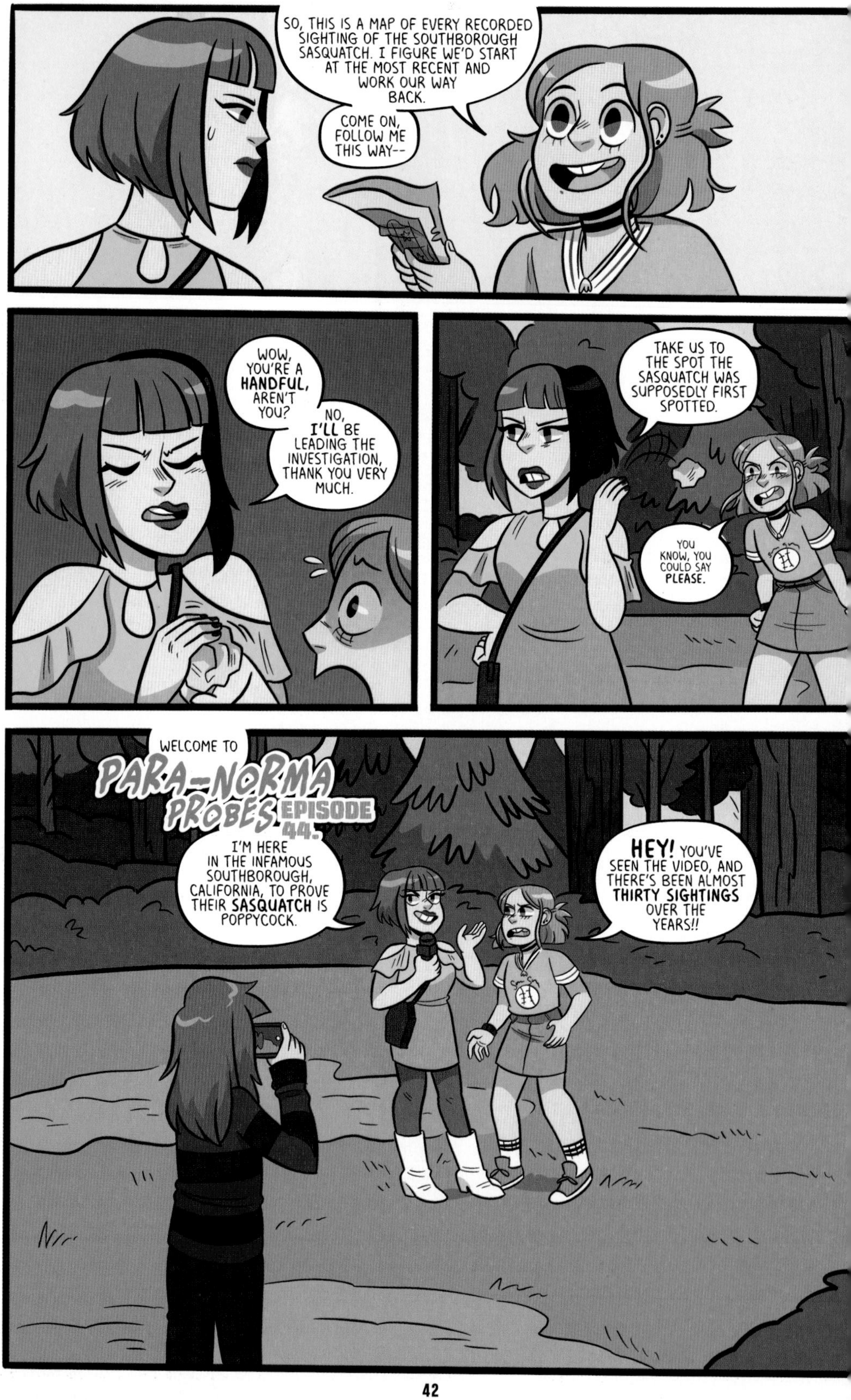
SO, THIS IS A MAP OF EVERY RECORDED SIGHTING OF THE SOUTHBOROUGH SASQUATCH. I FIGURE WE'D START AT THE MOST RECENT AND WORK OUR WAY BACK.
COME ON, FOLLOW ME THIS WAY--
WOW, YOU'RE A HANDFUL, AREN'T YOU?
NO, I'LL BE LEADING THE INVESTIGATION, THANK YOU VERY MUCH.
TAKE US TO THE SPOT THE SASQUATCH WAS SUPPOSEDLY FIRST SPOTTED.
YOU KNOW, YOU COULD SAY PLEASE.
WELCOME TO
PARA-NORMA PROBES EPISODE 44.
I'M HERE IN THE INFAMOUS SOUTHBOROUGH, CALIFORNIA, TO PROVE THEIR SASQUATCH IS POPPYCOCK.
HEY! YOU'VE SEEN THE VIDEO, AND THERE'S BEEN ALMOST THIRTY SIGHTINGS OVER THE YEARS!!

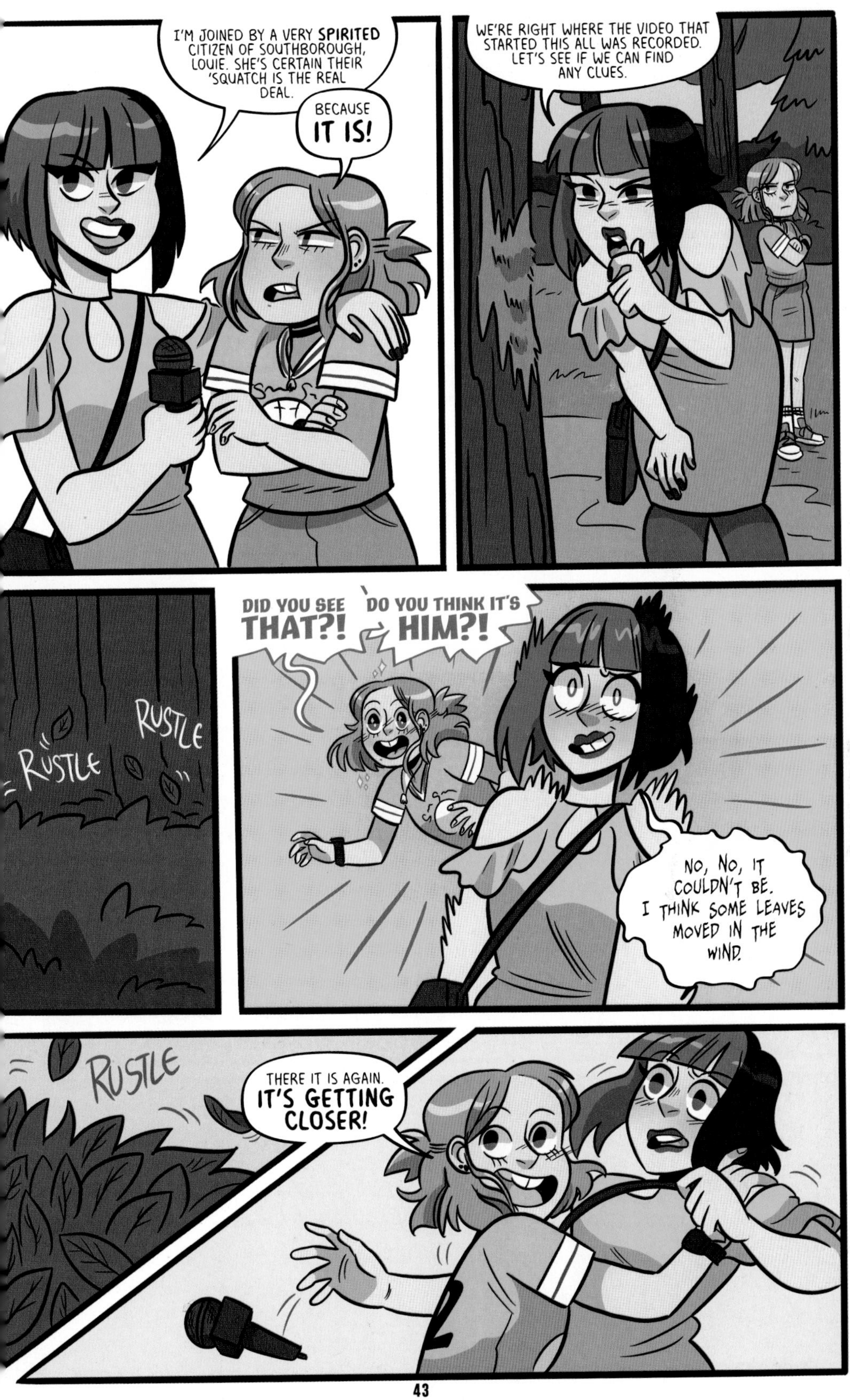
I'M JOINED BY A VERY SPIRITED CITIZEN OF SOUTHBOROUGH, LOUIE. SHE'S CERTAIN THEIR 'SQUATCH IS THE REAL DEAL.
BECAUSE IT IS!
WE'RE RIGHT WHERE THE VIDEO THAT STARTED THIS ALL WAS RECORDED. LET'S SEE IF WE CAN FIND ANY CLUES.
RUSTLE
RUSTLE
DID YOU SEE THAT?!
DO YOU THINK IT'S HIM?!
NO, NO, IT COULDN'T BE. I THINK SOME LEAVES MOVED IN THE WIND.
RUSTLE
THERE IT IS AGAIN. IT'S GETTING CLOSER!

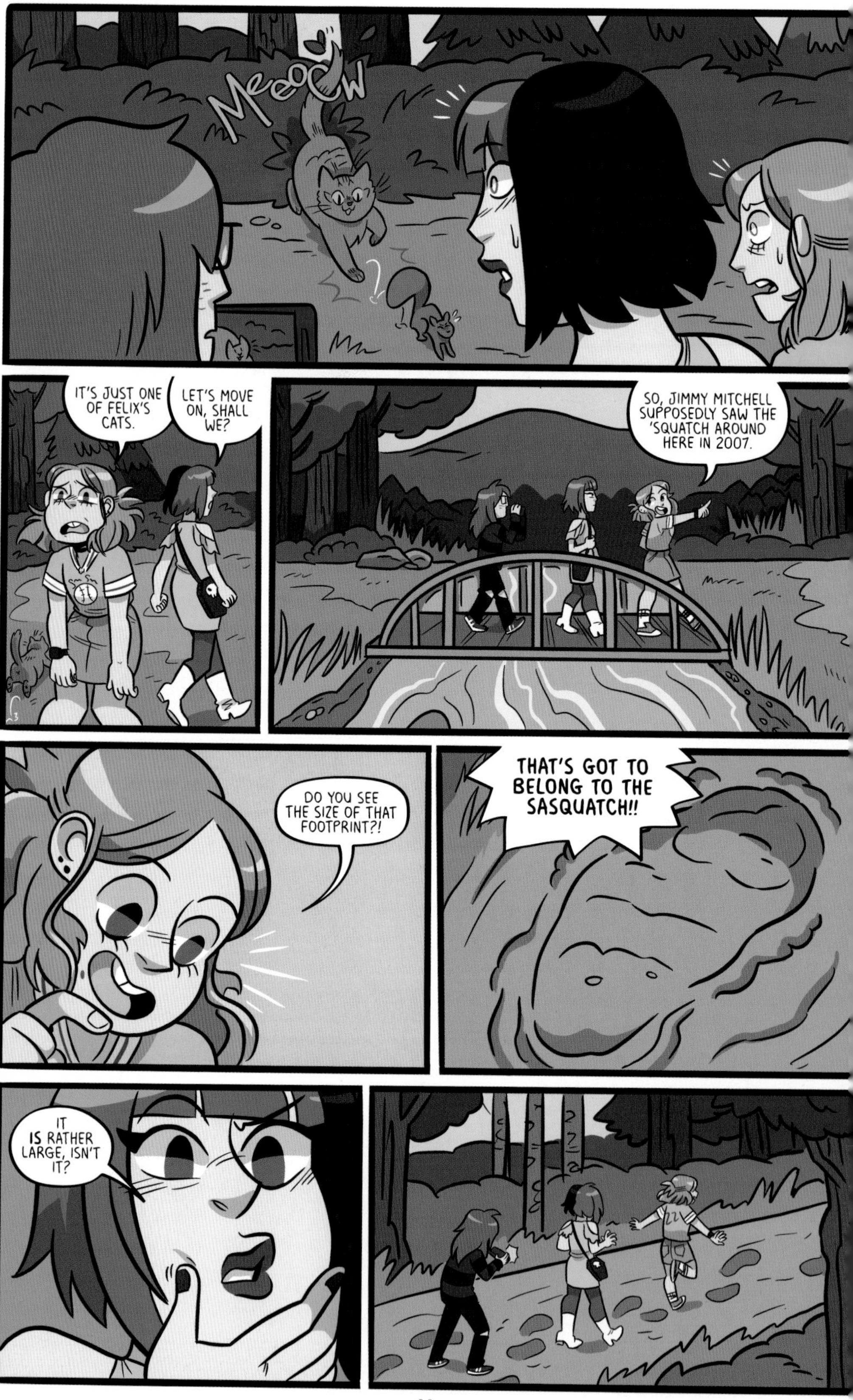
MEOOOW
IT'S JUST ONE OF FELIX'S CATS.
LET'S MOVE ON, SHALL WE?
SO, JIMMY MITCHELL SUPPOSEDLY SAW THE 'SQUATCH AROUND HERE IN 2007.
DO YOU SEE THE SIZE OF THAT FOOTPRINT?!
THAT'S GOT TO BELONG TO THE SASQUATCH!!
IT IS RATHER LARGE, ISN'T IT?

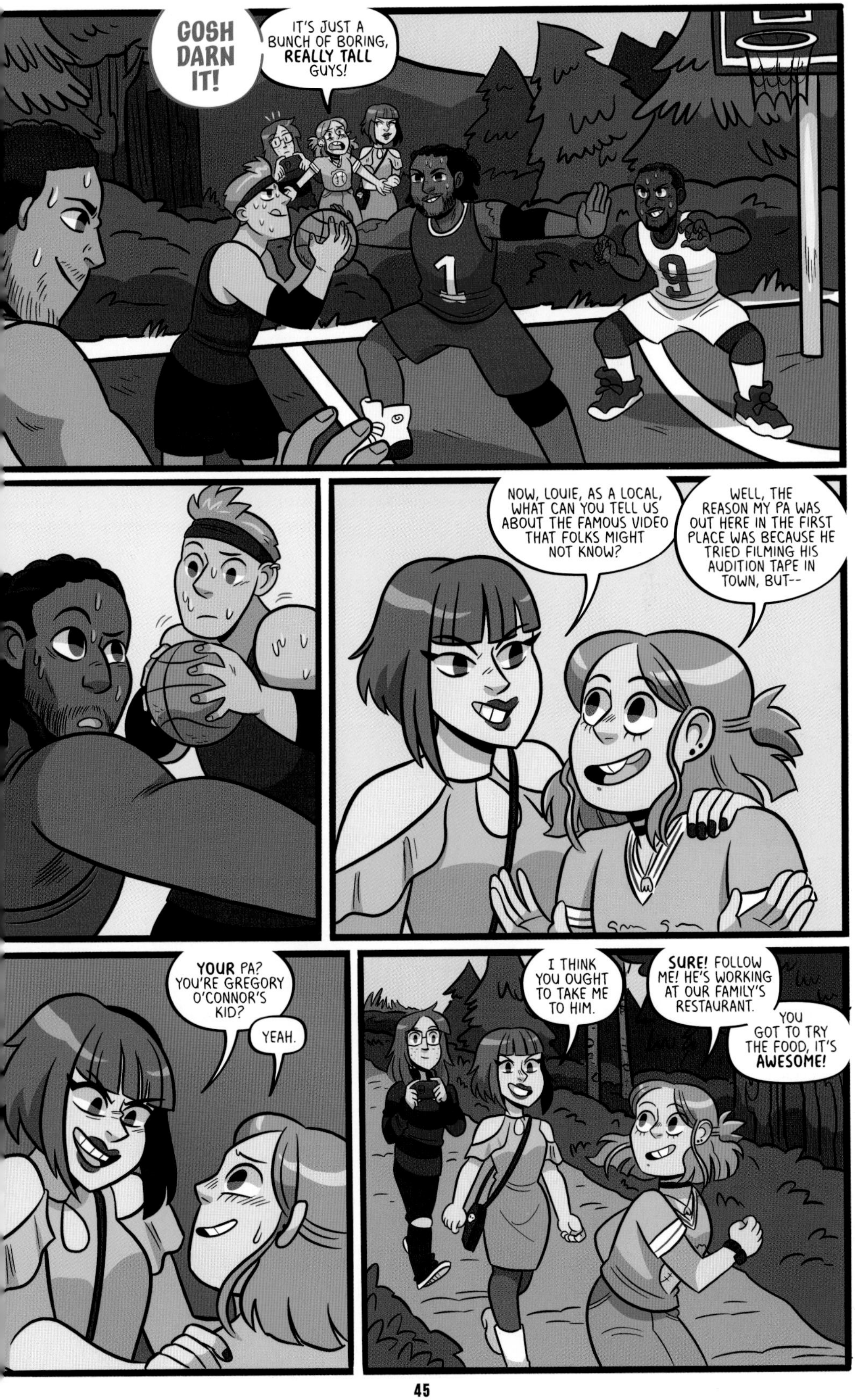
GOSH DARN IT!
IT'S JUST A BUNCH OF BORING, **REALLY TALL** GUYS!
NOW, LOUIE, AS A LOCAL, WHAT CAN YOU TELL US ABOUT THE FAMOUS VIDEO THAT FOLKS MIGHT NOT KNOW?
WELL, THE REASON MY PA WAS OUT HERE IN THE FIRST PLACE WAS BECAUSE HE TRIED FILMING HIS AUDITION TAPE IN TOWN, BUT--
YOUR PA? YOU'RE GREGORY O'CONNOR'S KID?
YEAH.
I THINK YOU OUGHT TO TAKE ME TO HIM.
SURE! FOLLOW ME! HE'S WORKING AT OUR FAMILY'S RESTAURANT.
YOU GOT TO TRY THE FOOD, IT'S **AWESOME!**

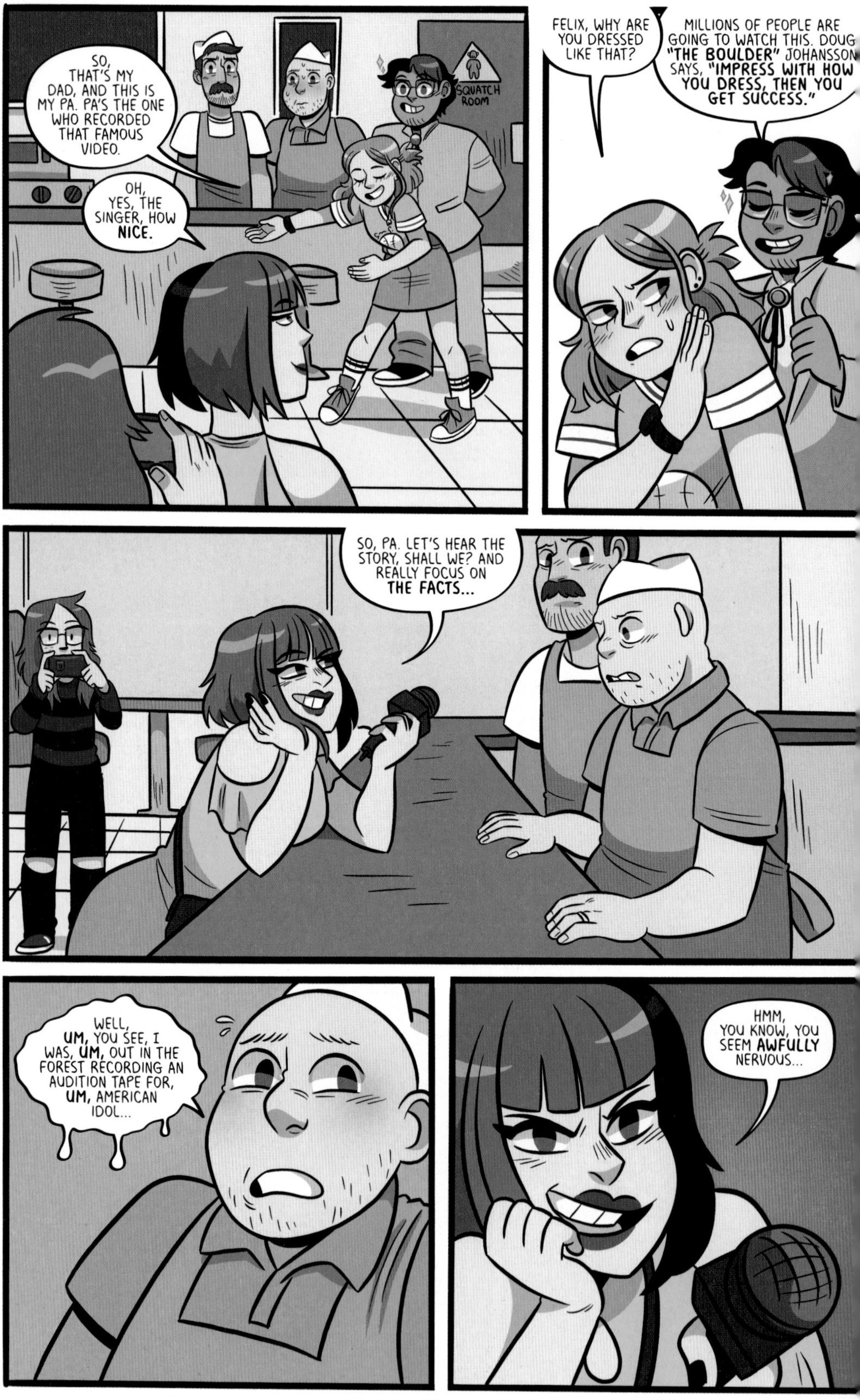
SO, THAT'S MY DAD, AND THIS IS MY PA. PA'S THE ONE WHO RECORDED THAT FAMOUS VIDEO.
OH, YES, THE SINGER, HOW **NICE**.
SQUATCH ROOM
FELIX, WHY ARE YOU DRESSED LIKE THAT?
MILLIONS OF PEOPLE ARE GOING TO WATCH THIS. DOUG **"THE BOULDER"** JOHANSSON SAYS, **"IMPRESS WITH HOW YOU DRESS, THEN YOU GET SUCCESS."**
SO, PA. LET'S HEAR THE STORY, SHALL WE? AND REALLY FOCUS ON **THE FACTS...**
WELL, **UM,** YOU SEE, I WAS, **UM,** OUT IN THE FOREST RECORDING AN AUDITION TAPE FOR, **UM,** AMERICAN IDOL...
HMM, YOU KNOW, YOU SEEM **AWFULLY** NERVOUS...

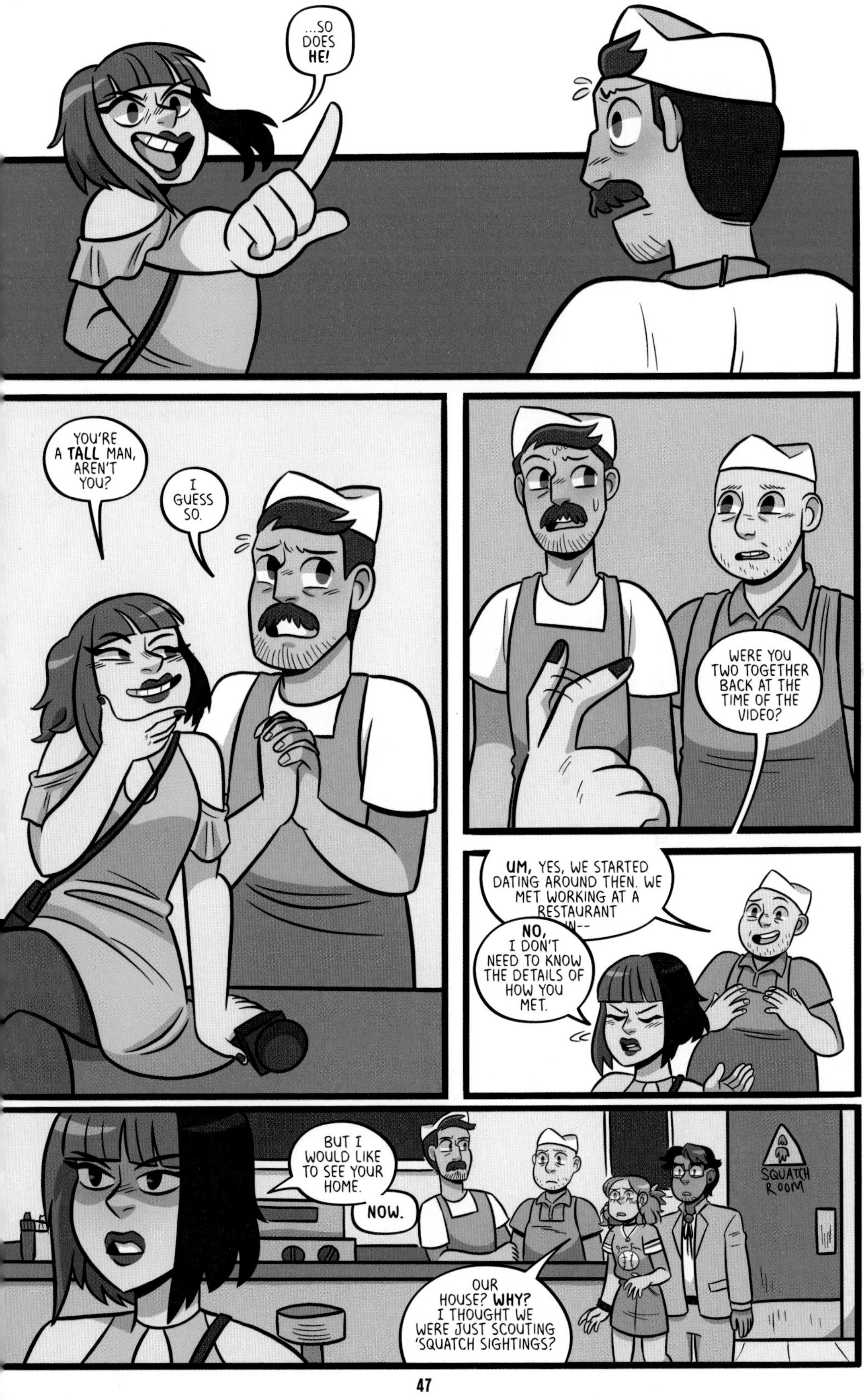
...SO DOES **HE!**
YOU'RE A **TALL** MAN, AREN'T YOU?
I GUESS SO.
WERE YOU TWO TOGETHER BACK AT THE TIME OF THE VIDEO?
UM, YES, WE STARTED DATING AROUND THEN. WE MET WORKING AT A RESTAURANT
NO, I DON'T NEED TO KNOW THE DETAILS OF HOW YOU MET.
BUT I WOULD LIKE TO SEE YOUR HOME.
NOW.
SQUATCH ROOM
OUR HOUSE? **WHY?** I THOUGHT WE WERE JUST SCOUTING 'SQUATCH SIGHTINGS?

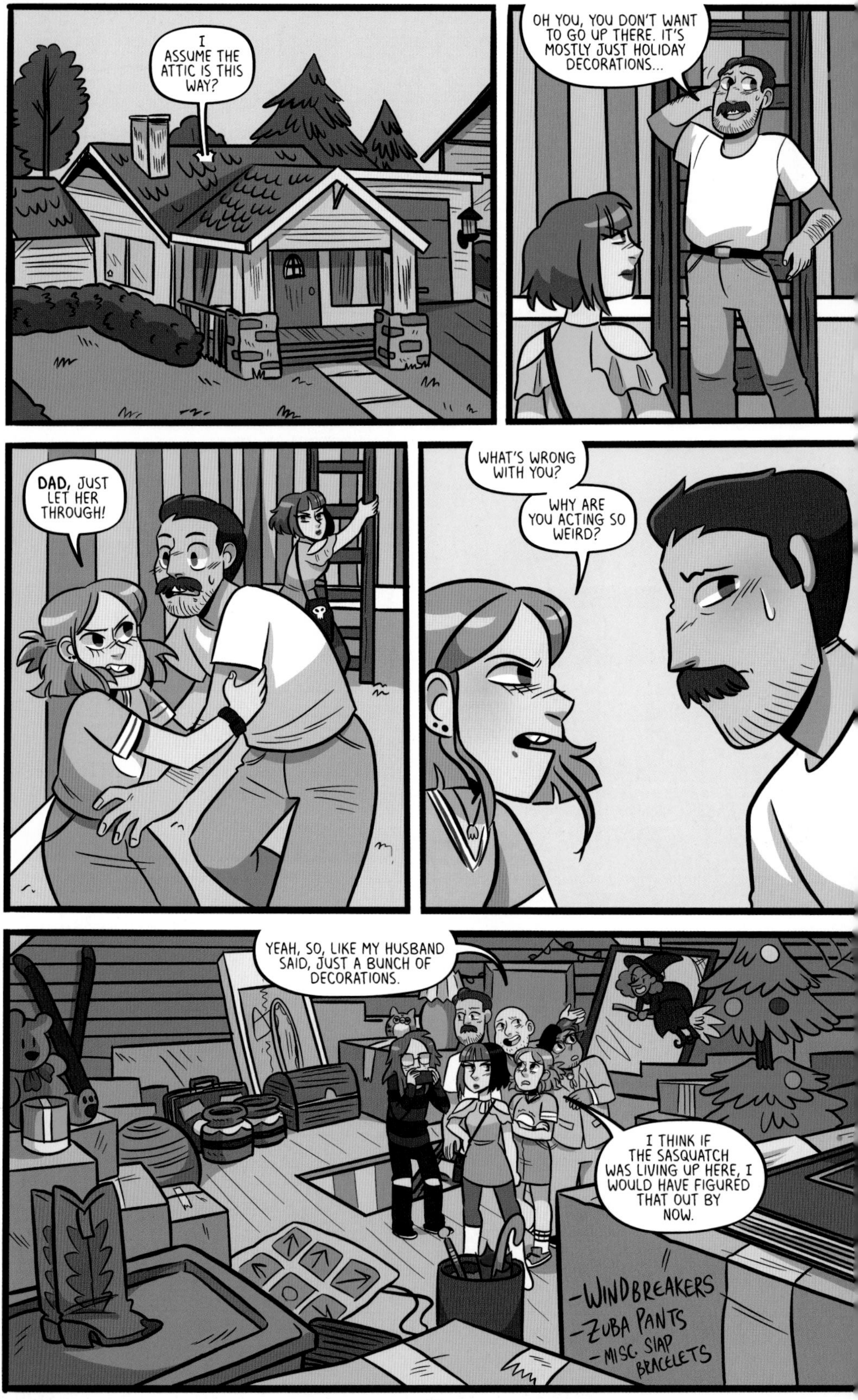
I ASSUME THE ATTIC IS THIS WAY?
OH YOU, YOU DON'T WANT TO GO UP THERE. IT'S MOSTLY JUST HOLIDAY DECORATIONS...
DAD, JUST LET HER THROUGH!
WHAT'S WRONG WITH YOU?
WHY ARE YOU ACTING SO WEIRD?
YEAH, SO, LIKE MY HUSBAND SAID, JUST A BUNCH OF DECORATIONS.
I THINK IF THE SASQUATCH WAS LIVING UP HERE, I WOULD HAVE FIGURED THAT OUT BY NOW.
-WINDBREAKERS
-ZUBA PANTS
-MISC. SLAP BRACELETS

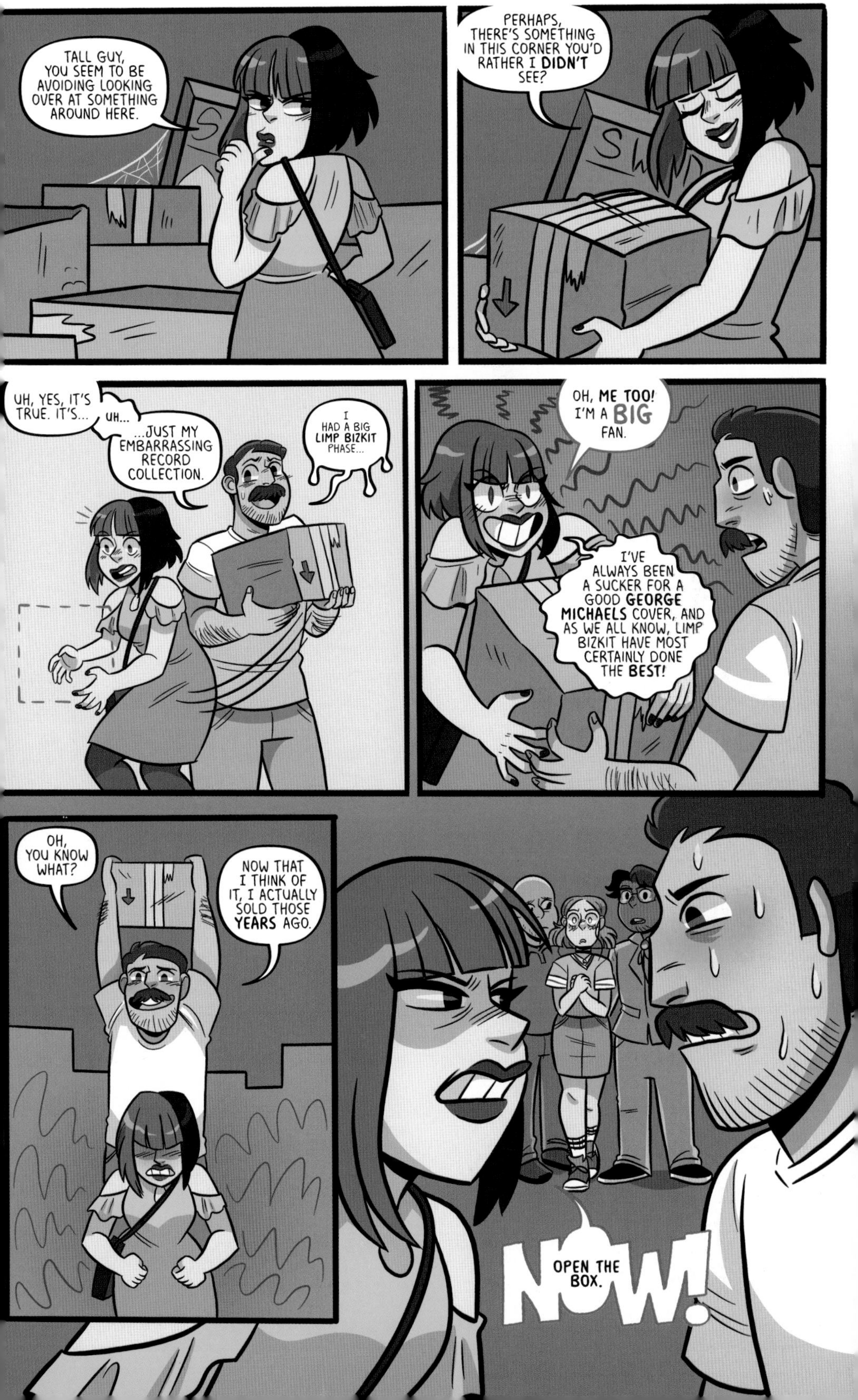
TALL GUY, YOU SEEM TO BE AVOIDING LOOKING OVER AT SOMETHING AROUND HERE.
PERHAPS, THERE'S SOMETHING IN THIS CORNER YOU'D RATHER I **DIDN'T** SEE?
UH, YES, IT'S TRUE. IT'S...
UH...
...JUST MY EMBARRASSING RECORD COLLECTION.
I HAD A BIG **LIMP BIZKIT** PHASE...
OH, **ME TOO!** I'M A **BIG** FAN.
I'VE ALWAYS BEEN A SUCKER FOR A GOOD **GEORGE MICHAELS** COVER, AND AS WE ALL KNOW, LIMP BIZKIT HAVE MOST CERTAINLY DONE THE **BEST!**
OH, YOU KNOW WHAT?
NOW THAT I THINK OF IT, I ACTUALLY SOLD THOSE **YEARS** AGO.
OPEN THE BOX.
NOW!

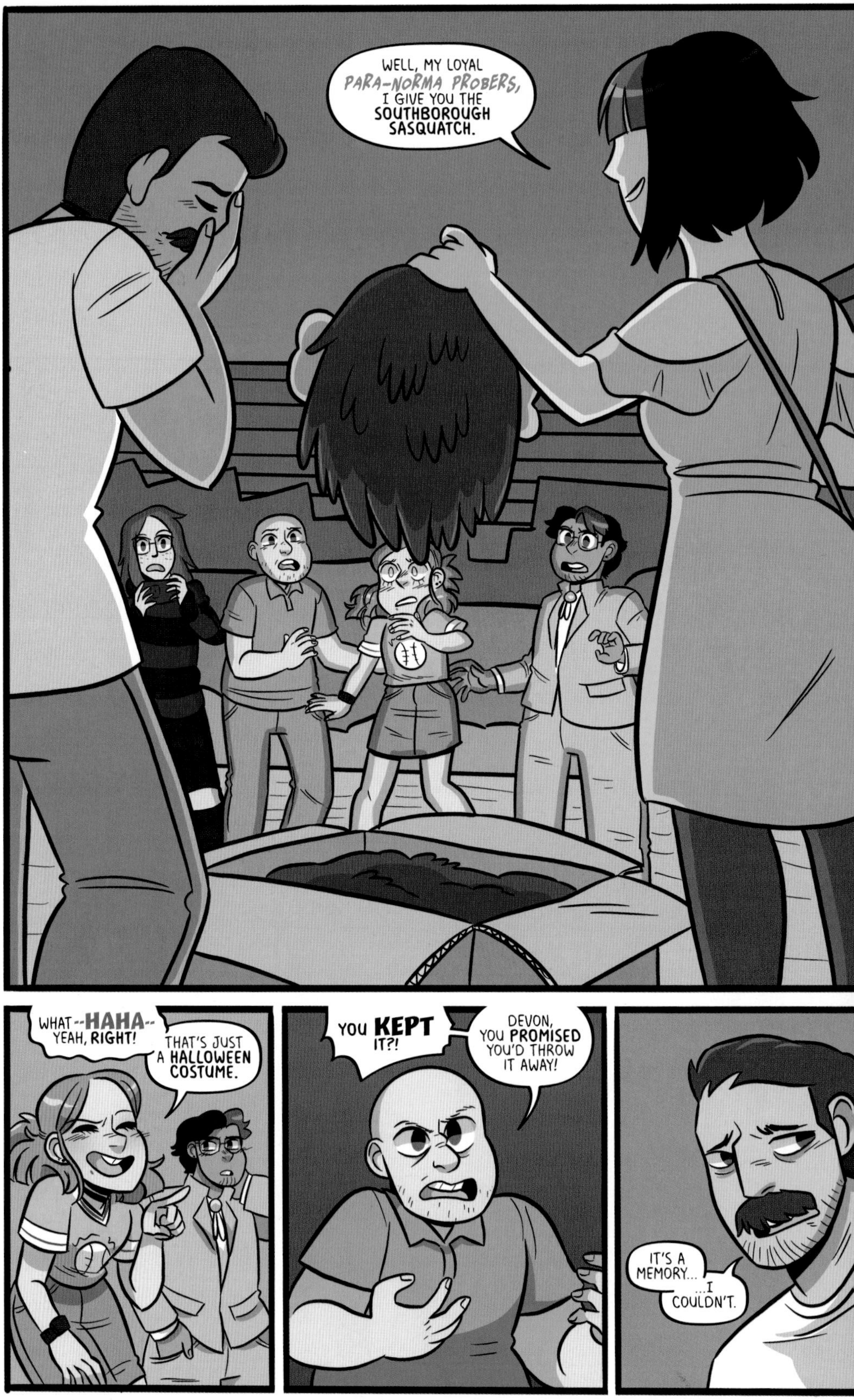
WELL, MY LOYAL PARA-NORMA PROBERS, I GIVE YOU THE SOUTHBOROUGH SASQUATCH.
WHAT--HAHA--YEAH, RIGHT!
THAT'S JUST A HALLOWEEN COSTUME.
YOU KEPT IT?!
DEVON, YOU PROMISED YOU'D THROW IT AWAY!
IT'S A MEMORY... ...I COULDN'T.

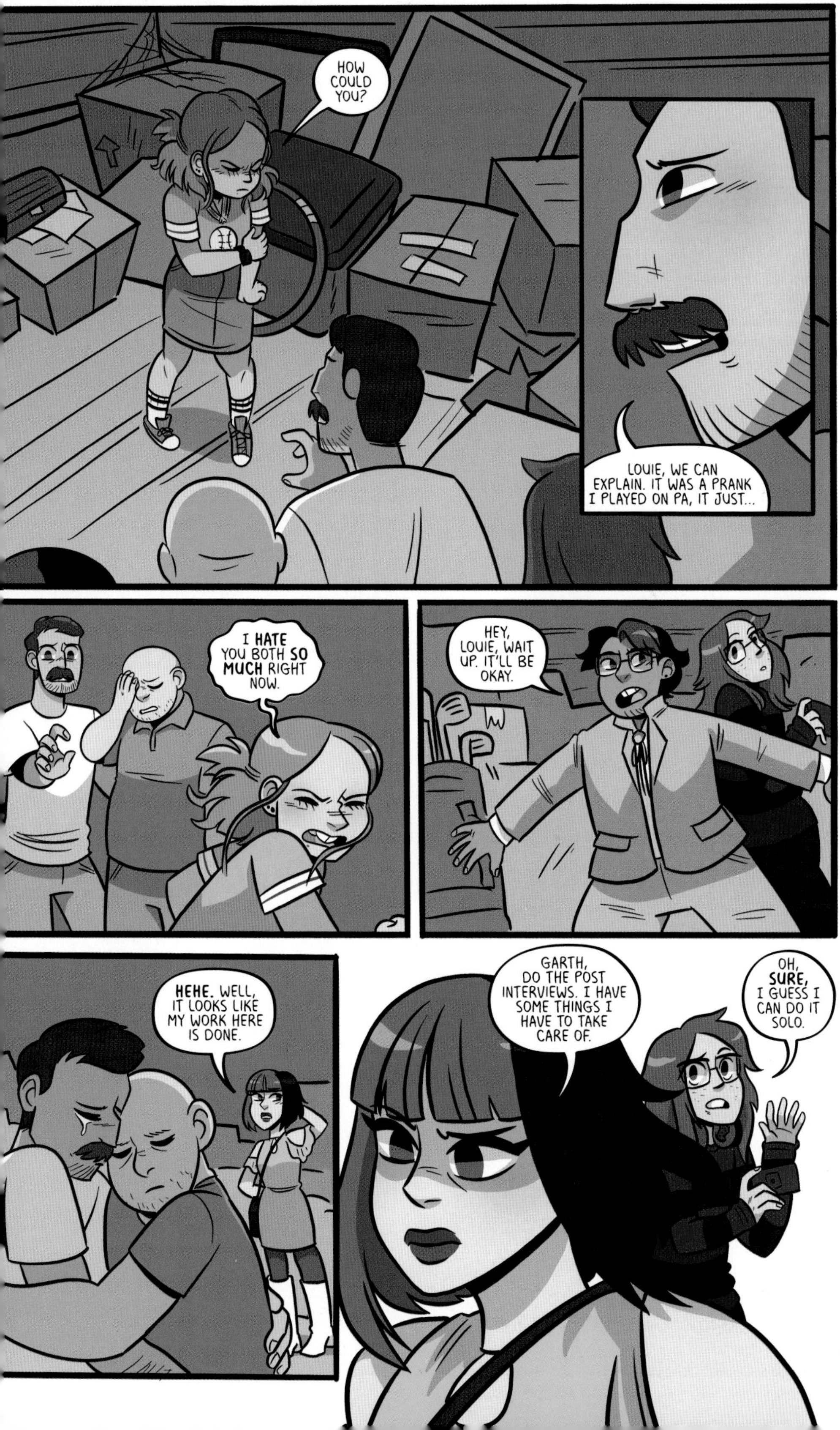
HOW COULD YOU?
LOUIE, WE CAN EXPLAIN. IT WAS A PRANK I PLAYED ON PA, IT JUST...
I **HATE** YOU BOTH **SO MUCH** RIGHT NOW.
HEY, LOUIE, WAIT UP. IT'LL BE OKAY.
HEHE. WELL, IT LOOKS LIKE MY WORK HERE IS DONE.
GARTH, DO THE POST INTERVIEWS. I HAVE SOME THINGS I HAVE TO TAKE CARE OF.
OH, **SURE,** I GUESS I CAN DO IT SOLO.

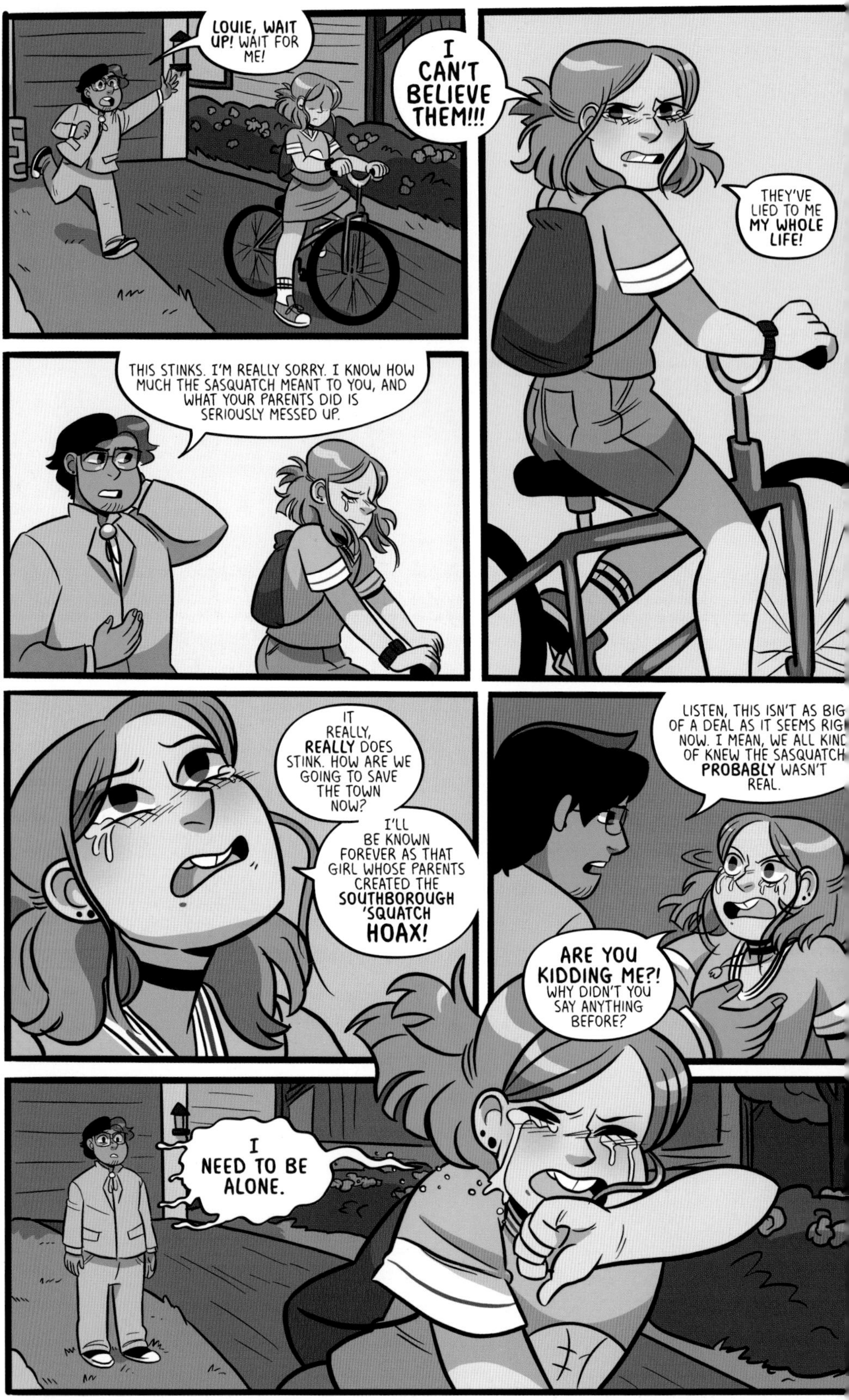
LOUIE, WAIT UP! WAIT FOR ME!
I CAN'T BELIEVE THEM!!!
THEY'VE LIED TO ME MY WHOLE LIFE!
THIS STINKS. I'M REALLY SORRY. I KNOW HOW MUCH THE SASQUATCH MEANT TO YOU, AND WHAT YOUR PARENTS DID IS SERIOUSLY MESSED UP.
IT REALLY, REALLY DOES STINK. HOW ARE WE GOING TO SAVE THE TOWN NOW?
I'LL BE KNOWN FOREVER AS THAT GIRL WHOSE PARENTS CREATED THE SOUTHBOROUGH 'SQUATCH HOAX!
ARE YOU KIDDING ME?! WHY DIDN'T YOU SAY ANYTHING BEFORE?
I NEED TO BE ALONE.

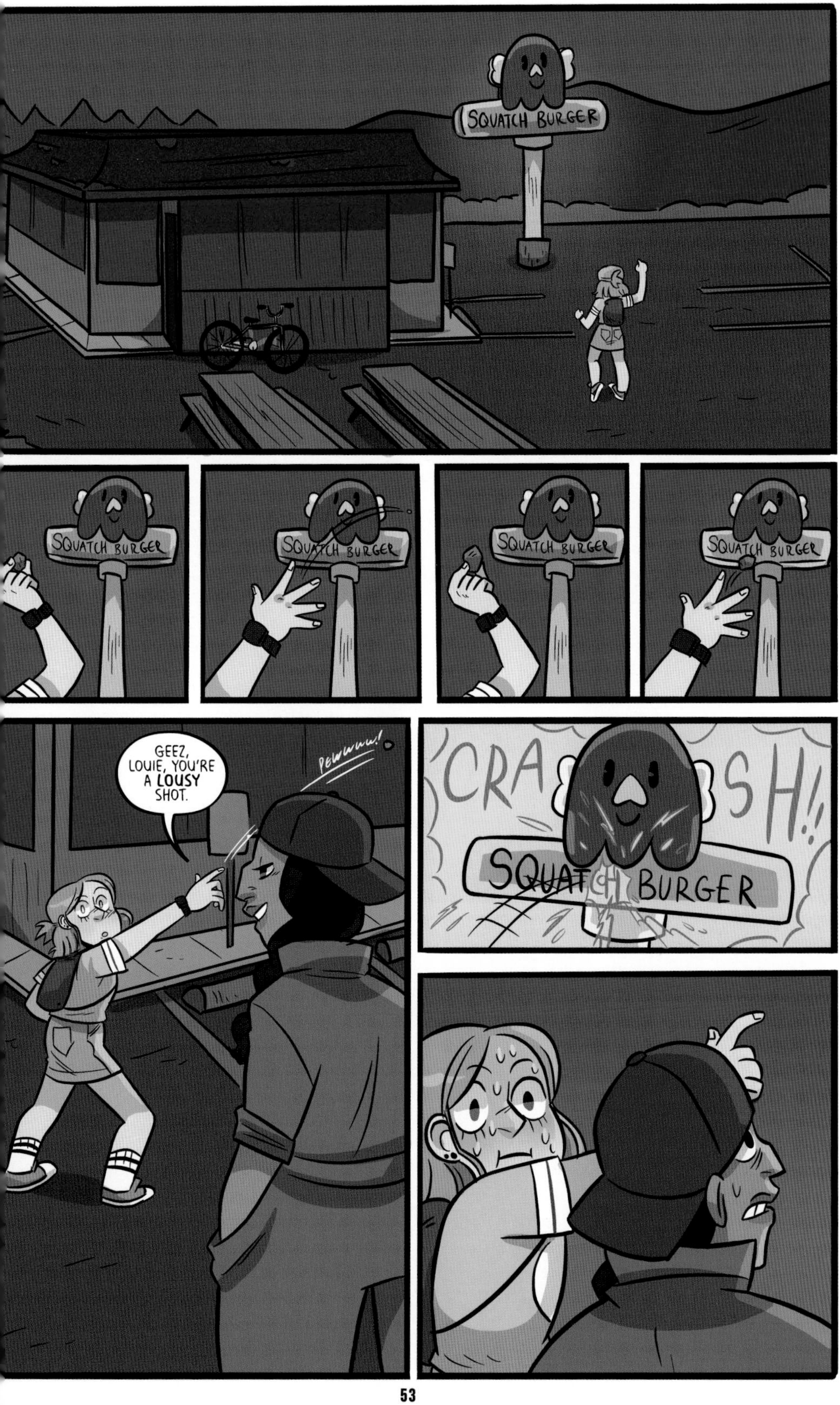
SQUATCH BURGER
SQUATCH BURGER
SQUATCH BURGER
SQUATCH BURGER
SQUATCH BURGER
GEEZ, LOUIE, YOU'RE A **LOUSY** SHOT.
PEWWWW!
CRASH!!
SQUATCH BURGER

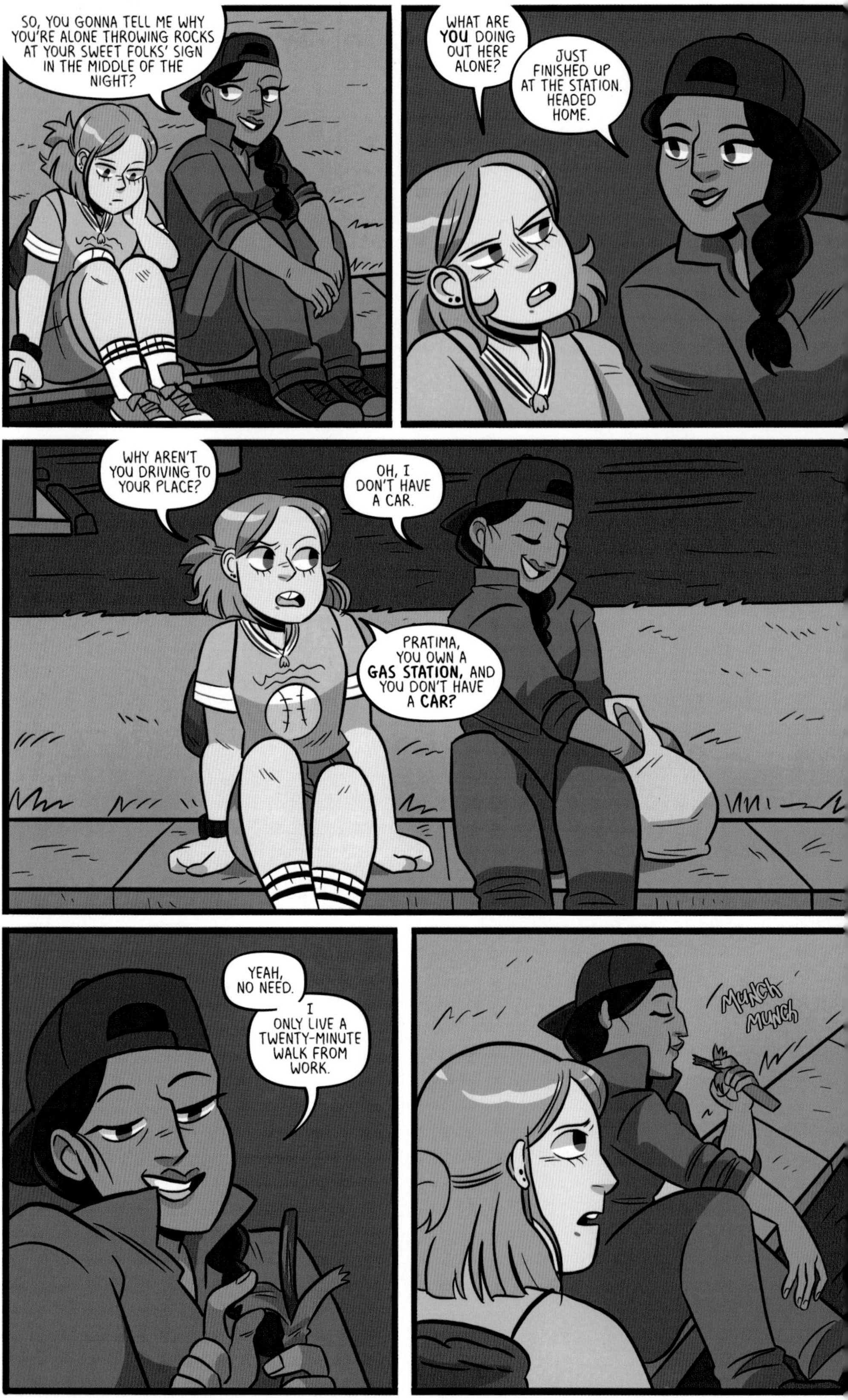
SO, YOU GONNA TELL ME WHY YOU'RE ALONE THROWING ROCKS AT YOUR SWEET FOLKS' SIGN IN THE MIDDLE OF THE NIGHT?
WHAT ARE YOU DOING OUT HERE ALONE?
JUST FINISHED UP AT THE STATION. HEADED HOME.
WHY AREN'T YOU DRIVING TO YOUR PLACE?
OH, I DON'T HAVE A CAR.
PRATIMA, YOU OWN A GAS STATION, AND YOU DON'T HAVE A CAR?
YEAH, NO NEED.
I ONLY LIVE A TWENTY-MINUTE WALK FROM WORK.
MUNCH MUNCH

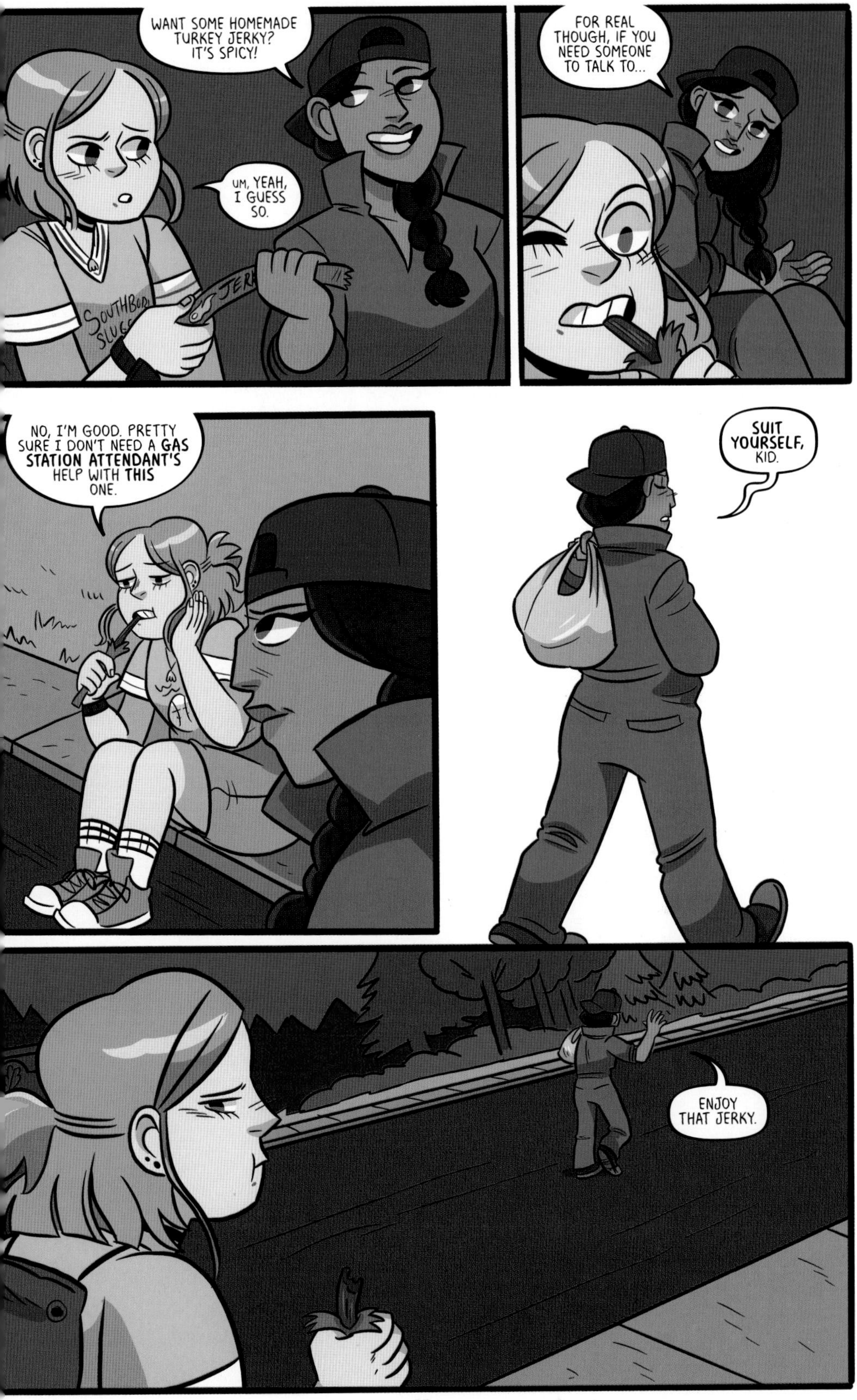
WANT SOME HOMEMADE TURKEY JERKY? IT'S SPICY!
UM, YEAH, I GUESS SO.
FOR REAL THOUGH, IF YOU NEED SOMEONE TO TALK TO...
NO, I'M GOOD. PRETTY SURE I DON'T NEED A **GAS STATION ATTENDANT'S** HELP WITH **THIS** ONE.
SUIT YOURSELF, KID.
ENJOY THAT JERKY.

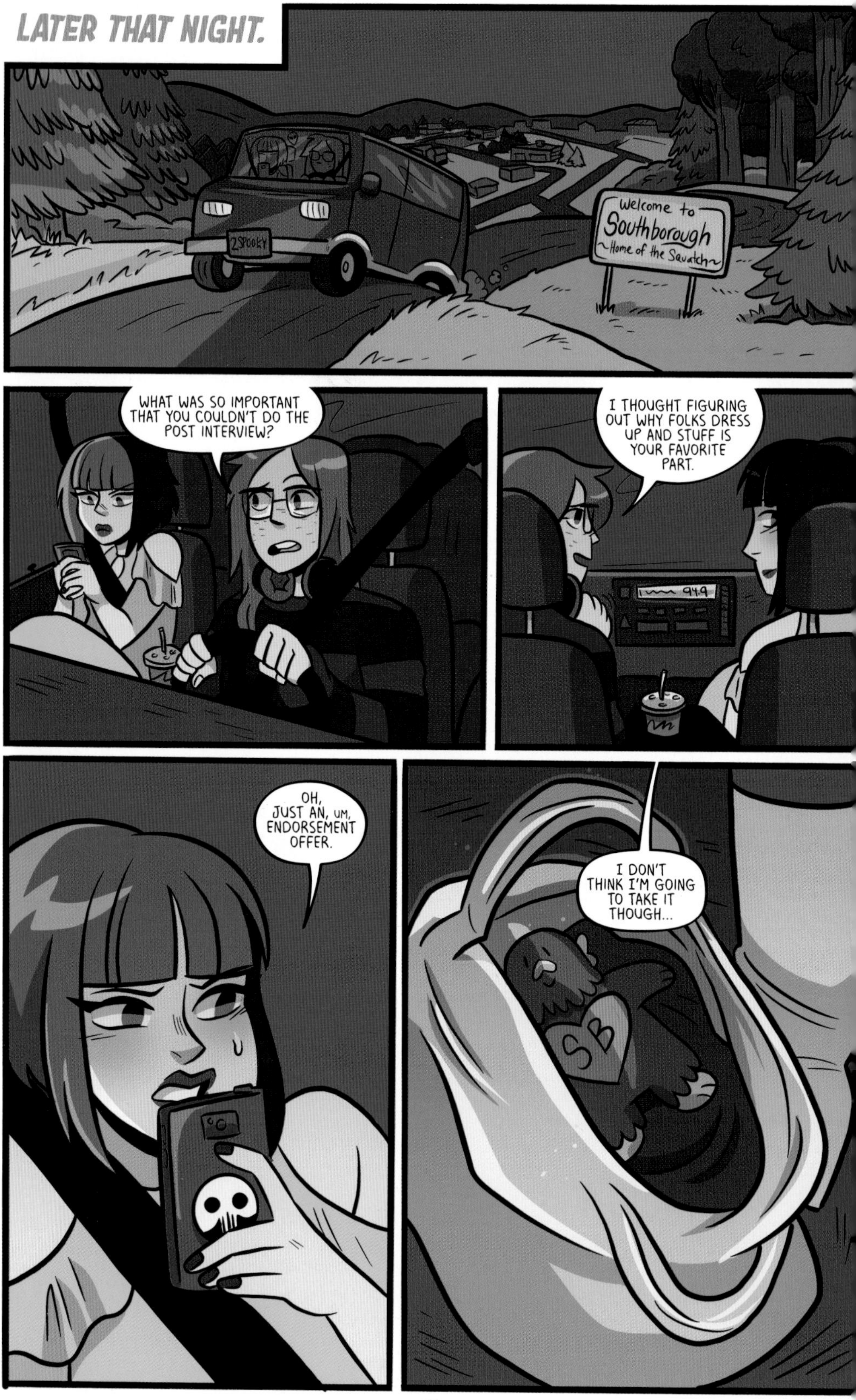
LATER THAT NIGHT.
2SPOOKY
Welcome to
Southborough
Home of the Sauatch
WHAT WAS SO IMPORTANT THAT YOU COULDN'T DO THE POST INTERVIEW?
I THOUGHT FIGURING OUT WHY FOLKS DRESS UP AND STUFF IS YOUR FAVORITE PART.
94.9
OH, JUST AN, UM, ENDORSEMENT OFFER.
I DON'T THINK I'M GOING TO TAKE IT THOUGH...
SB

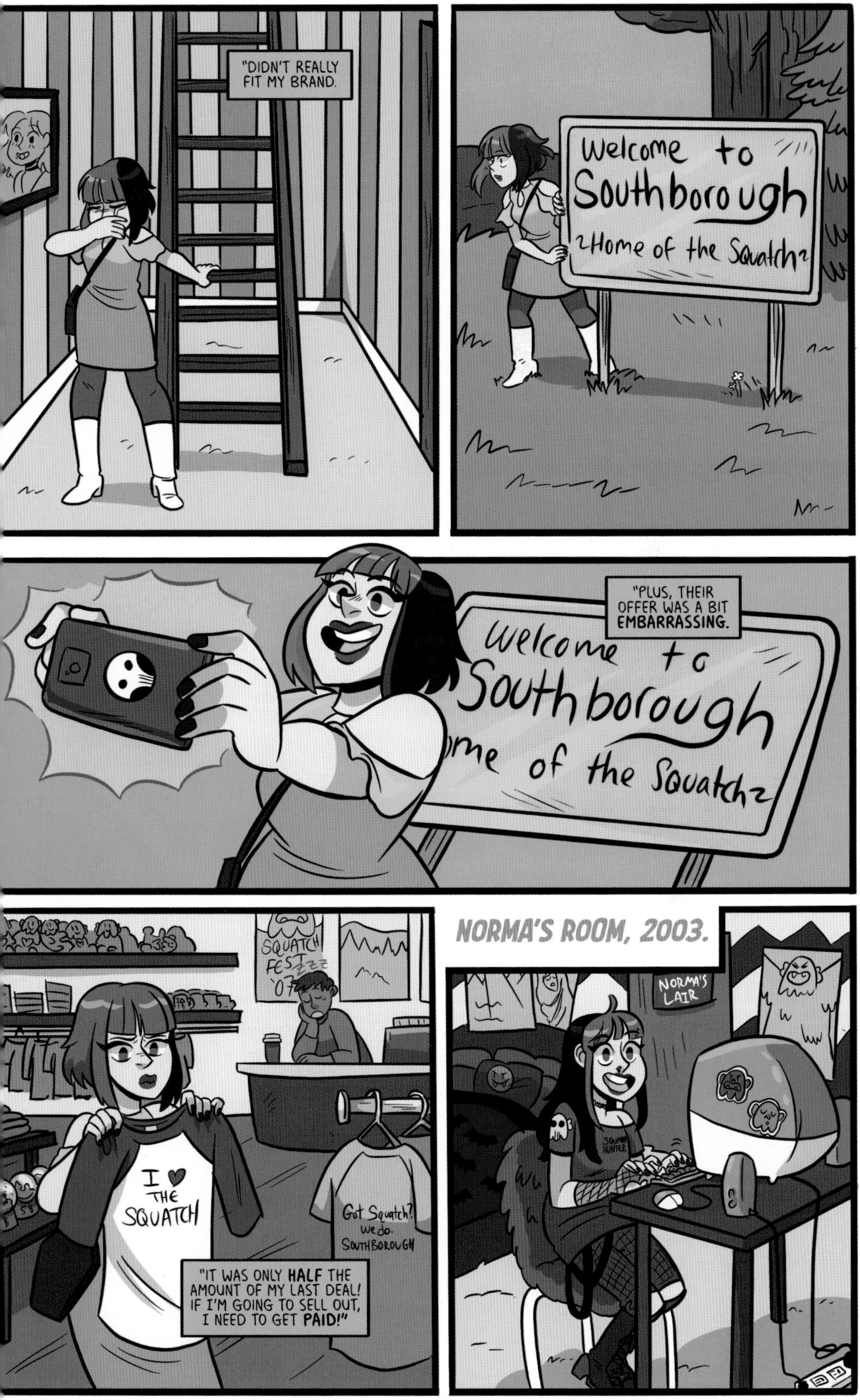
"DIDN'T REALLY FIT MY BRAND.
Welcome to Southborough
~Home of the Squatch~
"PLUS, THEIR OFFER WAS A BIT **EMBARRASSING.**
Welcome to Southborough
me of the Squatch~
SQUATCH FEST '07
I ♥ THE SQUATCH
Got Squatch? we do. SOUTHBOROUGH
"IT WAS ONLY **HALF** THE AMOUNT OF MY LAST DEAL! IF I'M GOING TO SELL OUT, I NEED TO GET **PAID!**"
NORMA'S ROOM, 2003.
NORMA'S LAIR

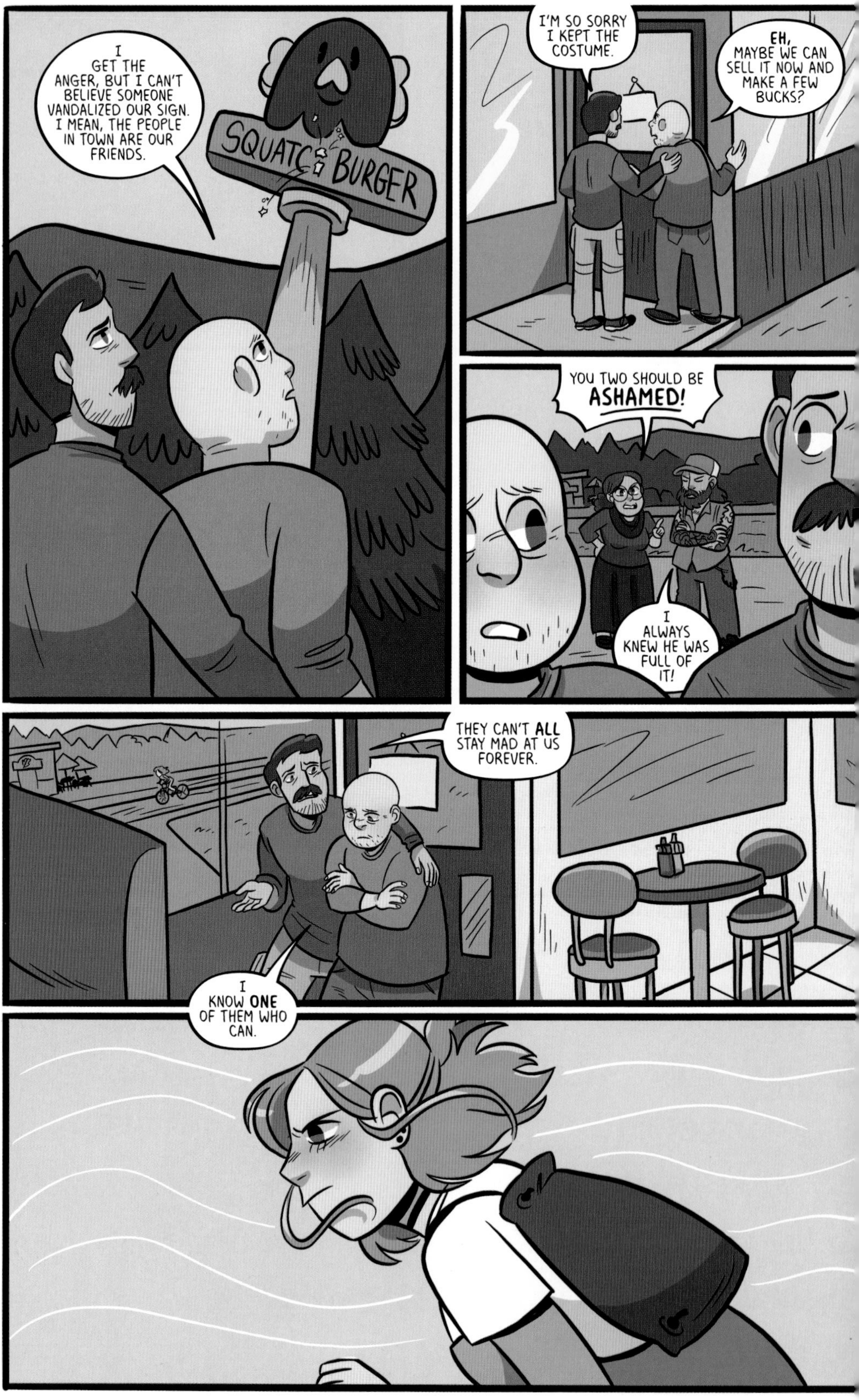

I GET THE ANGER, BUT I CAN'T BELIEVE SOMEONE VANDALIZED OUR SIGN. I MEAN, THE PEOPLE IN TOWN ARE OUR FRIENDS.
SQUATC BURGER
I'M SO SORRY I KEPT THE COSTUME.
EH, MAYBE WE CAN SELL IT NOW AND MAKE A FEW BUCKS?
YOU TWO SHOULD BE ASHAMED!
I ALWAYS KNEW HE WAS FULL OF IT!
THEY CAN'T ALL STAY MAD AT US FOREVER.
I KNOW ONE OF THEM WHO CAN.

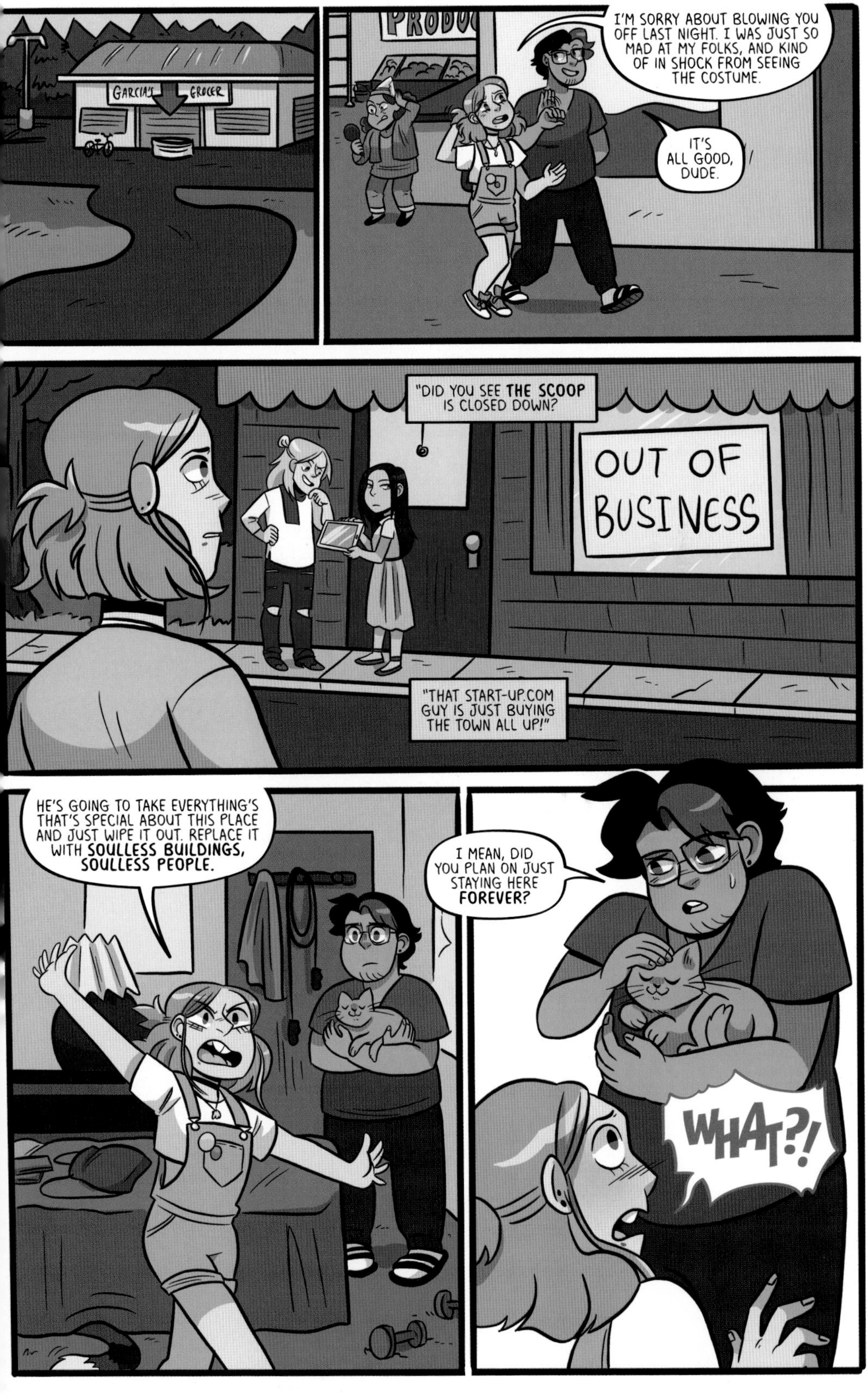
GARCIA'S GROCER
PRODUC
I'M SORRY ABOUT BLOWING YOU OFF LAST NIGHT. I WAS JUST SO MAD AT MY FOLKS, AND KIND OF IN SHOCK FROM SEEING THE COSTUME.
IT'S ALL GOOD, DUDE.
"DID YOU SEE **THE SCOOP** IS CLOSED DOWN?
OUT OF BUSINESS
"THAT START-UP.COM GUY IS JUST BUYING THE TOWN ALL UP!"
HE'S GOING TO TAKE EVERYTHING'S THAT'S SPECIAL ABOUT THIS PLACE AND JUST WIPE IT OUT. REPLACE IT WITH **SOULLESS BUILDINGS, SOULLESS PEOPLE.**
I MEAN, DID YOU PLAN ON JUST STAYING HERE **FOREVER?**
WHAT?!

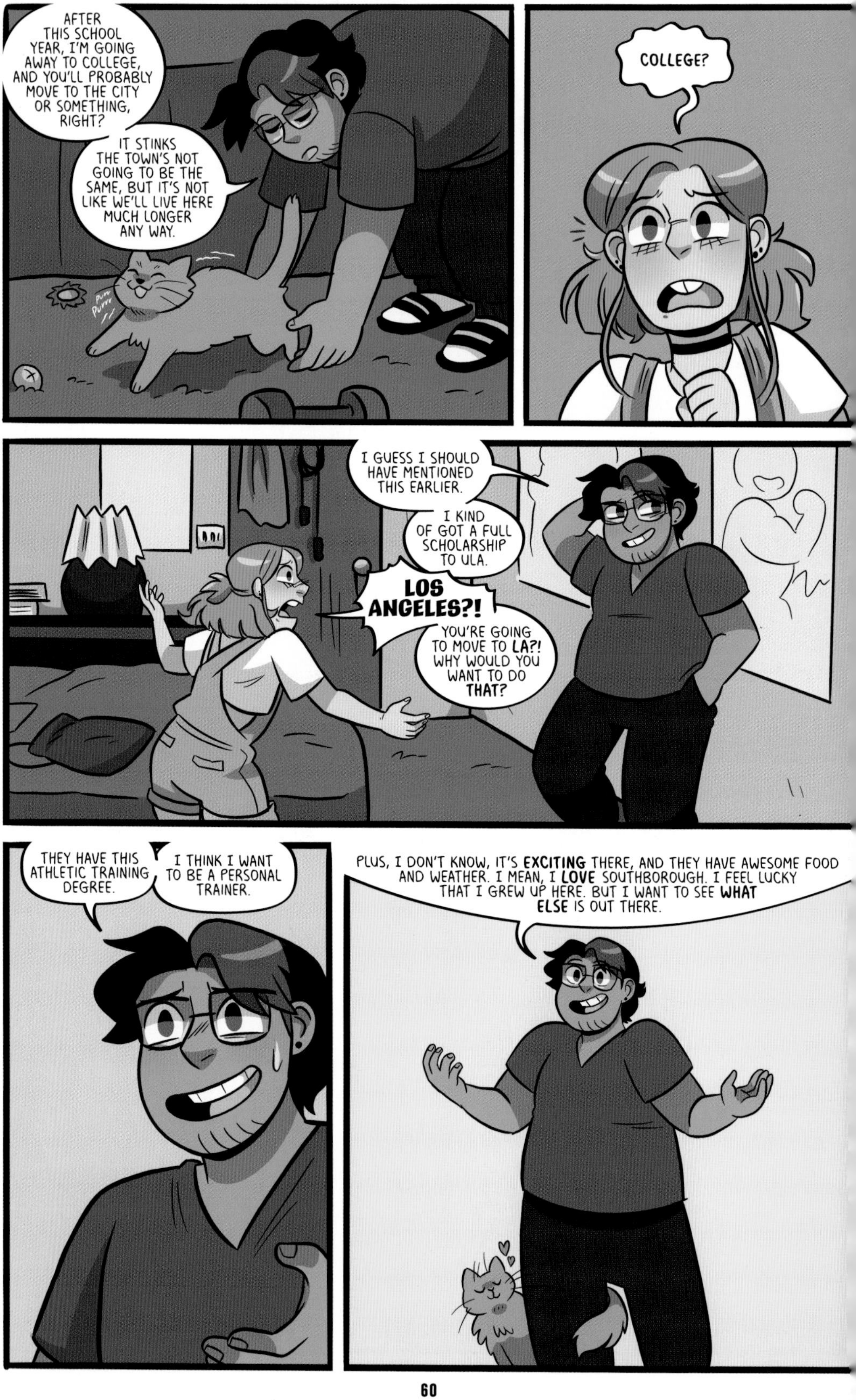
AFTER THIS SCHOOL YEAR, I'M GOING AWAY TO COLLEGE, AND YOU'LL PROBABLY MOVE TO THE CITY OR SOMETHING, RIGHT?
IT STINKS THE TOWN'S NOT GOING TO BE THE SAME, BUT IT'S NOT LIKE WE'LL LIVE HERE MUCH LONGER ANY WAY.
Purr Purrr
COLLEGE?
I GUESS I SHOULD HAVE MENTIONED THIS EARLIER.
I KIND OF GOT A FULL SCHOLARSHIP TO ULA.
LOS ANGELES?!
YOU'RE GOING TO MOVE TO LA?! WHY WOULD YOU WANT TO DO THAT?
THEY HAVE THIS ATHLETIC TRAINING DEGREE.
I THINK I WANT TO BE A PERSONAL TRAINER.
PLUS, I DON'T KNOW, IT'S EXCITING THERE, AND THEY HAVE AWESOME FOOD AND WEATHER. I MEAN, I LOVE SOUTHBOROUGH. I FEEL LUCKY THAT I GREW UP HERE. BUT I WANT TO SEE WHAT ELSE IS OUT THERE.

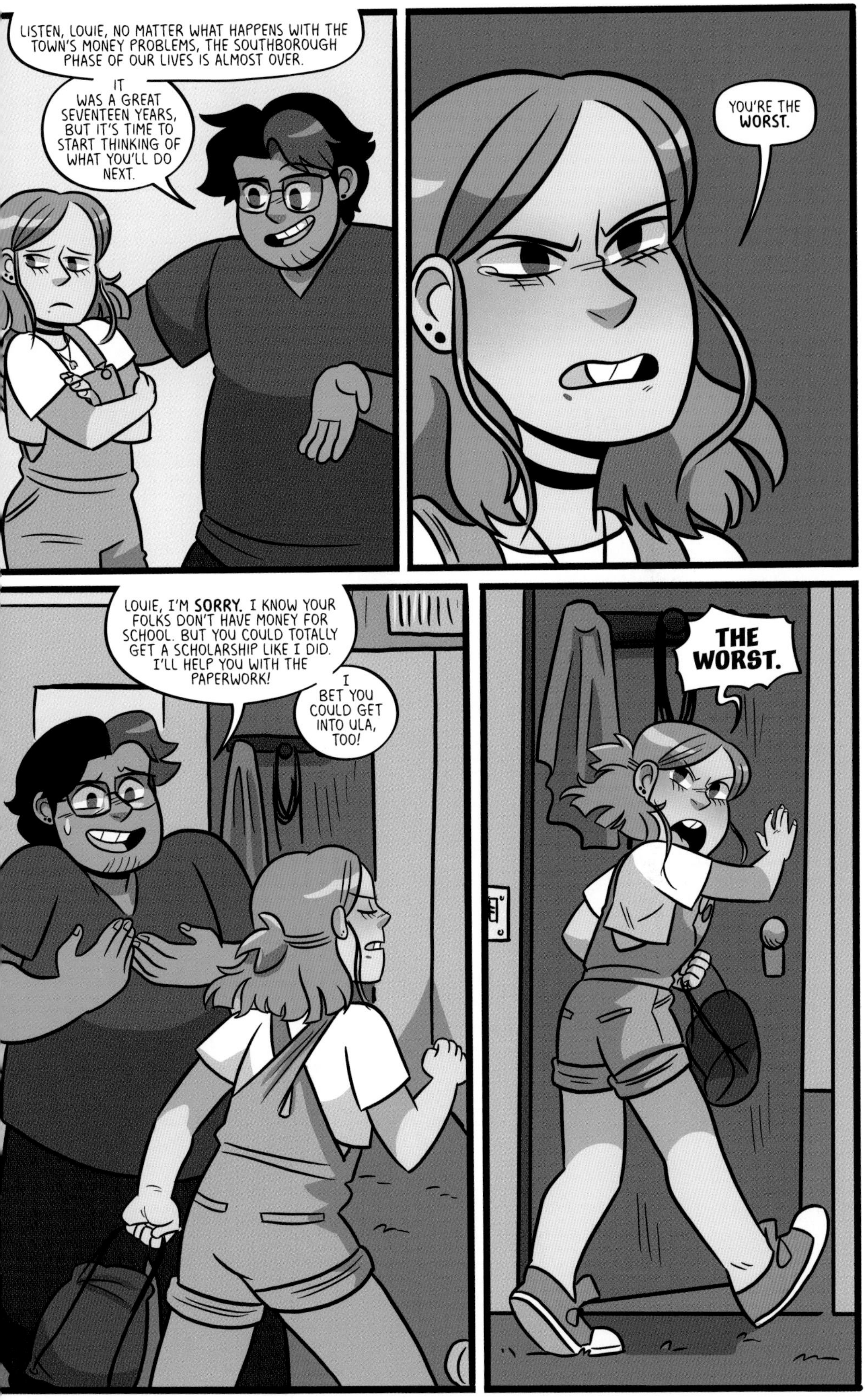
LISTEN, LOUIE, NO MATTER WHAT HAPPENS WITH THE TOWN'S MONEY PROBLEMS, THE SOUTHBOROUGH PHASE OF OUR LIVES IS ALMOST OVER.
IT WAS A GREAT SEVENTEEN YEARS, BUT IT'S TIME TO START THINKING OF WHAT YOU'LL DO NEXT.
YOU'RE THE **WORST.**
LOUIE, I'M **SORRY.** I KNOW YOUR FOLKS DON'T HAVE MONEY FOR SCHOOL. BUT YOU COULD TOTALLY GET A SCHOLARSHIP LIKE I DID. I'LL HELP YOU WITH THE PAPERWORK!
I BET YOU COULD GET INTO ULA, TOO!
THE WORST.

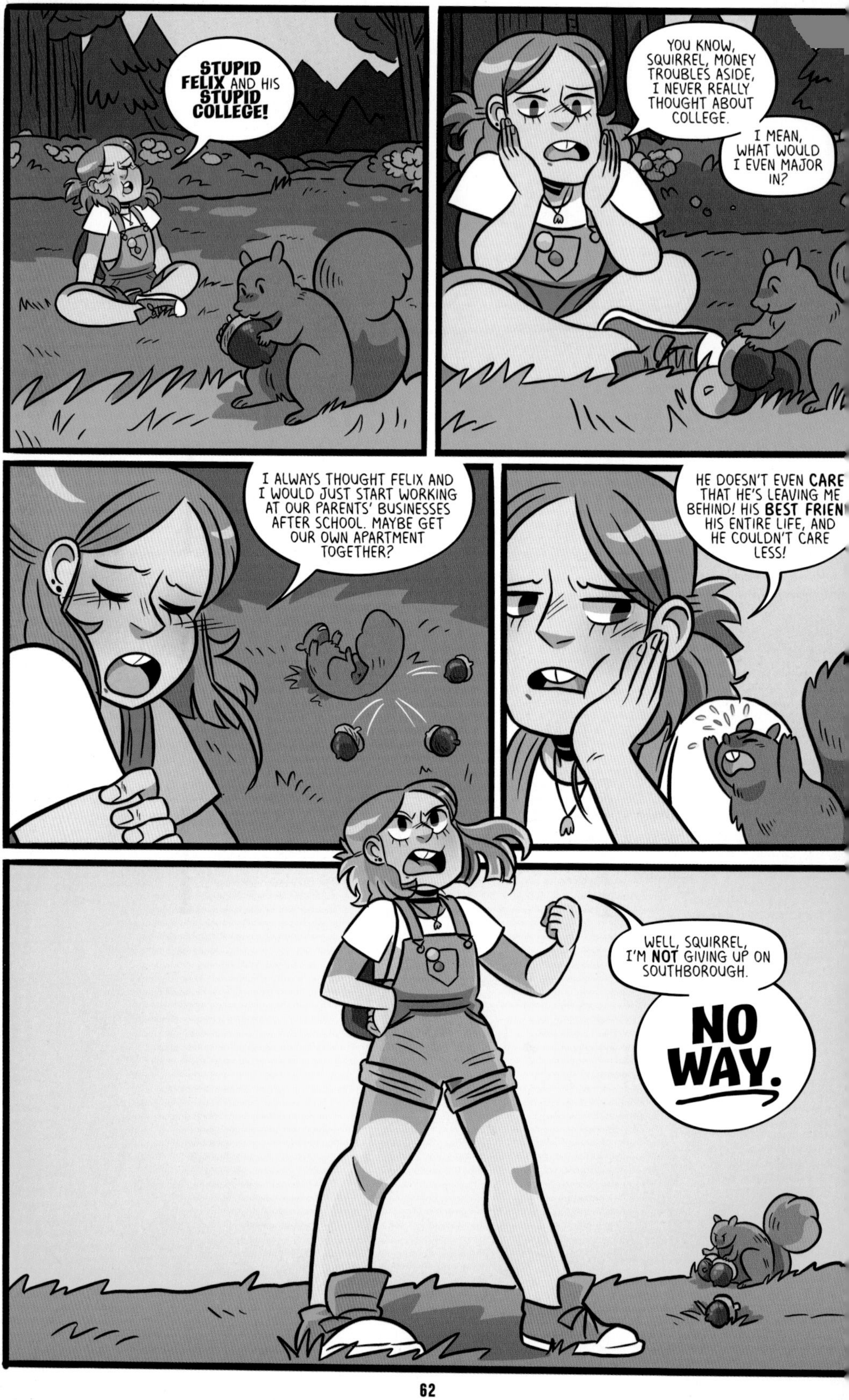
STUPID FELIX AND HIS STUPID COLLEGE!
YOU KNOW, SQUIRREL, MONEY TROUBLES ASIDE, I NEVER REALLY THOUGHT ABOUT COLLEGE.
I MEAN, WHAT WOULD I EVEN MAJOR IN?
I ALWAYS THOUGHT FELIX AND I WOULD JUST START WORKING AT OUR PARENTS' BUSINESSES AFTER SCHOOL. MAYBE GET OUR OWN APARTMENT TOGETHER?
HE DOESN'T EVEN CARE THAT HE'S LEAVING ME BEHIND! HIS BEST FRIEN HIS ENTIRE LIFE, AND HE COULDN'T CARE LESS!
WELL, SQUIRREL, I'M NOT GIVING UP ON SOUTHBOROUGH.
NO WAY.

CHAPTER 3

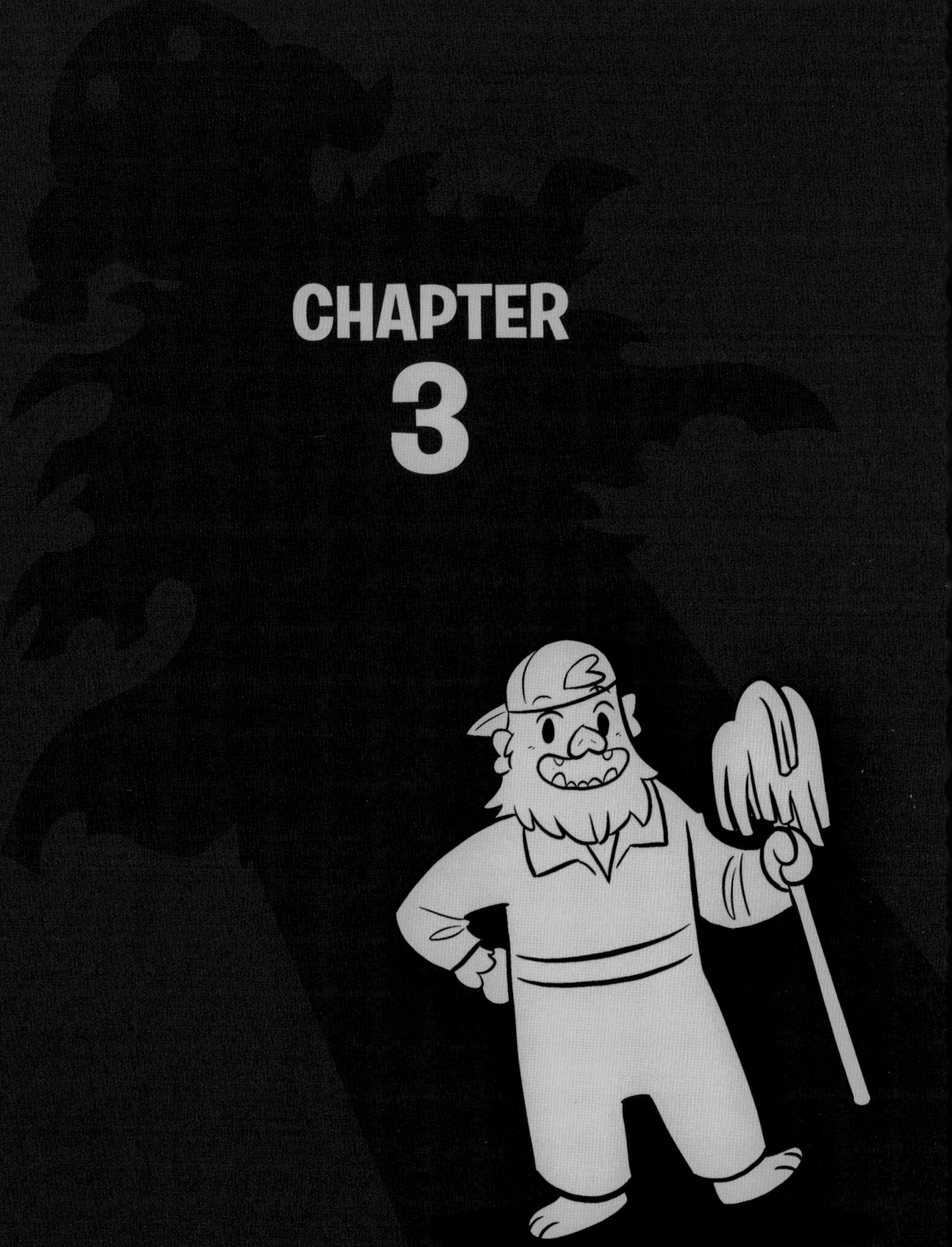

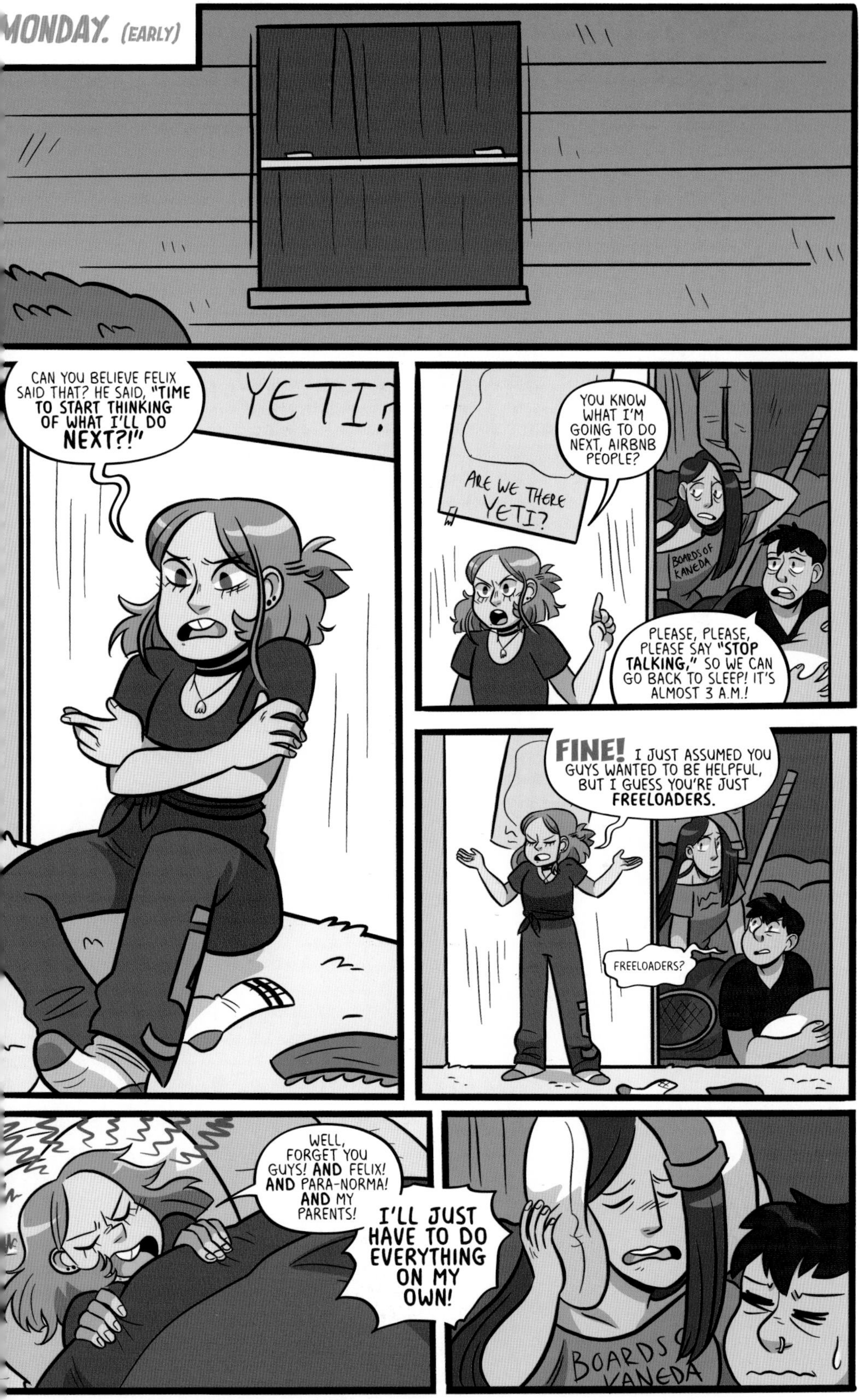
MONDAY. (EARLY)
CAN YOU BELIEVE FELIX SAID THAT? HE SAID, "TIME TO START THINKING OF WHAT I'LL DO NEXT?!"
YETI?
ARE WE THERE YETI?
YOU KNOW WHAT I'M GOING TO DO NEXT, AIRBNB PEOPLE?
BOARDS OF KANEDA
PLEASE, PLEASE, PLEASE SAY "STOP TALKING," SO WE CAN GO BACK TO SLEEP! IT'S ALMOST 3 A.M.!
FINE! I JUST ASSUMED YOU GUYS WANTED TO BE HELPFUL, BUT I GUESS YOU'RE JUST FREELOADERS.
FREELOADERS?
WELL, FORGET YOU GUYS! AND FELIX! AND PARA-NORMA! AND MY PARENTS!
I'LL JUST HAVE TO DO EVERYTHING ON MY OWN!
BOARDS OF KANEDA

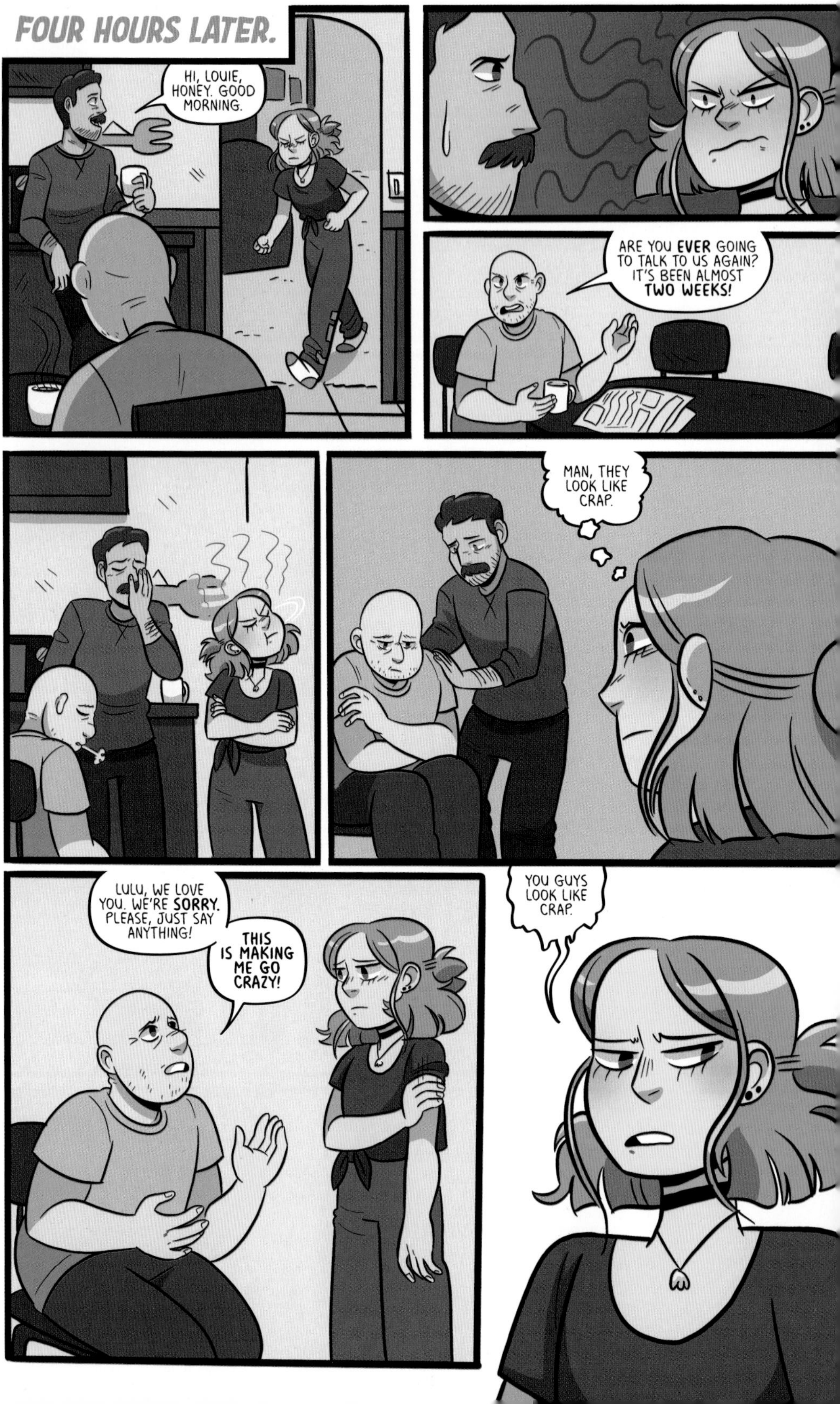
FOUR HOURS LATER.
HI, LOUIE, HONEY. GOOD MORNING.
ARE YOU EVER GOING TO TALK TO US AGAIN? IT'S BEEN ALMOST TWO WEEKS!
MAN, THEY LOOK LIKE CRAP.
LULU, WE LOVE YOU. WE'RE SORRY. PLEASE, JUST SAY ANYTHING!
THIS IS MAKING ME GO CRAZY!
YOU GUYS LOOK LIKE CRAP.

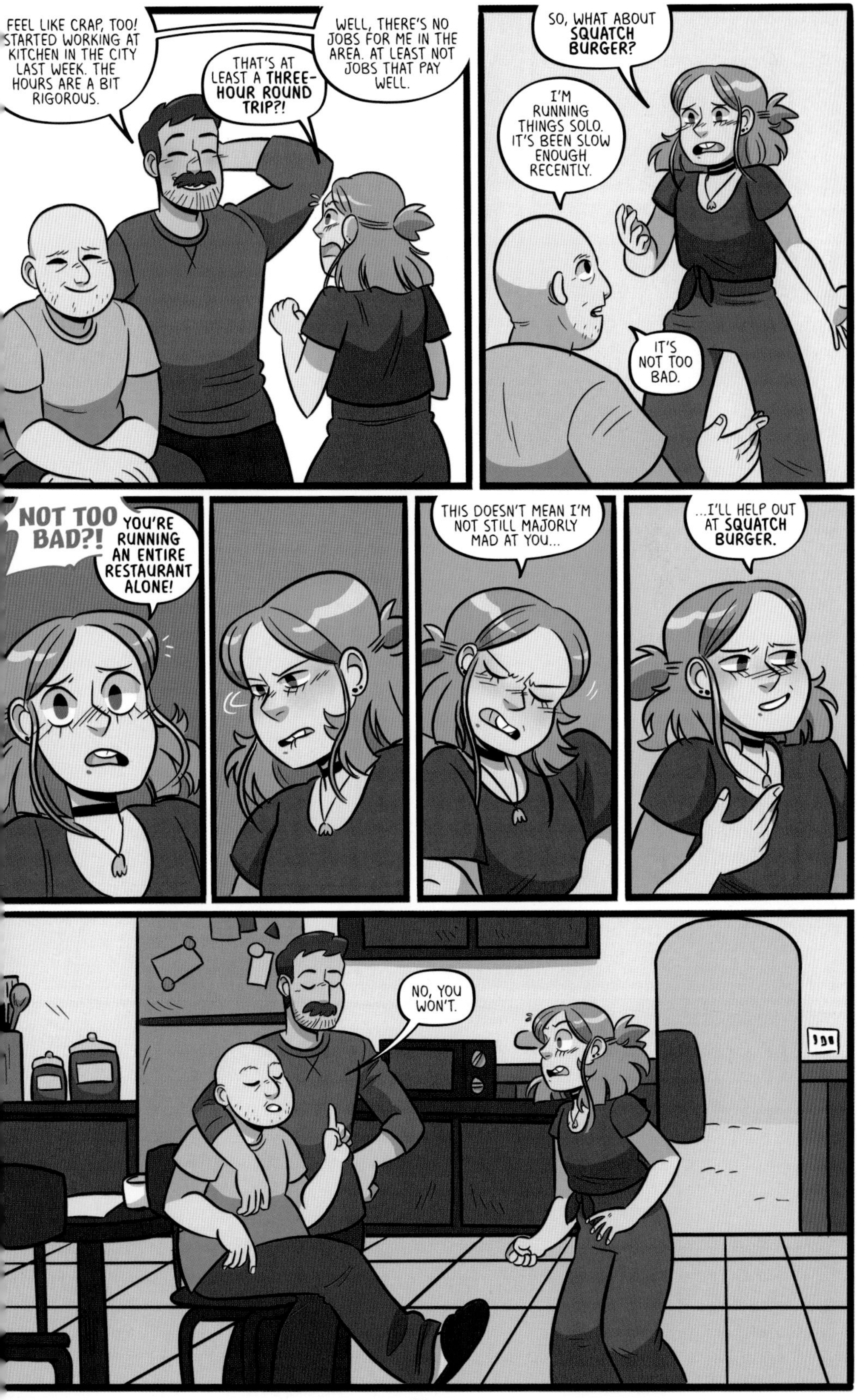
FEEL LIKE CRAP, TOO! STARTED WORKING AT KITCHEN IN THE CITY LAST WEEK. THE HOURS ARE A BIT RIGOROUS.
THAT'S AT LEAST A **THREE-HOUR ROUND TRIP?!**
WELL, THERE'S NO JOBS FOR ME IN THE AREA. AT LEAST NOT JOBS THAT PAY WELL.
SO, WHAT ABOUT **SQUATCH BURGER?**
I'M RUNNING THINGS SOLO. IT'S BEEN SLOW ENOUGH RECENTLY.
IT'S NOT TOO BAD.
NOT TOO BAD?! YOU'RE RUNNING AN ENTIRE RESTAURANT ALONE!
THIS DOESN'T MEAN I'M NOT STILL MAJORLY MAD AT YOU...
...I'LL HELP OUT AT **SQUATCH BURGER.**
NO, YOU WON'T.

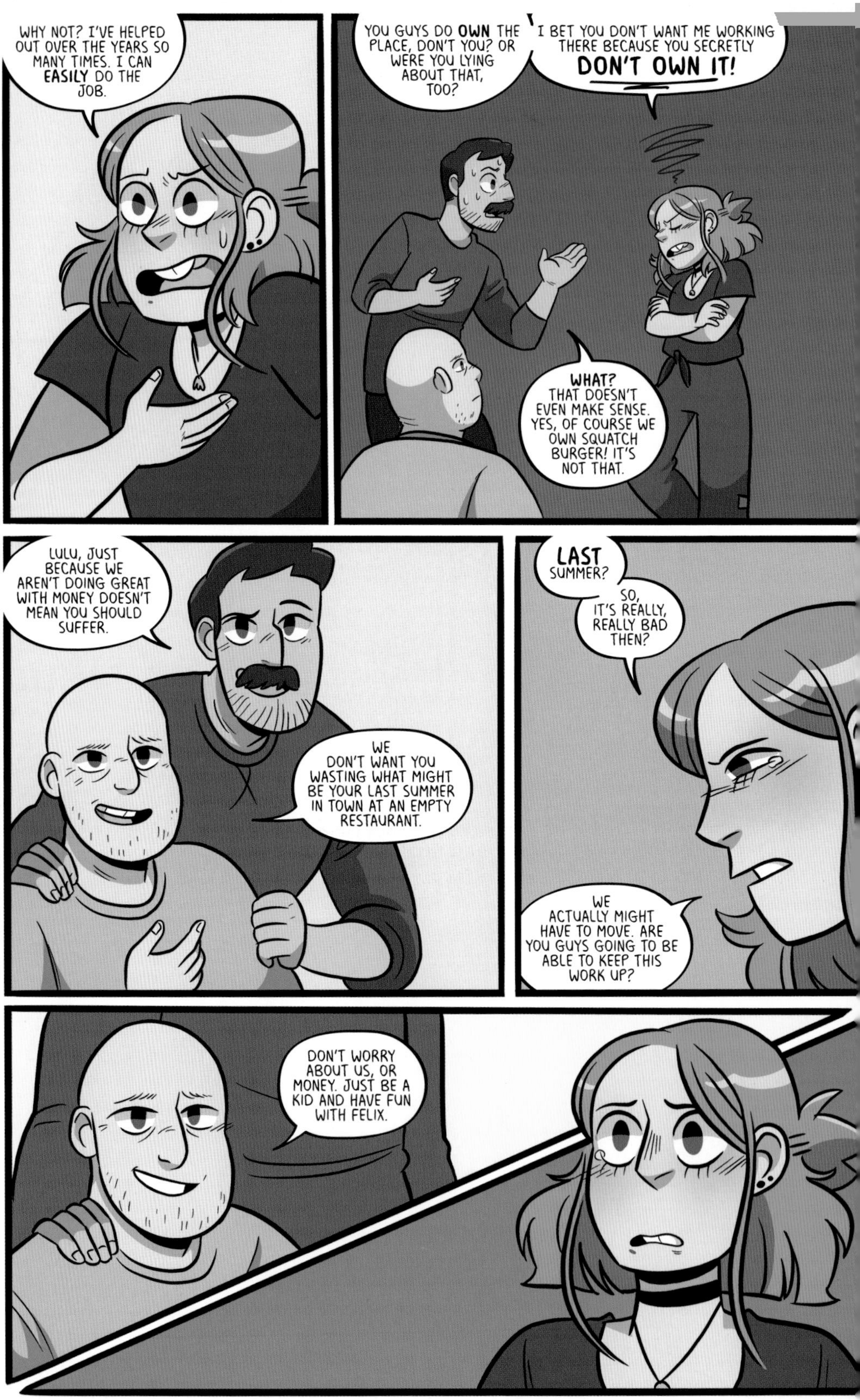
WHY NOT? I'VE HELPED OUT OVER THE YEARS SO MANY TIMES. I CAN **EASILY** DO THE JOB.
YOU GUYS DO **OWN** THE PLACE, DON'T YOU? OR WERE YOU LYING ABOUT THAT, TOO?
I BET YOU DON'T WANT ME WORKING THERE BECAUSE YOU SECRETLY **DON'T OWN IT!**
WHAT? THAT DOESN'T EVEN MAKE SENSE. YES, OF COURSE WE OWN SQUATCH BURGER! IT'S NOT THAT.
LULU, JUST BECAUSE WE AREN'T DOING GREAT WITH MONEY DOESN'T MEAN YOU SHOULD SUFFER.
WE DON'T WANT YOU WASTING WHAT MIGHT BE YOUR LAST SUMMER IN TOWN AT AN EMPTY RESTAURANT.
LAST SUMMER?
SO, IT'S REALLY, REALLY BAD THEN?
WE ACTUALLY MIGHT HAVE TO MOVE. ARE YOU GUYS GOING TO BE ABLE TO KEEP THIS WORK UP?
DON'T WORRY ABOUT US, OR MONEY. JUST BE A KID AND HAVE FUN WITH FELIX.

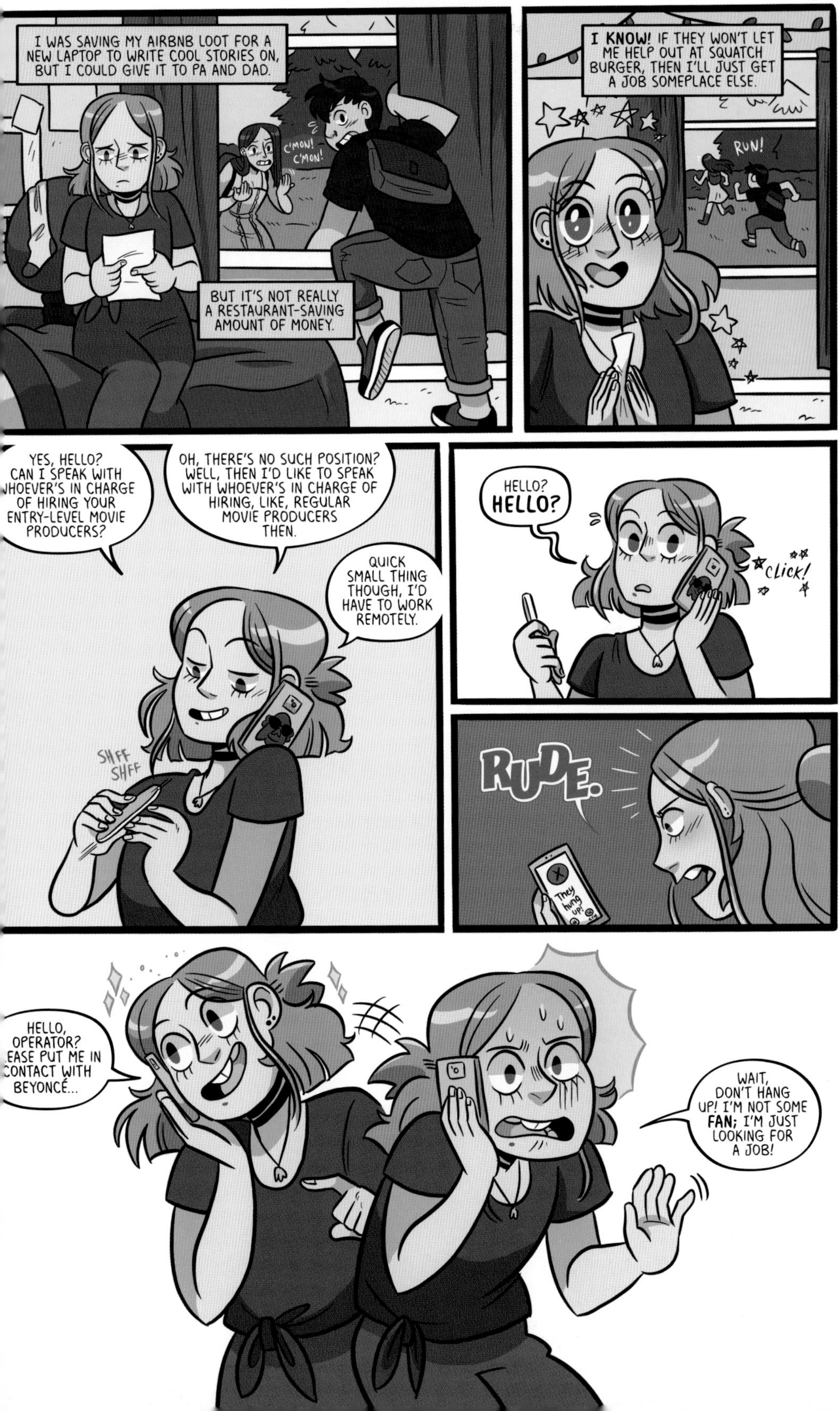

I WAS SAVING MY AIRBNB LOOT FOR A NEW LAPTOP TO WRITE COOL STORIES ON, BUT I COULD GIVE IT TO PA AND DAD.
C'MON! C'MON!
BUT IT'S NOT REALLY A RESTAURANT-SAVING AMOUNT OF MONEY.
I KNOW! IF THEY WON'T LET ME HELP OUT AT SQUATCH BURGER, THEN I'LL JUST GET A JOB SOMEPLACE ELSE.
RUN!
YES, HELLO? CAN I SPEAK WITH WHOEVER'S IN CHARGE OF HIRING YOUR ENTRY-LEVEL MOVIE PRODUCERS?
OH, THERE'S NO SUCH POSITION? WELL, THEN I'D LIKE TO SPEAK WITH WHOEVER'S IN CHARGE OF HIRING, LIKE, REGULAR MOVIE PRODUCERS THEN.
QUICK SMALL THING THOUGH, I'D HAVE TO WORK REMOTELY.
SHFF SHFF
HELLO? HELLO?
CLICK!
RUDE.
They hung up!
HELLO, OPERATOR? EASE PUT ME IN CONTACT WITH BEYONCÉ...
WAIT, DON'T HANG UP! I'M NOT SOME FAN; I'M JUST LOOKING FOR A JOB!

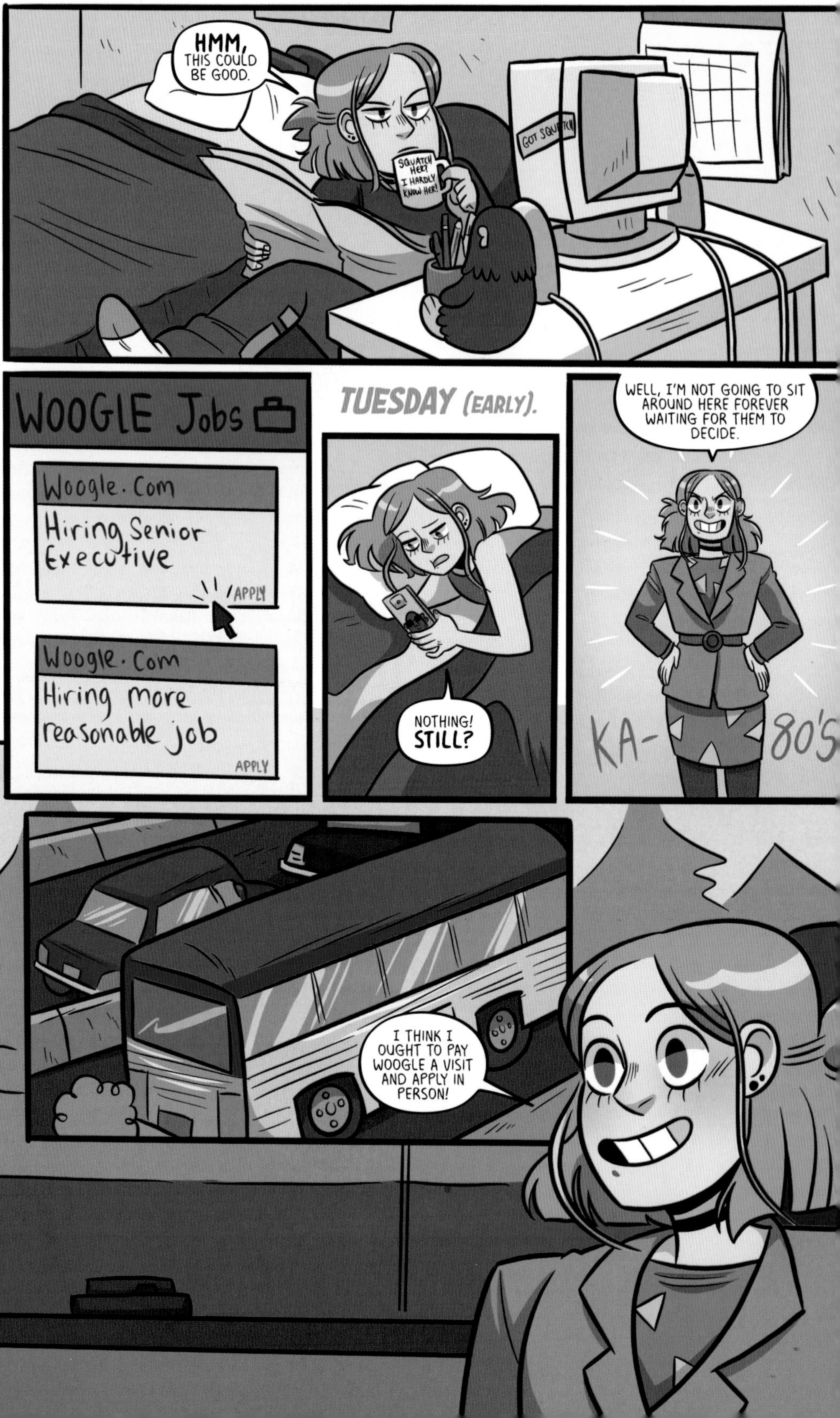
HMM, THIS COULD BE GOOD.
SQUATCH HER? I HARDLY KNOW HER!
GOT SQUATCH
WOOGLE Jobs
Woogle.Com
Hiring Senior Executive
APPLY
Woogle.Com
Hiring more reasonable job
APPLY
TUESDAY (EARLY).
NOTHING! STILL?
WELL, I'M NOT GOING TO SIT AROUND HERE FOREVER WAITING FOR THEM TO DECIDE.
KA-80'S
I THINK I OUGHT TO PAY WOOGLE A VISIT AND APPLY IN PERSON!

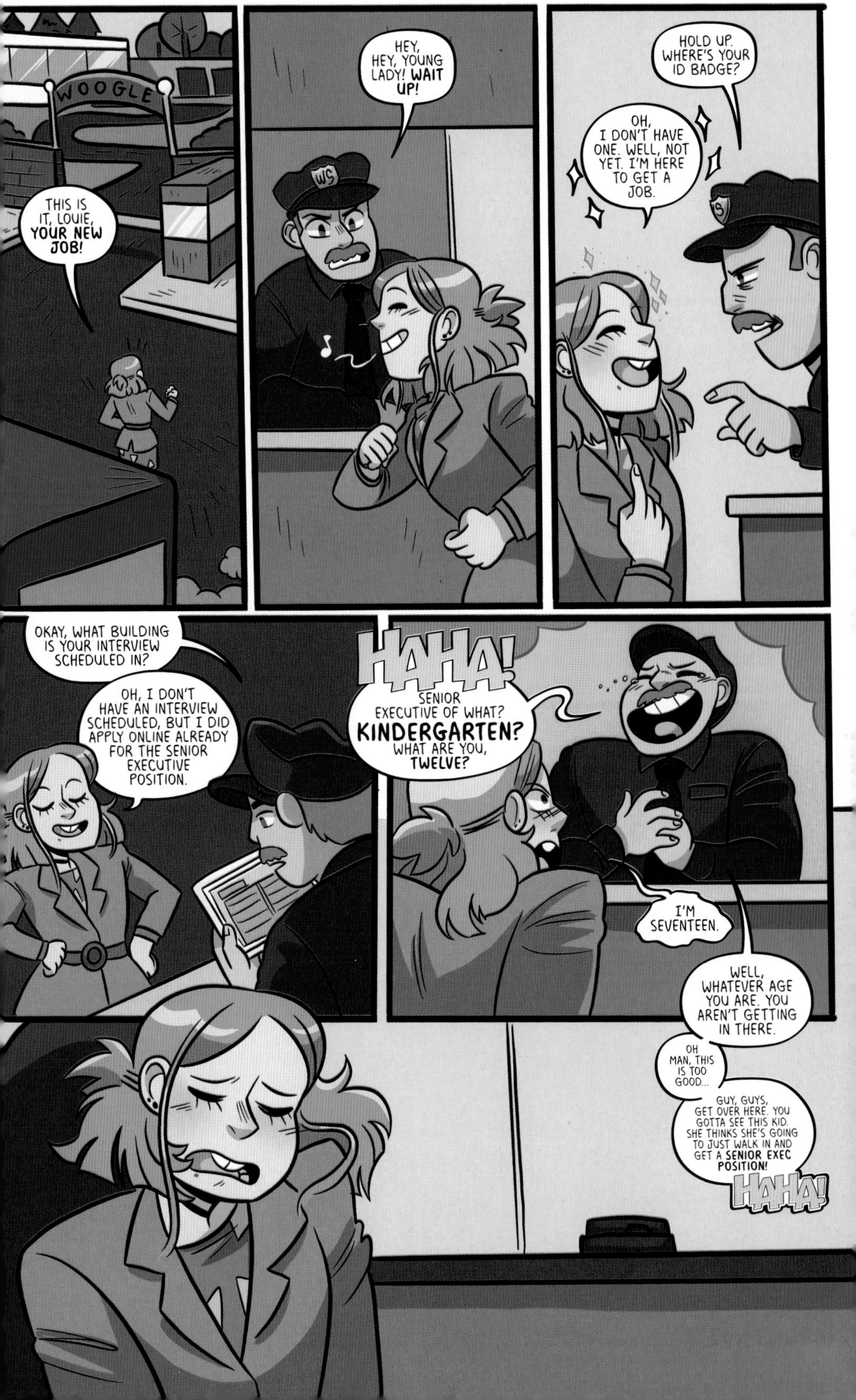

WOOGLE
THIS IS IT, LOUIE, **YOUR NEW JOB!**
HEY, HEY, YOUNG LADY! **WAIT UP!**
HOLD UP. WHERE'S YOUR ID BADGE?
OH, I DON'T HAVE ONE. WELL, NOT YET. I'M HERE TO GET A JOB.
OKAY, WHAT BUILDING IS YOUR INTERVIEW SCHEDULED IN?
OH, I DON'T HAVE AN INTERVIEW SCHEDULED, BUT I DID APPLY ONLINE ALREADY FOR THE SENIOR EXECUTIVE POSITION.
HAHA!
SENIOR EXECUTIVE OF WHAT? **KINDERGARTEN?** WHAT ARE YOU, **TWELVE?**
I'M SEVENTEEN.
WELL, WHATEVER AGE YOU ARE. YOU AREN'T GETTING IN THERE.
OH MAN, THIS IS TOO GOOD...
GUY, GUYS, GET OVER HERE. YOU GOTTA SEE THIS KID. SHE THINKS SHE'S GOING TO JUST WALK IN AND GET A **SENIOR EXEC POSITION!**
HAHA!

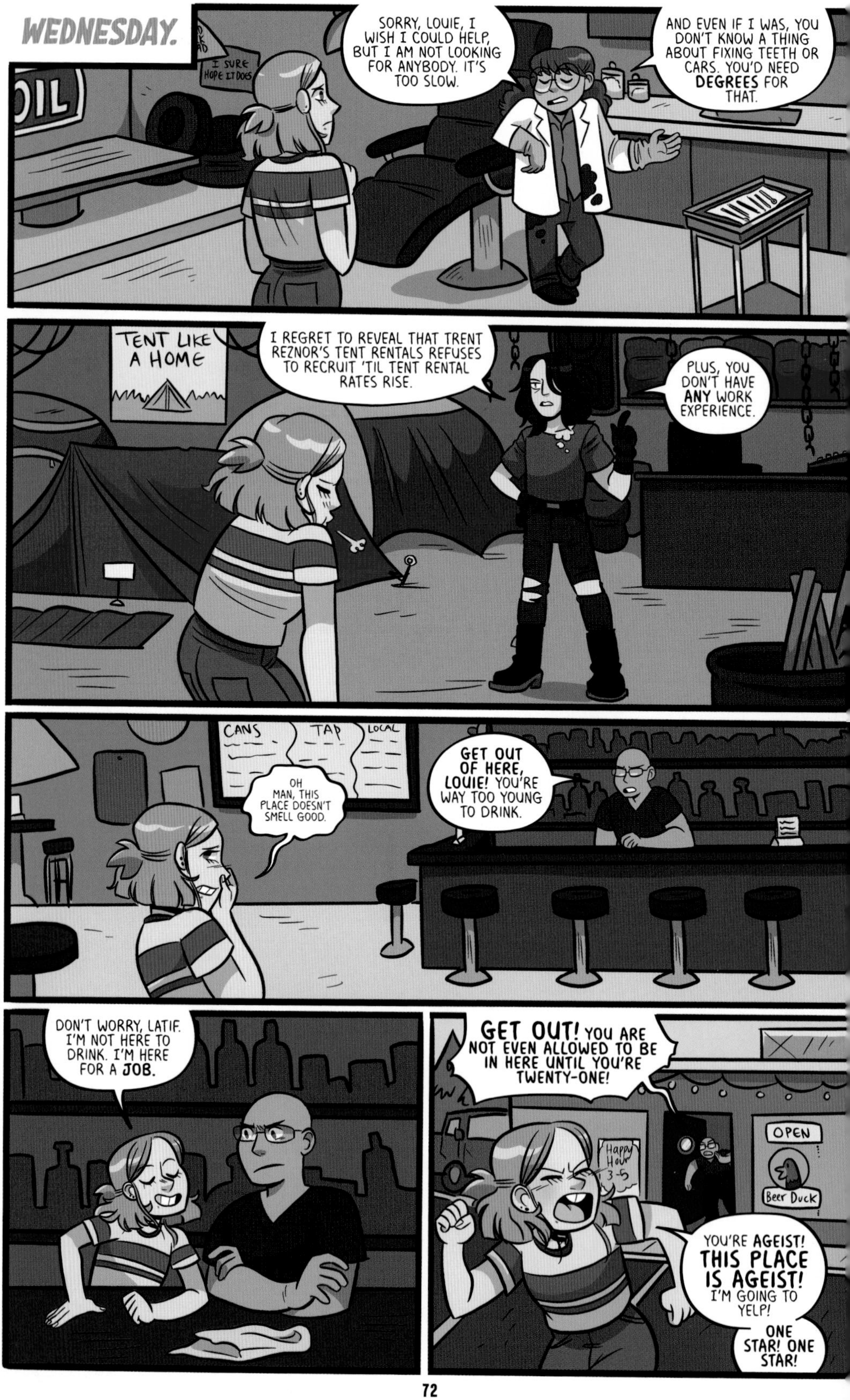
WEDNESDAY.
I SURE HOPE IT DOES
OIL
SORRY, LOUIE, I WISH I COULD HELP, BUT I AM NOT LOOKING FOR ANYBODY. IT'S TOO SLOW.
AND EVEN IF I WAS, YOU DON'T KNOW A THING ABOUT FIXING TEETH OR CARS. YOU'D NEED **DEGREES** FOR THAT.
TENT LIKE A HOME
I REGRET TO REVEAL THAT TRENT REZNOR'S TENT RENTALS REFUSES TO RECRUIT 'TIL TENT RENTAL RATES RISE.
PLUS, YOU DON'T HAVE **ANY** WORK EXPERIENCE.
CANS
TAP
LOCAL
OH MAN, THIS PLACE DOESN'T SMELL GOOD.
GET OUT OF HERE, LOUIE! YOU'RE WAY TOO YOUNG TO DRINK.
DON'T WORRY, LATIF. I'M NOT HERE TO DRINK. I'M HERE FOR A **JOB.**
GET OUT! YOU ARE NOT EVEN ALLOWED TO BE IN HERE UNTIL YOU'RE TWENTY-ONE!
Happy Hour 3-5
OPEN
Beer Duck
YOU'RE **AGEIST! THIS PLACE IS AGEIST!** I'M GOING TO YELP!
ONE STAR! ONE STAR!

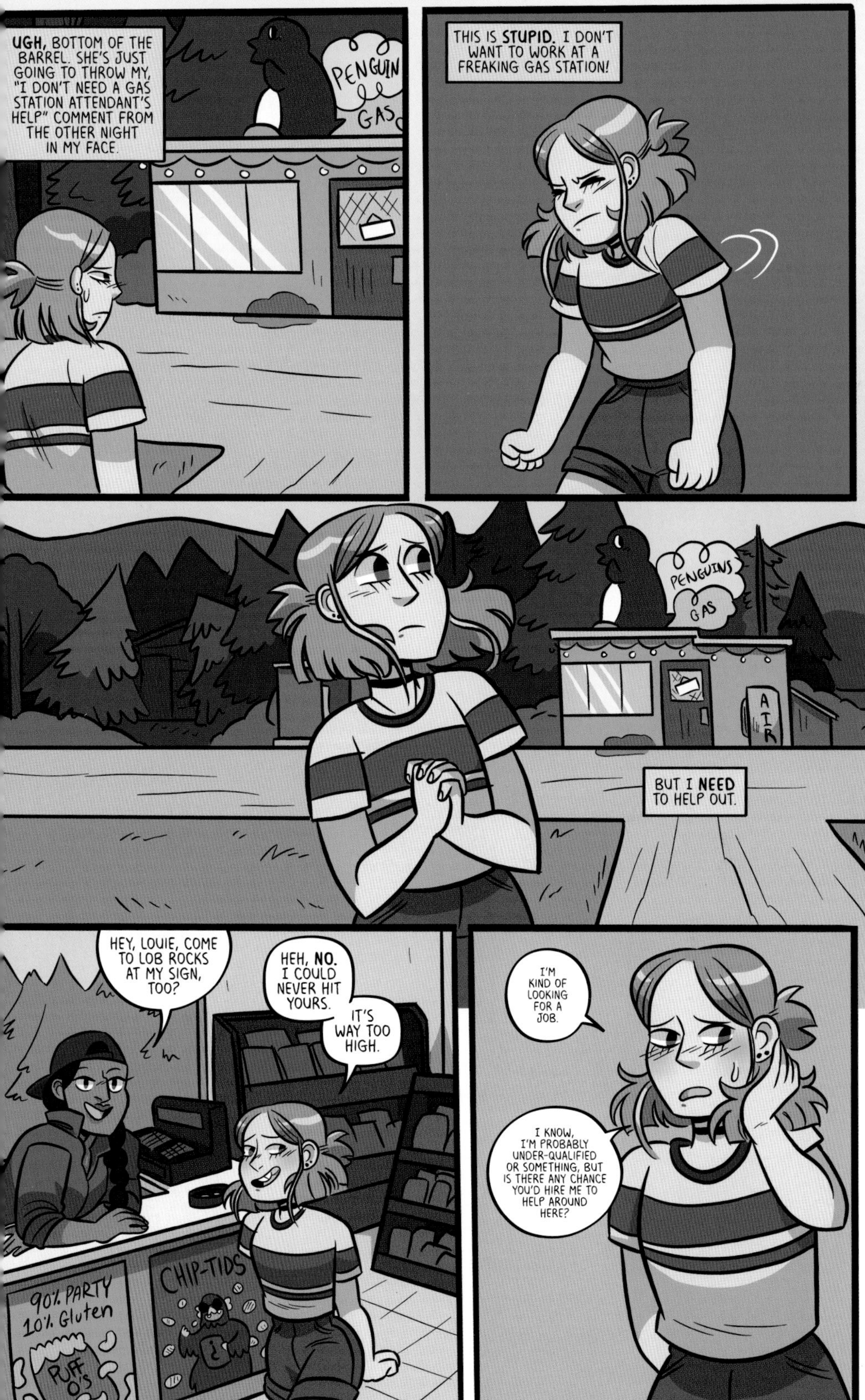
UGH, BOTTOM OF THE BARREL. SHE'S JUST GOING TO THROW MY, "I DON'T NEED A GAS STATION ATTENDANT'S HELP" COMMENT FROM THE OTHER NIGHT IN MY FACE.
PENGUIN GAS
THIS IS STUPID. I DON'T WANT TO WORK AT A FREAKING GAS STATION!
PENGUINS GAS
AIR
BUT I NEED TO HELP OUT.
HEY, LOUIE, COME TO LOB ROCKS AT MY SIGN, TOO?
HEH, NO. I COULD NEVER HIT YOURS.
IT'S WAY TOO HIGH.
90% PARTY 10% Gluten
PUFF O's
CHIP-TIDS
I'M KIND OF LOOKING FOR A JOB.
I KNOW, I'M PROBABLY UNDER-QUALIFIED OR SOMETHING, BUT IS THERE ANY CHANCE YOU'D HIRE ME TO HELP AROUND HERE?

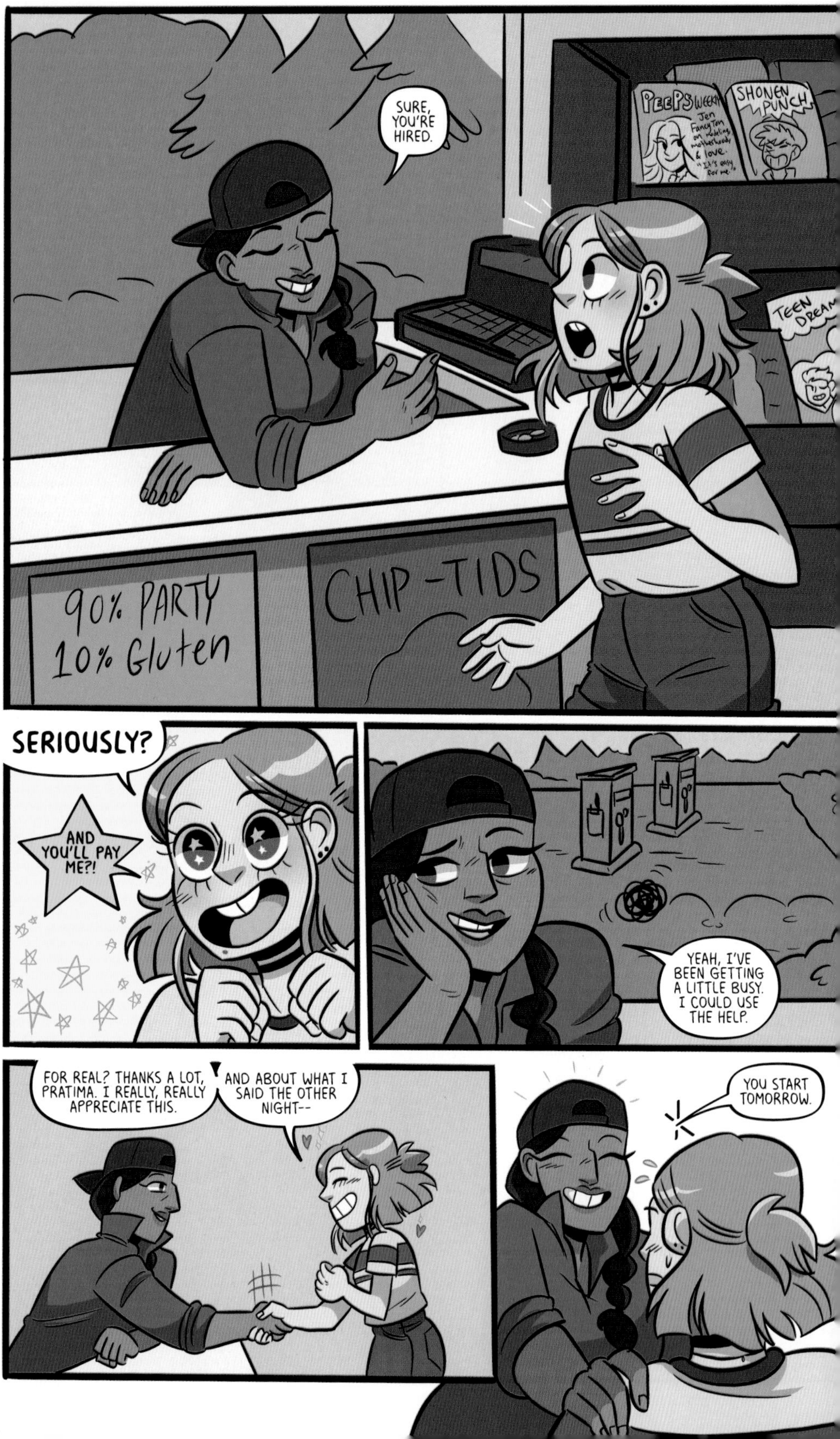

PEEPS WEEKLY
Jen FancyTon on modeling, motherhood & love. "It's easy for me."
SHONEN PUNCH
TEEN DREAM
SURE, YOU'RE HIRED.
90% PARTY
10% Gluten
CHIP-TIDS
SERIOUSLY?
AND YOU'LL PAY ME?!
YEAH, I'VE BEEN GETTING A LITTLE BUSY. I COULD USE THE HELP.
FOR REAL? THANKS A LOT, PRATIMA. I REALLY, REALLY APPRECIATE THIS.
AND ABOUT WHAT I SAID THE OTHER NIGHT--
YOU START TOMORROW.

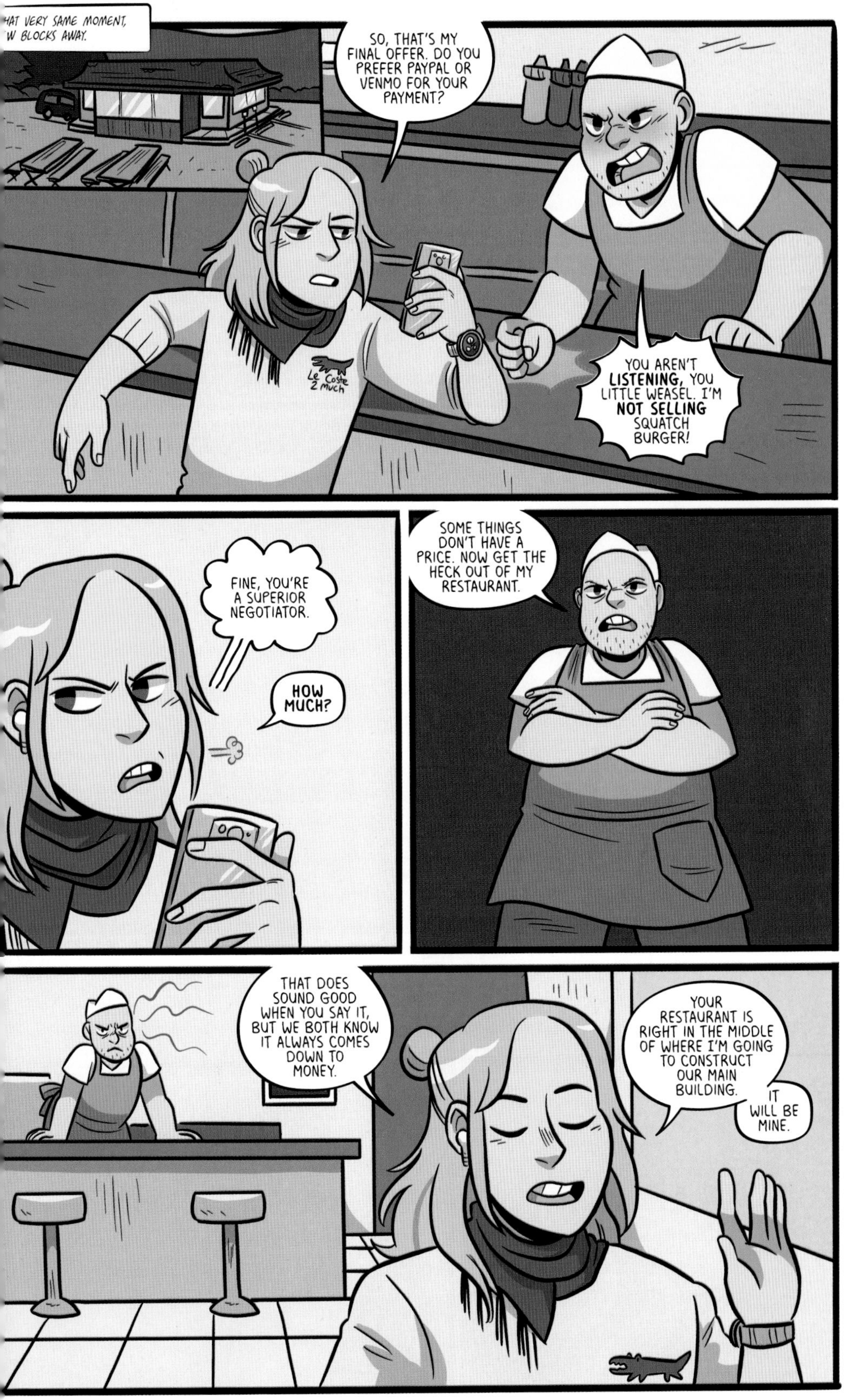
HAT VERY SAME MOMENT,
W BLOCKS AWAY.
SO, THAT'S MY FINAL OFFER. DO YOU PREFER PAYPAL OR VENMO FOR YOUR PAYMENT?
Le Coste 2 Much
YOU AREN'T **LISTENING,** YOU LITTLE WEASEL. I'M **NOT SELLING** SQUATCH BURGER!
FINE, YOU'RE A SUPERIOR NEGOTIATOR.
HOW MUCH?
SOME THINGS DON'T HAVE A PRICE. NOW GET THE HECK OUT OF MY RESTAURANT.
THAT DOES SOUND GOOD WHEN YOU SAY IT, BUT WE BOTH KNOW IT ALWAYS COMES DOWN TO MONEY.
YOUR RESTAURANT IS RIGHT IN THE MIDDLE OF WHERE I'M GOING TO CONSTRUCT OUR MAIN BUILDING.
IT WILL BE MINE.

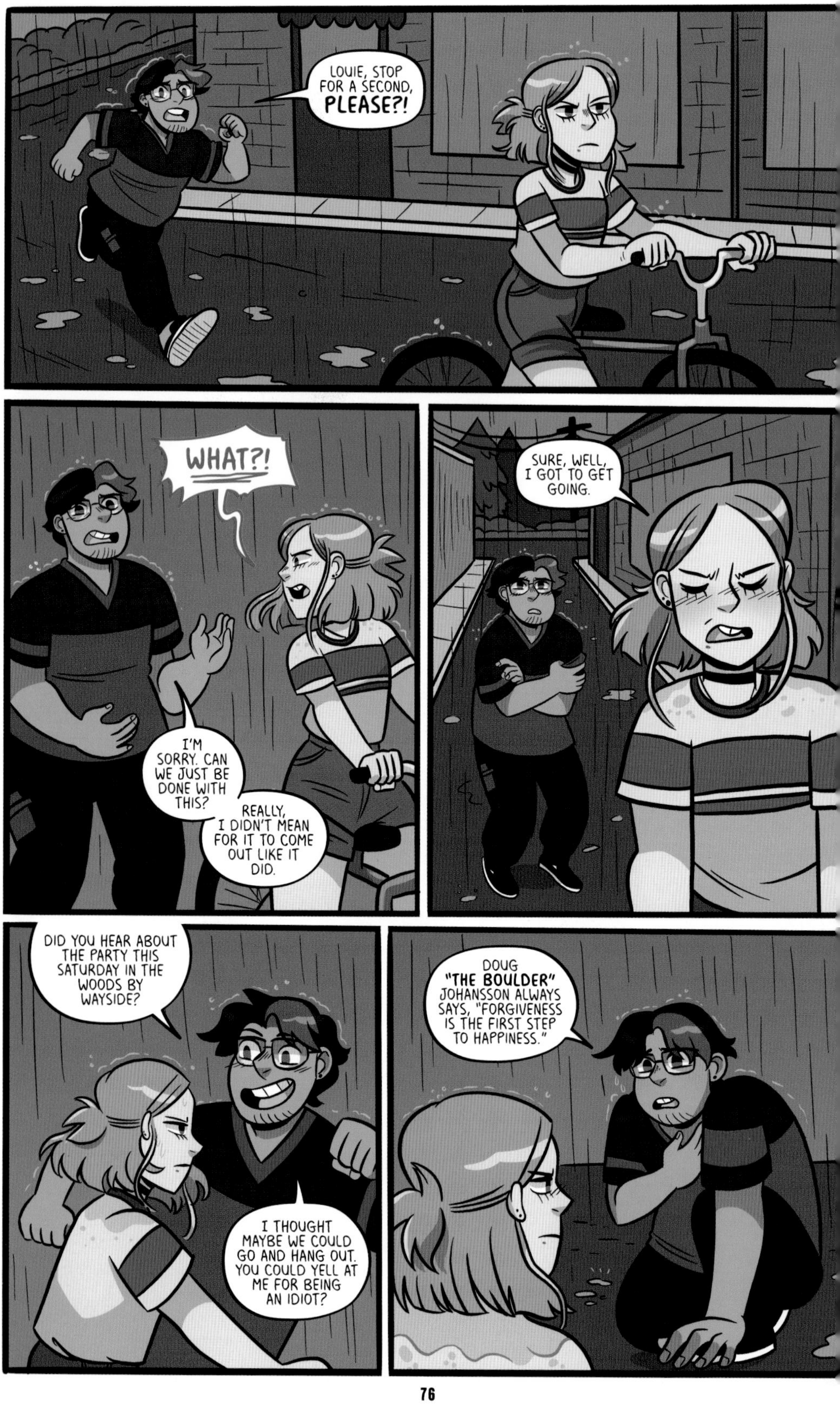
LOUIE, STOP FOR A SECOND, **PLEASE?!**
WHAT?!
I'M SORRY. CAN WE JUST BE DONE WITH THIS?
REALLY, I DIDN'T MEAN FOR IT TO COME OUT LIKE IT DID.
SURE, WELL, I GOT TO GET GOING.
DID YOU HEAR ABOUT THE PARTY THIS SATURDAY IN THE WOODS BY WAYSIDE?
I THOUGHT MAYBE WE COULD GO AND HANG OUT. YOU COULD YELL AT ME FOR BEING AN IDIOT?
DOUG **"THE BOULDER"** JOHANSSON ALWAYS SAYS, "FORGIVENESS IS THE FIRST STEP TO HAPPINESS."

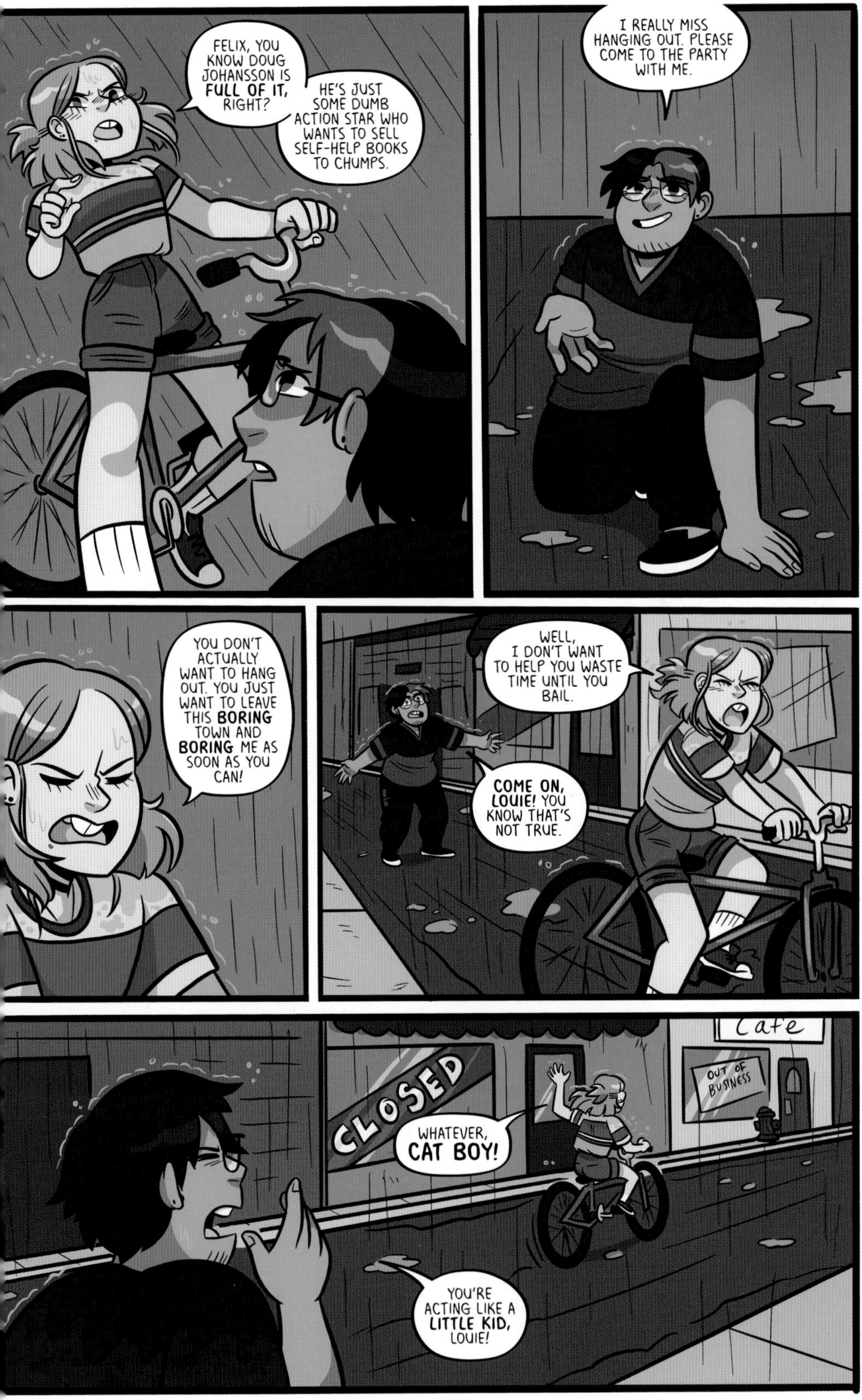
FELIX, YOU KNOW DOUG JOHANSSON IS **FULL OF IT,** RIGHT?
HE'S JUST SOME DUMB ACTION STAR WHO WANTS TO SELL SELF-HELP BOOKS TO CHUMPS.
I REALLY MISS HANGING OUT. PLEASE COME TO THE PARTY WITH ME.
YOU DON'T ACTUALLY WANT TO HANG OUT. YOU JUST WANT TO LEAVE THIS **BORING** TOWN AND **BORING** ME AS SOON AS YOU CAN!
WELL, I DON'T WANT TO HELP YOU WASTE TIME UNTIL YOU BAIL.
COME ON, LOUIE! YOU KNOW THAT'S NOT TRUE.
CLOSED
Cafe
OUT OF BUSINESS
WHATEVER, **CAT BOY!**
YOU'RE ACTING LIKE A **LITTLE KID,** LOUIE!

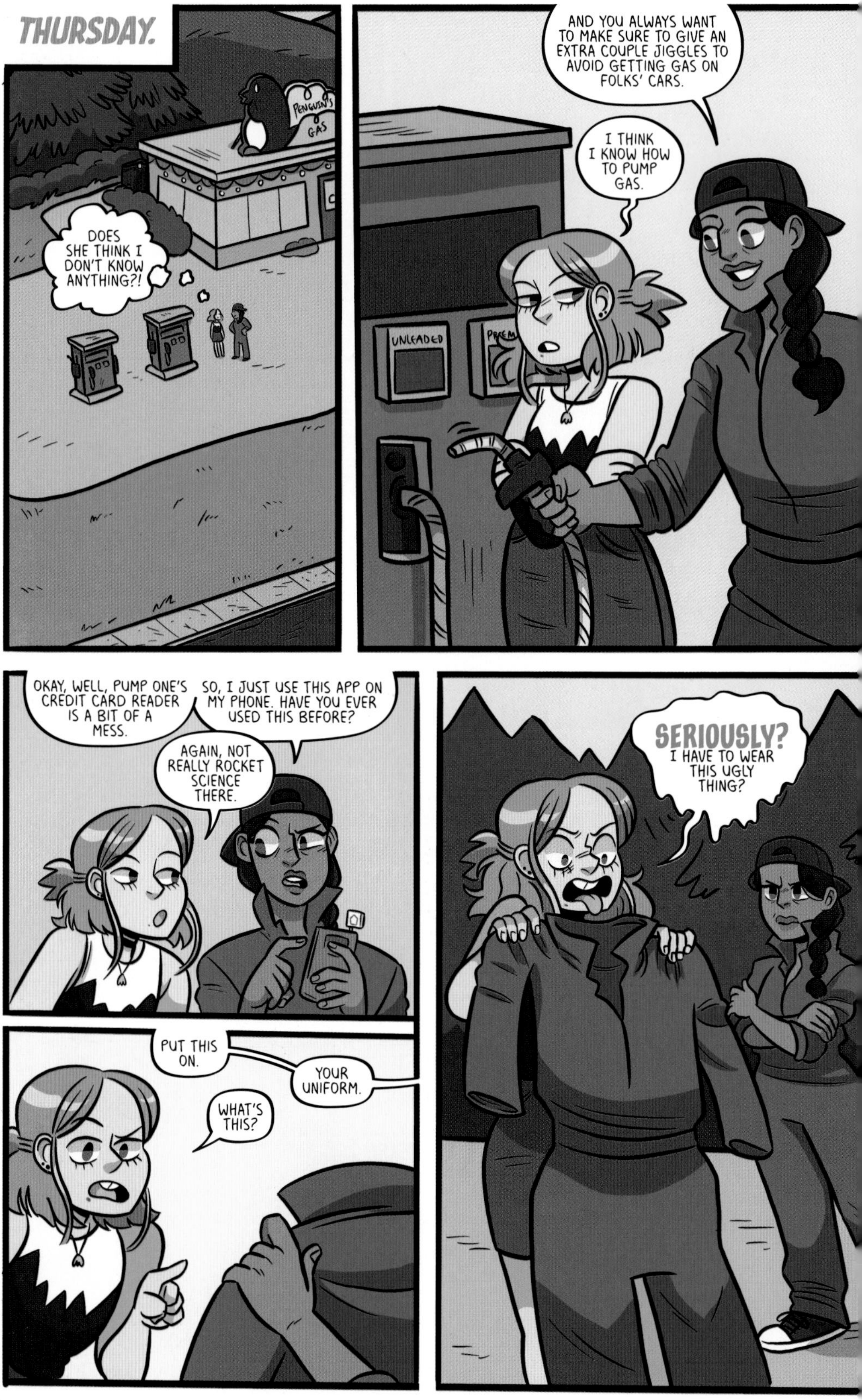
THURSDAY.
PENGUIN'S GAS
DOES SHE THINK I DON'T KNOW ANYTHING?!
AND YOU ALWAYS WANT TO MAKE SURE TO GIVE AN EXTRA COUPLE JIGGLES TO AVOID GETTING GAS ON FOLKS' CARS.
I THINK I KNOW HOW TO PUMP GAS.
UNLEADED
OKAY, WELL, PUMP ONE'S CREDIT CARD READER IS A BIT OF A MESS.
SO, I JUST USE THIS APP ON MY PHONE. HAVE YOU EVER USED THIS BEFORE?
AGAIN, NOT REALLY ROCKET SCIENCE THERE.
PUT THIS ON.
YOUR UNIFORM.
WHAT'S THIS?
SERIOUSLY? I HAVE TO WEAR THIS UGLY THING?

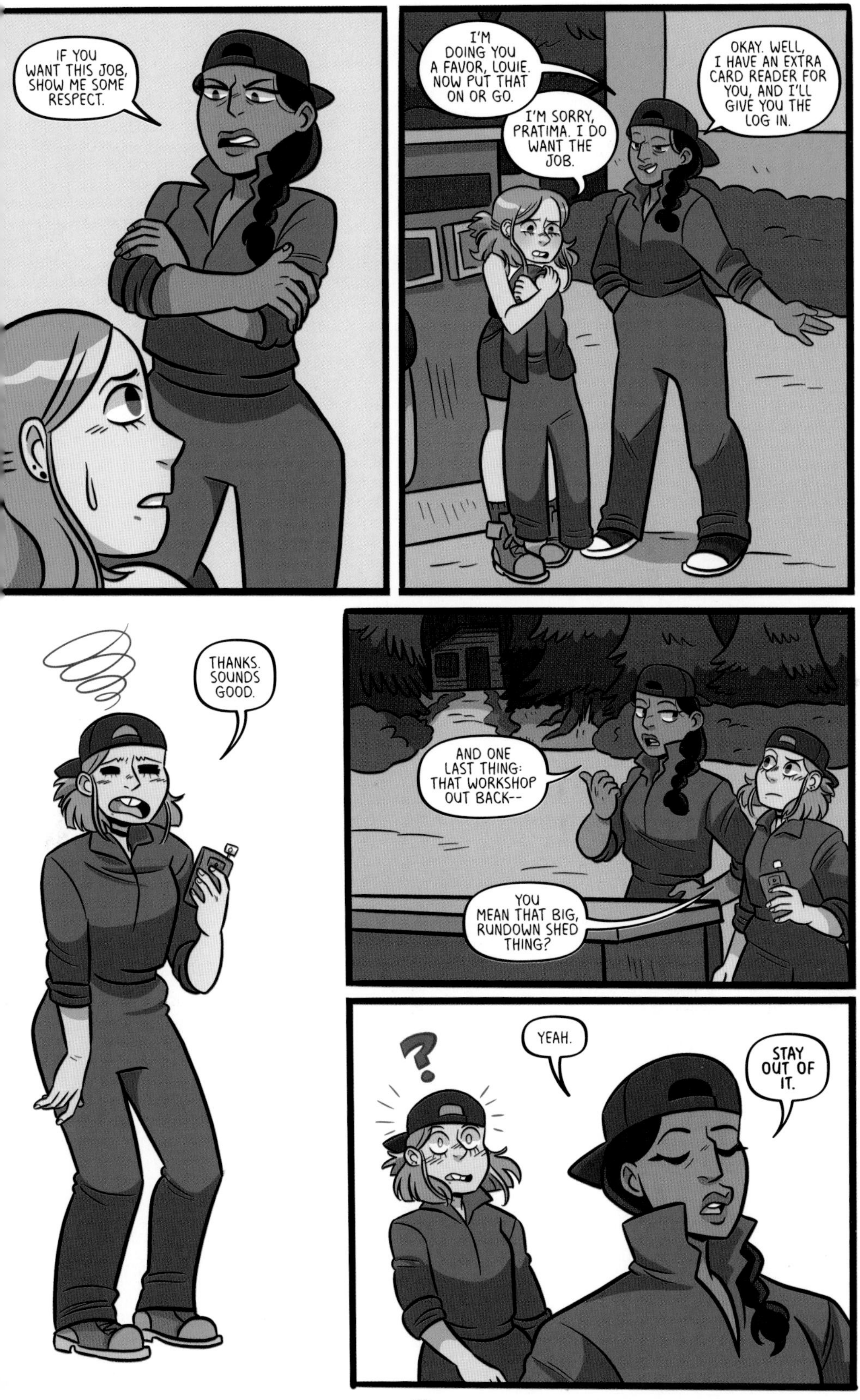
IF YOU WANT THIS JOB, SHOW ME SOME RESPECT.
I'M DOING YOU A FAVOR, LOUIE. NOW PUT THAT ON OR GO.
I'M SORRY, PRATIMA. I DO WANT THE JOB.
OKAY. WELL, I HAVE AN EXTRA CARD READER FOR YOU, AND I'LL GIVE YOU THE LOG IN.
THANKS. SOUNDS GOOD.
AND ONE LAST THING: THAT WORKSHOP OUT BACK--
YOU MEAN THAT BIG, RUNDOWN SHED THING?
YEAH.
STAY OUT OF IT.

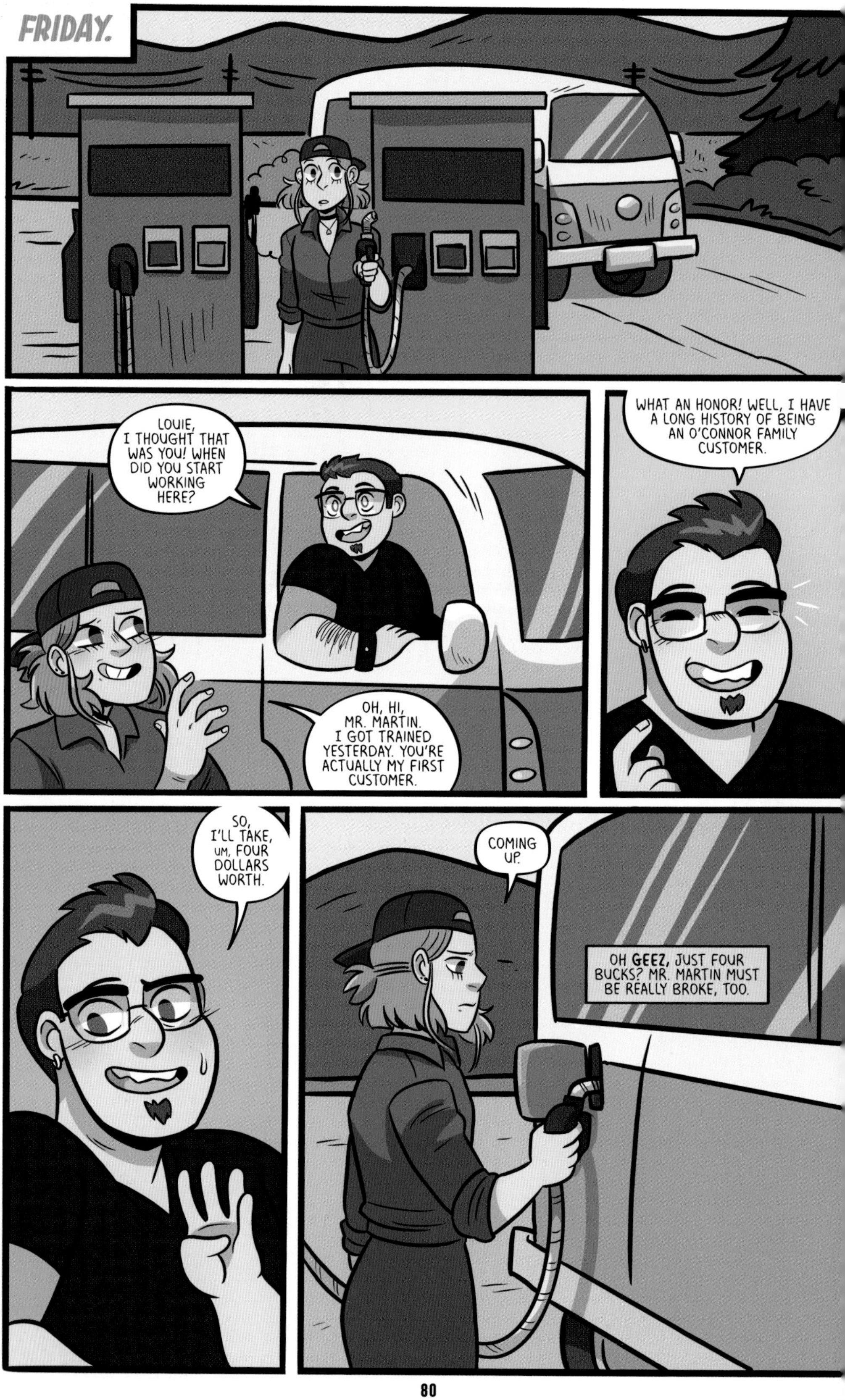
FRIDAY.
LOUIE, I THOUGHT THAT WAS YOU! WHEN DID YOU START WORKING HERE?
OH, HI, MR. MARTIN. I GOT TRAINED YESTERDAY. YOU'RE ACTUALLY MY FIRST CUSTOMER.
WHAT AN HONOR! WELL, I HAVE A LONG HISTORY OF BEING AN O'CONNOR FAMILY CUSTOMER.
SO, I'LL TAKE, UM, FOUR DOLLARS WORTH.
COMING UP.
OH **GEEZ,** JUST FOUR BUCKS? MR. MARTIN MUST BE REALLY BROKE, TOO.

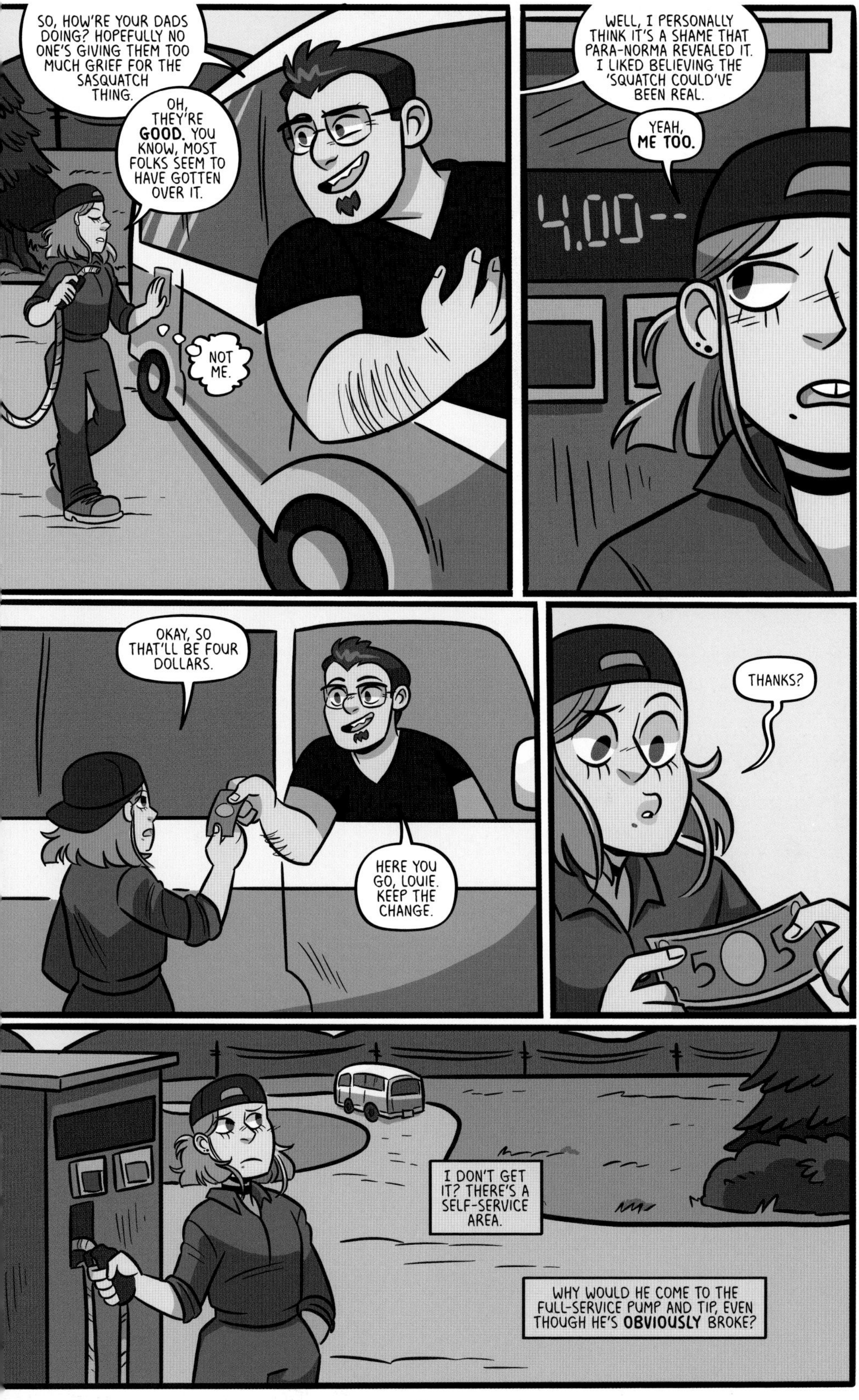
SO, HOW'RE YOUR DADS DOING? HOPEFULLY NO ONE'S GIVING THEM TOO MUCH GRIEF FOR THE SASQUATCH THING.
OH, THEY'RE **GOOD.** YOU KNOW, MOST FOLKS SEEM TO HAVE GOTTEN OVER IT.
NOT ME.
WELL, I PERSONALLY THINK IT'S A SHAME THAT PARA-NORMA REVEALED IT. I LIKED BELIEVING THE 'SQUATCH COULD'VE BEEN REAL.
YEAH, **ME TOO.**
4.00--
OKAY, SO THAT'LL BE FOUR DOLLARS.
HERE YOU GO, LOUIE. KEEP THE CHANGE.
THANKS?
I DON'T GET IT? THERE'S A SELF-SERVICE AREA.
WHY WOULD HE COME TO THE FULL-SERVICE PUMP AND TIP, EVEN THOUGH HE'S **OBVIOUSLY** BROKE?

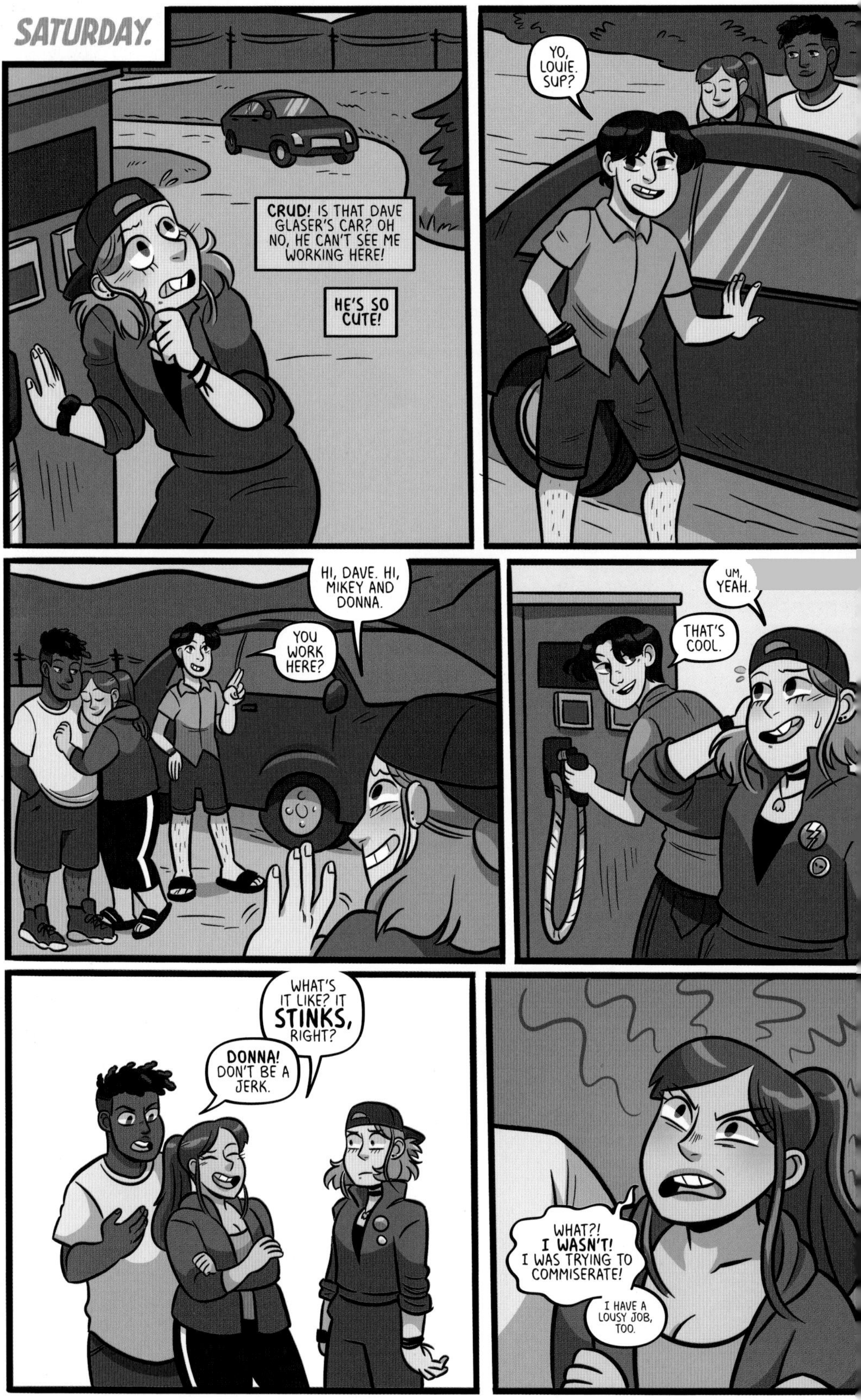
SATURDAY.
CRUD! IS THAT DAVE GLASER'S CAR? OH NO, HE CAN'T SEE ME WORKING HERE!
HE'S SO CUTE!
YO, LOUIE. SUP?
HI, DAVE. HI, MIKEY AND DONNA.
YOU WORK HERE?
UM, YEAH.
THAT'S COOL.
WHAT'S IT LIKE? IT STINKS, RIGHT?
DONNA! DON'T BE A JERK.
WHAT?! I WASN'T! I WAS TRYING TO COMMISERATE!
I HAVE A LOUSY JOB, TOO.

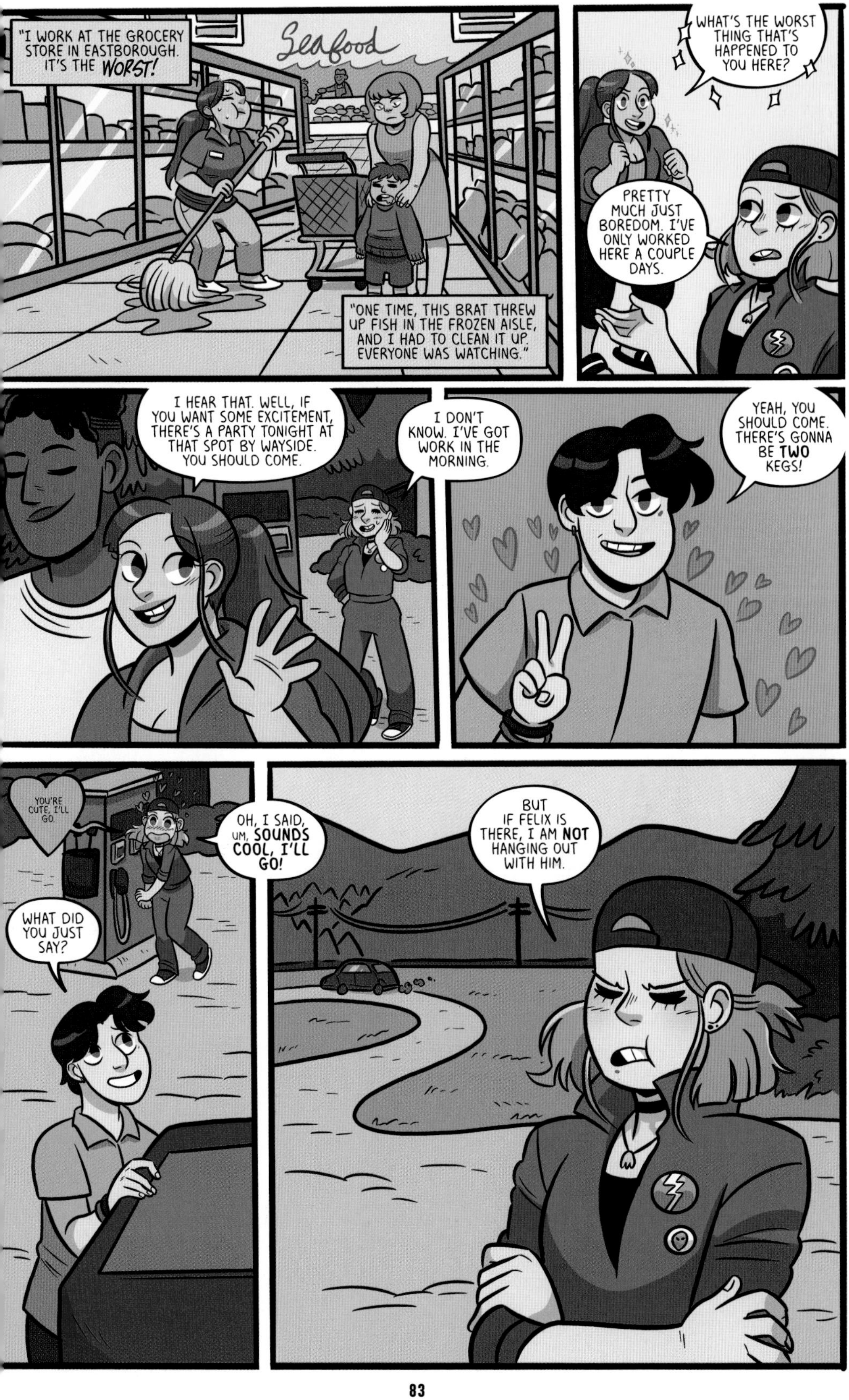
"I WORK AT THE GROCERY STORE IN EASTBOROUGH. IT'S THE WORST!
Seafood
"ONE TIME, THIS BRAT THREW UP FISH IN THE FROZEN AISLE, AND I HAD TO CLEAN IT UP. EVERYONE WAS WATCHING."
WHAT'S THE WORST THING THAT'S HAPPENED TO YOU HERE?
PRETTY MUCH JUST BOREDOM. I'VE ONLY WORKED HERE A COUPLE DAYS.
I HEAR THAT. WELL, IF YOU WANT SOME EXCITEMENT, THERE'S A PARTY TONIGHT AT THAT SPOT BY WAYSIDE. YOU SHOULD COME.
I DON'T KNOW. I'VE GOT WORK IN THE MORNING.
YEAH, YOU SHOULD COME. THERE'S GONNA BE TWO KEGS!
YOU'RE CUTE, I'LL GO.
WHAT DID YOU JUST SAY?
OH, I SAID, UM, SOUNDS COOL, I'LL GO!
BUT IF FELIX IS THERE, I AM NOT HANGING OUT WITH HIM.

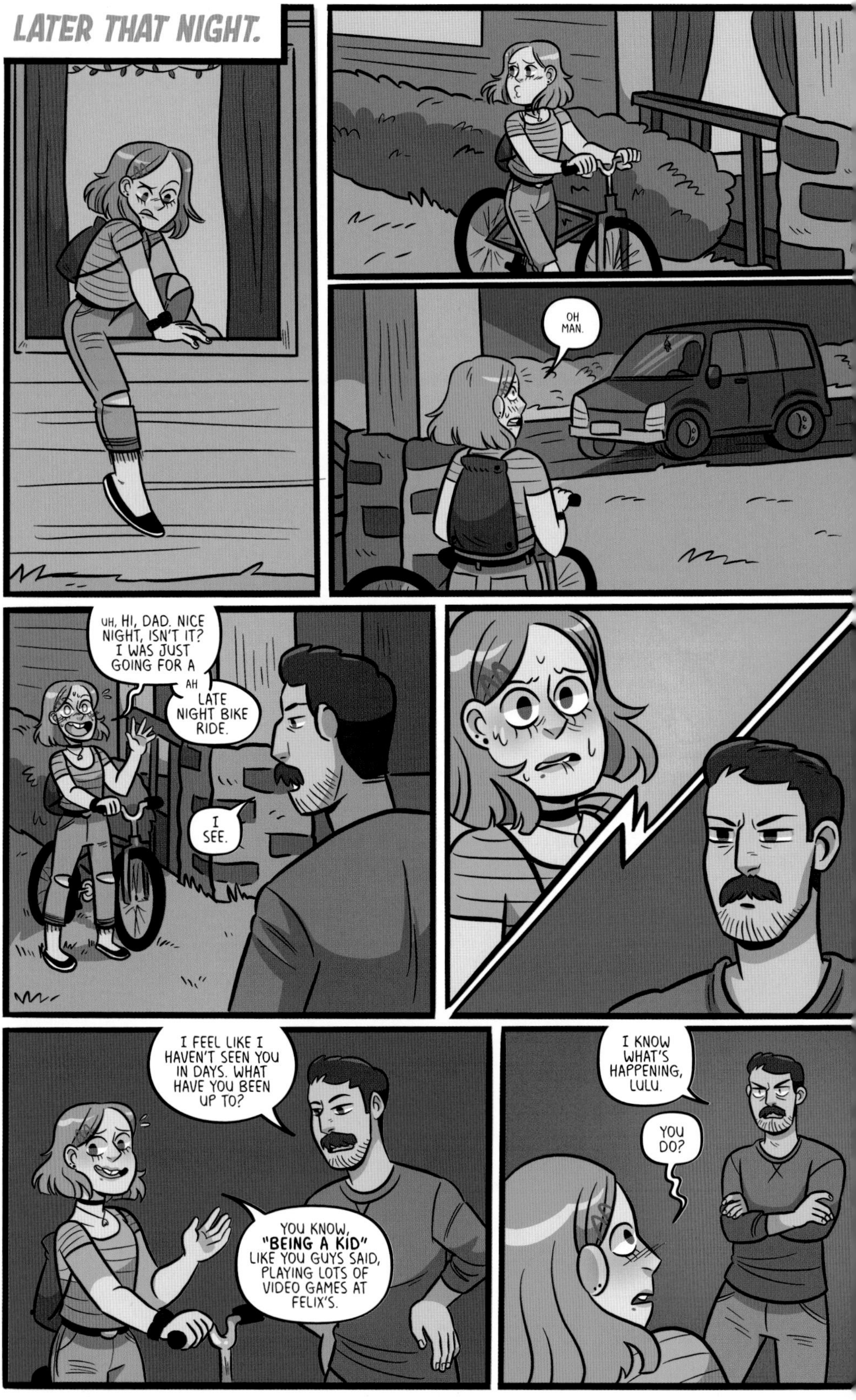
LATER THAT NIGHT.
OH MAN.
UH, HI, DAD. NICE NIGHT, ISN'T IT? I WAS JUST GOING FOR A
AH
LATE NIGHT BIKE RIDE.
I SEE.
I FEEL LIKE I HAVEN'T SEEN YOU IN DAYS. WHAT HAVE YOU BEEN UP TO?
YOU KNOW, "BEING A KID" LIKE YOU GUYS SAID, PLAYING LOTS OF VIDEO GAMES AT FELIX'S.
I KNOW WHAT'S HAPPENING, LULU.
YOU DO?

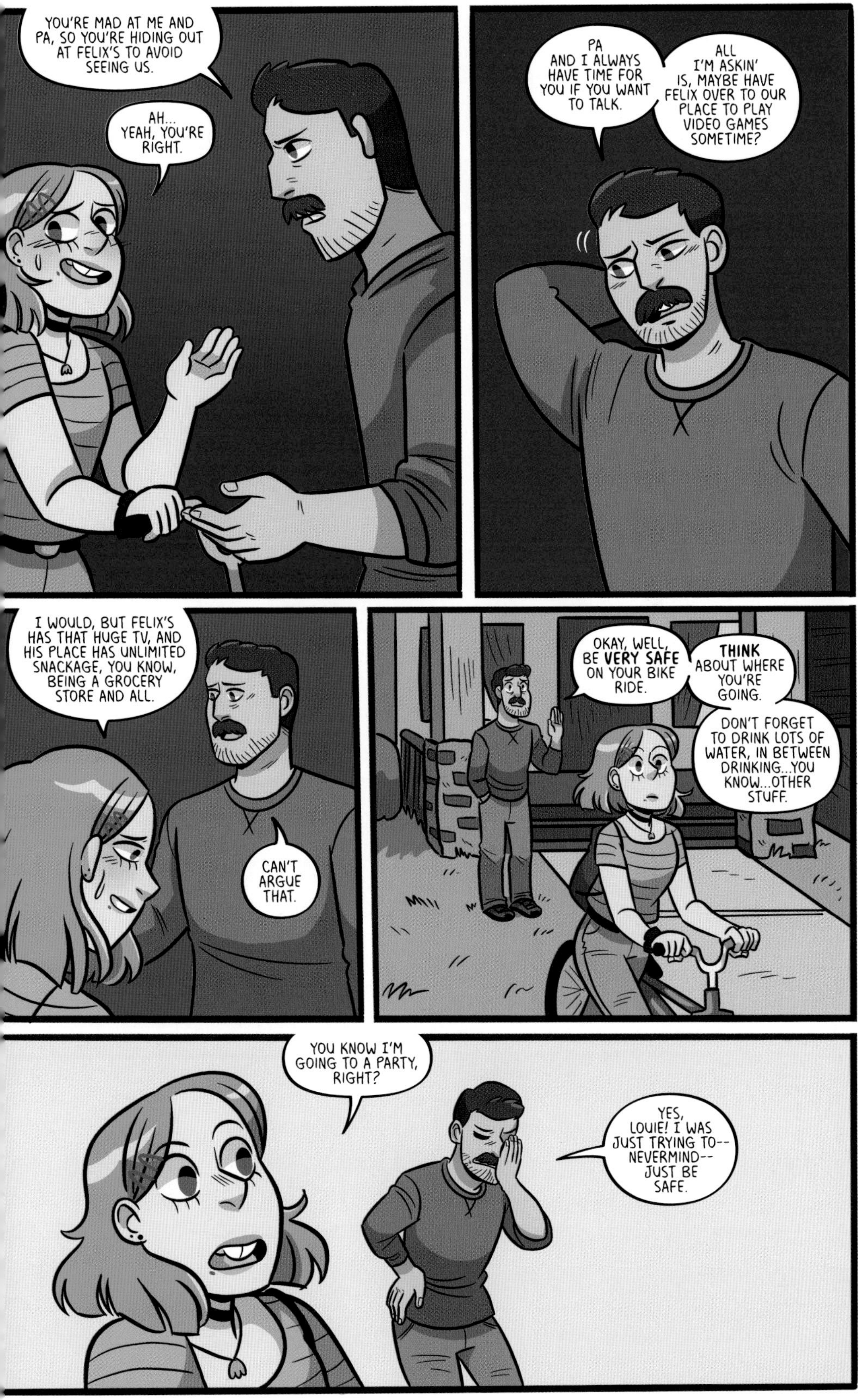
YOU'RE MAD AT ME AND PA, SO YOU'RE HIDING OUT AT FELIX'S TO AVOID SEEING US.
AH... YEAH, YOU'RE RIGHT.
PA AND I ALWAYS HAVE TIME FOR YOU IF YOU WANT TO TALK.
ALL I'M ASKIN' IS, MAYBE HAVE FELIX OVER TO OUR PLACE TO PLAY VIDEO GAMES SOMETIME?
I WOULD, BUT FELIX'S HAS THAT HUGE TV, AND HIS PLACE HAS UNLIMITED SNACKAGE, YOU KNOW, BEING A GROCERY STORE AND ALL.
CAN'T ARGUE THAT.
OKAY, WELL, BE **VERY SAFE** ON YOUR BIKE RIDE.
THINK ABOUT WHERE YOU'RE GOING.
DON'T FORGET TO DRINK LOTS OF WATER, IN BETWEEN DRINKING...YOU KNOW...OTHER STUFF.
YOU KNOW I'M GOING TO A PARTY, RIGHT?
YES, LOUIE! I WAS JUST TRYING TO-- NEVERMIND-- JUST BE SAFE.

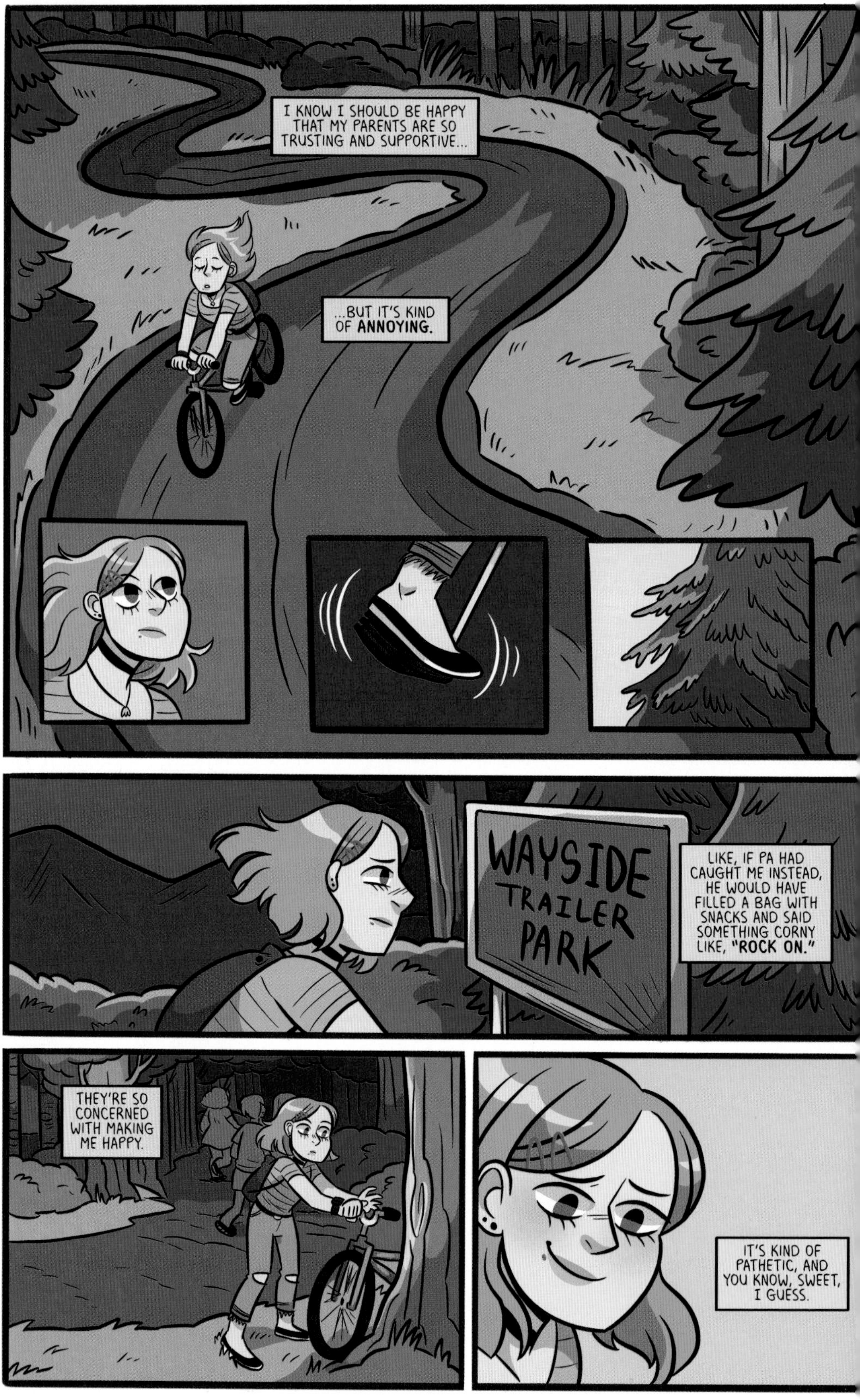
I KNOW I SHOULD BE HAPPY THAT MY PARENTS ARE SO TRUSTING AND SUPPORTIVE...
...BUT IT'S KIND OF **ANNOYING.**
WAYSIDE TRAILER PARK
LIKE, IF PA HAD CAUGHT ME INSTEAD, HE WOULD HAVE FILLED A BAG WITH SNACKS AND SAID SOMETHING CORNY LIKE, **"ROCK ON."**
THEY'RE SO CONCERNED WITH MAKING ME HAPPY.
IT'S KIND OF PATHETIC, AND YOU KNOW, SWEET, I GUESS.

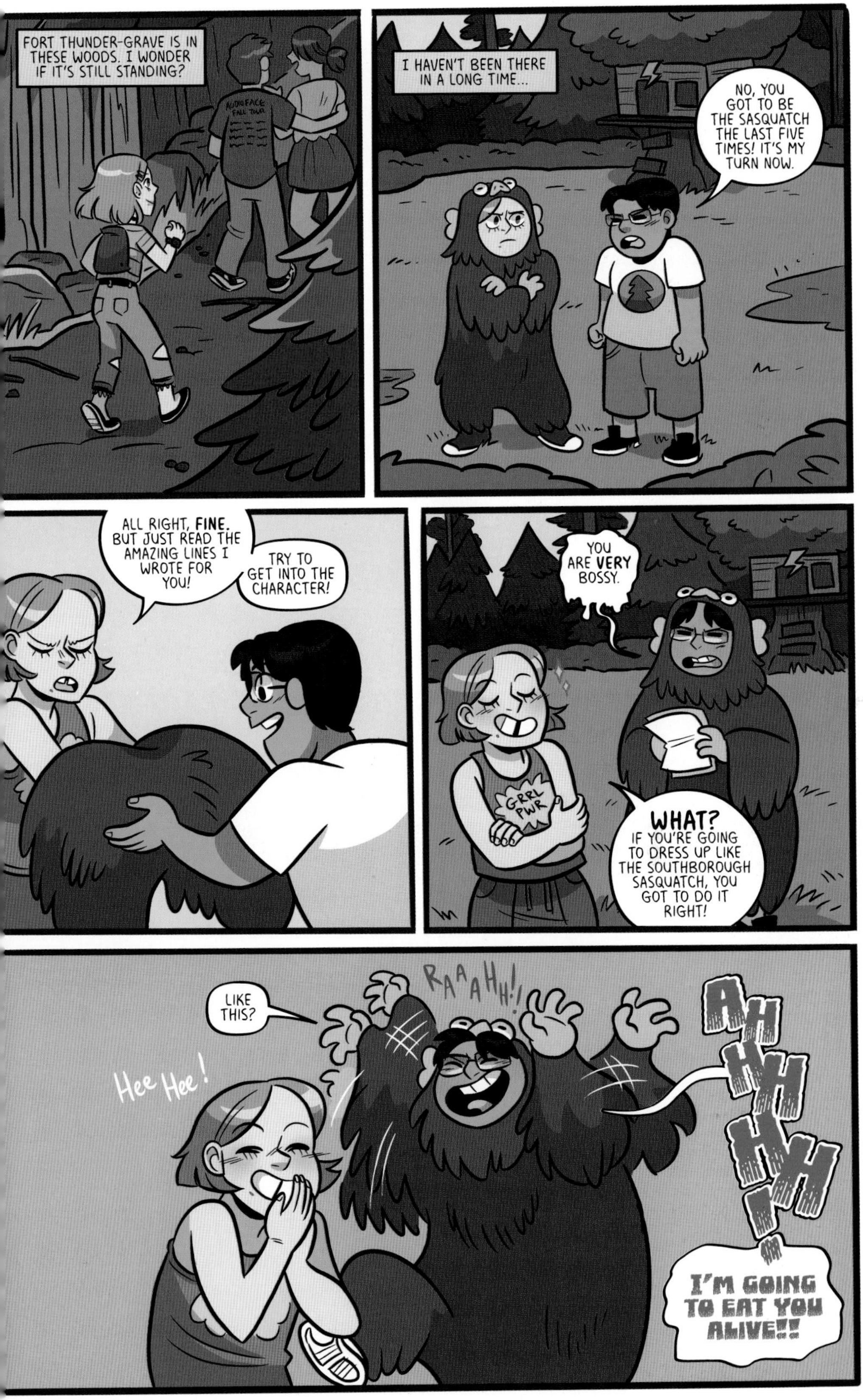

FORT THUNDER-GRAVE IS IN THESE WOODS. I WONDER IF IT'S STILL STANDING?
AUDIOFACE FALL TOUR
I HAVEN'T BEEN THERE IN A LONG TIME...
NO, YOU GOT TO BE THE SASQUATCH THE LAST FIVE TIMES! IT'S MY TURN NOW.
ALL RIGHT, FINE. BUT JUST READ THE AMAZING LINES I WROTE FOR YOU!
TRY TO GET INTO THE CHARACTER!
YOU ARE VERY BOSSY.
GRRL PWR
WHAT? IF YOU'RE GOING TO DRESS UP LIKE THE SOUTHBOROUGH SASQUATCH, YOU GOT TO DO IT RIGHT!
LIKE THIS?
RAAAHH!!
Hee Hee!
AHHHHHH!
I'M GOING TO EAT YOU ALIVE!!

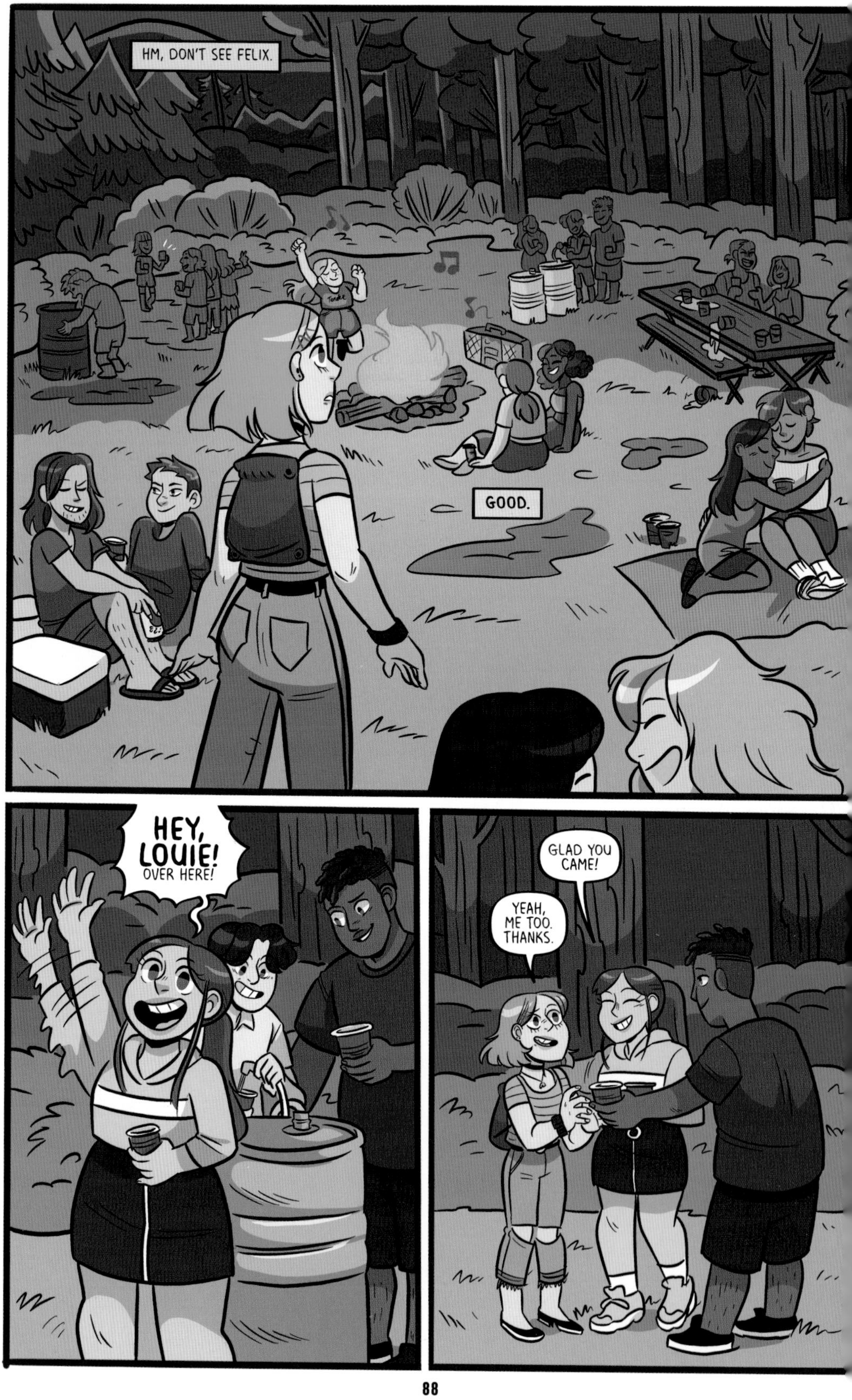
HM, DON'T SEE FELIX.
GOOD.
HEY, LOUIE! OVER HERE!
GLAD YOU CAME!
YEAH, ME TOO. THANKS.

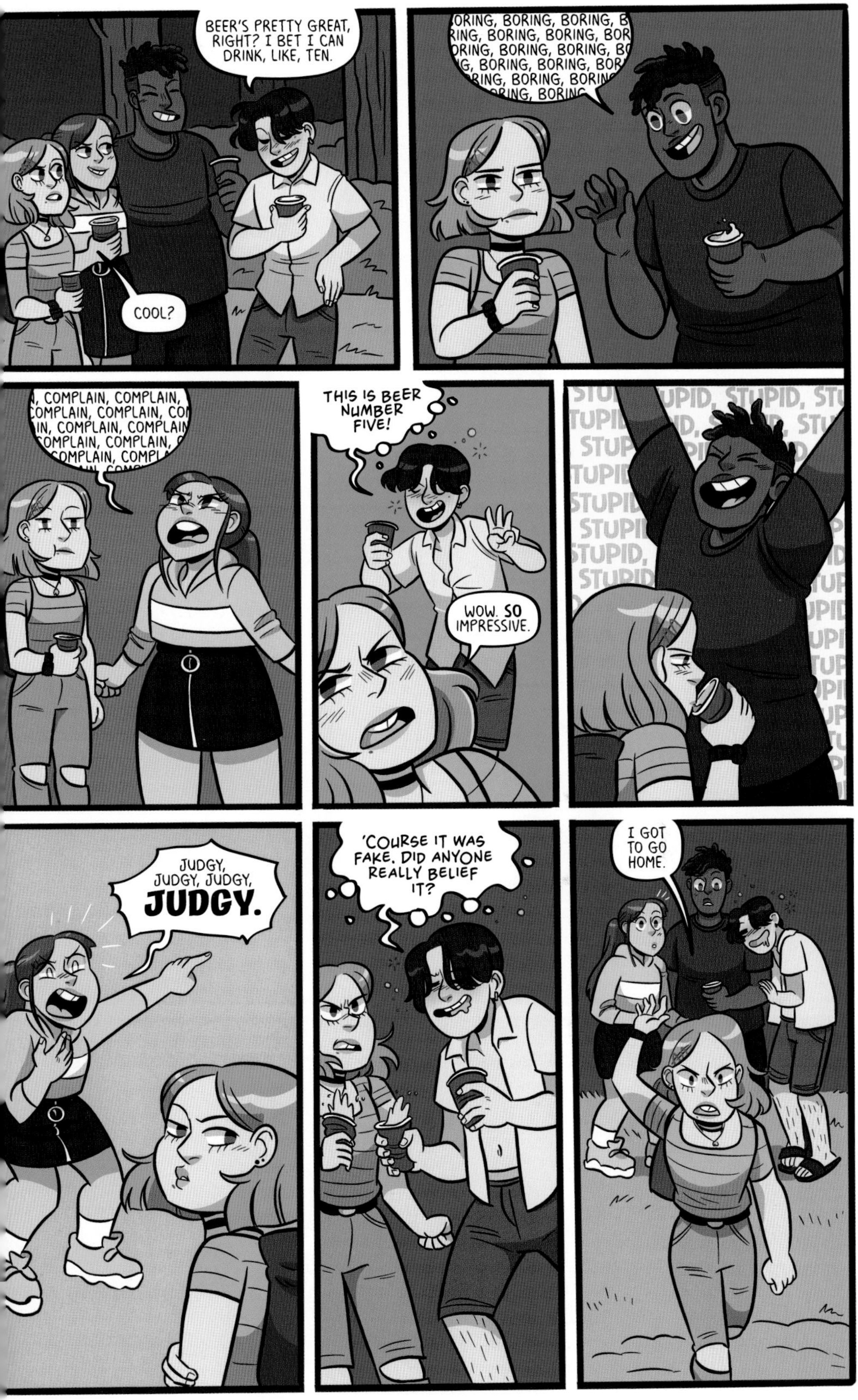
BEER'S PRETTY GREAT, RIGHT? I BET I CAN DRINK, LIKE, TEN.
COOL?
BORING, BORING, BORING, BORING, BORING, BORING, BORING, BORING, BORING, BORING, BORING, BORING, BORING, BORING, BORING
COMPLAIN, COMPLAIN, COMPLAIN, COMPLAIN, COMPLAIN, COMPLAIN, COMPLAIN, COMPLAIN, COMPLAIN
THIS IS BEER NUMBER FIVE!
WOW. SO IMPRESSIVE.
STUPID, STUPID, STUPID, STUPID, STUPID, STUPID
JUDGY, JUDGY, JUDGY, JUDGY.
'COURSE IT WAS FAKE. DID ANYONE REALLY BELIEF IT?
I GOT TO GO HOME.

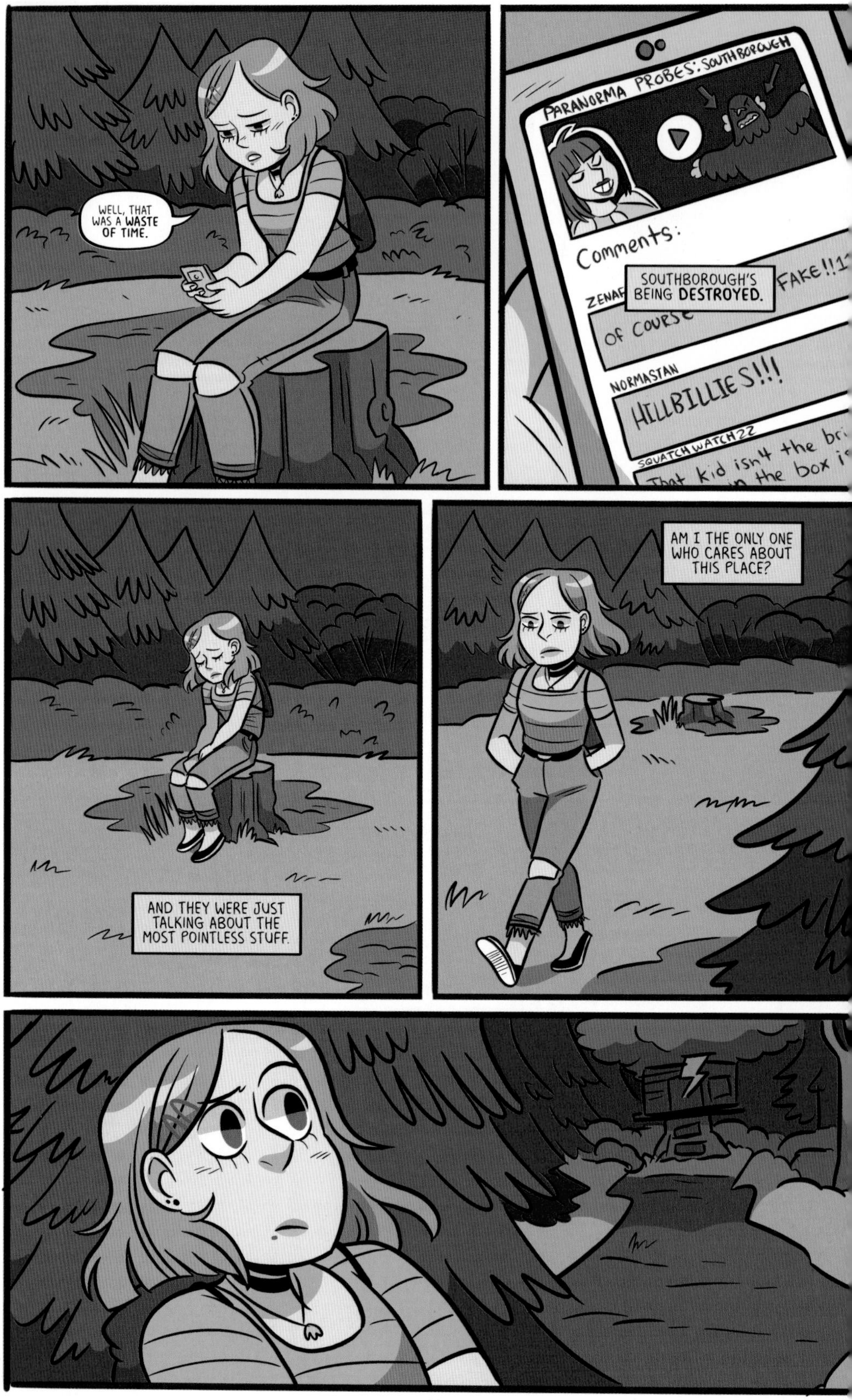
WELL, THAT WAS A WASTE OF TIME.
PARANORMA PROBES: SOUTHBOROUGH
Comments:
SOUTHBOROUGH'S BEING DESTROYED.
of course
NORMASTAN
HILLBILLIES!!!
SQUATCHWATCH22
That kid isn't the
in the box
AND THEY WERE JUST TALKING ABOUT THE MOST POINTLESS STUFF.
AM I THE ONLY ONE WHO CARES ABOUT THIS PLACE?

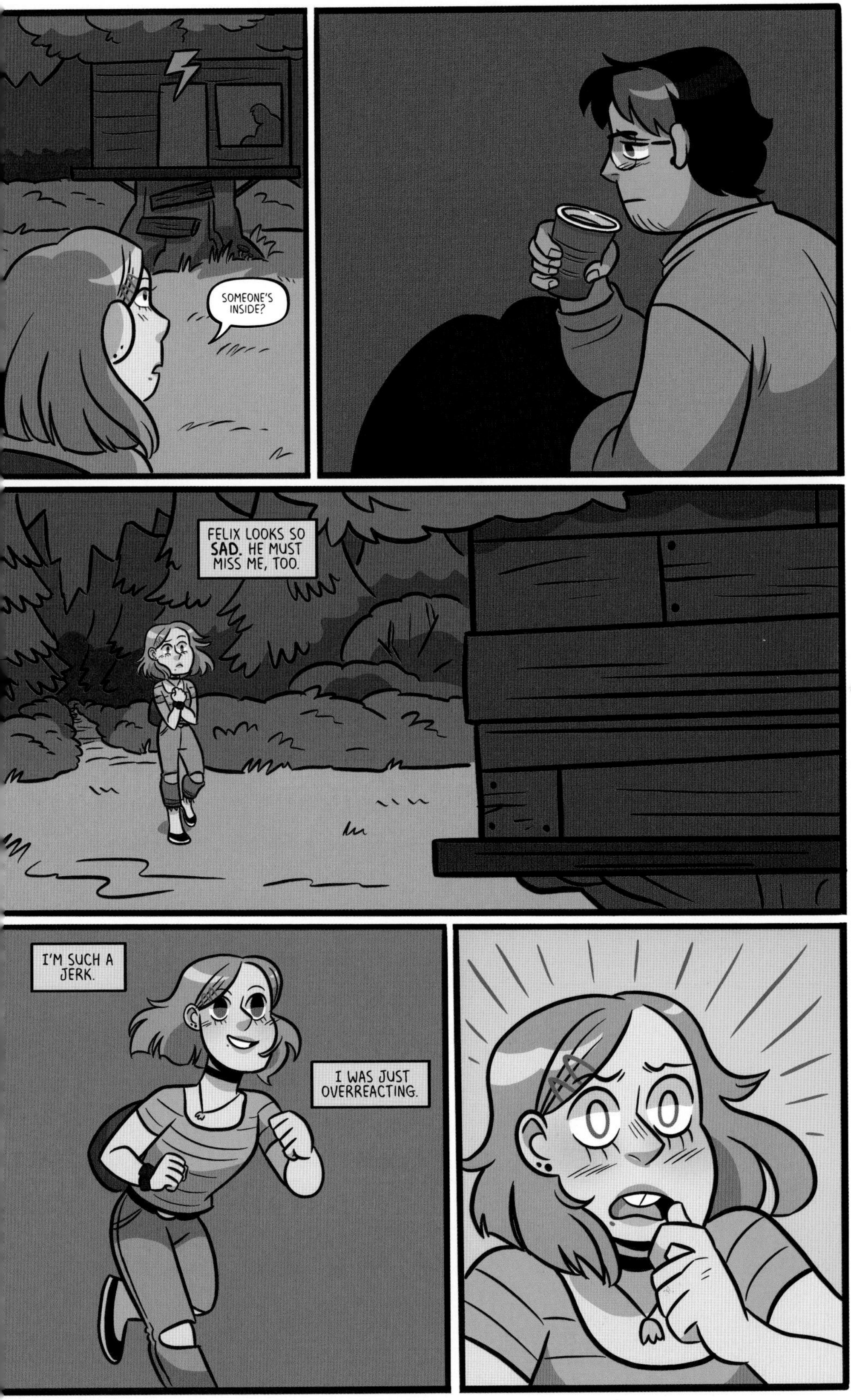
SOMEONE'S INSIDE?
FELIX LOOKS SO **SAD.** HE MUST MISS ME, TOO.
I'M SUCH A JERK.
I WAS JUST OVERREACTING.

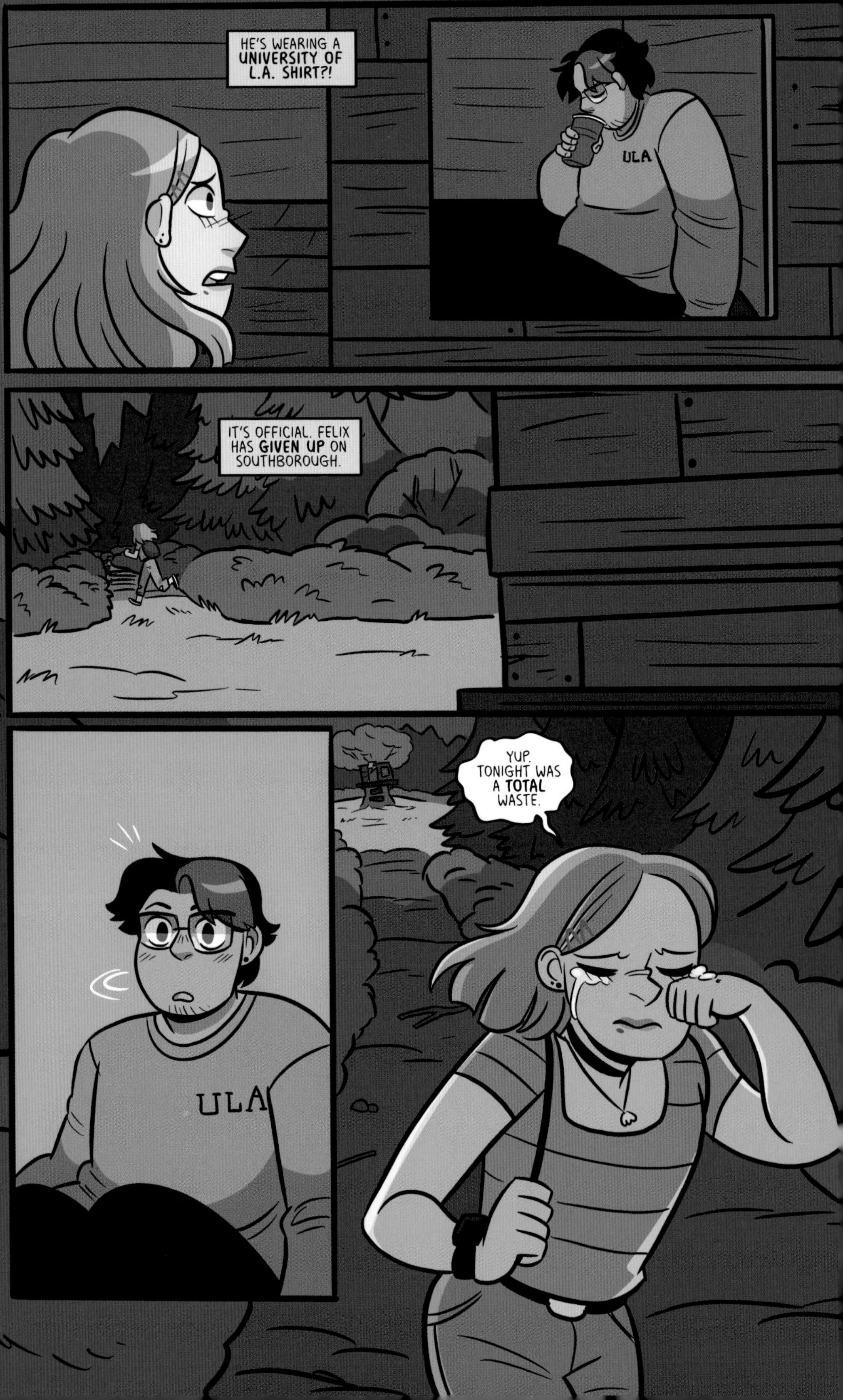
HE'S WEARING A UNIVERSITY OF L.A. SHIRT?!
ULA
IT'S OFFICIAL. FELIX HAS GIVEN UP ON SOUTHBOROUGH.
YUP. TONIGHT WAS A TOTAL WASTE.
ULA

CHAPTER 4

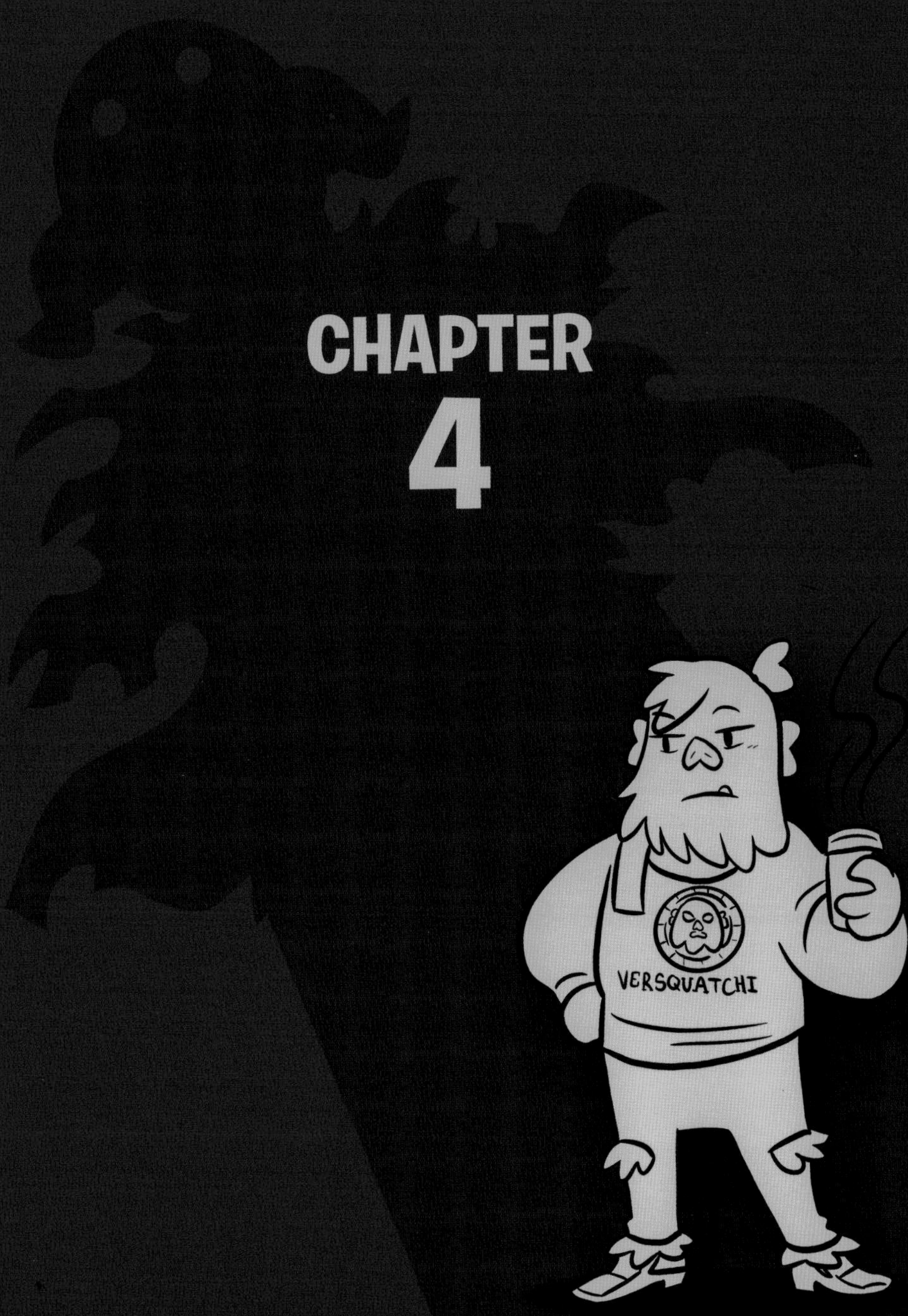
VERSQUATCHI

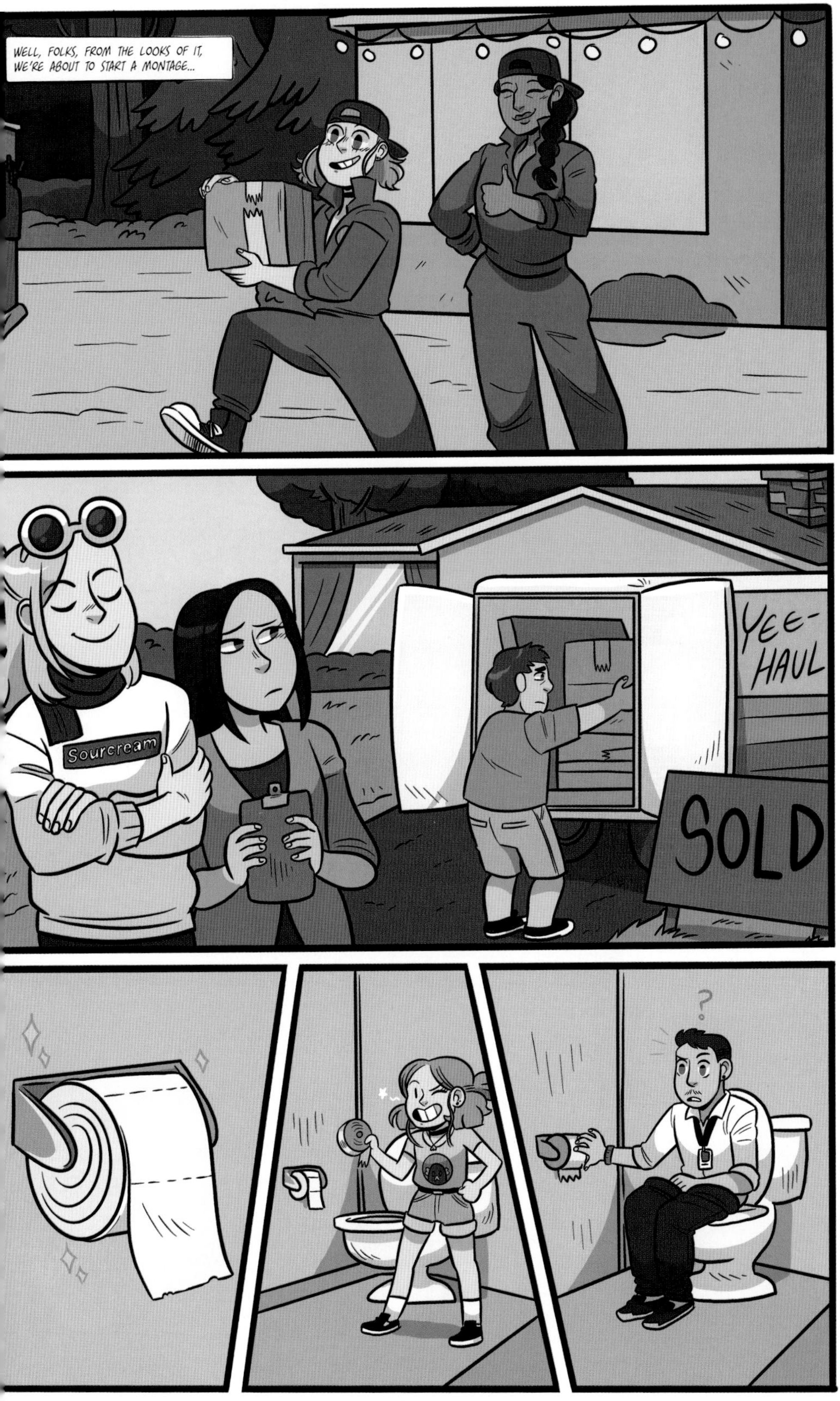

WELL, FOLKS, FROM THE LOOKS OF IT, WE'RE ABOUT TO START A MONTAGE...
Sourcream
YEE-HAUL
SOLD
?

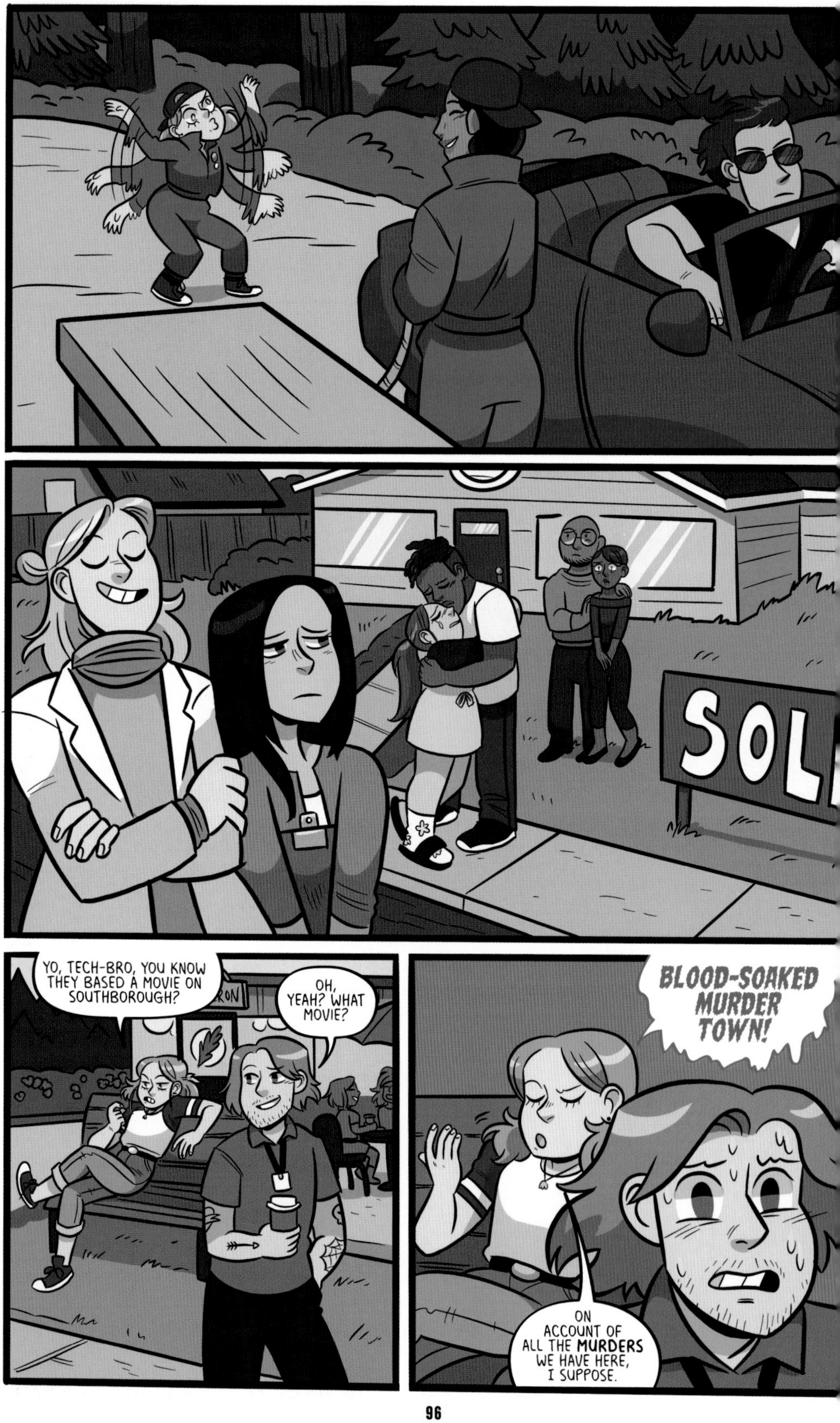
SOL
YO, TECH-BRO, YOU KNOW THEY BASED A MOVIE ON SOUTHBOROUGH?
OH, YEAH? WHAT MOVIE?
BLOOD-SOAKED MURDER TOWN!
ON ACCOUNT OF ALL THE **MURDERS** WE HAVE HERE, I SUPPOSE.

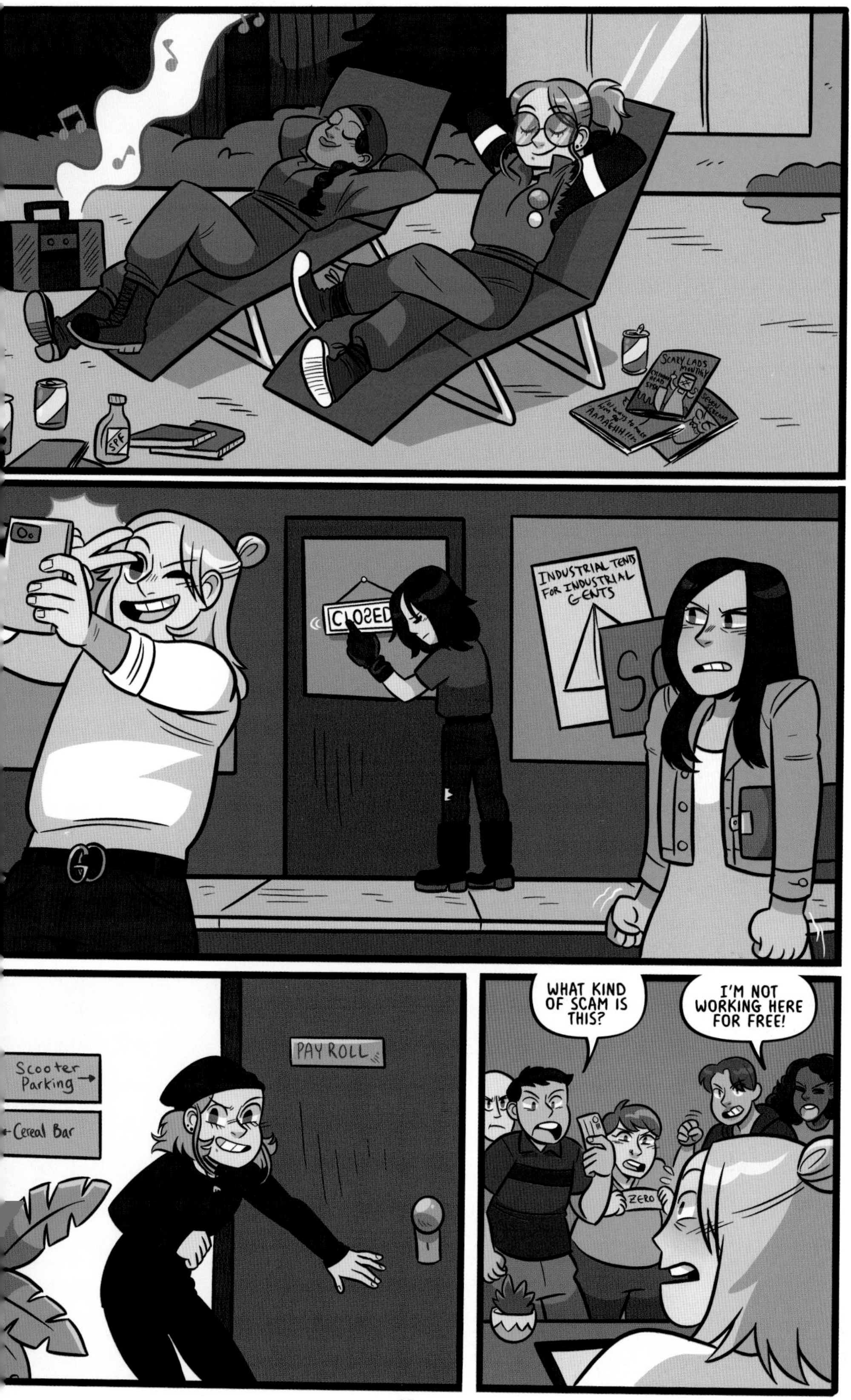
SPF
SCARY LADS MONTHLY
CLOSED
INDUSTRIAL TENTS FOR INDUSTRIAL GENTS
PAYROLL
Scooter Parking →
← Cereal Bar
WHAT KIND OF SCAM IS THIS?
I'M NOT WORKING HERE FOR FREE!
ZERO

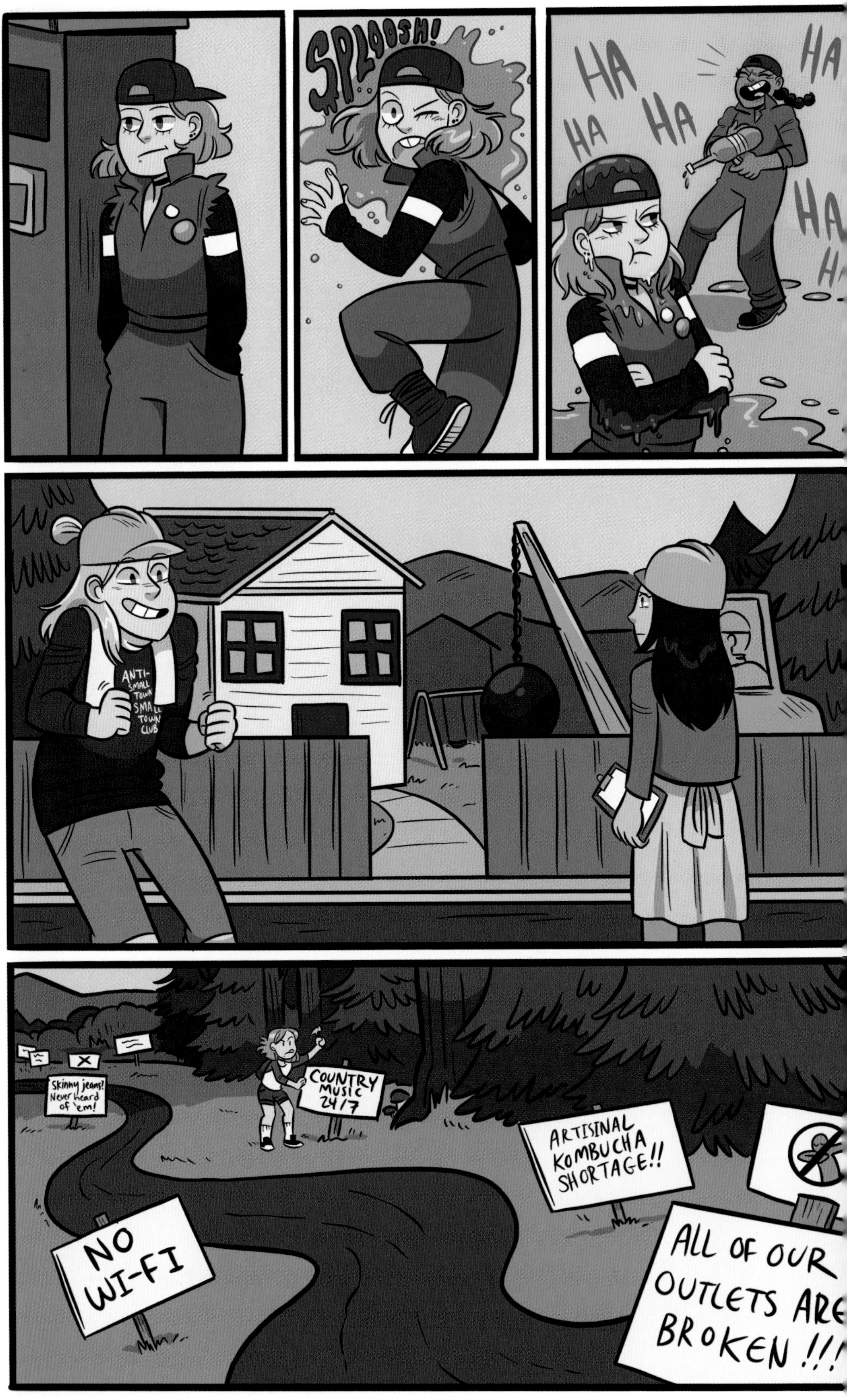
SPLOOSH!
HA HA HA HA HA
ANTI-SMALL TOWN SMALL TOWN CLUB
Skinny jeans? Never heard of 'em!
COUNTRY MUSIC 24/7
ARTISINAL KOMBUCHA SHORTAGE!!
NO WI-FI
ALL OF OUR OUTLETS ARE BROKEN!!!

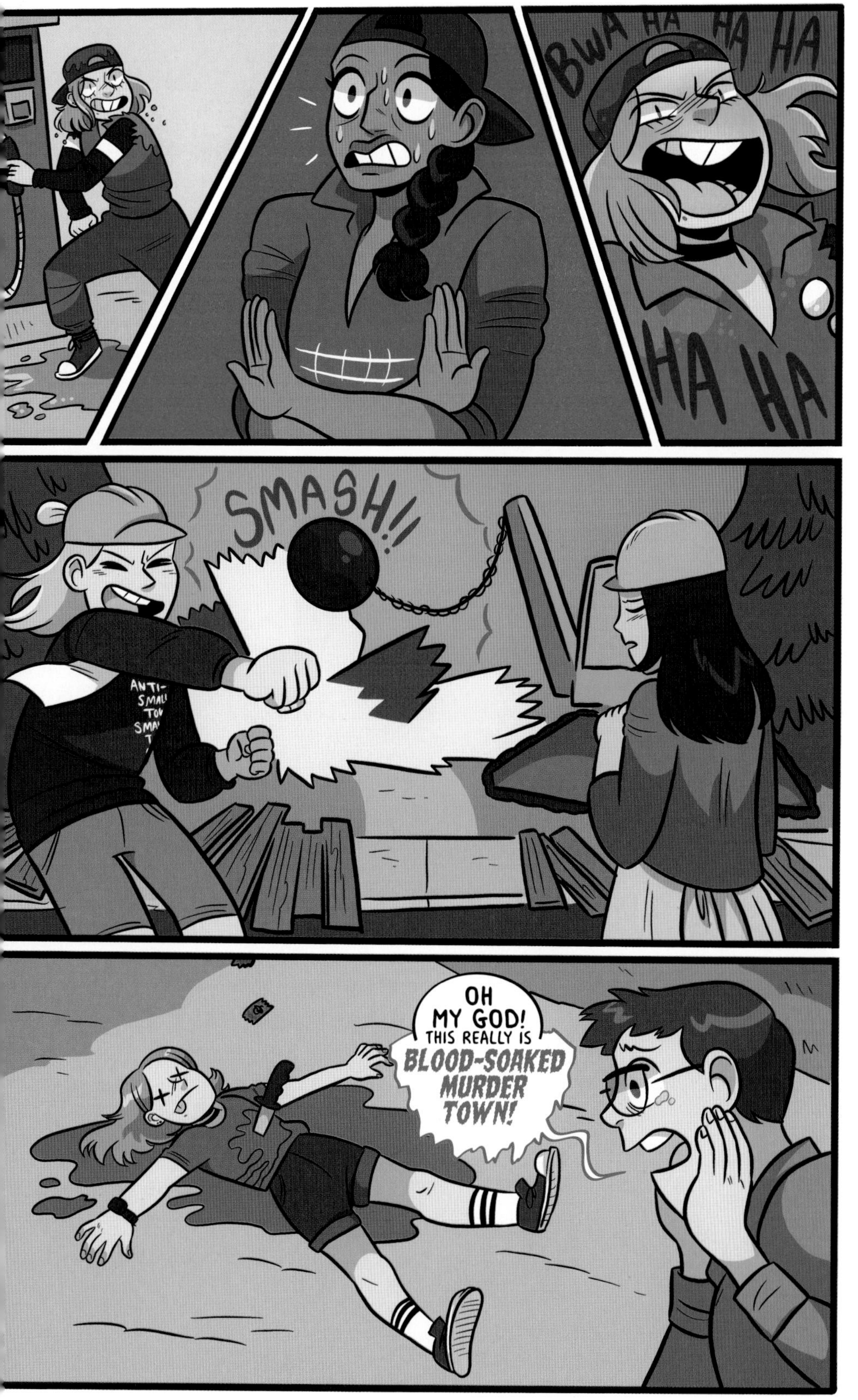
BWA HA HA HA
HA HA
SMASH!!
OH MY GOD! THIS REALLY IS BLOOD-SOAKED MURDER TOWN!

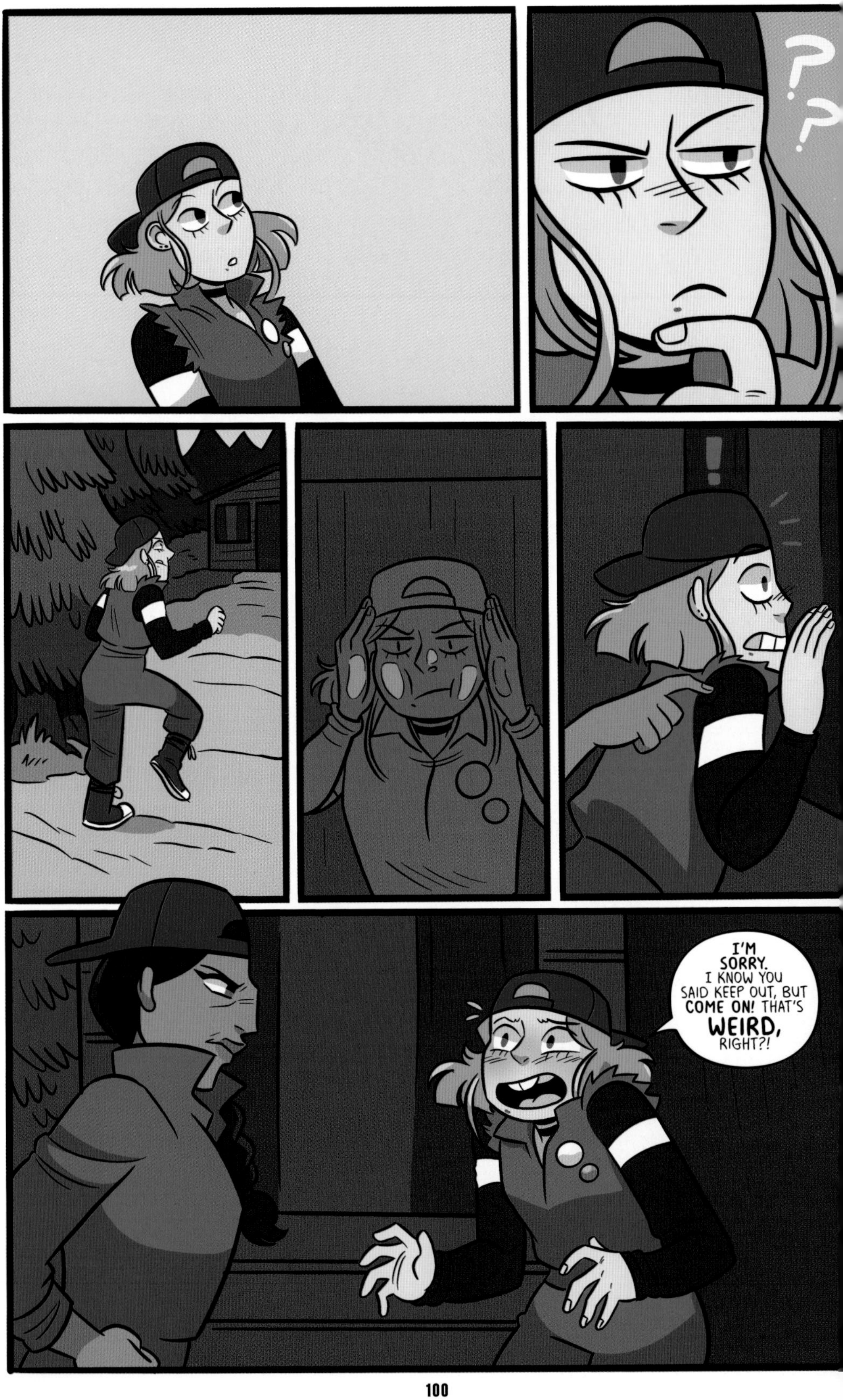
??
!
I'M SORRY. I KNOW YOU SAID KEEP OUT, BUT COME ON! THAT'S WEIRD, RIGHT?!

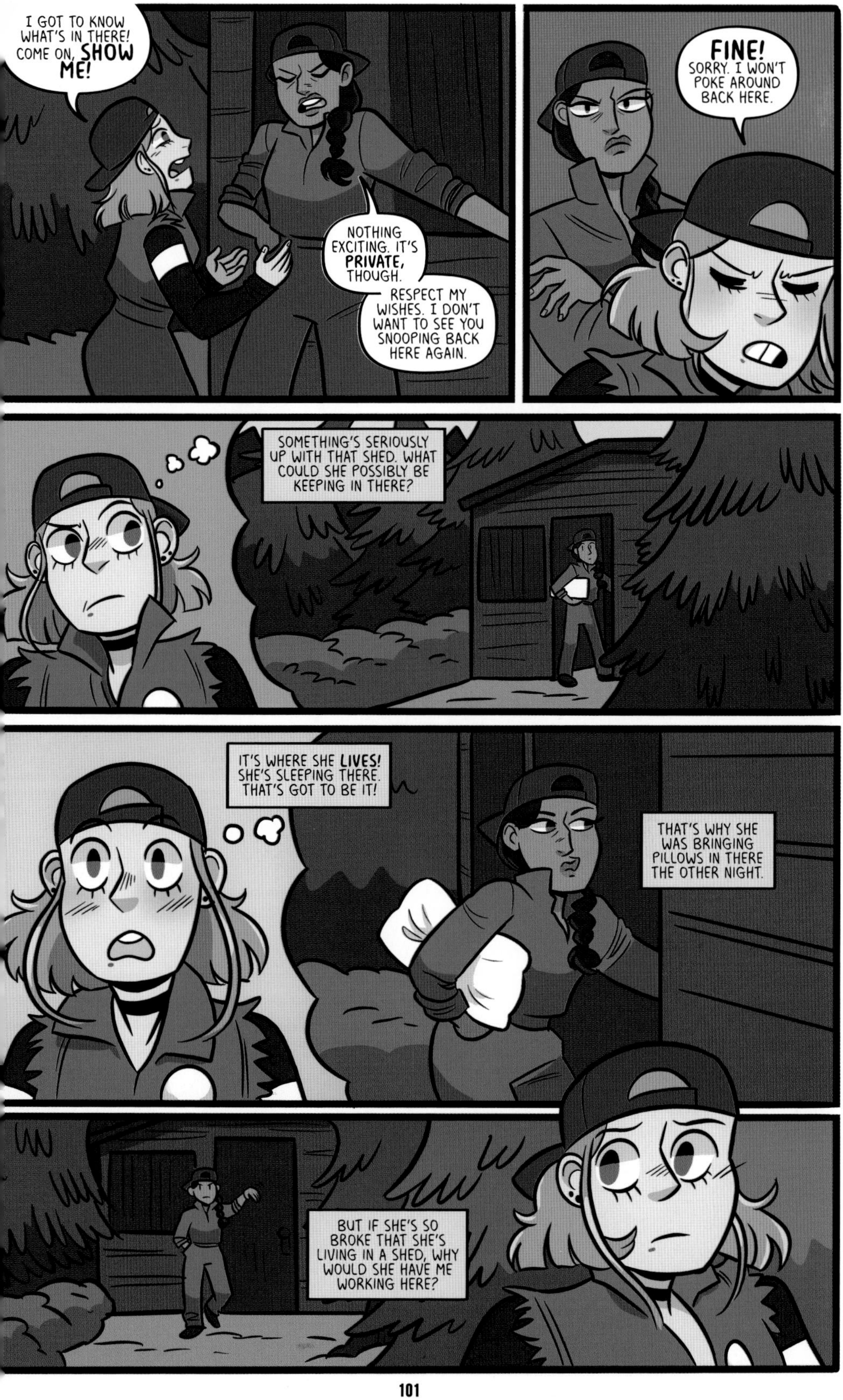
I GOT TO KNOW WHAT'S IN THERE! COME ON, SHOW ME!
NOTHING EXCITING. IT'S PRIVATE, THOUGH.
RESPECT MY WISHES. I DON'T WANT TO SEE YOU SNOOPING BACK HERE AGAIN.
FINE! SORRY. I WON'T POKE AROUND BACK HERE.
SOMETHING'S SERIOUSLY UP WITH THAT SHED. WHAT COULD SHE POSSIBLY BE KEEPING IN THERE?
IT'S WHERE SHE LIVES! SHE'S SLEEPING THERE. THAT'S GOT TO BE IT!
THAT'S WHY SHE WAS BRINGING PILLOWS IN THERE THE OTHER NIGHT.
BUT IF SHE'S SO BROKE THAT SHE'S LIVING IN A SHED, WHY WOULD SHE HAVE ME WORKING HERE?

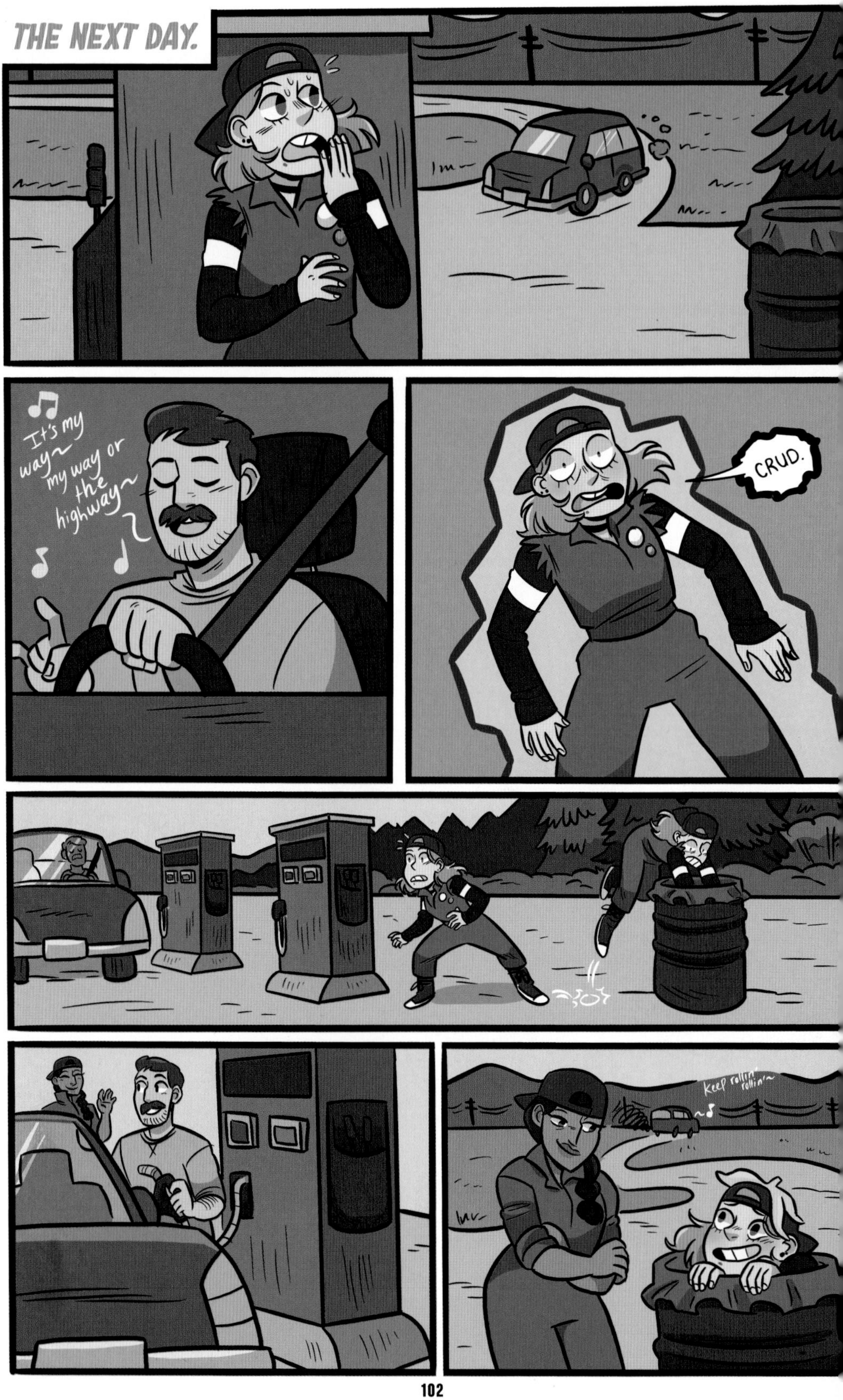
THE NEXT DAY.
It's my way~ my way or the highway~
CRUD.
Keep rollin' rollin'~

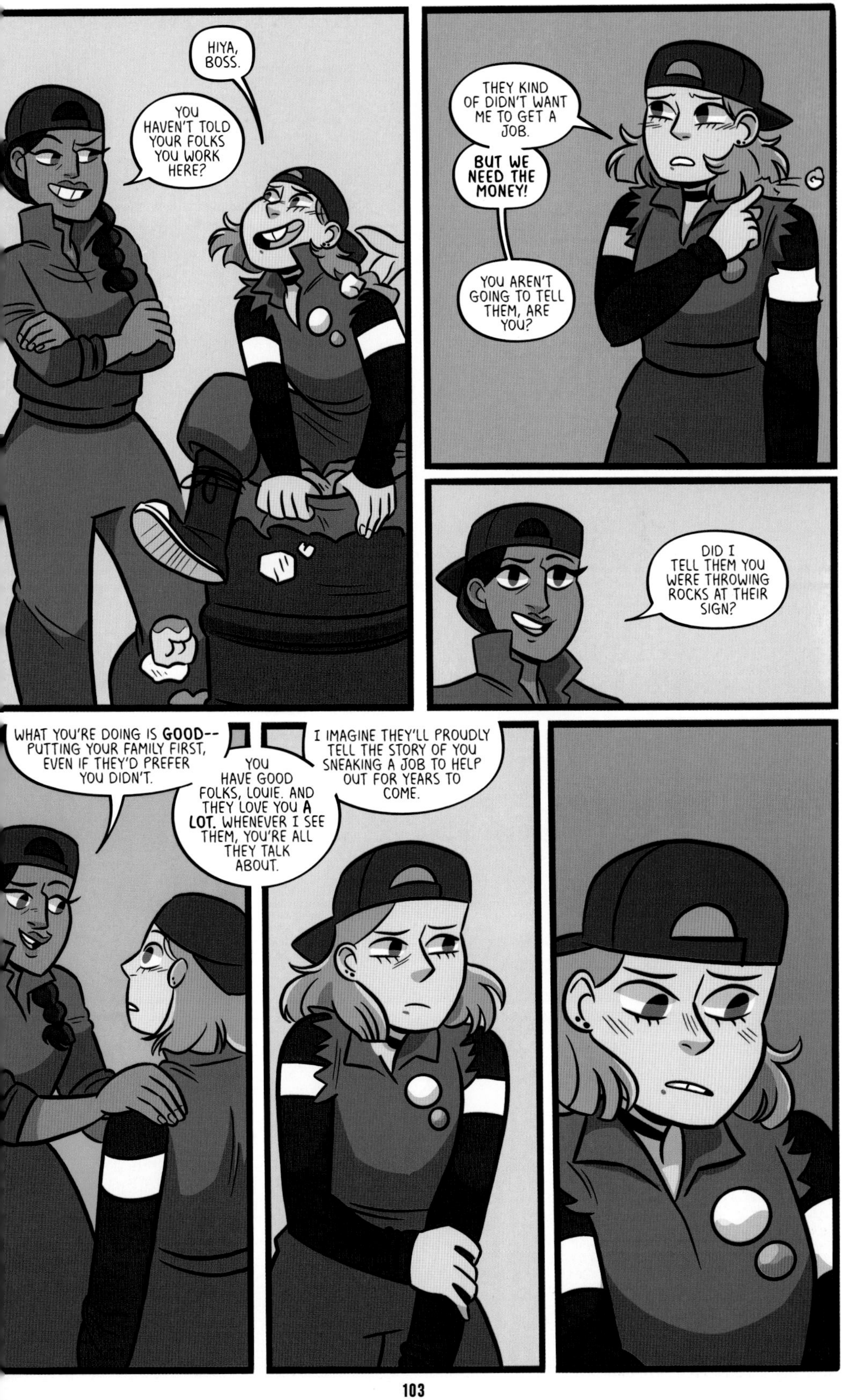
HIYA, BOSS.
YOU HAVEN'T TOLD YOUR FOLKS YOU WORK HERE?
THEY KIND OF DIDN'T WANT ME TO GET A JOB.
BUT WE NEED THE MONEY!
YOU AREN'T GOING TO TELL THEM, ARE YOU?
DID I TELL THEM YOU WERE THROWING ROCKS AT THEIR SIGN?
WHAT YOU'RE DOING IS GOOD-- PUTTING YOUR FAMILY FIRST, EVEN IF THEY'D PREFER YOU DIDN'T.
YOU HAVE GOOD FOLKS, LOUIE. AND THEY LOVE YOU A LOT. WHENEVER I SEE THEM, YOU'RE ALL THEY TALK ABOUT.
I IMAGINE THEY'LL PROUDLY TELL THE STORY OF YOU SNEAKING A JOB TO HELP OUT FOR YEARS TO COME.

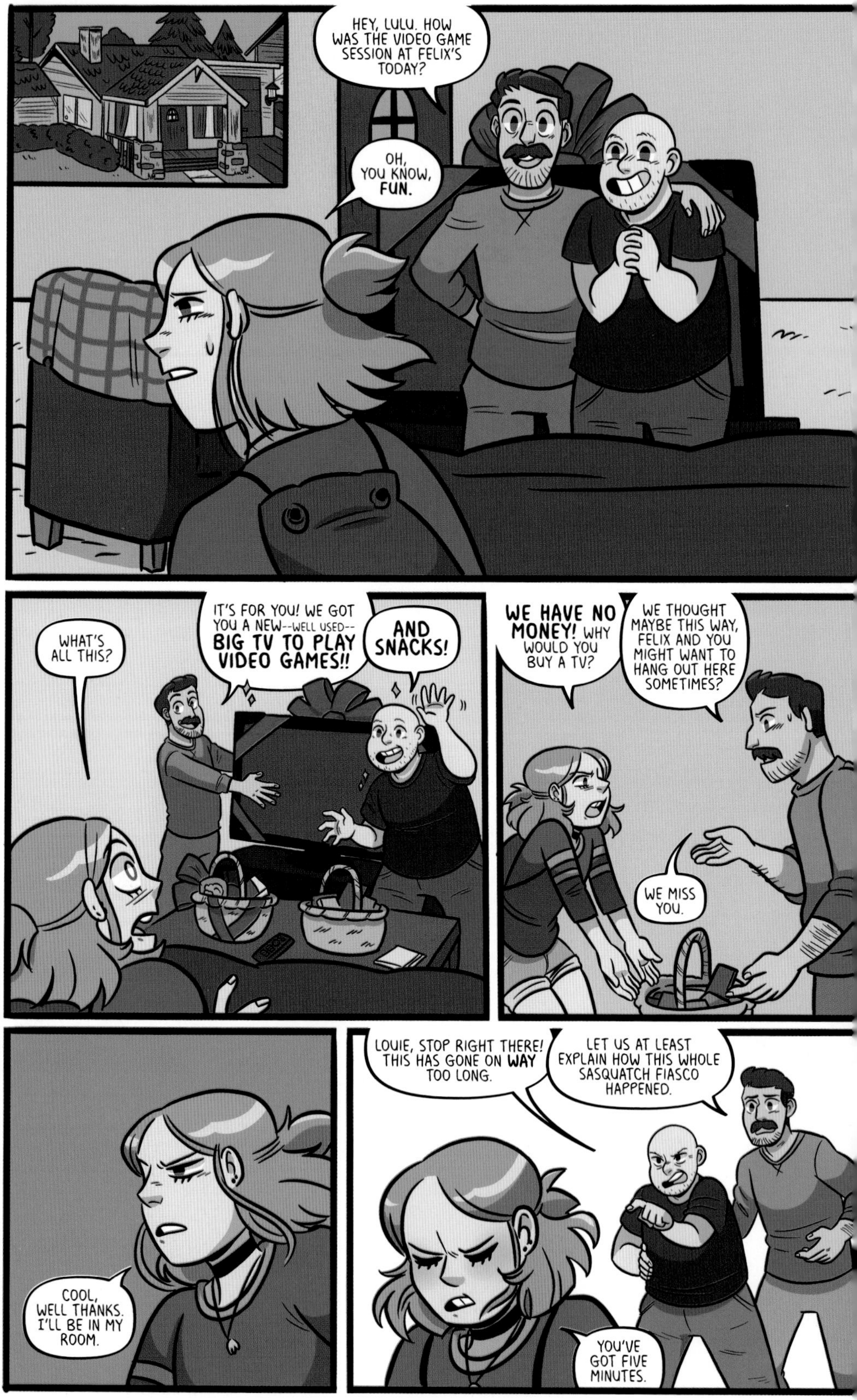
HEY, LULU. HOW WAS THE VIDEO GAME SESSION AT FELIX'S TODAY?
OH, YOU KNOW, **FUN.**
WHAT'S ALL THIS?
IT'S FOR YOU! WE GOT YOU A NEW--WELL USED-- **BIG TV TO PLAY VIDEO GAMES!!**
AND SNACKS!
WE HAVE NO MONEY! WHY WOULD YOU BUY A TV?
WE THOUGHT MAYBE THIS WAY, FELIX AND YOU MIGHT WANT TO HANG OUT HERE SOMETIMES?
WE MISS YOU.
COOL, WELL THANKS. I'LL BE IN MY ROOM.
LOUIE, STOP RIGHT THERE! THIS HAS GONE ON **WAY** TOO LONG.
LET US AT LEAST EXPLAIN HOW THIS WHOLE SASQUATCH FIASCO HAPPENED.
YOU'VE GOT FIVE MINUTES.

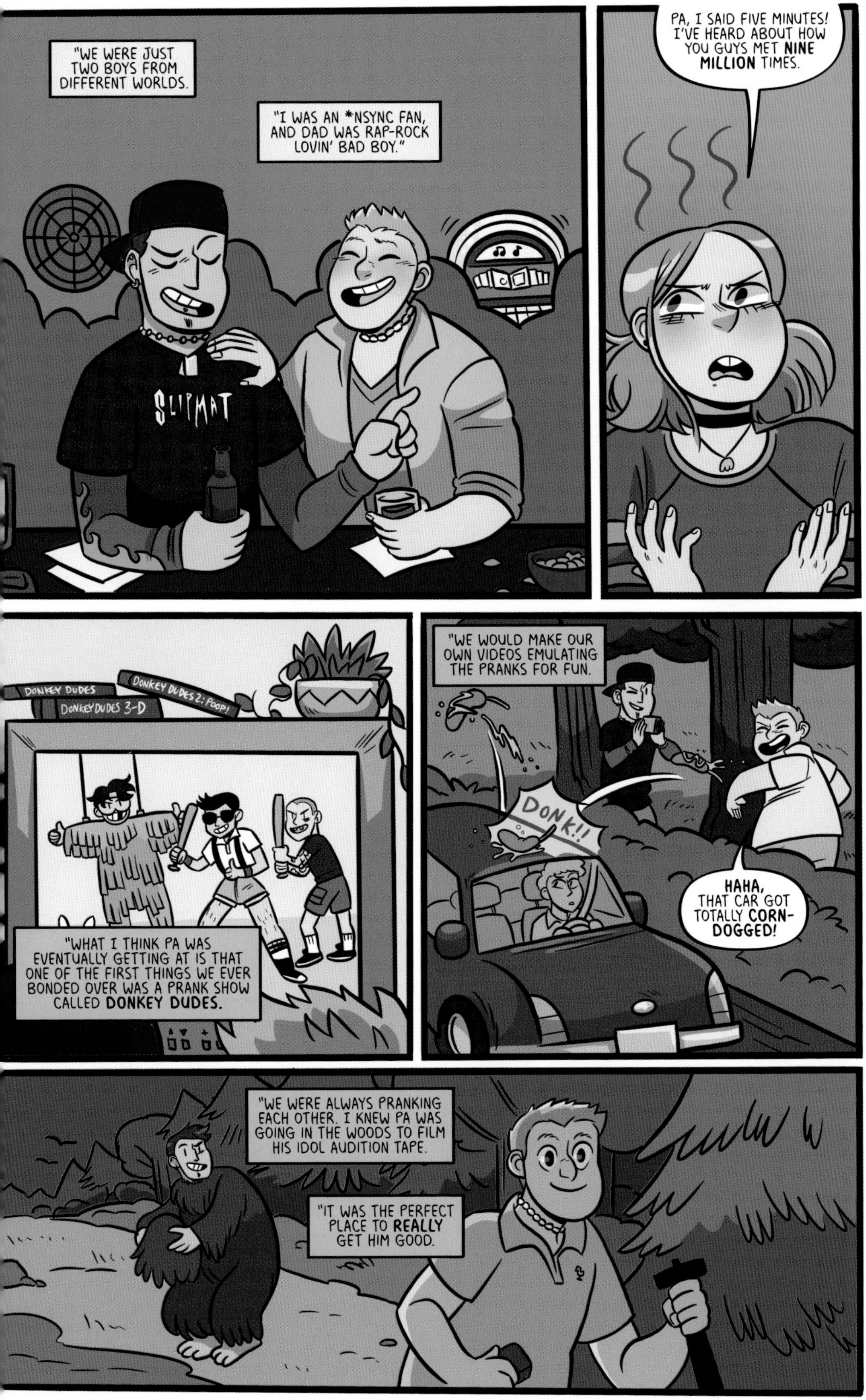

"WE WERE JUST TWO BOYS FROM DIFFERENT WORLDS.
"I WAS AN *NSYNC FAN, AND DAD WAS RAP-ROCK LOVIN' BAD BOY."
SLIPMAT
PA, I SAID FIVE MINUTES! I'VE HEARD ABOUT HOW YOU GUYS MET **NINE MILLION** TIMES.
DONKEY DUDES
DONKEY DUDES 2: POOP!
DONKEY DUDES 3-D
"WHAT I THINK PA WAS EVENTUALLY GETTING AT IS THAT ONE OF THE FIRST THINGS WE EVER BONDED OVER WAS A PRANK SHOW CALLED **DONKEY DUDES.**
"WE WOULD MAKE OUR OWN VIDEOS EMULATING THE PRANKS FOR FUN.
DONK!!
HAHA, THAT CAR GOT TOTALLY **CORN-DOGGED!**
"WE WERE ALWAYS PRANKING EACH OTHER. I KNEW PA WAS GOING IN THE WOODS TO FILM HIS IDOL AUDITION TAPE.
"IT WAS THE PERFECT PLACE TO **REALLY** GET HIM GOOD.

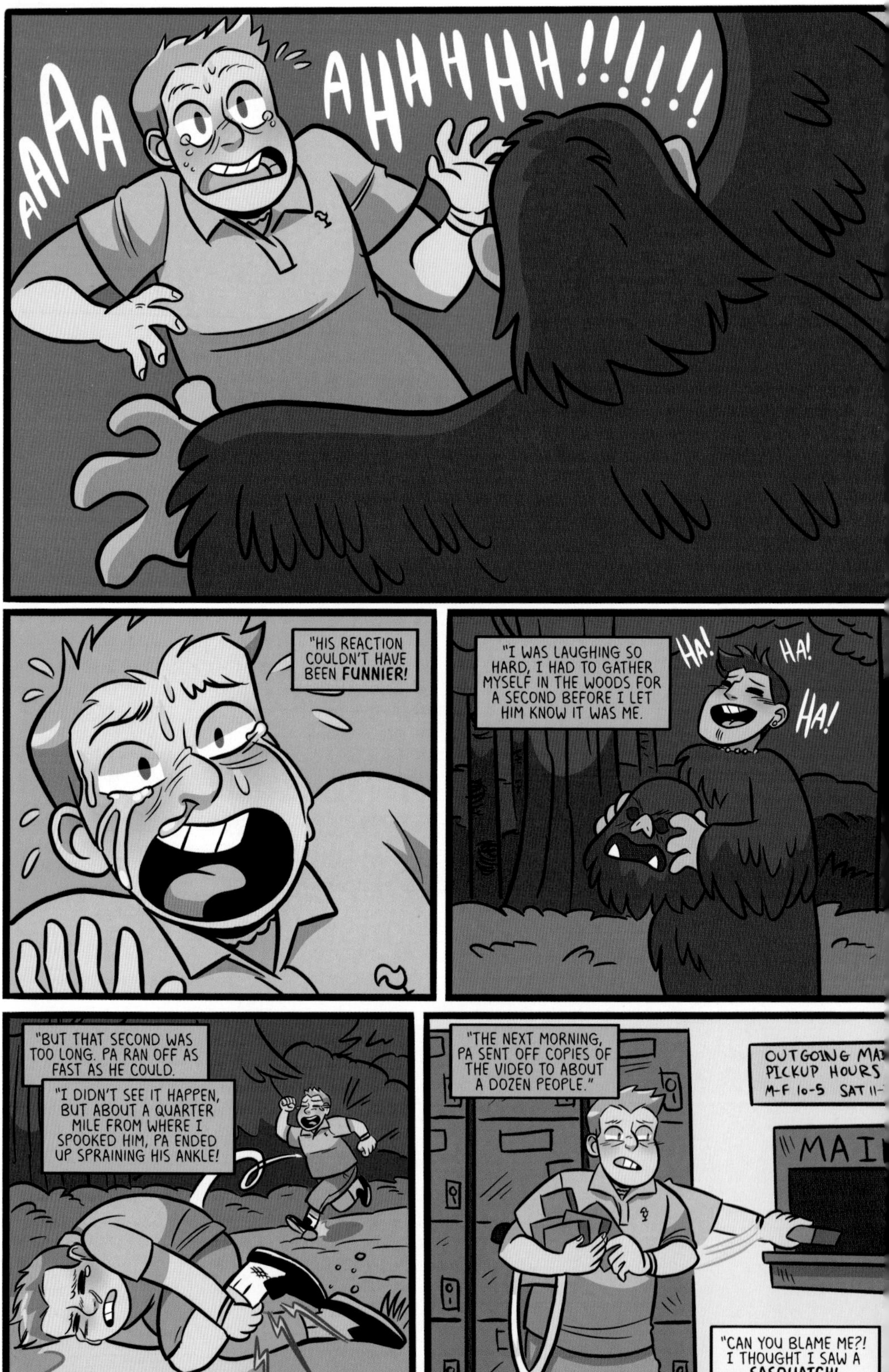
AAAAHHHHHH!!!!!!
"HIS REACTION COULDN'T HAVE BEEN **FUNNIER**!
"I WAS LAUGHING SO HARD, I HAD TO GATHER MYSELF IN THE WOODS FOR A SECOND BEFORE I LET HIM KNOW IT WAS ME.
HA! HA! HA!
"BUT THAT SECOND WAS TOO LONG. PA RAN OFF AS FAST AS HE COULD.
"I DIDN'T SEE IT HAPPEN, BUT ABOUT A QUARTER MILE FROM WHERE I SPOOKED HIM, PA ENDED UP SPRAINING HIS ANKLE!
"THE NEXT MORNING, PA SENT OFF COPIES OF THE VIDEO TO ABOUT A DOZEN PEOPLE."
OUTGOING MA PICKUP HOURS M-F 10-5 SAT 11-
MAI
"CAN YOU BLAME ME?! I THOUGHT I SAW A **SASQUATCH**!

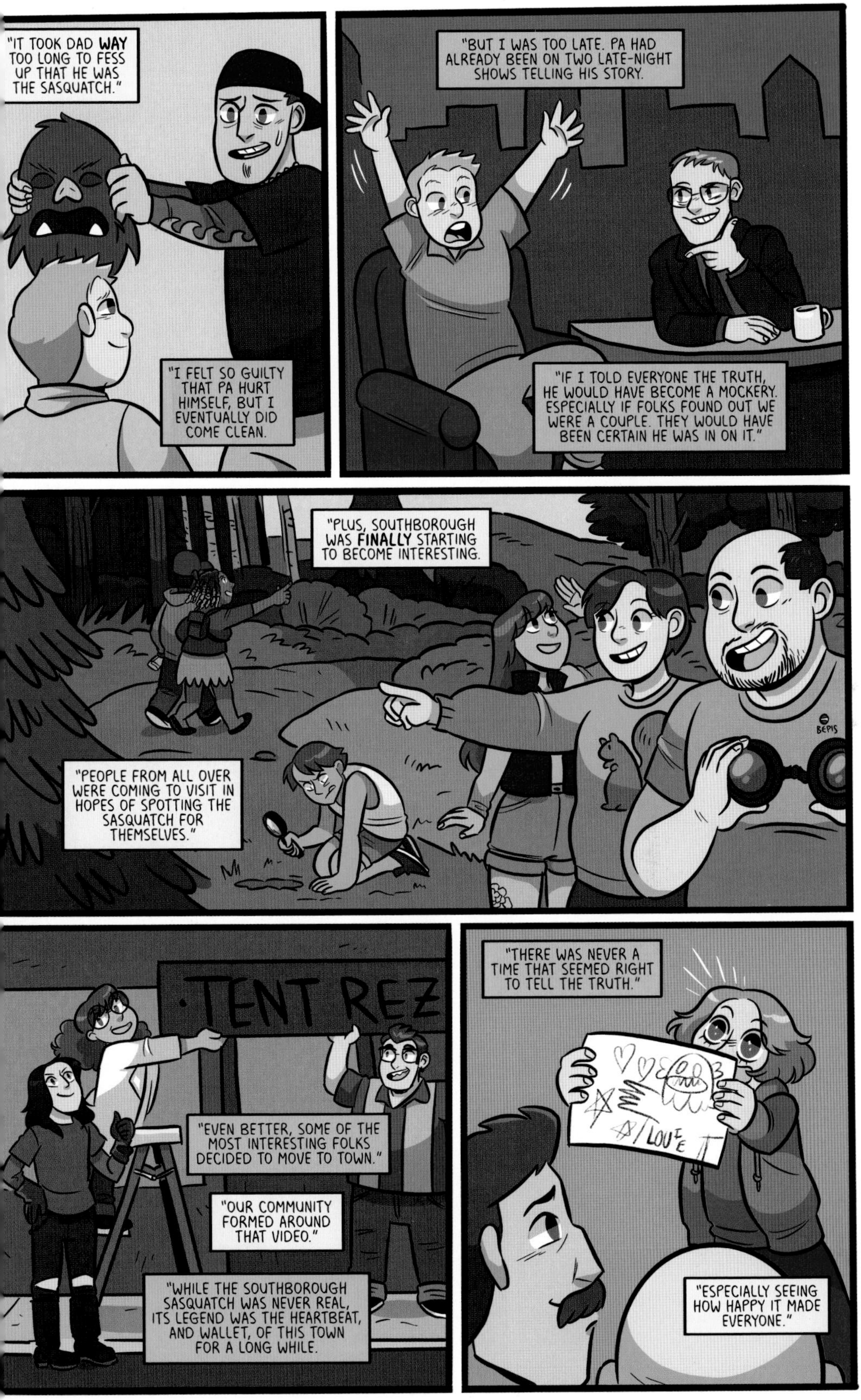
"IT TOOK DAD WAY TOO LONG TO FESS UP THAT HE WAS THE SASQUATCH."
"I FELT SO GUILTY THAT PA HURT HIMSELF, BUT I EVENTUALLY DID COME CLEAN.
"BUT I WAS TOO LATE. PA HAD ALREADY BEEN ON TWO LATE-NIGHT SHOWS TELLING HIS STORY.
"IF I TOLD EVERYONE THE TRUTH, HE WOULD HAVE BECOME A MOCKERY. ESPECIALLY IF FOLKS FOUND OUT WE WERE A COUPLE. THEY WOULD HAVE BEEN CERTAIN HE WAS IN ON IT."
"PLUS, SOUTHBOROUGH WAS FINALLY STARTING TO BECOME INTERESTING.
BEPIS
"PEOPLE FROM ALL OVER WERE COMING TO VISIT IN HOPES OF SPOTTING THE SASQUATCH FOR THEMSELVES."
TENT REZ
"EVEN BETTER, SOME OF THE MOST INTERESTING FOLKS DECIDED TO MOVE TO TOWN."
"OUR COMMUNITY FORMED AROUND THAT VIDEO."
"WHILE THE SOUTHBOROUGH SASQUATCH WAS NEVER REAL, ITS LEGEND WAS THE HEARTBEAT, AND WALLET, OF THIS TOWN FOR A LONG WHILE.
"THERE WAS NEVER A TIME THAT SEEMED RIGHT TO TELL THE TRUTH."
LOUIE
"ESPECIALLY SEEING HOW HAPPY IT MADE EVERYONE."

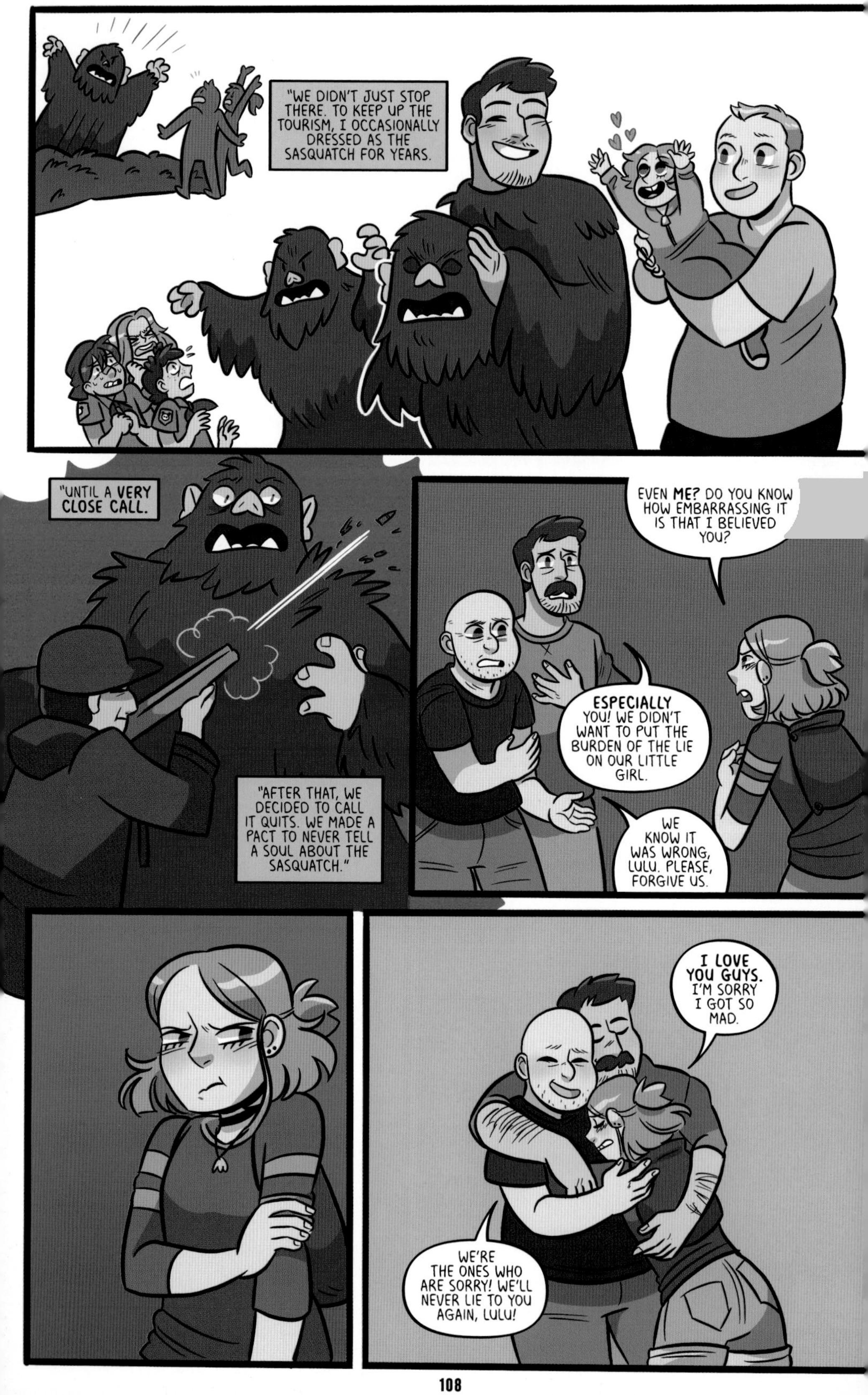
"WE DIDN'T JUST STOP THERE. TO KEEP UP THE TOURISM, I OCCASIONALLY DRESSED AS THE SASQUATCH FOR YEARS.
"UNTIL A VERY CLOSE CALL.
"AFTER THAT, WE DECIDED TO CALL IT QUITS. WE MADE A PACT TO NEVER TELL A SOUL ABOUT THE SASQUATCH."
EVEN ME? DO YOU KNOW HOW EMBARRASSING IT IS THAT I BELIEVED YOU?
ESPECIALLY YOU! WE DIDN'T WANT TO PUT THE BURDEN OF THE LIE ON OUR LITTLE GIRL.
WE KNOW IT WAS WRONG, LULU. PLEASE, FORGIVE US.
I LOVE YOU GUYS. I'M SORRY I GOT SO MAD.
WE'RE THE ONES WHO ARE SORRY! WE'LL NEVER LIE TO YOU AGAIN, LULU!

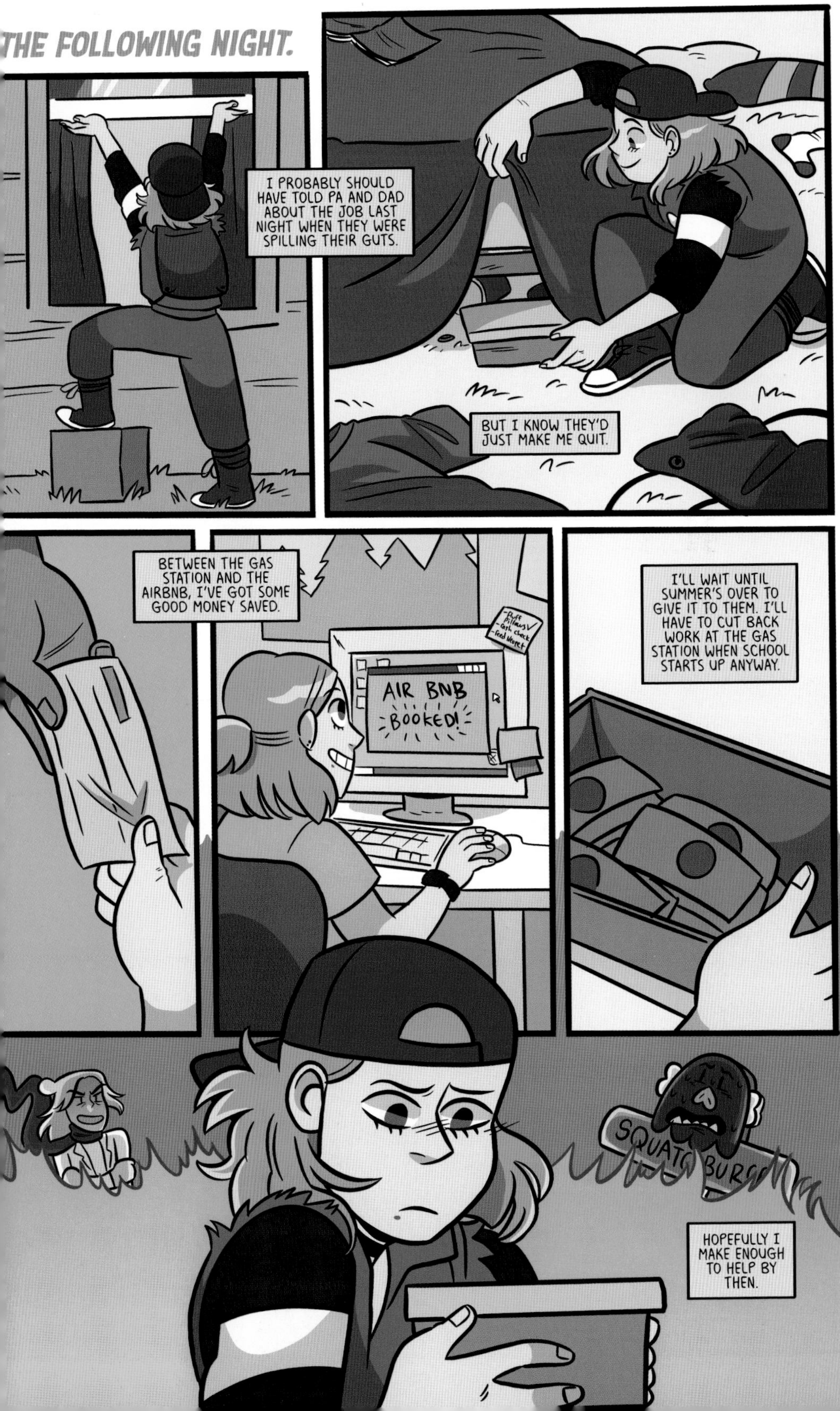
THE FOLLOWING NIGHT.
I PROBABLY SHOULD HAVE TOLD PA AND DAD ABOUT THE JOB LAST NIGHT WHEN THEY WERE SPILLING THEIR GUTS.
BUT I KNOW THEY'D JUST MAKE ME QUIT.
BETWEEN THE GAS STATION AND THE AIRBNB, I'VE GOT SOME GOOD MONEY SAVED.
AIR BNB BOOKED!
I'LL WAIT UNTIL SUMMER'S OVER TO GIVE IT TO THEM. I'LL HAVE TO CUT BACK WORK AT THE GAS STATION WHEN SCHOOL STARTS UP ANYWAY.
HOPEFULLY I MAKE ENOUGH TO HELP BY THEN.

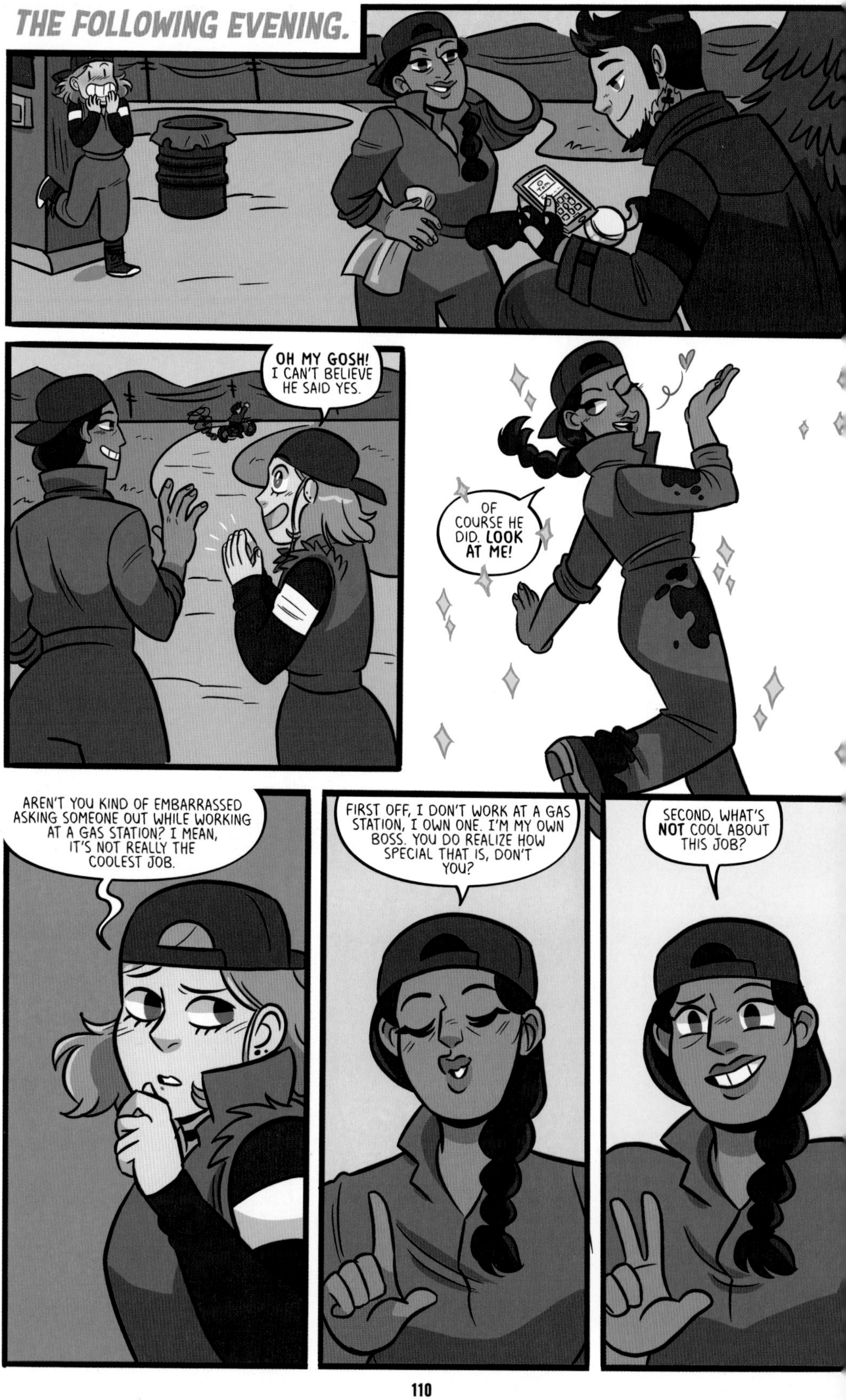
THE FOLLOWING EVENING.
OH MY GOSH! I CAN'T BELIEVE HE SAID YES.
OF COURSE HE DID. LOOK AT ME!
AREN'T YOU KIND OF EMBARRASSED ASKING SOMEONE OUT WHILE WORKING AT A GAS STATION? I MEAN, IT'S NOT REALLY THE COOLEST JOB.
FIRST OFF, I DON'T WORK AT A GAS STATION, I OWN ONE. I'M MY OWN BOSS. YOU DO REALIZE HOW SPECIAL THAT IS, DON'T YOU?
SECOND, WHAT'S NOT COOL ABOUT THIS JOB?

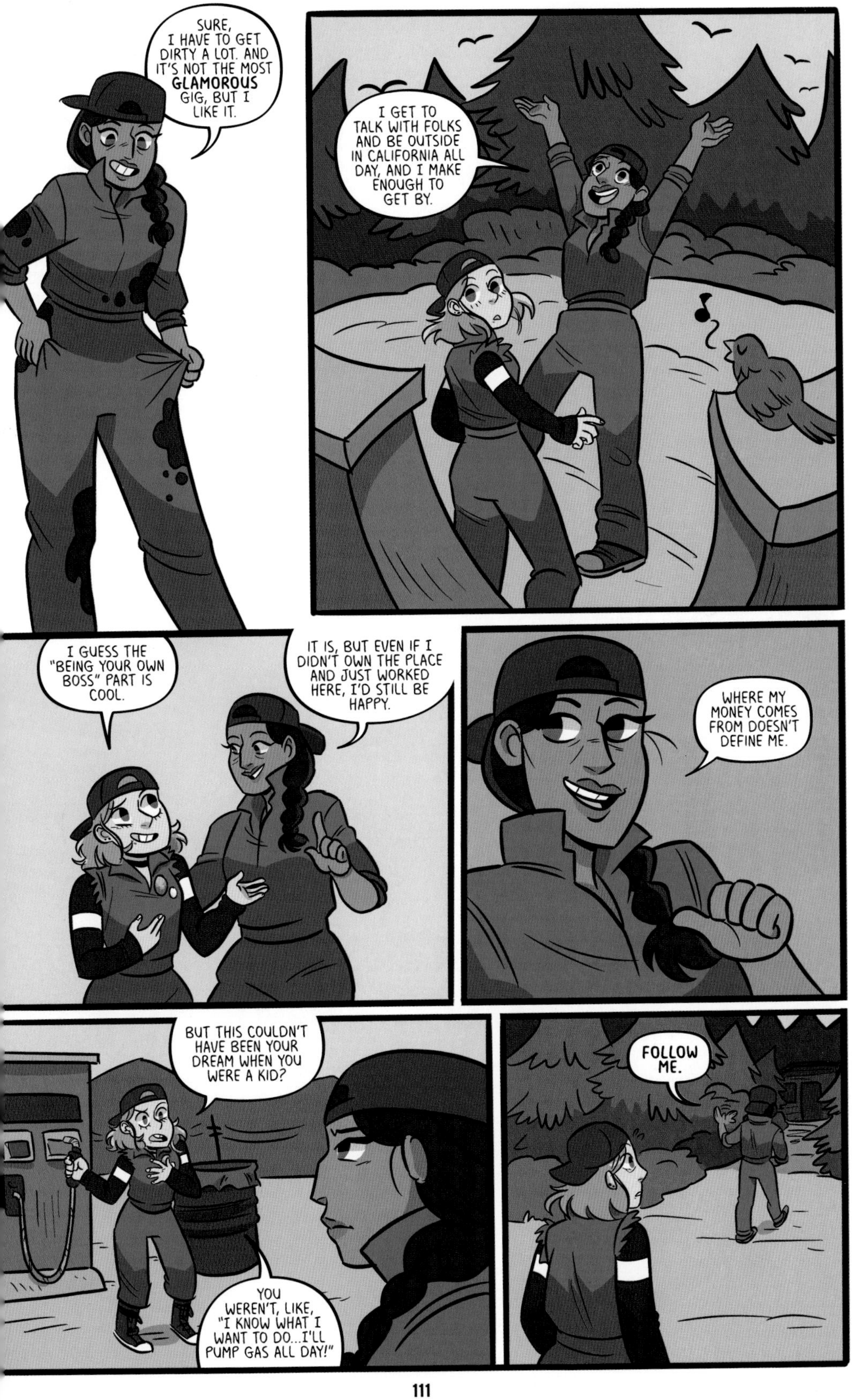
SURE, I HAVE TO GET DIRTY A LOT. AND IT'S NOT THE MOST **GLAMOROUS** GIG, BUT I LIKE IT.
I GET TO TALK WITH FOLKS AND BE OUTSIDE IN CALIFORNIA ALL DAY, AND I MAKE ENOUGH TO GET BY.
I GUESS THE "BEING YOUR OWN BOSS" PART IS COOL.
IT IS, BUT EVEN IF I DIDN'T OWN THE PLACE AND JUST WORKED HERE, I'D STILL BE HAPPY.
WHERE MY MONEY COMES FROM DOESN'T DEFINE ME.
BUT THIS COULDN'T HAVE BEEN YOUR DREAM WHEN YOU WERE A KID?
YOU WEREN'T, LIKE, "I KNOW WHAT I WANT TO DO...I'LL PUMP GAS ALL DAY!"
FOLLOW ME.

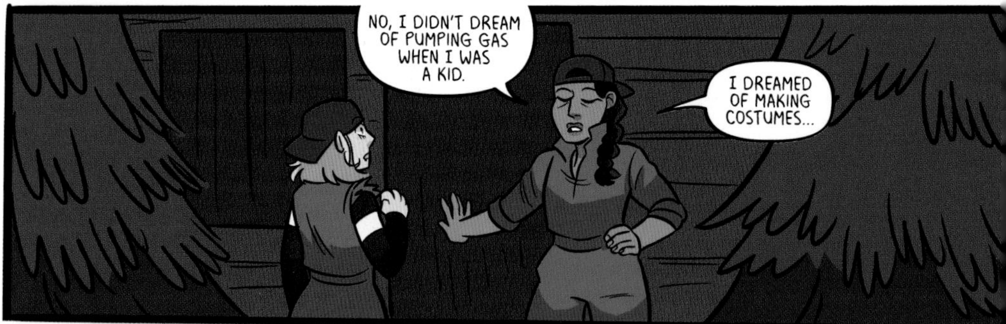
NO, I DIDN'T DREAM OF PUMPING GAS WHEN I WAS A KID.
I DREAMED OF MAKING COSTUMES...

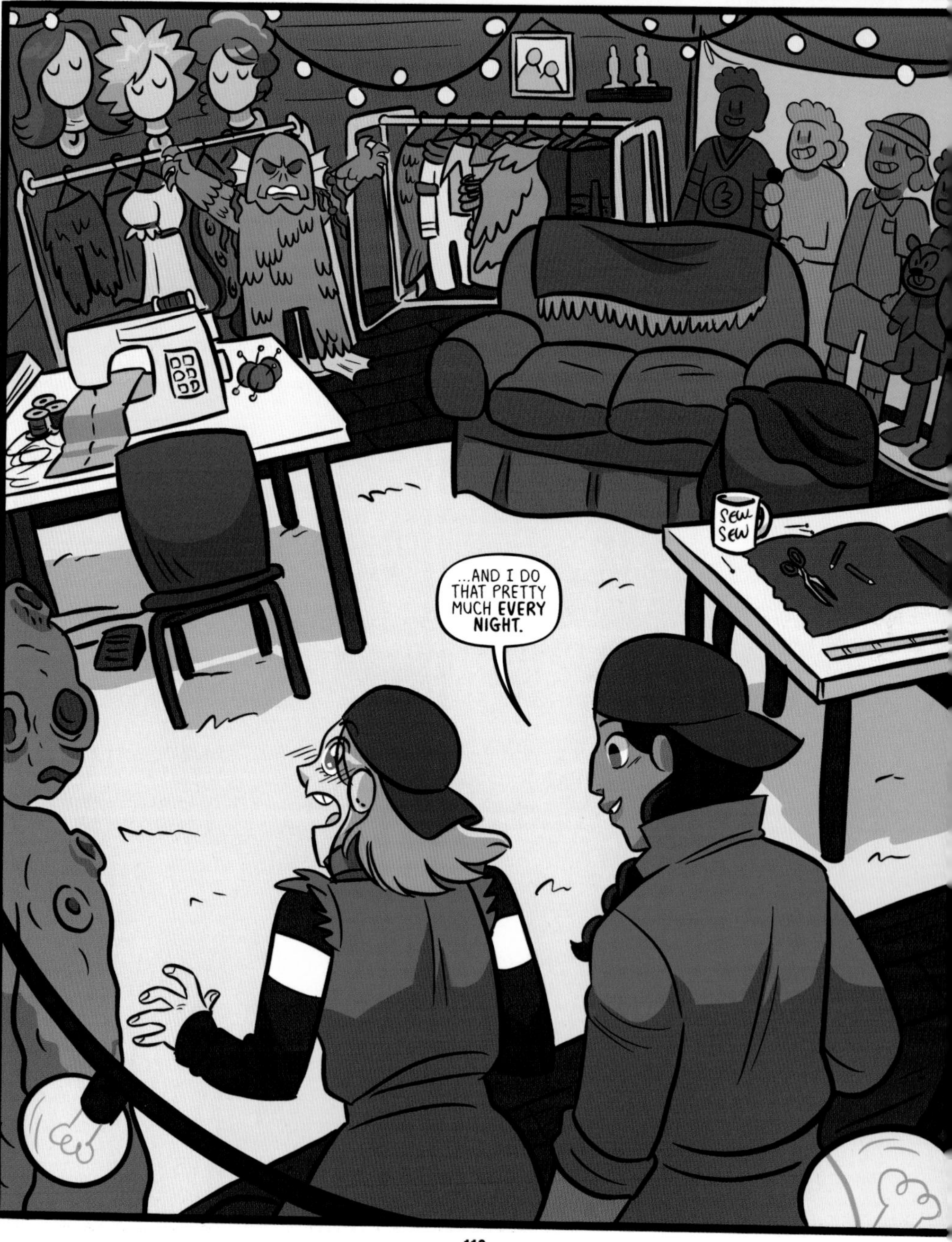
SEW SEW
...AND I DO THAT PRETTY MUCH EVERY NIGHT.

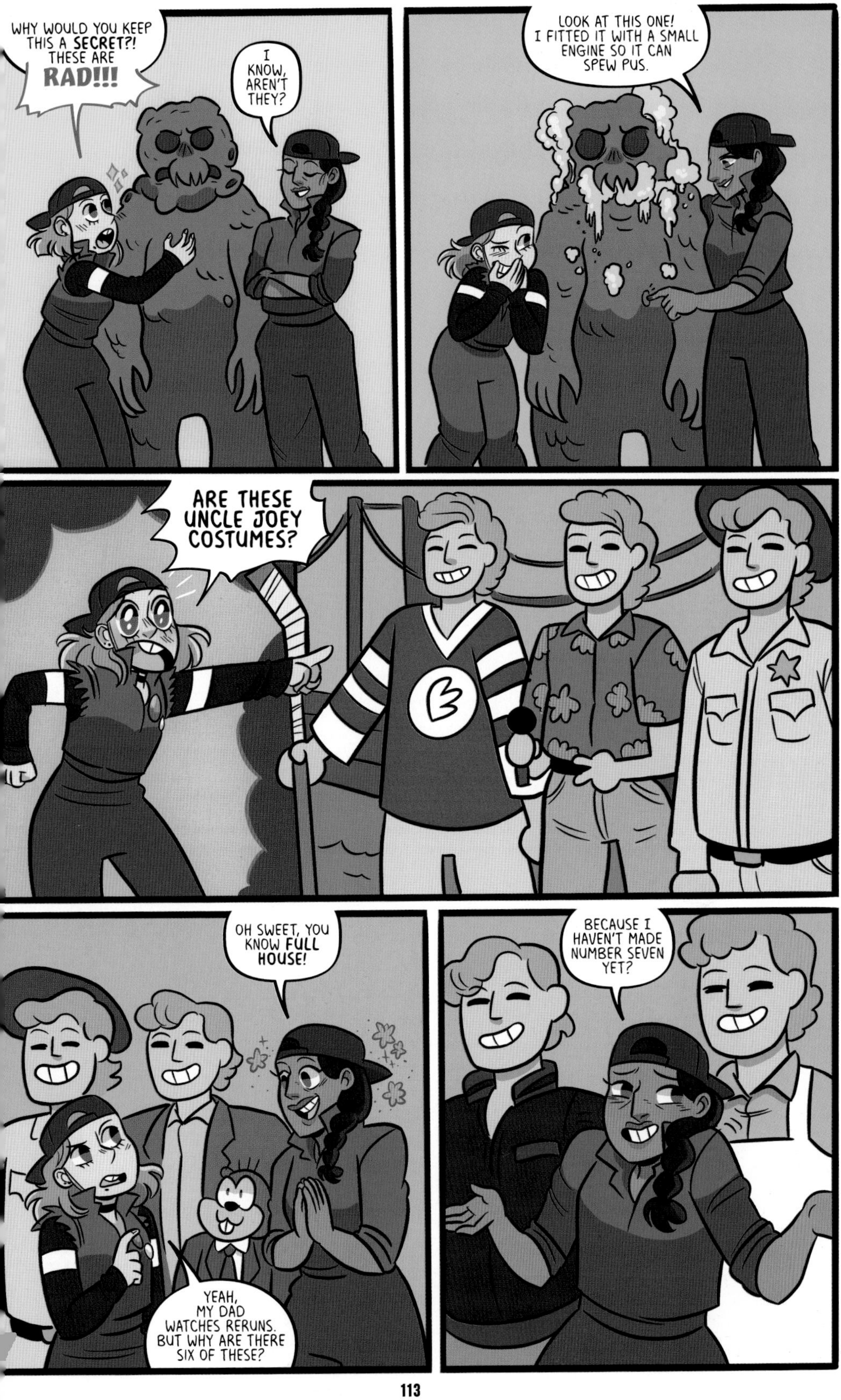

WHY WOULD YOU KEEP THIS A **SECRET?!** THESE ARE **RAD!!!**
I KNOW, AREN'T THEY?
LOOK AT THIS ONE! I FITTED IT WITH A SMALL ENGINE SO IT CAN SPEW PUS.
ARE THESE UNCLE JOEY COSTUMES?
OH SWEET, YOU KNOW **FULL HOUSE!**
YEAH, MY DAD WATCHES RERUNS. BUT WHY ARE THERE SIX OF THESE?
BECAUSE I HAVEN'T MADE NUMBER SEVEN YET?

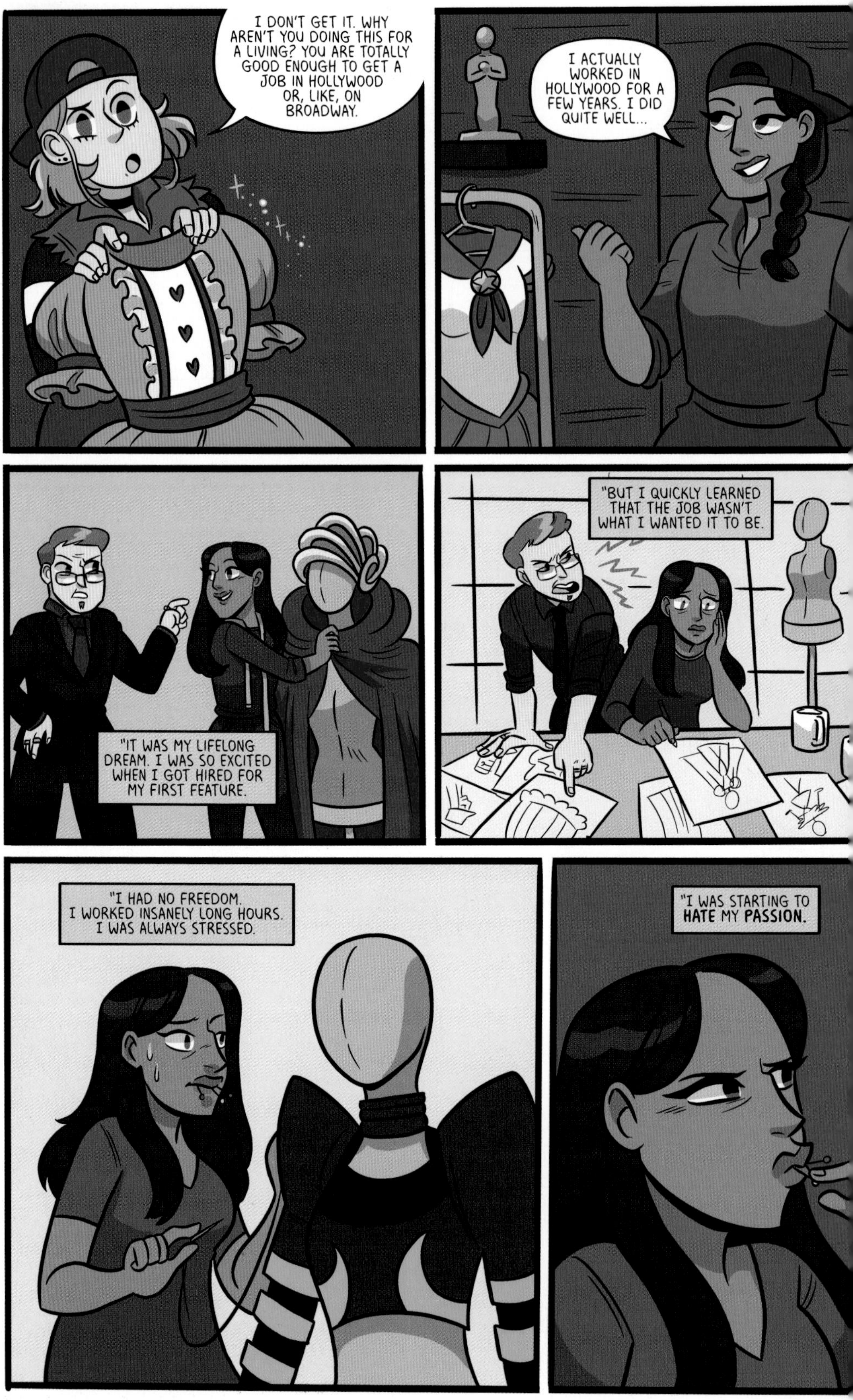
I DON'T GET IT. WHY AREN'T YOU DOING THIS FOR A LIVING? YOU ARE TOTALLY GOOD ENOUGH TO GET A JOB IN HOLLYWOOD OR, LIKE, ON BROADWAY.
I ACTUALLY WORKED IN HOLLYWOOD FOR A FEW YEARS. I DID QUITE WELL...
"IT WAS MY LIFELONG DREAM. I WAS SO EXCITED WHEN I GOT HIRED FOR MY FIRST FEATURE.
"BUT I QUICKLY LEARNED THAT THE JOB WASN'T WHAT I WANTED IT TO BE.
"I HAD NO FREEDOM. I WORKED INSANELY LONG HOURS. I WAS ALWAYS STRESSED.
"I WAS STARTING TO **HATE** MY **PASSION.**

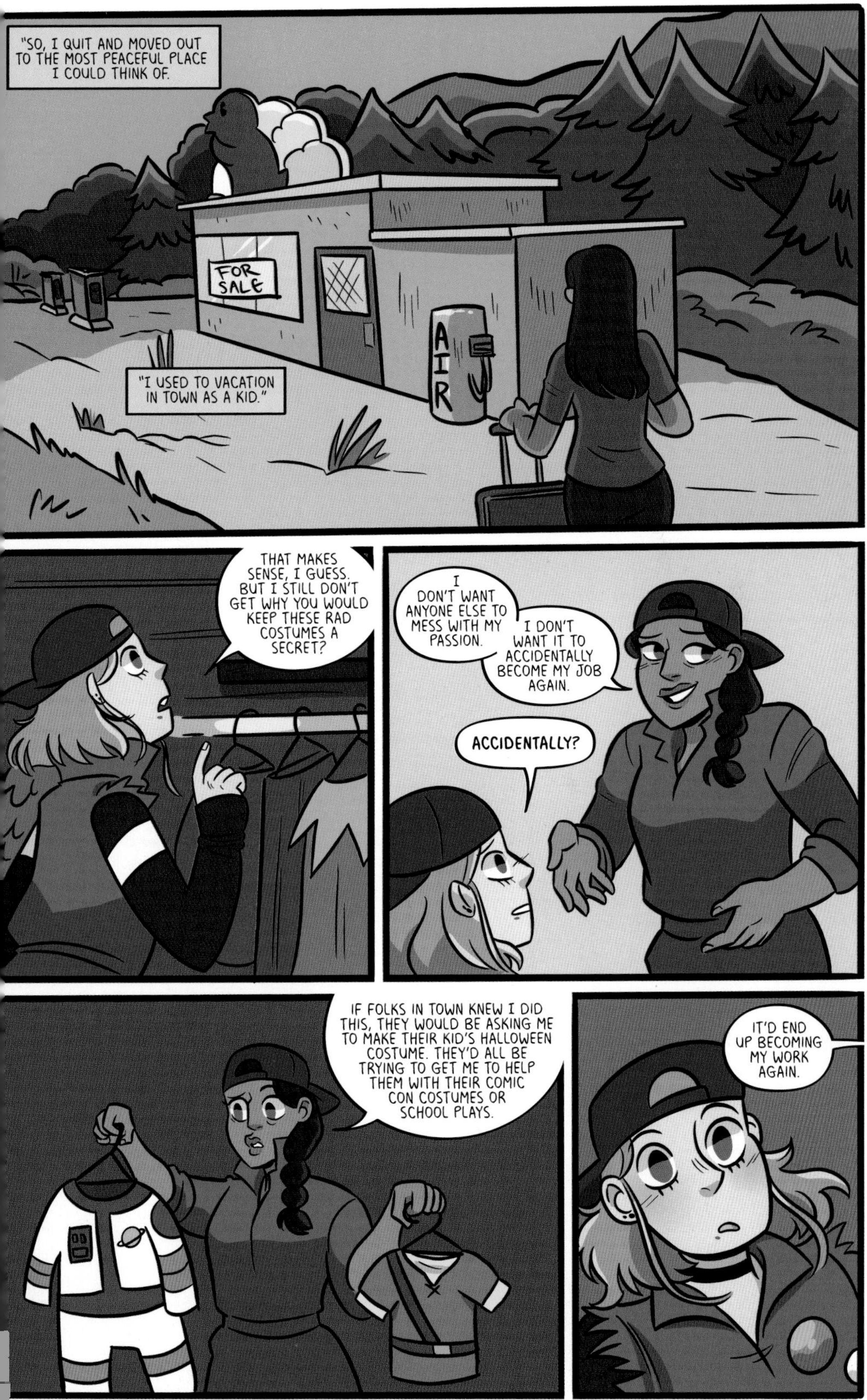
"SO, I QUIT AND MOVED OUT TO THE MOST PEACEFUL PLACE I COULD THINK OF.
FOR SALE
AIR
"I USED TO VACATION IN TOWN AS A KID."
THAT MAKES SENSE, I GUESS. BUT I STILL DON'T GET WHY YOU WOULD KEEP THESE RAD COSTUMES A SECRET?
I DON'T WANT ANYONE ELSE TO MESS WITH MY PASSION.
I DON'T WANT IT TO ACCIDENTALLY BECOME MY JOB AGAIN.
ACCIDENTALLY?
IF FOLKS IN TOWN KNEW I DID THIS, THEY WOULD BE ASKING ME TO MAKE THEIR KID'S HALLOWEEN COSTUME. THEY'D ALL BE TRYING TO GET ME TO HELP THEM WITH THEIR COMIC CON COSTUMES OR SCHOOL PLAYS.
IT'D END UP BECOMING MY WORK AGAIN.

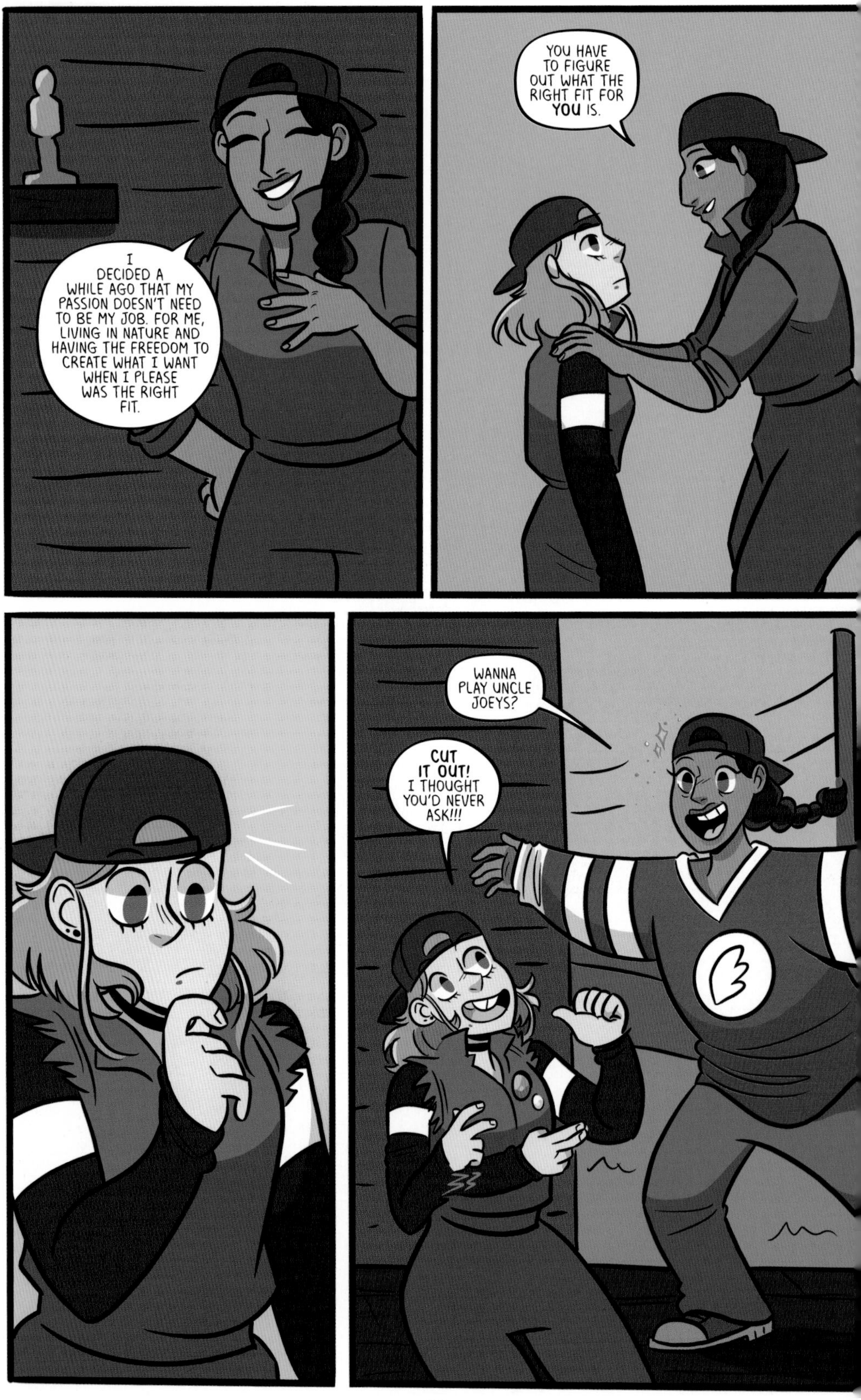
I DECIDED A WHILE AGO THAT MY PASSION DOESN'T NEED TO BE MY JOB. FOR ME, LIVING IN NATURE AND HAVING THE FREEDOM TO CREATE WHAT I WANT WHEN I PLEASE WAS THE RIGHT FIT.
YOU HAVE TO FIGURE OUT WHAT THE RIGHT FIT FOR **YOU** IS.
WANNA PLAY UNCLE JOEYS?
CUT IT OUT! I THOUGHT YOU'D NEVER ASK!!!

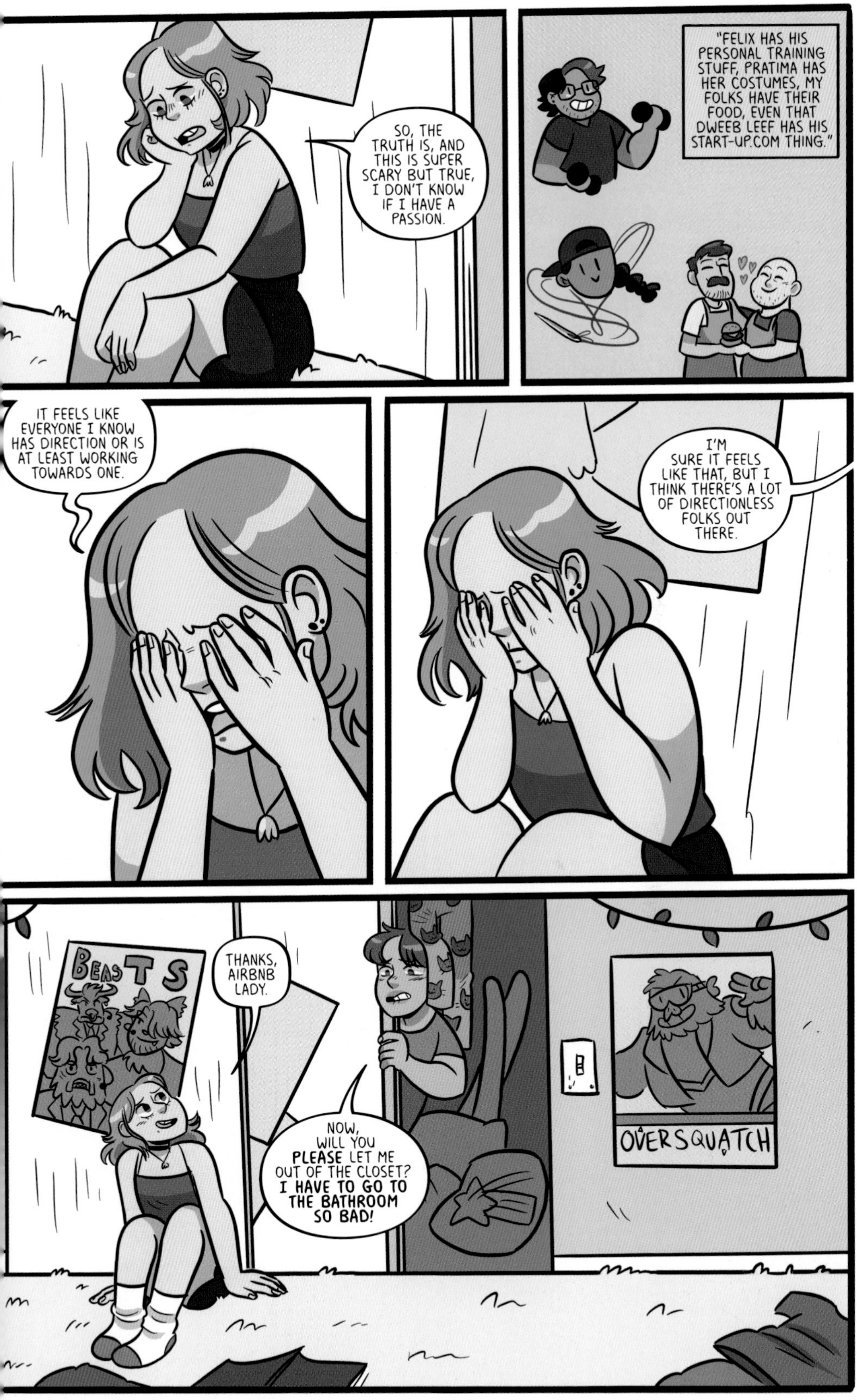
SO, THE TRUTH IS, AND THIS IS SUPER SCARY BUT TRUE, I DON'T KNOW IF I HAVE A PASSION.
"FELIX HAS HIS PERSONAL TRAINING STUFF, PRATIMA HAS HER COSTUMES, MY FOLKS HAVE THEIR FOOD, EVEN THAT DWEEB LEEF HAS HIS START-UP.COM THING."
IT FEELS LIKE EVERYONE I KNOW HAS DIRECTION OR IS AT LEAST WORKING TOWARDS ONE.
I'M SURE IT FEELS LIKE THAT, BUT I THINK THERE'S A LOT OF DIRECTIONLESS FOLKS OUT THERE.
BEASTS
THANKS, AIRBNB LADY.
NOW, WILL YOU **PLEASE** LET ME OUT OF THE CLOSET? **I HAVE TO GO TO THE BATHROOM SO BAD!**
OVERSQUATCH

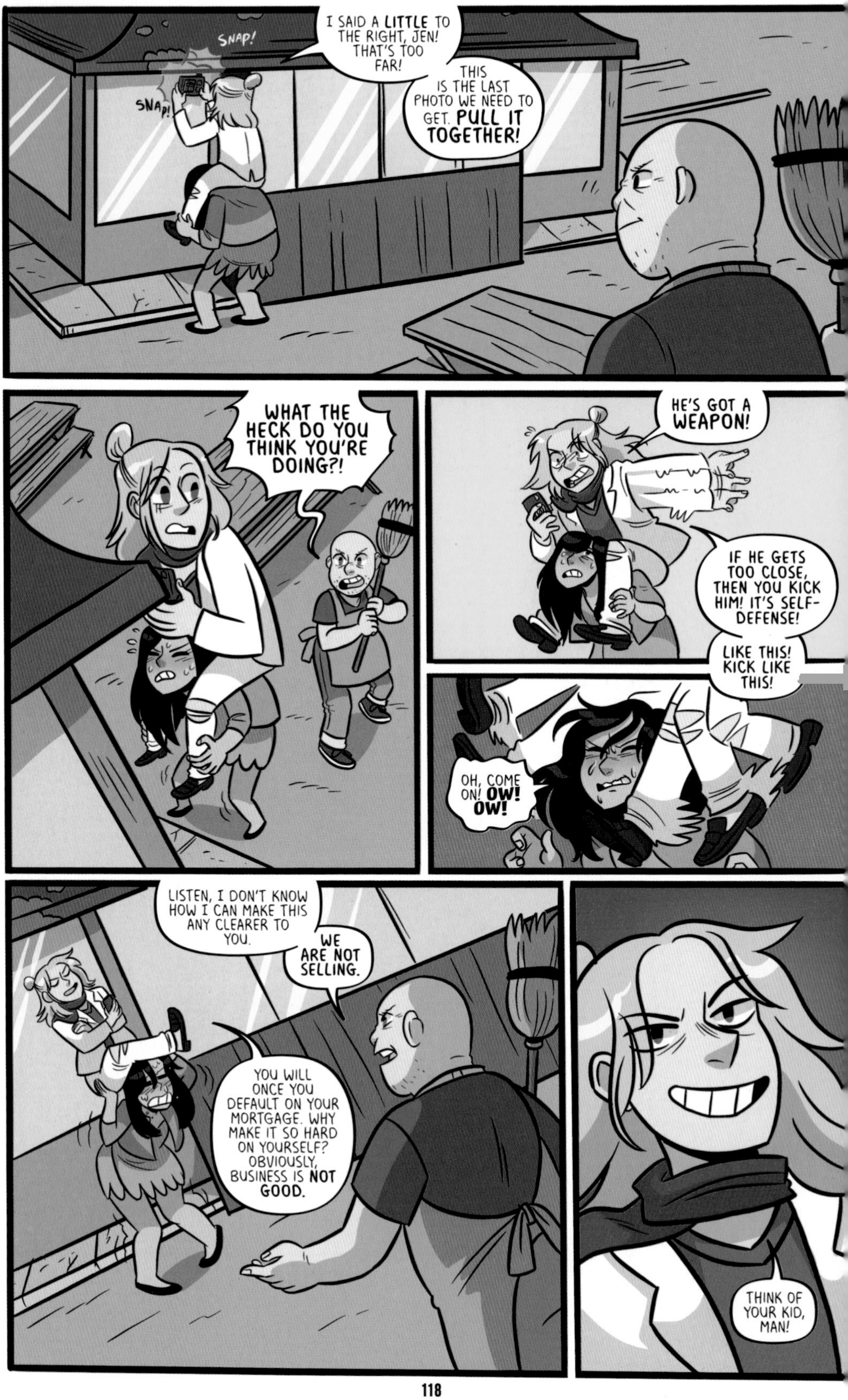
SNAP!
SNAP!
I SAID A LITTLE TO THE RIGHT, JEN! THAT'S TOO FAR!
THIS IS THE LAST PHOTO WE NEED TO GET. PULL IT TOGETHER!
WHAT THE HECK DO YOU THINK YOU'RE DOING?!
HE'S GOT A WEAPON!
IF HE GETS TOO CLOSE, THEN YOU KICK HIM! IT'S SELF-DEFENSE!
LIKE THIS! KICK LIKE THIS!
OH, COME ON! OW! OW!
LISTEN, I DON'T KNOW HOW I CAN MAKE THIS ANY CLEARER TO YOU.
WE ARE NOT SELLING.
YOU WILL ONCE YOU DEFAULT ON YOUR MORTGAGE. WHY MAKE IT SO HARD ON YOURSELF? OBVIOUSLY, BUSINESS IS NOT GOOD.
THINK OF YOUR KID, MAN!

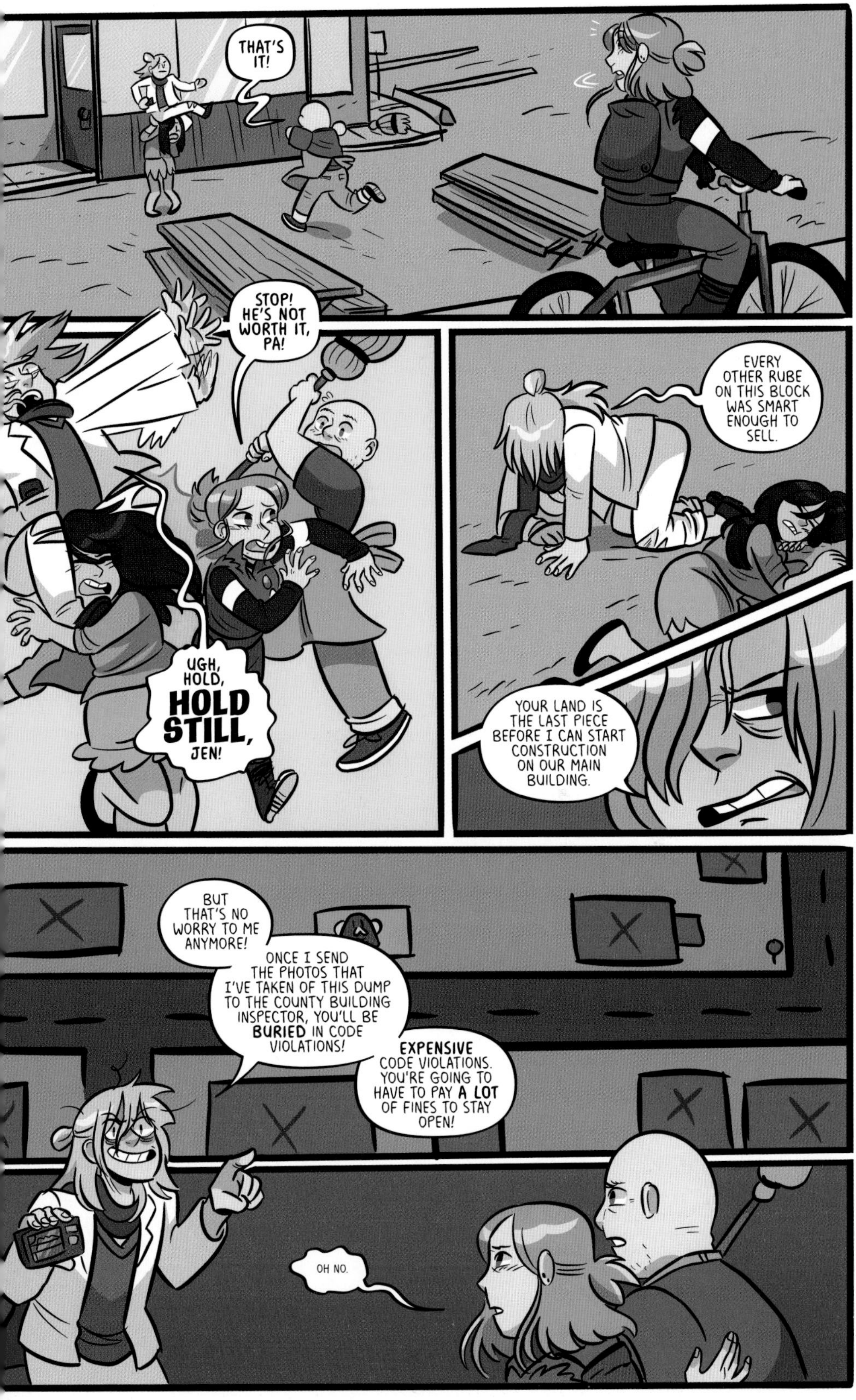

THAT'S IT!
STOP! HE'S NOT WORTH IT, PA!
UGH, HOLD, **HOLD STILL,** JEN!
EVERY OTHER RUBE ON THIS BLOCK WAS SMART ENOUGH TO SELL.
YOUR LAND IS THE LAST PIECE BEFORE I CAN START CONSTRUCTION ON OUR MAIN BUILDING.
BUT THAT'S NO WORRY TO ME ANYMORE!
ONCE I SEND THE PHOTOS THAT I'VE TAKEN OF THIS DUMP TO THE COUNTY BUILDING INSPECTOR, YOU'LL BE **BURIED** IN CODE VIOLATIONS!
EXPENSIVE CODE VIOLATIONS. YOU'RE GOING TO HAVE TO PAY **A LOT** OF FINES TO STAY OPEN!
OH NO.

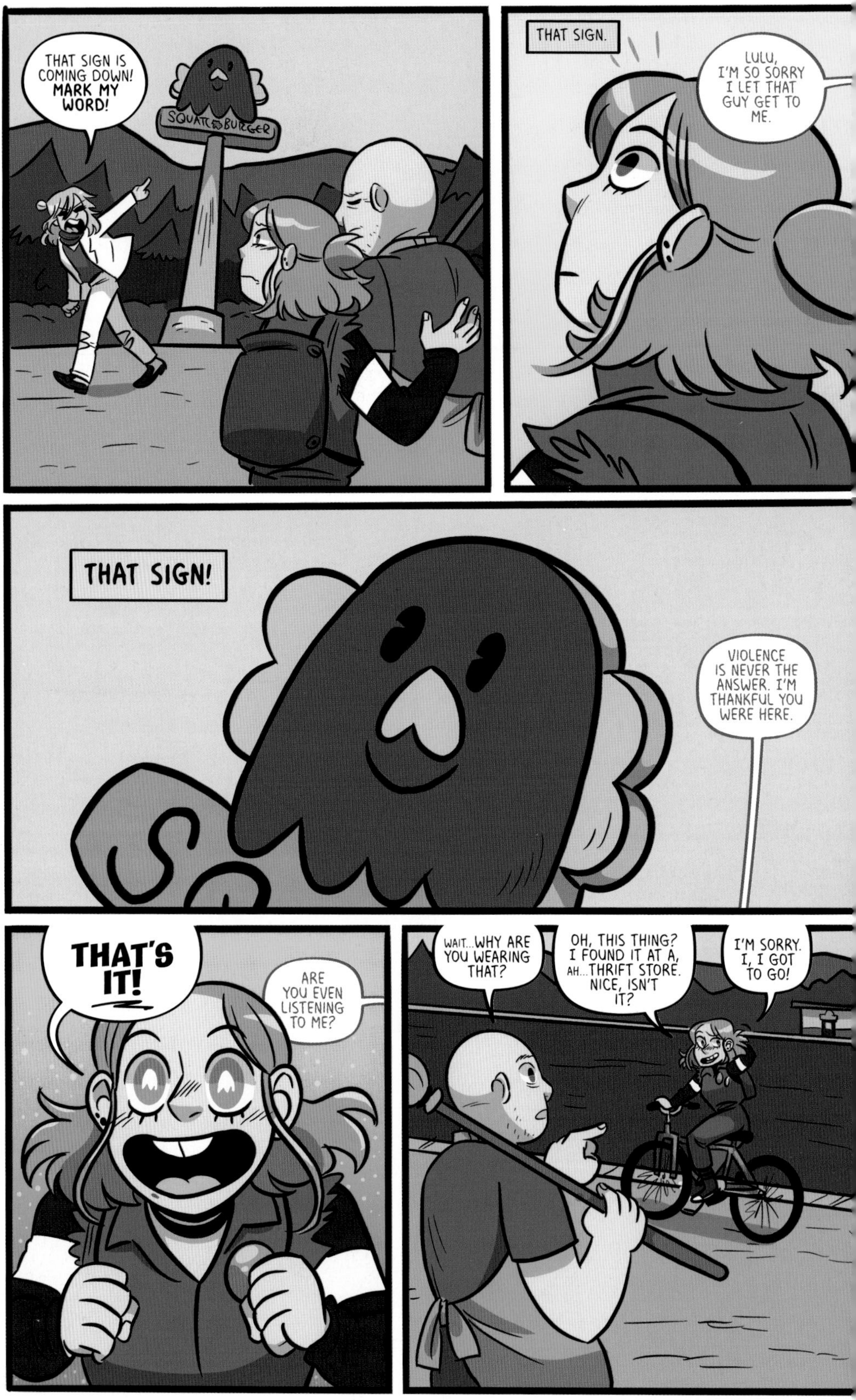
THAT SIGN IS COMING DOWN! MARK MY WORD!
SQUATCH BURGER
THAT SIGN.
LULU, I'M SO SORRY I LET THAT GUY GET TO ME.
THAT SIGN!
VIOLENCE IS NEVER THE ANSWER. I'M THANKFUL YOU WERE HERE.
THAT'S IT!
ARE YOU EVEN LISTENING TO ME?
WAIT...WHY ARE YOU WEARING THAT?
OH, THIS THING? I FOUND IT AT A, AH...THRIFT STORE. NICE, ISN'T IT?
I'M SORRY. I, I GOT TO GO!

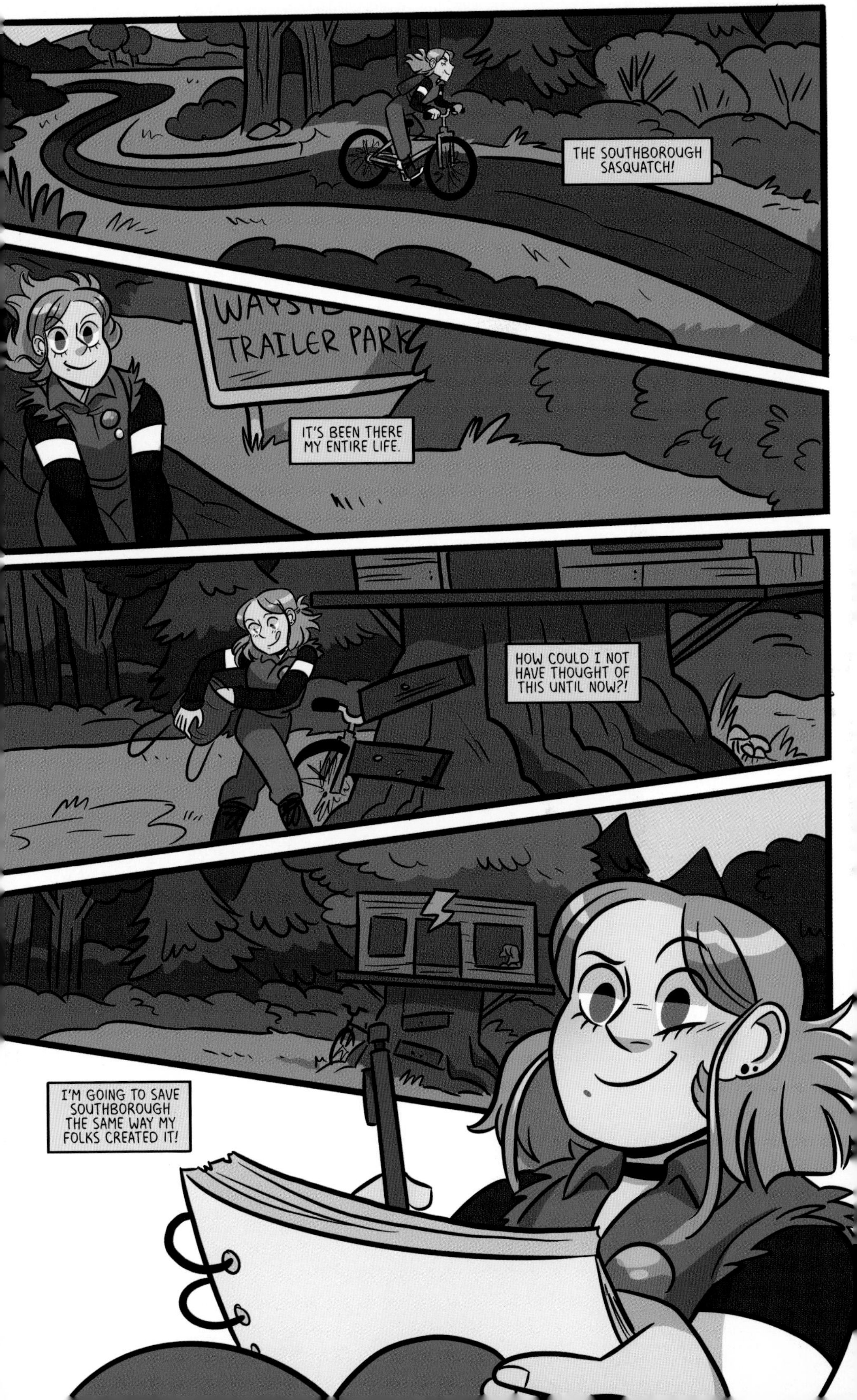
THE SOUTHBOROUGH SASQUATCH!
WAYSID
TRAILER PARK
IT'S BEEN THERE MY ENTIRE LIFE.
HOW COULD I NOT HAVE THOUGHT OF THIS UNTIL NOW?!
I'M GOING TO SAVE SOUTHBOROUGH THE SAME WAY MY FOLKS CREATED IT!

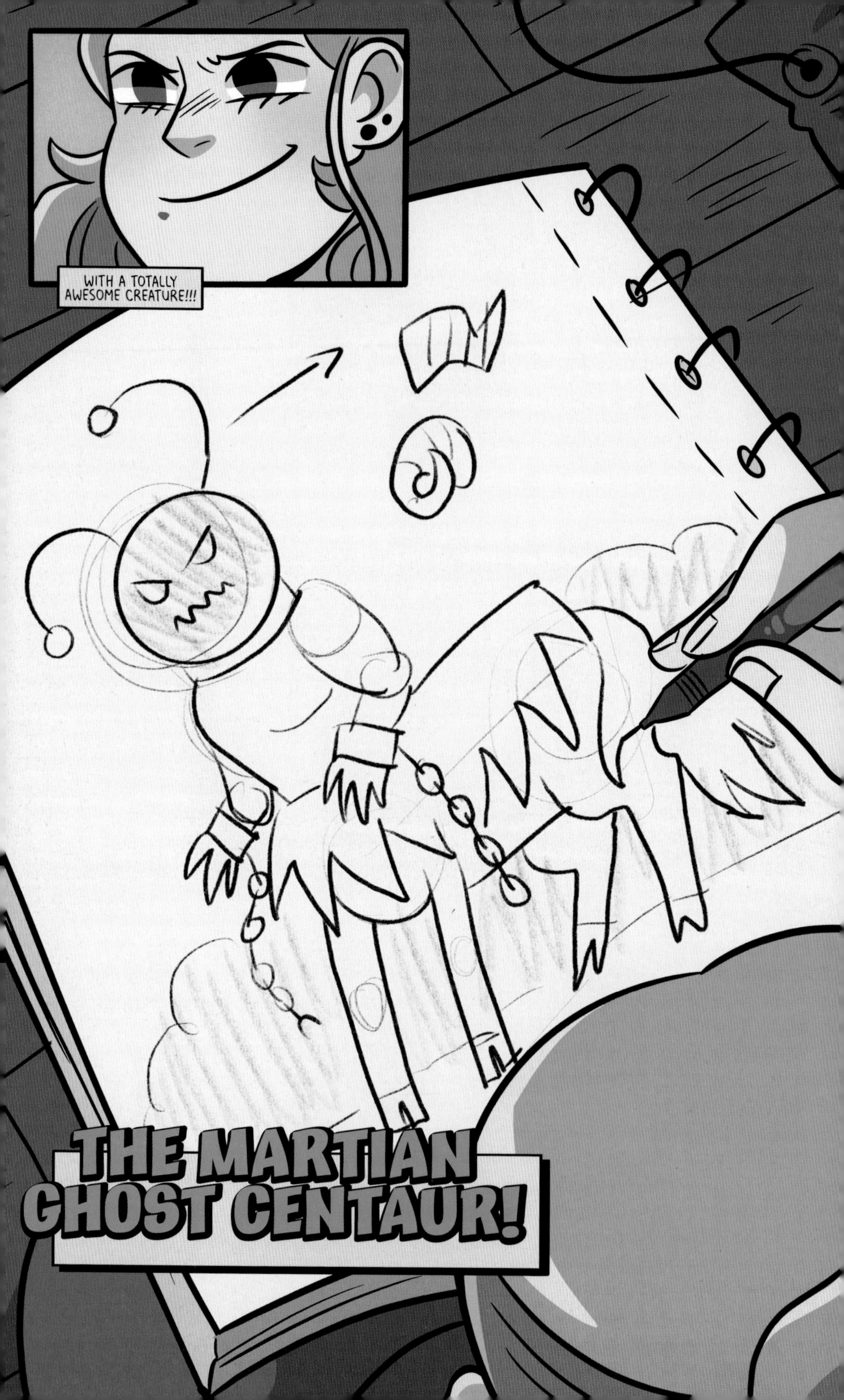
WITH A TOTALLY AWESOME CREATURE!!!
THE MARTIAN GHOST CENTAUR!

CHAPTER
5

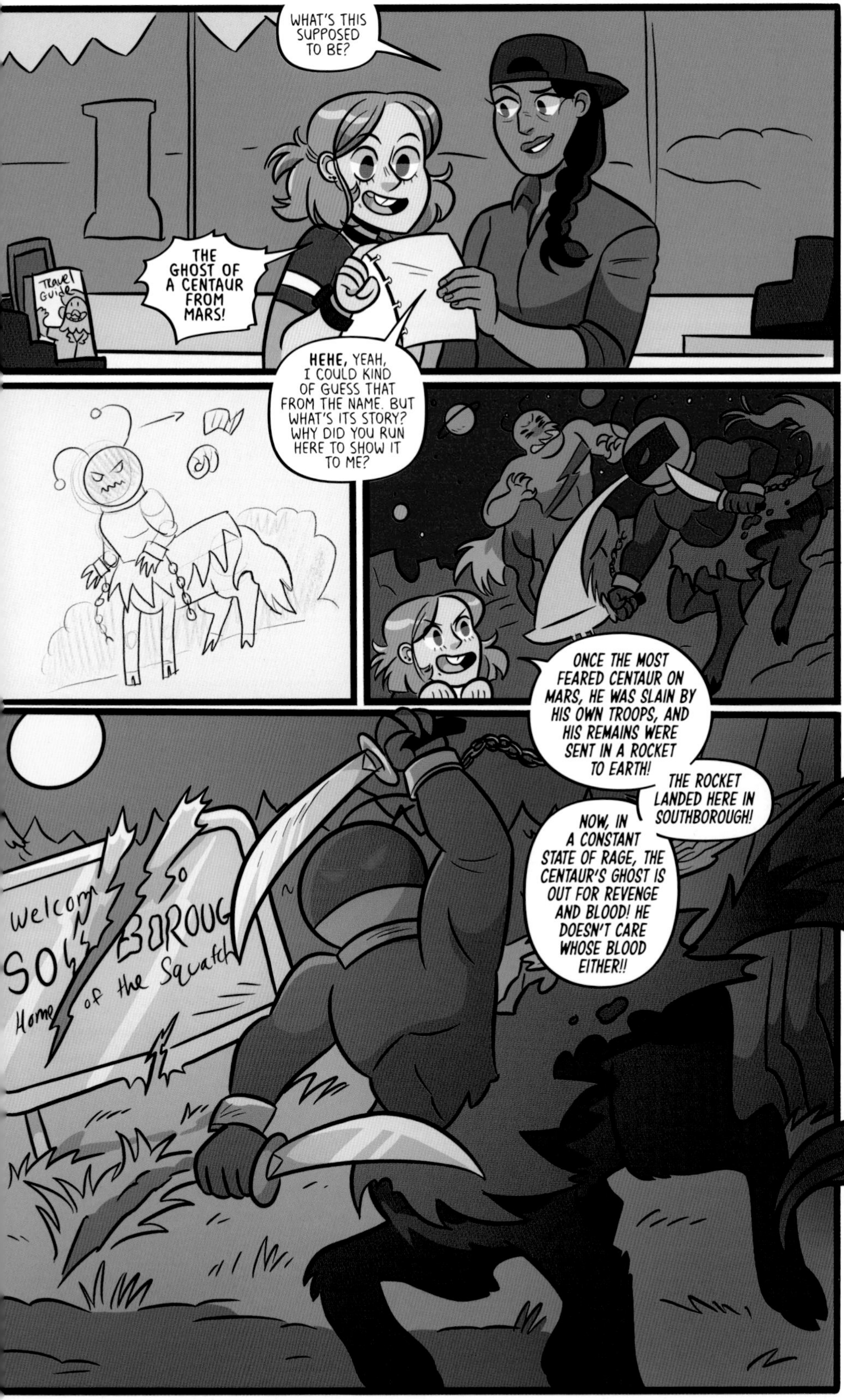

WHAT'S THIS SUPPOSED TO BE?
THE GHOST OF A CENTAUR FROM MARS!
TRAVEL GUIDE
HEHE, YEAH, I COULD KIND OF GUESS THAT FROM THE NAME. BUT WHAT'S ITS STORY? WHY DID YOU RUN HERE TO SHOW IT TO ME?
ONCE THE MOST FEARED CENTAUR ON MARS, HE WAS SLAIN BY HIS OWN TROOPS, AND HIS REMAINS WERE SENT IN A ROCKET TO EARTH!
THE ROCKET LANDED HERE IN SOUTHBOROUGH!
NOW, IN A CONSTANT STATE OF RAGE, THE CENTAUR'S GHOST IS OUT FOR REVENGE AND BLOOD! HE DOESN'T CARE WHOSE BLOOD EITHER!!
Welcom
SO BOROUG
Home of the Squatch

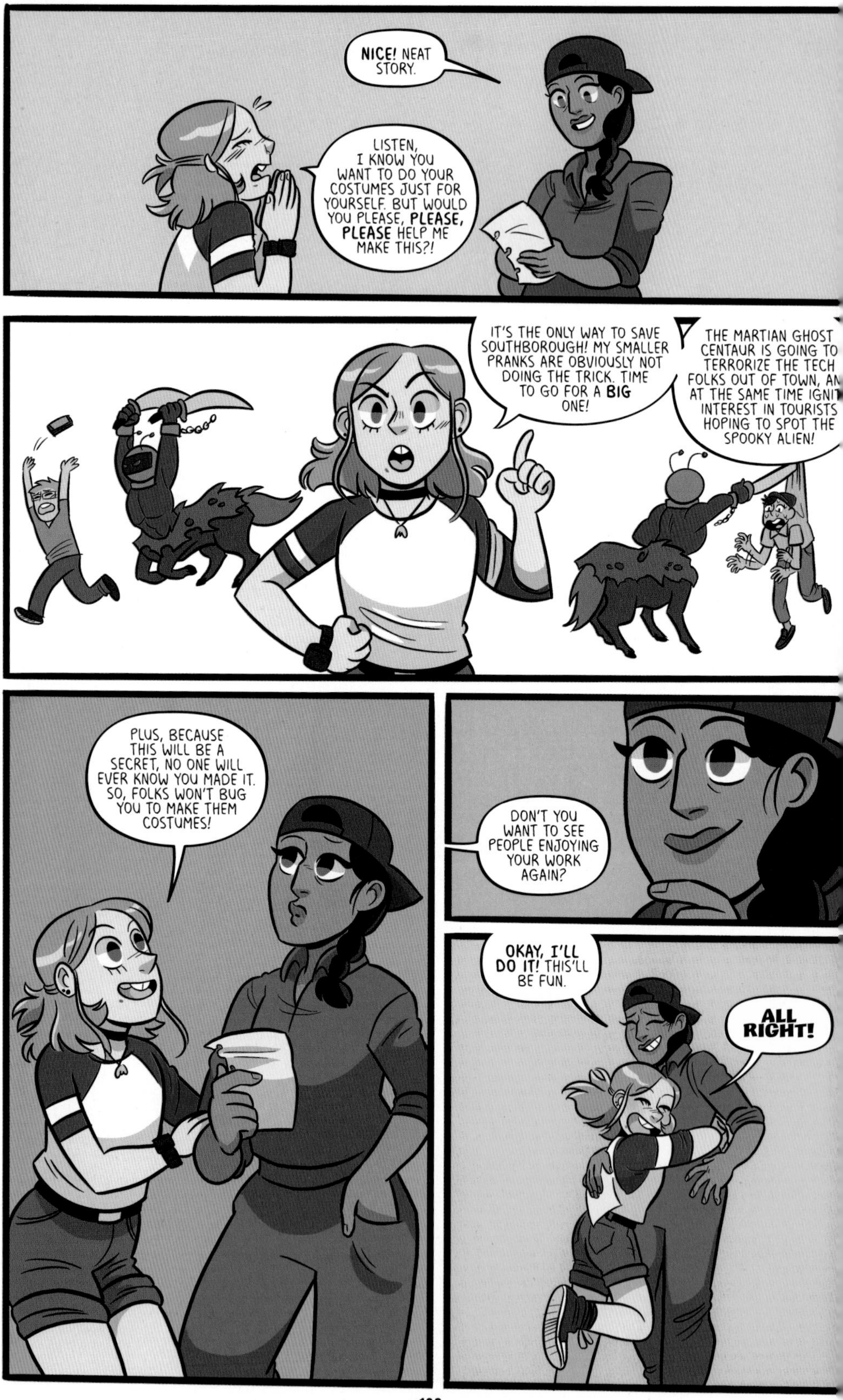
NICE! NEAT STORY.
LISTEN, I KNOW YOU WANT TO DO YOUR COSTUMES JUST FOR YOURSELF. BUT WOULD YOU PLEASE, PLEASE, PLEASE HELP ME MAKE THIS?!
IT'S THE ONLY WAY TO SAVE SOUTHBOROUGH! MY SMALLER PRANKS ARE OBVIOUSLY NOT DOING THE TRICK. TIME TO GO FOR A BIG ONE!
THE MARTIAN GHOST CENTAUR IS GOING TO TERRORIZE THE TECH FOLKS OUT OF TOWN, AN AT THE SAME TIME IGNIT INTEREST IN TOURISTS HOPING TO SPOT THE SPOOKY ALIEN!
PLUS, BECAUSE THIS WILL BE A SECRET, NO ONE WILL EVER KNOW YOU MADE IT. SO, FOLKS WON'T BUG YOU TO MAKE THEM COSTUMES!
DON'T YOU WANT TO SEE PEOPLE ENJOYING YOUR WORK AGAIN?
OKAY, I'LL DO IT! THIS'LL BE FUN.
ALL RIGHT!

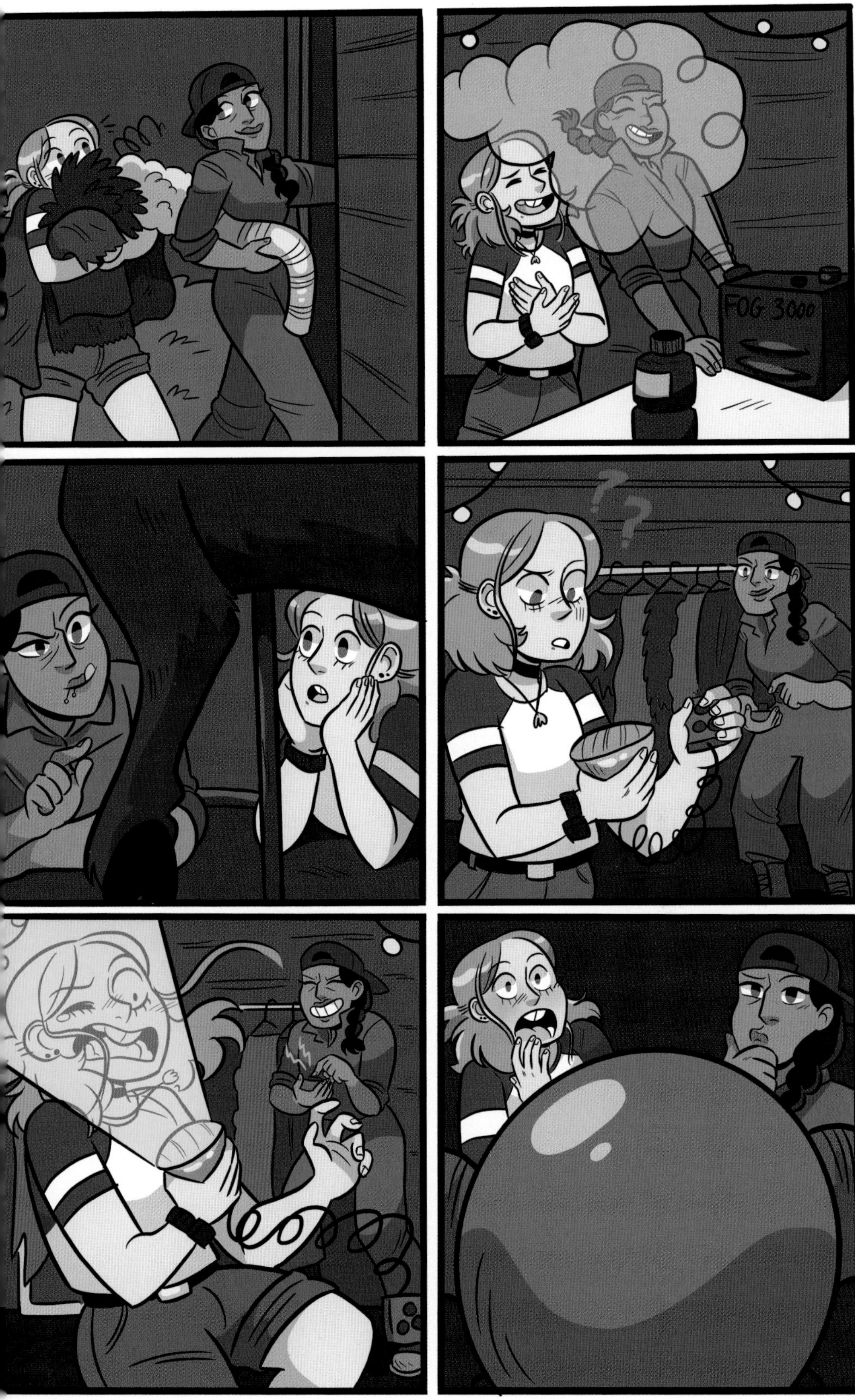
FOG 3000

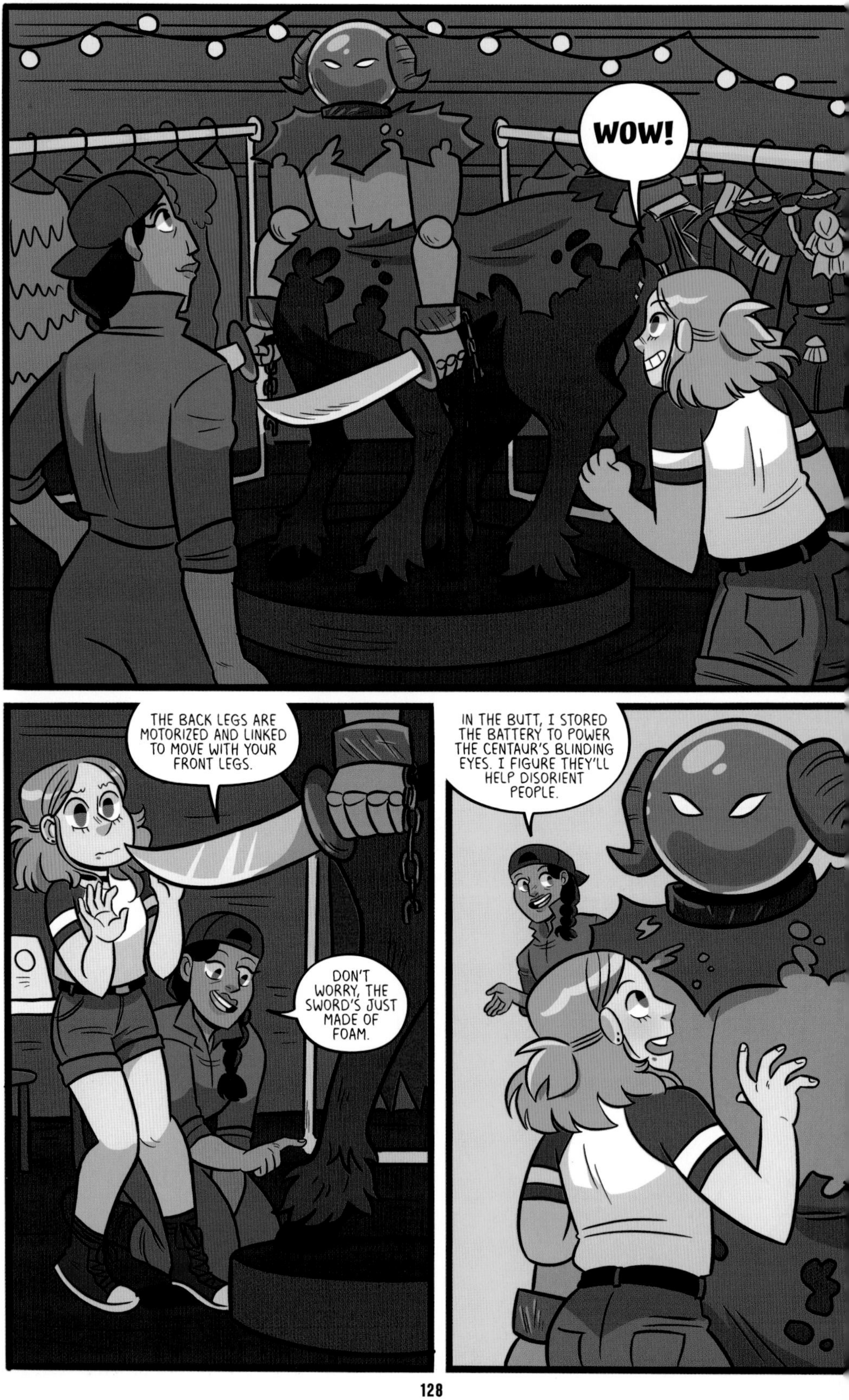
WOW!
THE BACK LEGS ARE MOTORIZED AND LINKED TO MOVE WITH YOUR FRONT LEGS.
DON'T WORRY, THE SWORD'S JUST MADE OF FOAM.
IN THE BUTT, I STORED THE BATTERY TO POWER THE CENTAUR'S BLINDING EYES. I FIGURE THEY'LL HELP DISORIENT PEOPLE.

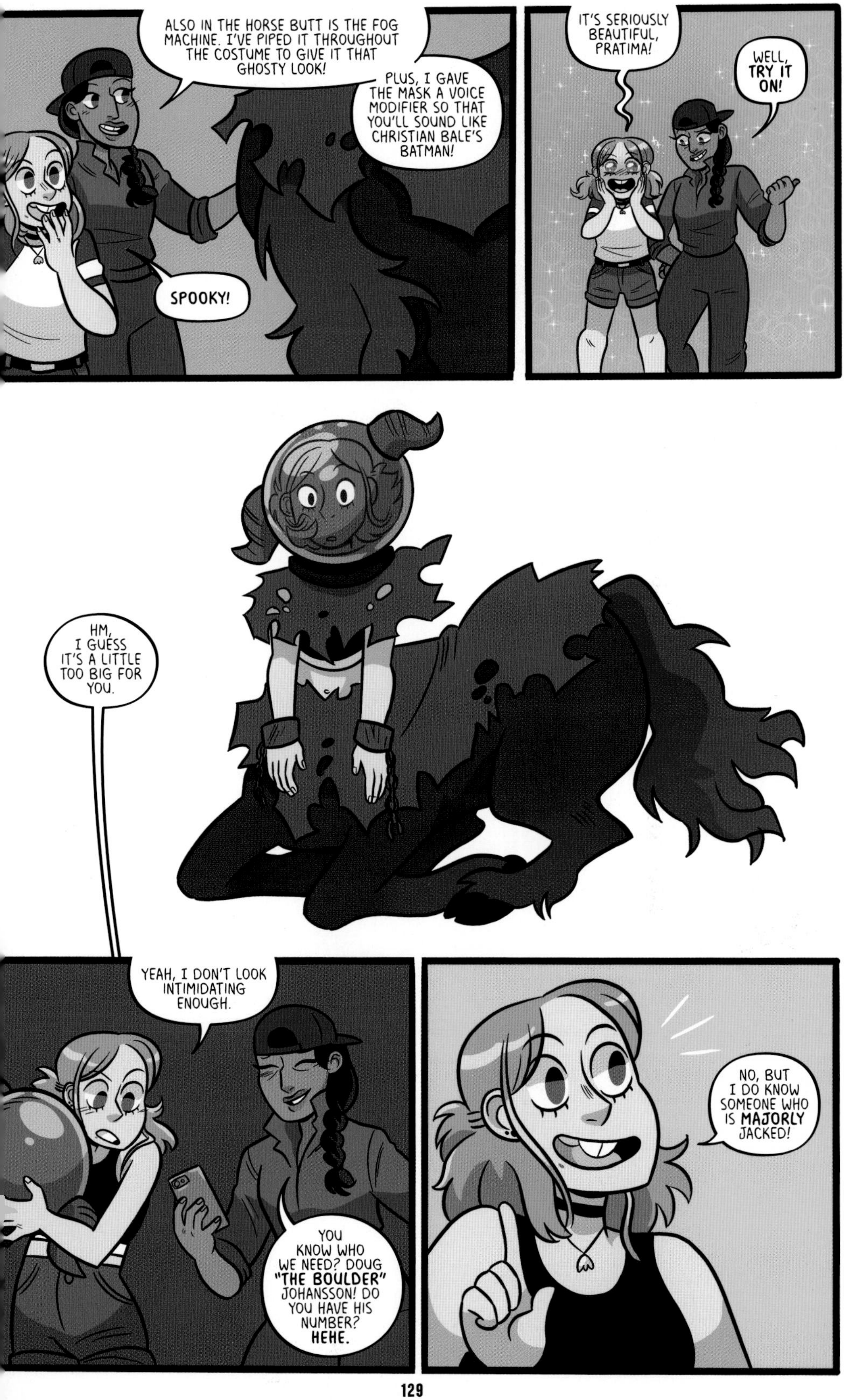
ALSO IN THE HORSE BUTT IS THE FOG MACHINE. I'VE PIPED IT THROUGHOUT THE COSTUME TO GIVE IT THAT GHOSTY LOOK!
PLUS, I GAVE THE MASK A VOICE MODIFIER SO THAT YOU'LL SOUND LIKE CHRISTIAN BALE'S BATMAN!
SPOOKY!
IT'S SERIOUSLY BEAUTIFUL, PRATIMA!
WELL, **TRY IT ON!**
HM, I GUESS IT'S A LITTLE TOO BIG FOR YOU.
YEAH, I DON'T LOOK INTIMIDATING ENOUGH.
YOU KNOW WHO WE NEED? DOUG **"THE BOULDER"** JOHANSSON! DO YOU HAVE HIS NUMBER? **HEHE.**
NO, BUT I DO KNOW SOMEONE WHO IS **MAJORLY** JACKED!

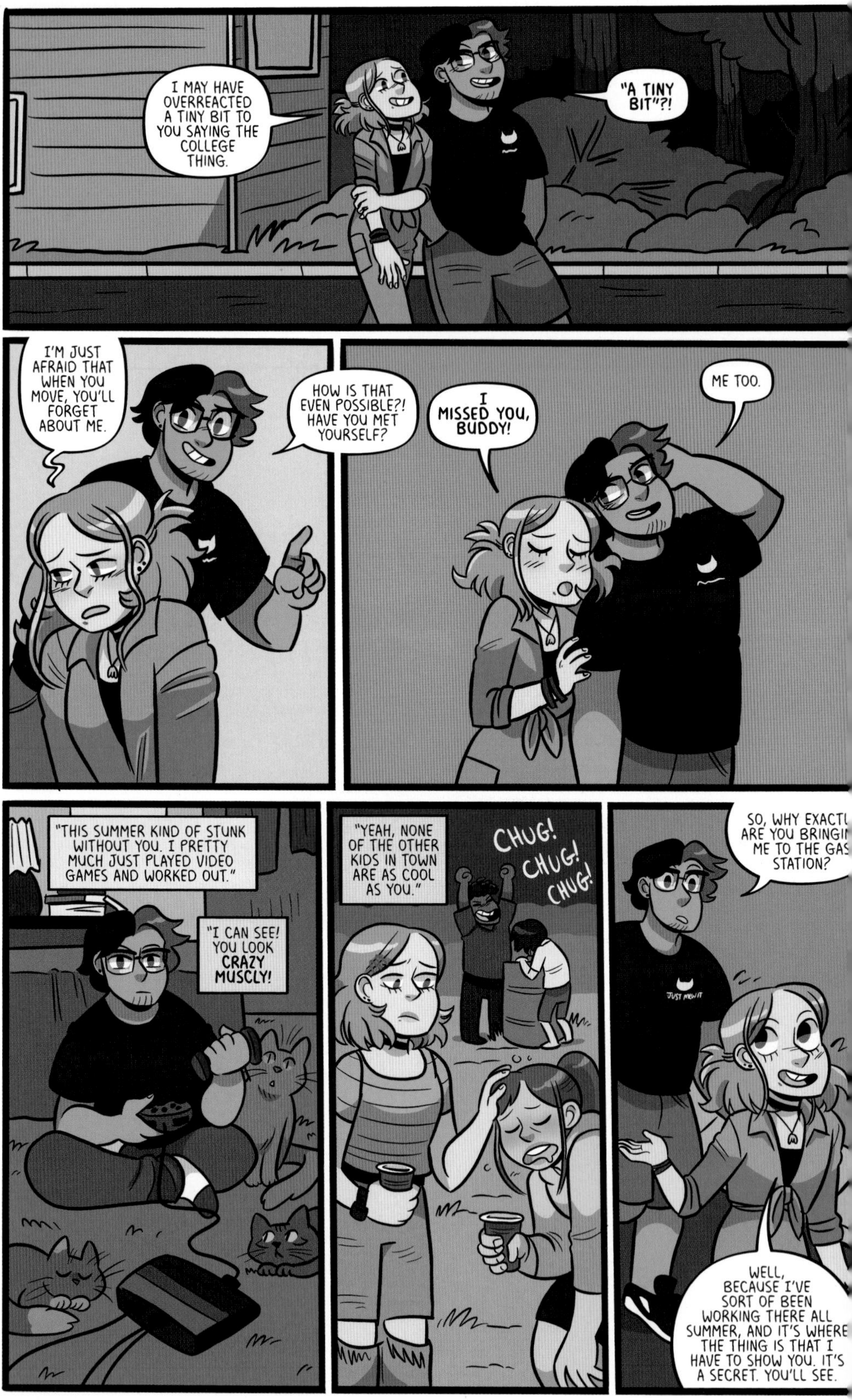

I MAY HAVE OVERREACTED A TINY BIT TO YOU SAYING THE COLLEGE THING.
"A TINY BIT"?!
I'M JUST AFRAID THAT WHEN YOU MOVE, YOU'LL FORGET ABOUT ME.
HOW IS THAT EVEN POSSIBLE?! HAVE YOU MET YOURSELF?
I MISSED YOU, BUDDY!
ME TOO.
"THIS SUMMER KIND OF STUNK WITHOUT YOU. I PRETTY MUCH JUST PLAYED VIDEO GAMES AND WORKED OUT."
"I CAN SEE! YOU LOOK CRAZY MUSCLY!
"YEAH, NONE OF THE OTHER KIDS IN TOWN ARE AS COOL AS YOU."
CHUG! CHUG! CHUG!
SO, WHY EXACTL ARE YOU BRINGI ME TO THE GAS STATION?
WELL, BECAUSE I'VE SORT OF BEEN WORKING THERE ALL SUMMER, AND IT'S WHERE THE THING IS THAT I HAVE TO SHOW YOU. IT'S A SECRET. YOU'LL SEE.

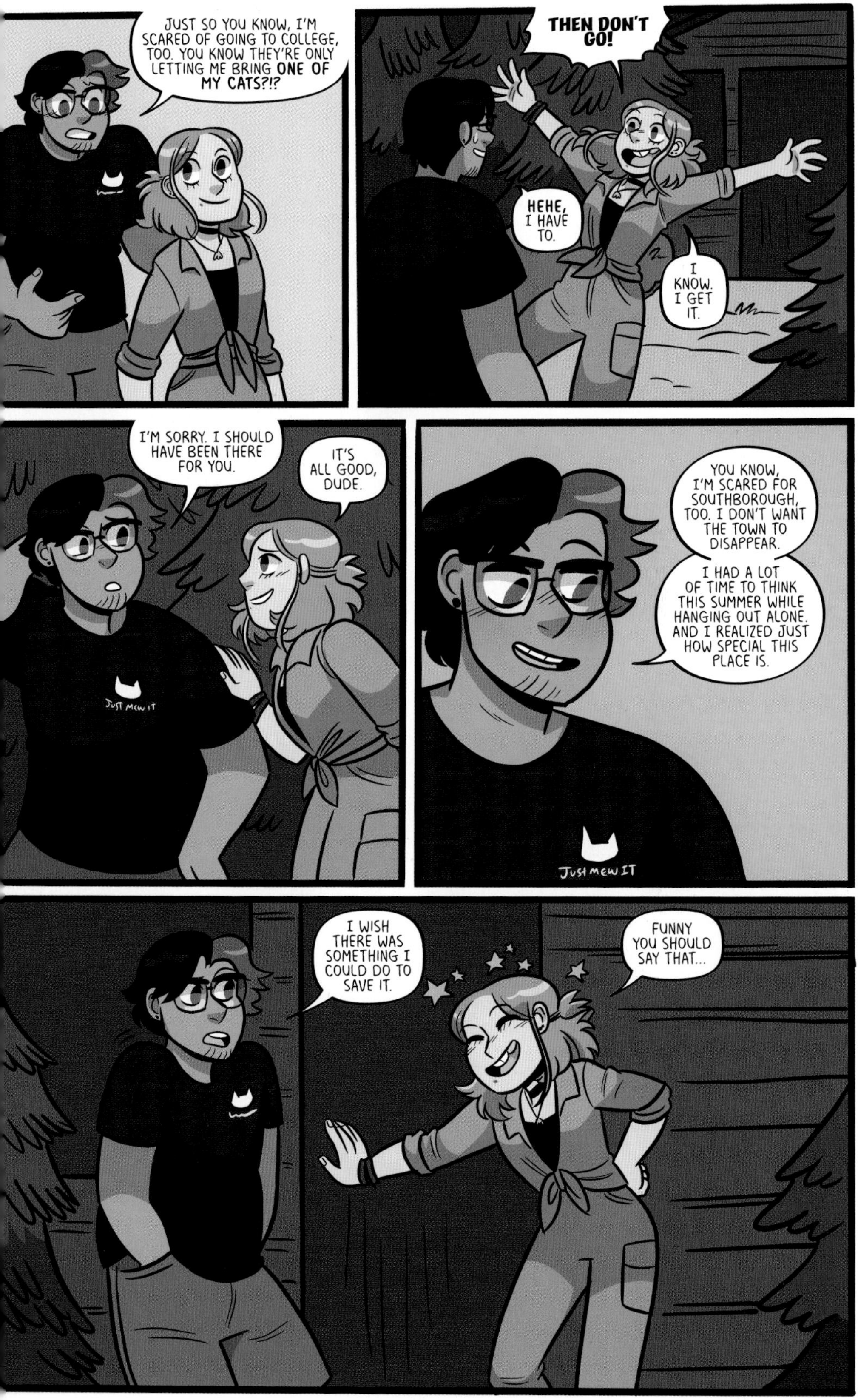
JUST SO YOU KNOW, I'M SCARED OF GOING TO COLLEGE, TOO. YOU KNOW THEY'RE ONLY LETTING ME BRING ONE OF MY CATS?!?
THEN DON'T GO!
HEHE, I HAVE TO.
I KNOW. I GET IT.
I'M SORRY. I SHOULD HAVE BEEN THERE FOR YOU.
IT'S ALL GOOD, DUDE.
JUST MEW IT
YOU KNOW, I'M SCARED FOR SOUTHBOROUGH, TOO. I DON'T WANT THE TOWN TO DISAPPEAR.
I HAD A LOT OF TIME TO THINK THIS SUMMER WHILE HANGING OUT ALONE. AND I REALIZED JUST HOW SPECIAL THIS PLACE IS.
JUST MEW IT
I WISH THERE WAS SOMETHING I COULD DO TO SAVE IT.
FUNNY YOU SHOULD SAY THAT...

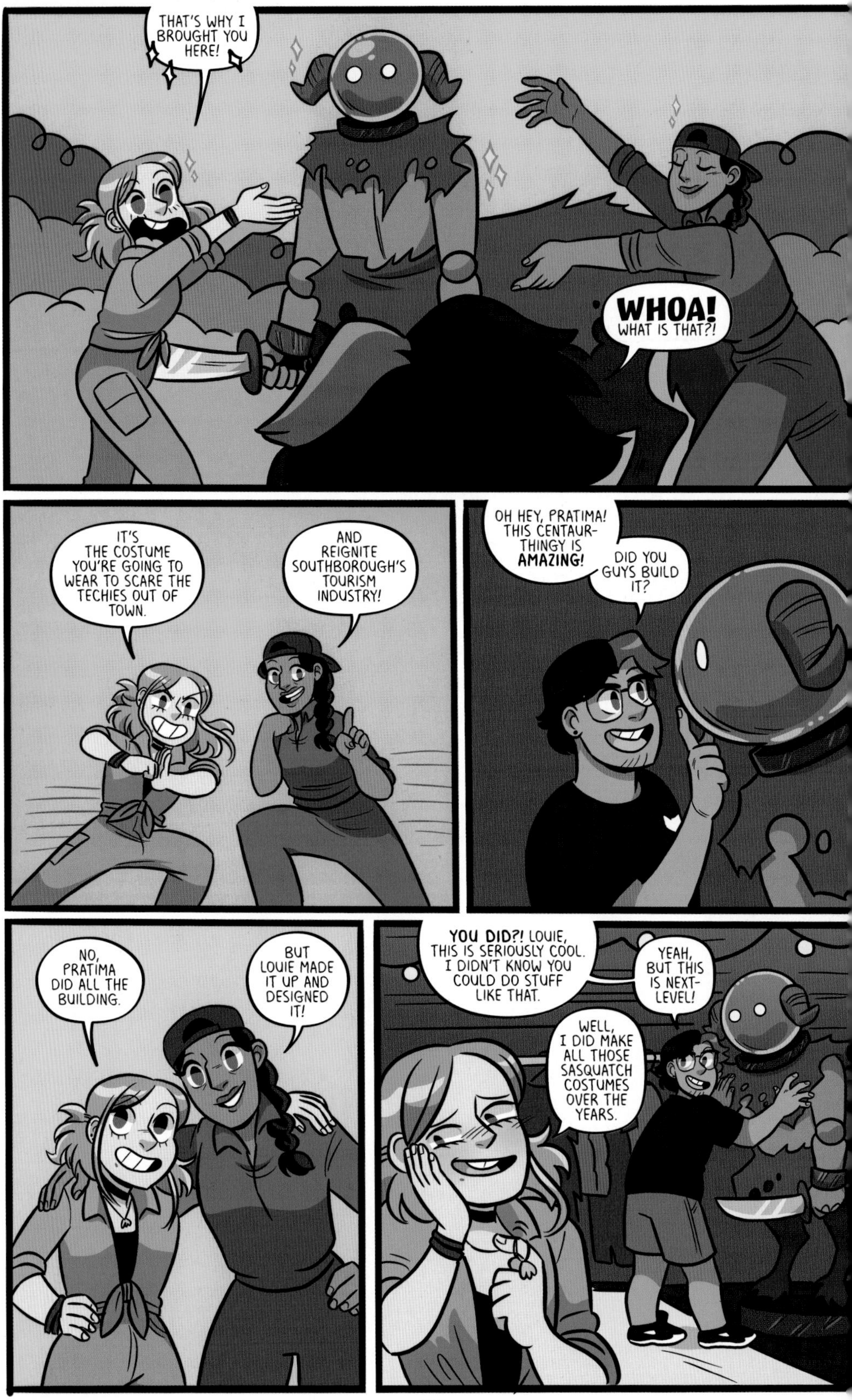
THAT'S WHY I BROUGHT YOU HERE!
WHOA! WHAT IS THAT?!
IT'S THE COSTUME YOU'RE GOING TO WEAR TO SCARE THE TECHIES OUT OF TOWN.
AND REIGNITE SOUTHBOROUGH'S TOURISM INDUSTRY!
OH HEY, PRATIMA! THIS CENTAUR-THINGY IS AMAZING!
DID YOU GUYS BUILD IT?
NO, PRATIMA DID ALL THE BUILDING.
BUT LOUIE MADE IT UP AND DESIGNED IT!
YOU DID?! LOUIE, THIS IS SERIOUSLY COOL. I DIDN'T KNOW YOU COULD DO STUFF LIKE THAT.
WELL, I DID MAKE ALL THOSE SASQUATCH COSTUMES OVER THE YEARS.
YEAH, BUT THIS IS NEXT-LEVEL!

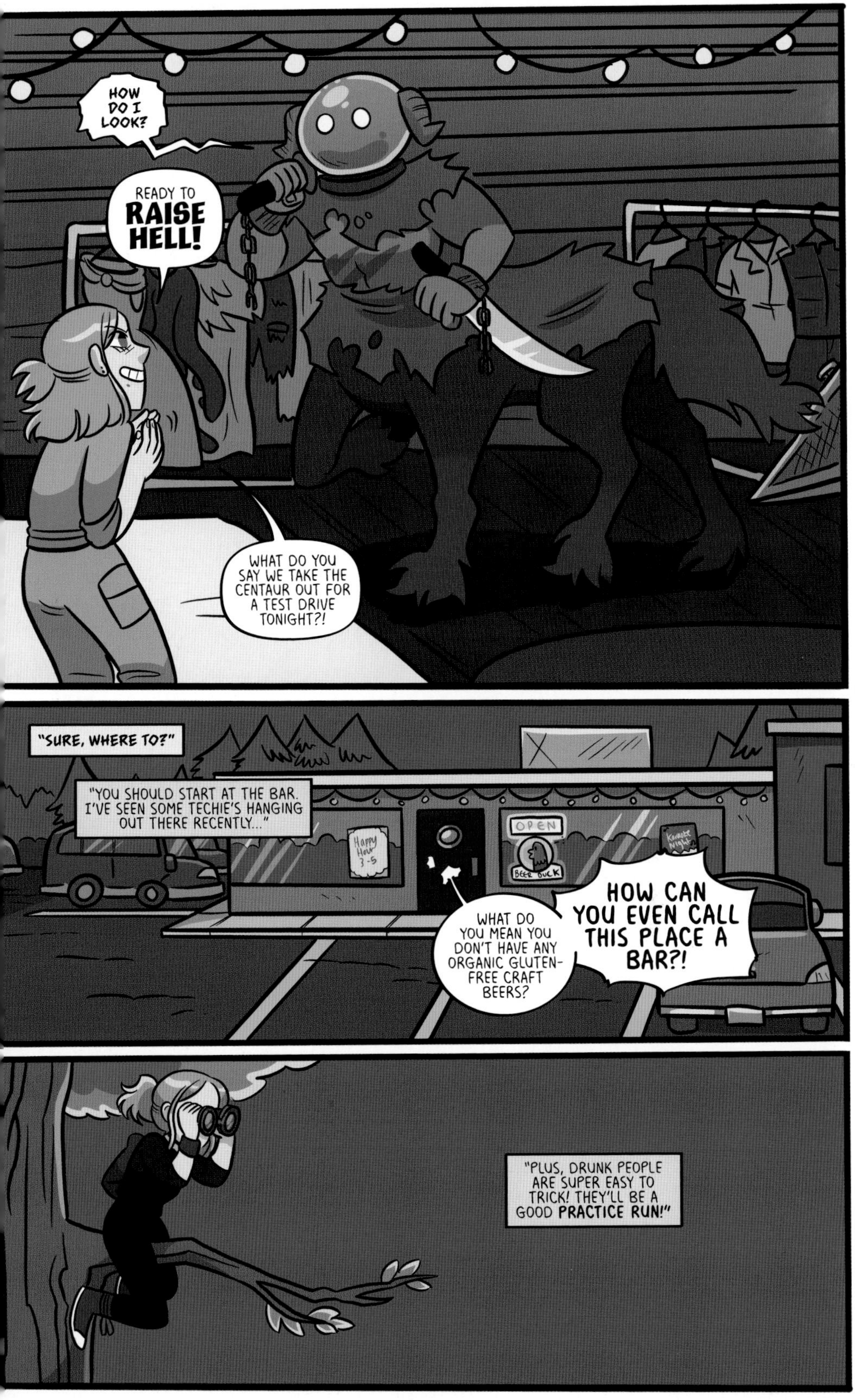
HOW DO I LOOK?
READY TO RAISE HELL!
WHAT DO YOU SAY WE TAKE THE CENTAUR OUT FOR A TEST DRIVE TONIGHT?!
"SURE, WHERE TO?"
"YOU SHOULD START AT THE BAR. I'VE SEEN SOME TECHIE'S HANGING OUT THERE RECENTLY..."
OPEN
BEER DUCK
WHAT DO YOU MEAN YOU DON'T HAVE ANY ORGANIC GLUTEN-FREE CRAFT BEERS?
HOW CAN YOU EVEN CALL THIS PLACE A BAR?!
"PLUS, DRUNK PEOPLE ARE SUPER EASY TO TRICK! THEY'LL BE A GOOD PRACTICE RUN!"

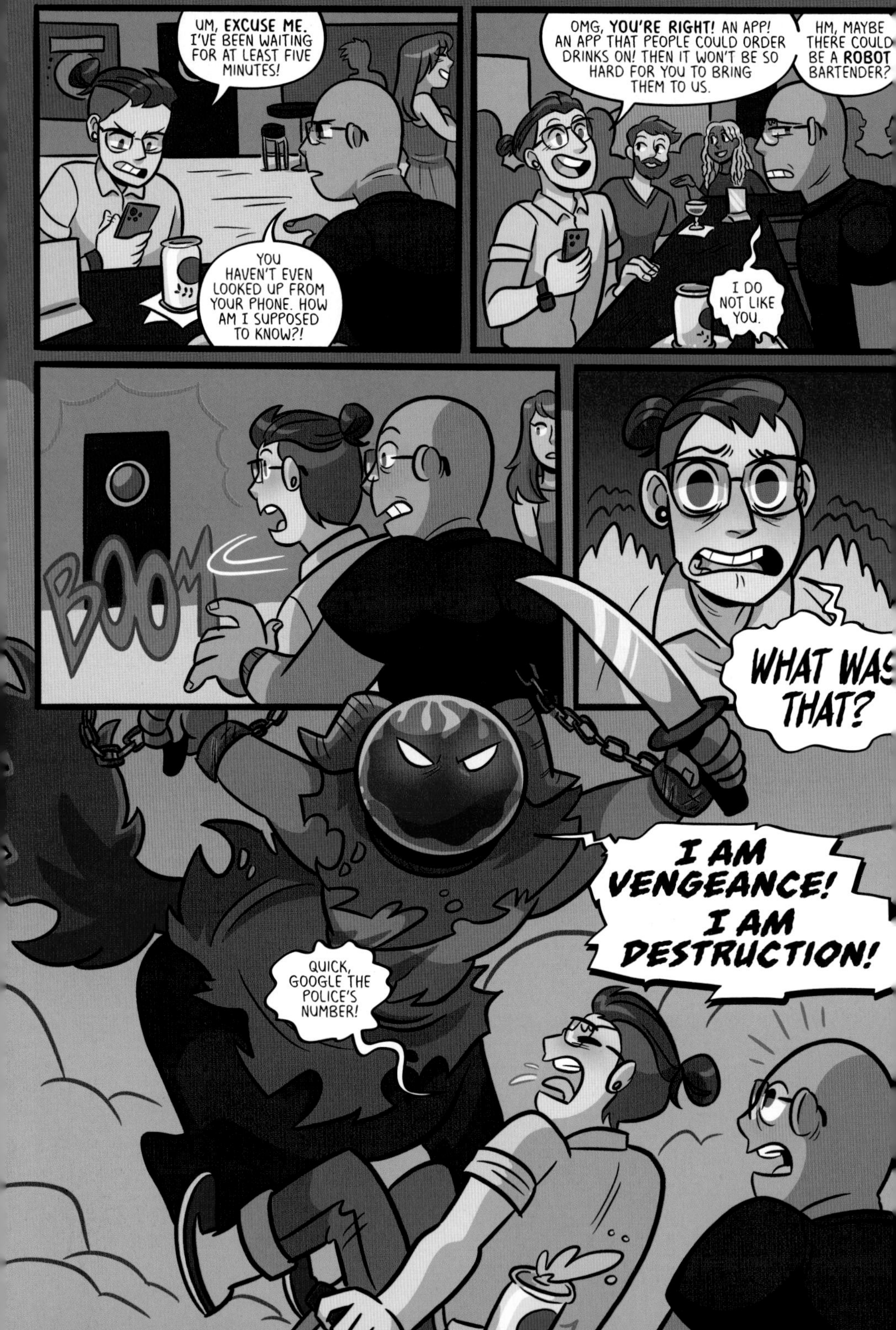
UM, EXCUSE ME. I'VE BEEN WAITING FOR AT LEAST FIVE MINUTES!
YOU HAVEN'T EVEN LOOKED UP FROM YOUR PHONE. HOW AM I SUPPOSED TO KNOW?!
OMG, YOU'RE RIGHT! AN APP! AN APP THAT PEOPLE COULD ORDER DRINKS ON! THEN IT WON'T BE SO HARD FOR YOU TO BRING THEM TO US.
HM, MAYBE THERE COULD BE A ROBOT BARTENDER?
I DO NOT LIKE YOU.
BOOM
WHAT WAS THAT?
I AM VENGEANCE! I AM DESTRUCTION!
QUICK, GOOGLE THE POLICE'S NUMBER!

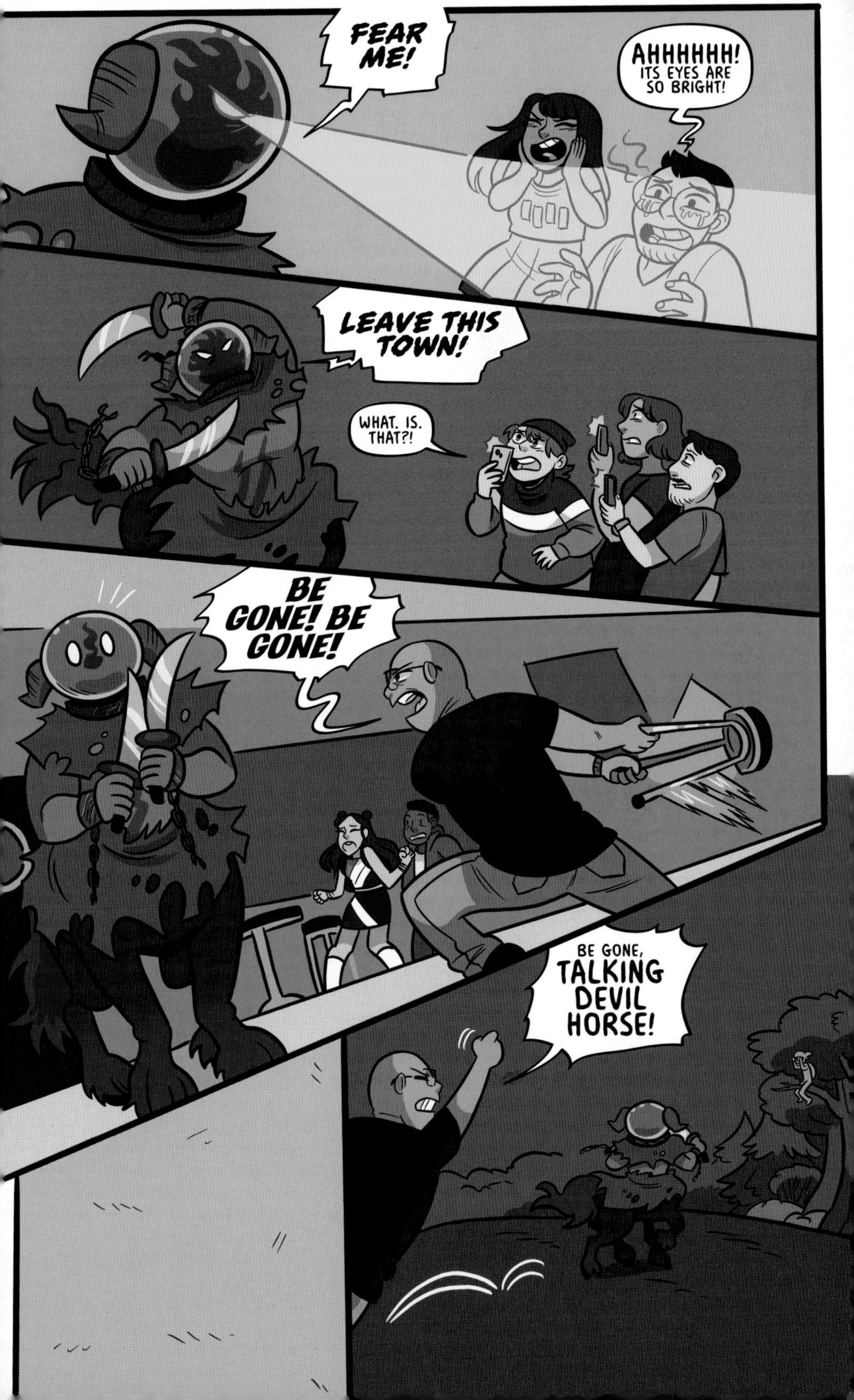
FEAR ME!
AHHHHHH! ITS EYES ARE SO BRIGHT!
LEAVE THIS TOWN!
WHAT. IS. THAT?!
BE GONE! BE GONE!
BE GONE, TALKING DEVIL HORSE!

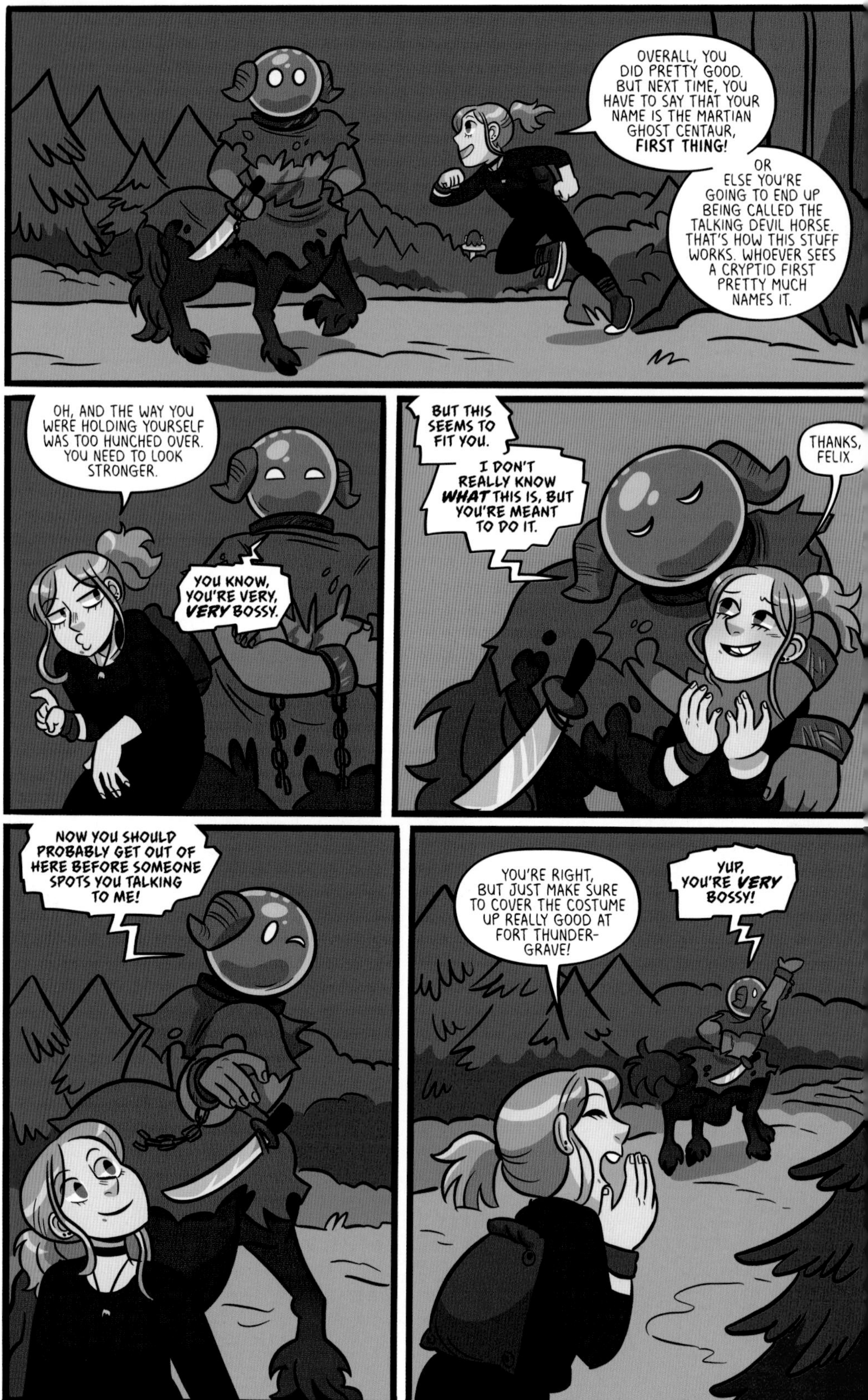
OVERALL, YOU DID PRETTY GOOD. BUT NEXT TIME, YOU HAVE TO SAY THAT YOUR NAME IS THE MARTIAN GHOST CENTAUR, **FIRST THING!**
OR ELSE YOU'RE GOING TO END UP BEING CALLED THE TALKING DEVIL HORSE. THAT'S HOW THIS STUFF WORKS. WHOEVER SEES A CRYPTID FIRST PRETTY MUCH NAMES IT.
OH, AND THE WAY YOU WERE HOLDING YOURSELF WAS TOO HUNCHED OVER. YOU NEED TO LOOK STRONGER.
YOU KNOW, YOU'RE VERY, ***VERY*** BOSSY.
BUT THIS SEEMS TO FIT YOU.
I DON'T REALLY KNOW ***WHAT*** THIS IS, BUT YOU'RE MEANT TO DO IT.
THANKS, FELIX.
NOW YOU SHOULD PROBABLY GET OUT OF HERE BEFORE SOMEONE SPOTS YOU TALKING TO ME!
YOU'RE RIGHT, BUT JUST MAKE SURE TO COVER THE COSTUME UP REALLY GOOD AT FORT THUNDER-GRAVE!
YUP, YOU'RE ***VERY*** BOSSY!

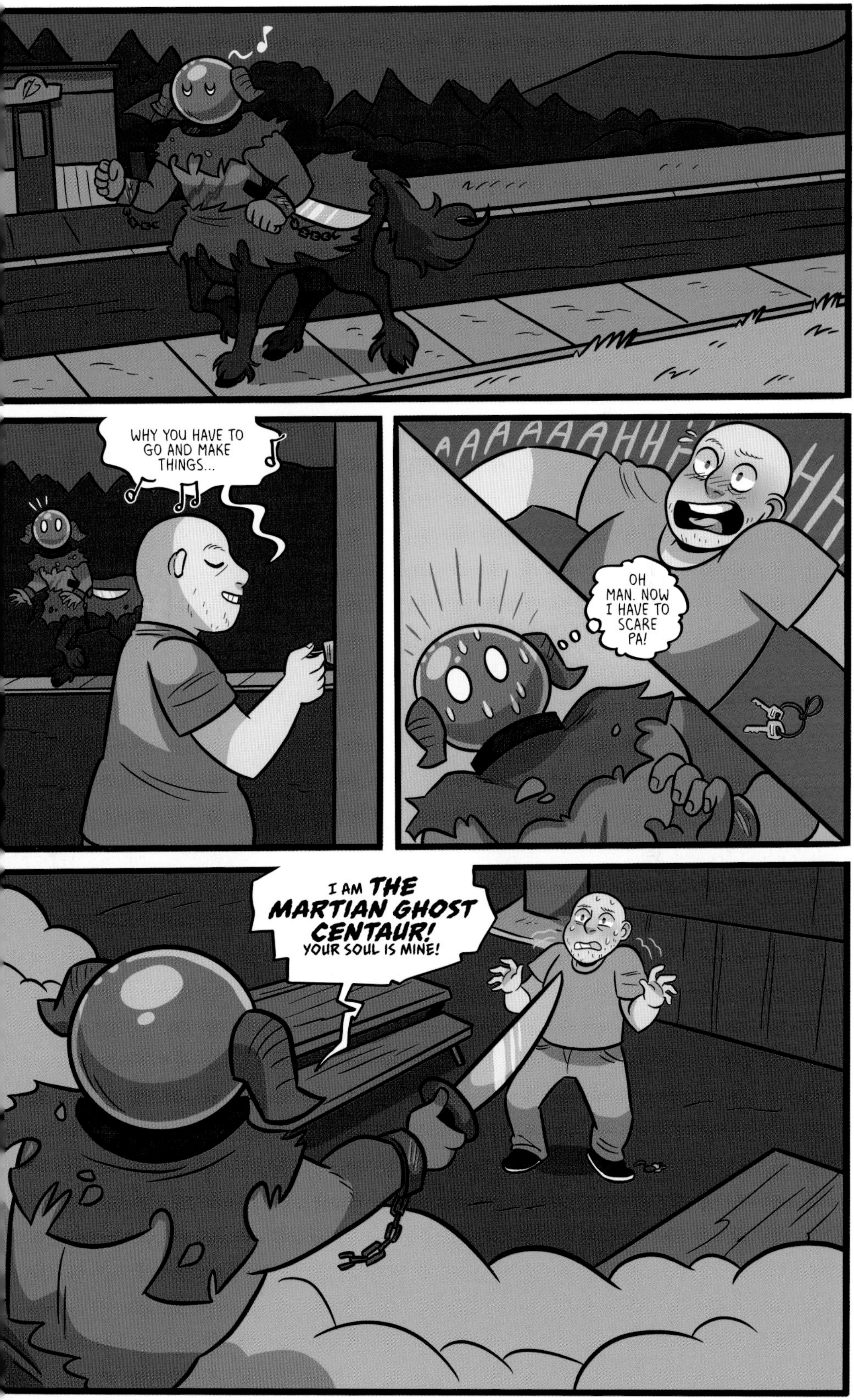

WHY YOU HAVE TO GO AND MAKE THINGS...
AAAAAAAHHH
OH MAN. NOW I HAVE TO SCARE PA!
I AM THE MARTIAN GHOST CENTAUR! YOUR SOUL IS MINE!

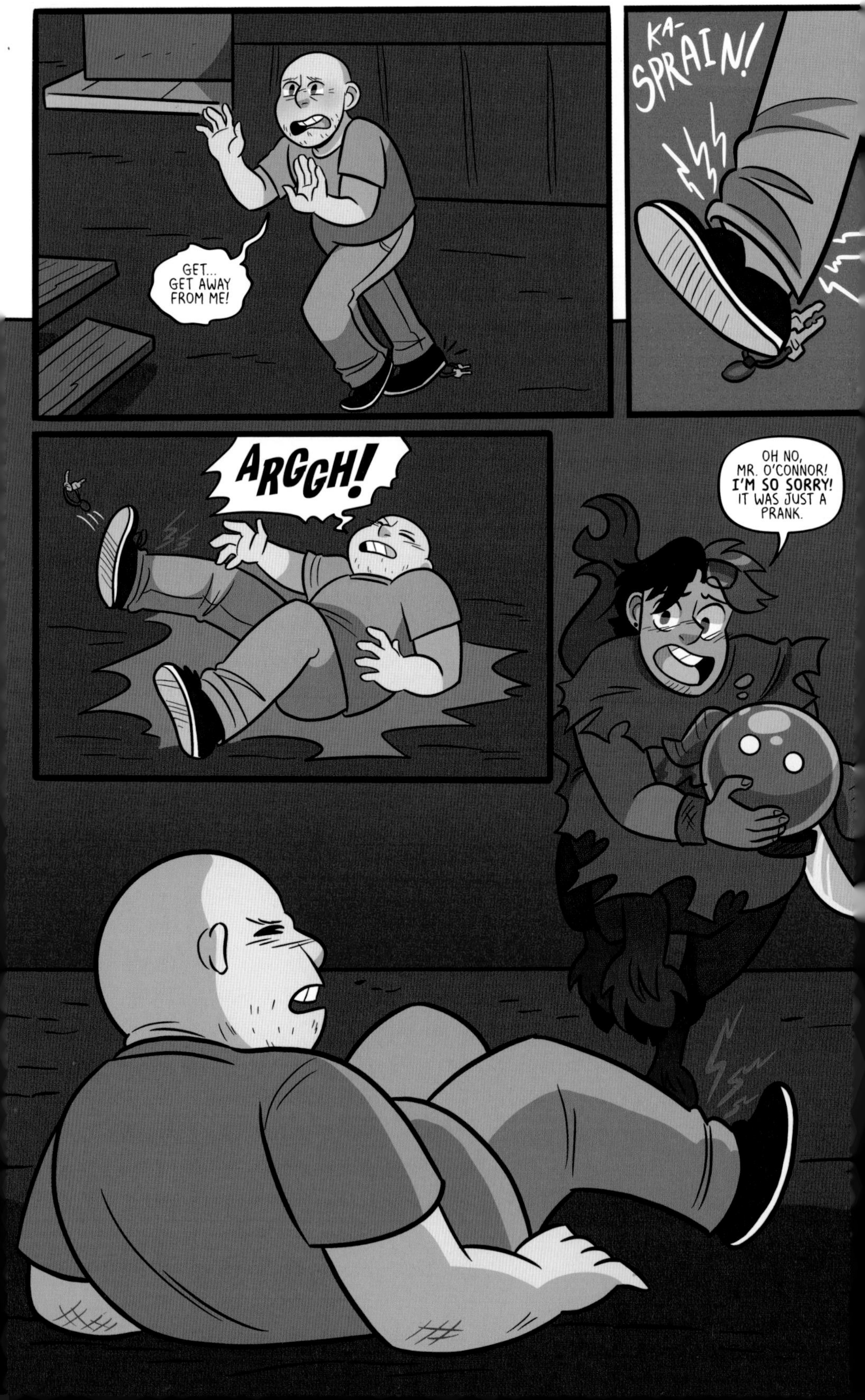
GET... GET AWAY FROM ME!
KA-SPRAIN!
ARGGH!
OH NO, MR. O'CONNOR! **I'M SO SORRY!** IT WAS JUST A PRANK.

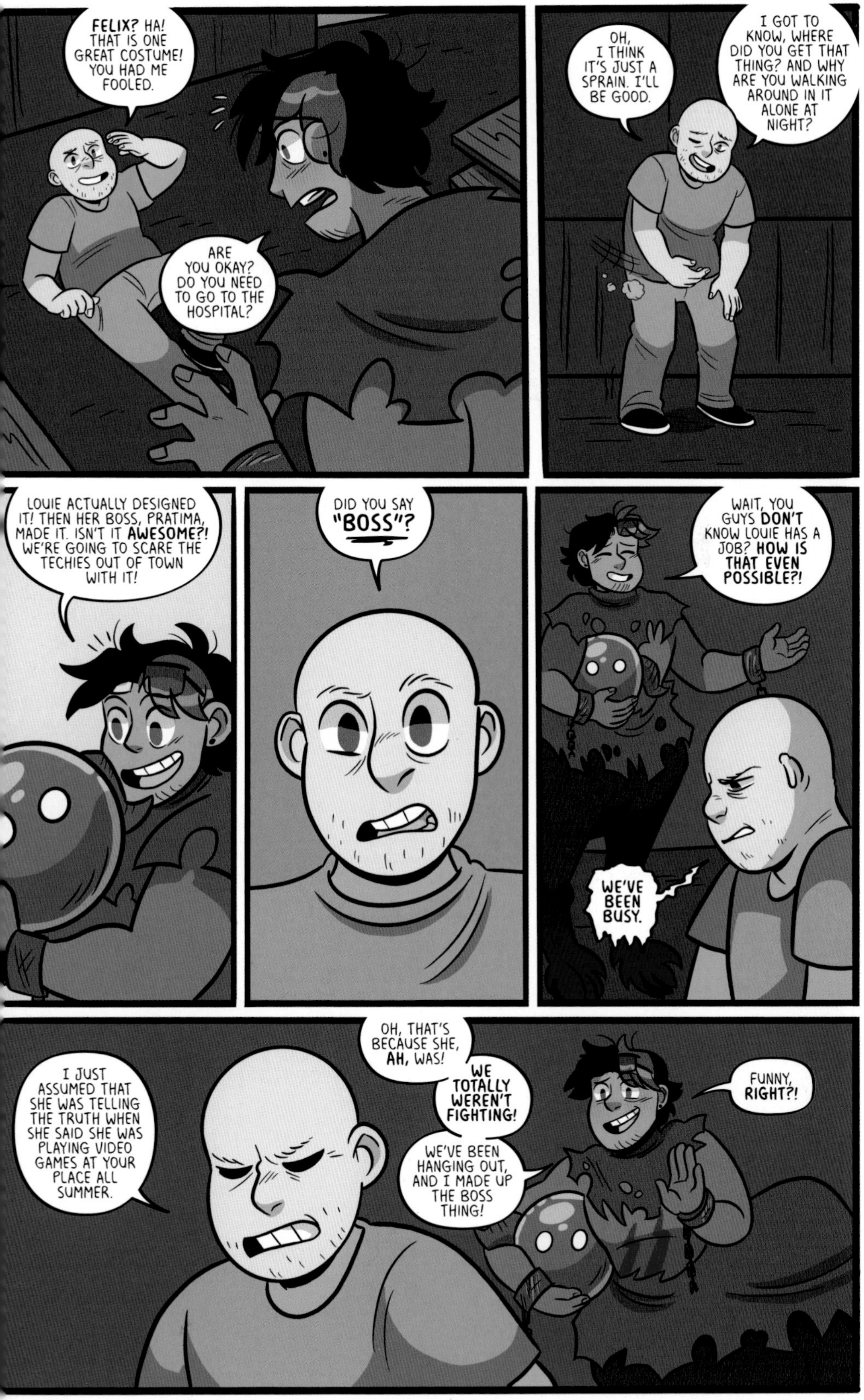
FELIX? HA! THAT IS ONE GREAT COSTUME! YOU HAD ME FOOLED.
ARE YOU OKAY? DO YOU NEED TO GO TO THE HOSPITAL?
OH, I THINK IT'S JUST A SPRAIN. I'LL BE GOOD.
I GOT TO KNOW, WHERE DID YOU GET THAT THING? AND WHY ARE YOU WALKING AROUND IN IT ALONE AT NIGHT?
LOUIE ACTUALLY DESIGNED IT! THEN HER BOSS, PRATIMA, MADE IT. ISN'T IT AWESOME?! WE'RE GOING TO SCARE THE TECHIES OUT OF TOWN WITH IT!
DID YOU SAY "BOSS"?
WAIT, YOU GUYS DON'T KNOW LOUIE HAS A JOB? HOW IS THAT EVEN POSSIBLE?!
WE'VE BEEN BUSY.
I JUST ASSUMED THAT SHE WAS TELLING THE TRUTH WHEN SHE SAID SHE WAS PLAYING VIDEO GAMES AT YOUR PLACE ALL SUMMER.
OH, THAT'S BECAUSE SHE, AH, WAS!
WE TOTALLY WEREN'T FIGHTING!
WE'VE BEEN HANGING OUT, AND I MADE UP THE BOSS THING!
FUNNY, RIGHT?!

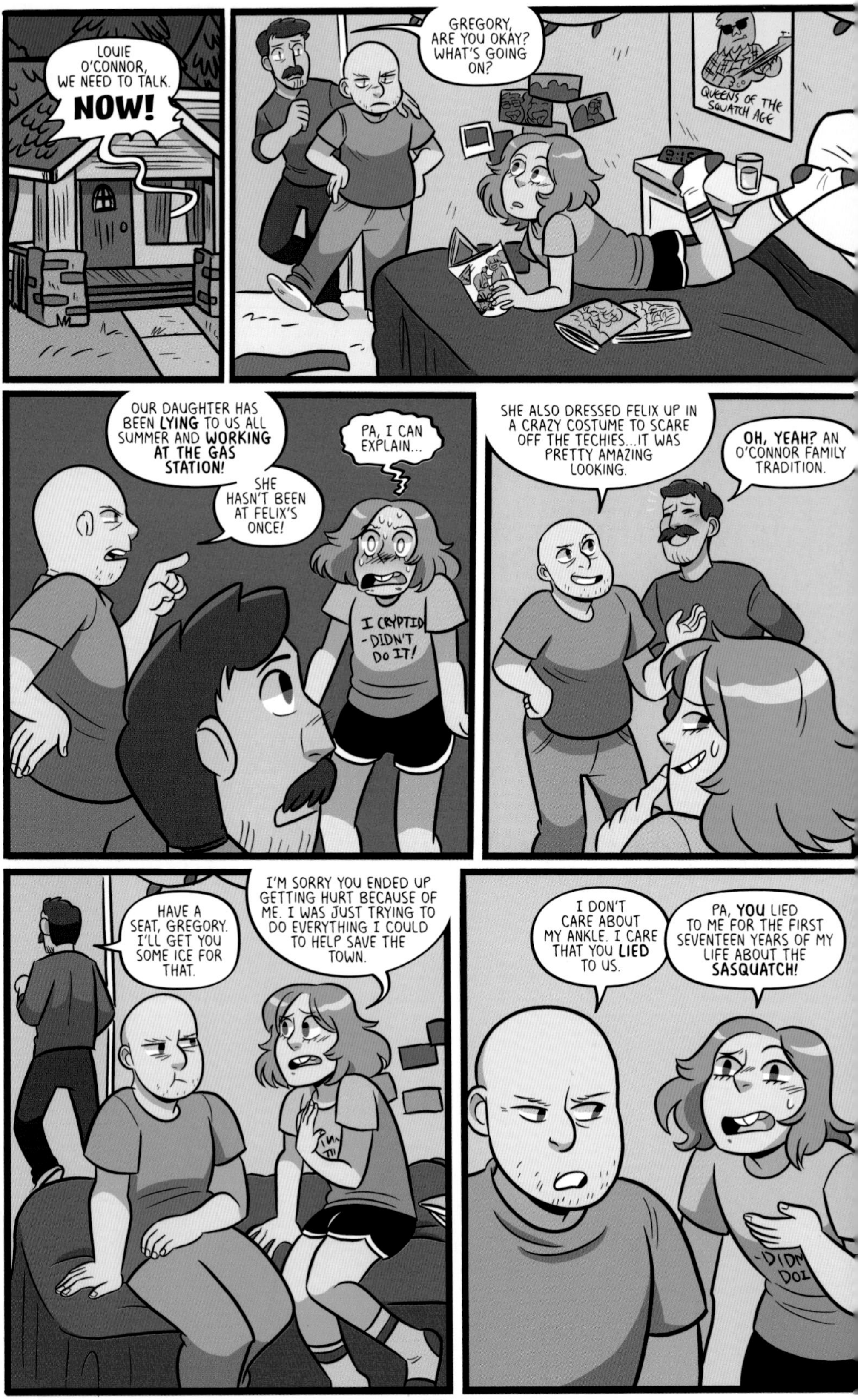
LOUIE O'CONNOR, WE NEED TO TALK.
NOW!
GREGORY, ARE YOU OKAY? WHAT'S GOING ON?
QUEENS OF THE SQUATCH AGE
OUR DAUGHTER HAS BEEN LYING TO US ALL SUMMER AND WORKING AT THE GAS STATION!
SHE HASN'T BEEN AT FELIX'S ONCE!
PA, I CAN EXPLAIN...
I CRYPTID -DIDN'T DO IT!
SHE ALSO DRESSED FELIX UP IN A CRAZY COSTUME TO SCARE OFF THE TECHIES...IT WAS PRETTY AMAZING LOOKING.
OH, YEAH? AN O'CONNOR FAMILY TRADITION.
HAVE A SEAT, GREGORY. I'LL GET YOU SOME ICE FOR THAT.
I'M SORRY YOU ENDED UP GETTING HURT BECAUSE OF ME. I WAS JUST TRYING TO DO EVERYTHING I COULD TO HELP SAVE THE TOWN.
I DON'T CARE ABOUT MY ANKLE. I CARE THAT YOU LIED TO US.
PA, YOU LIED TO ME FOR THE FIRST SEVENTEEN YEARS OF MY LIFE ABOUT THE SASQUATCH!

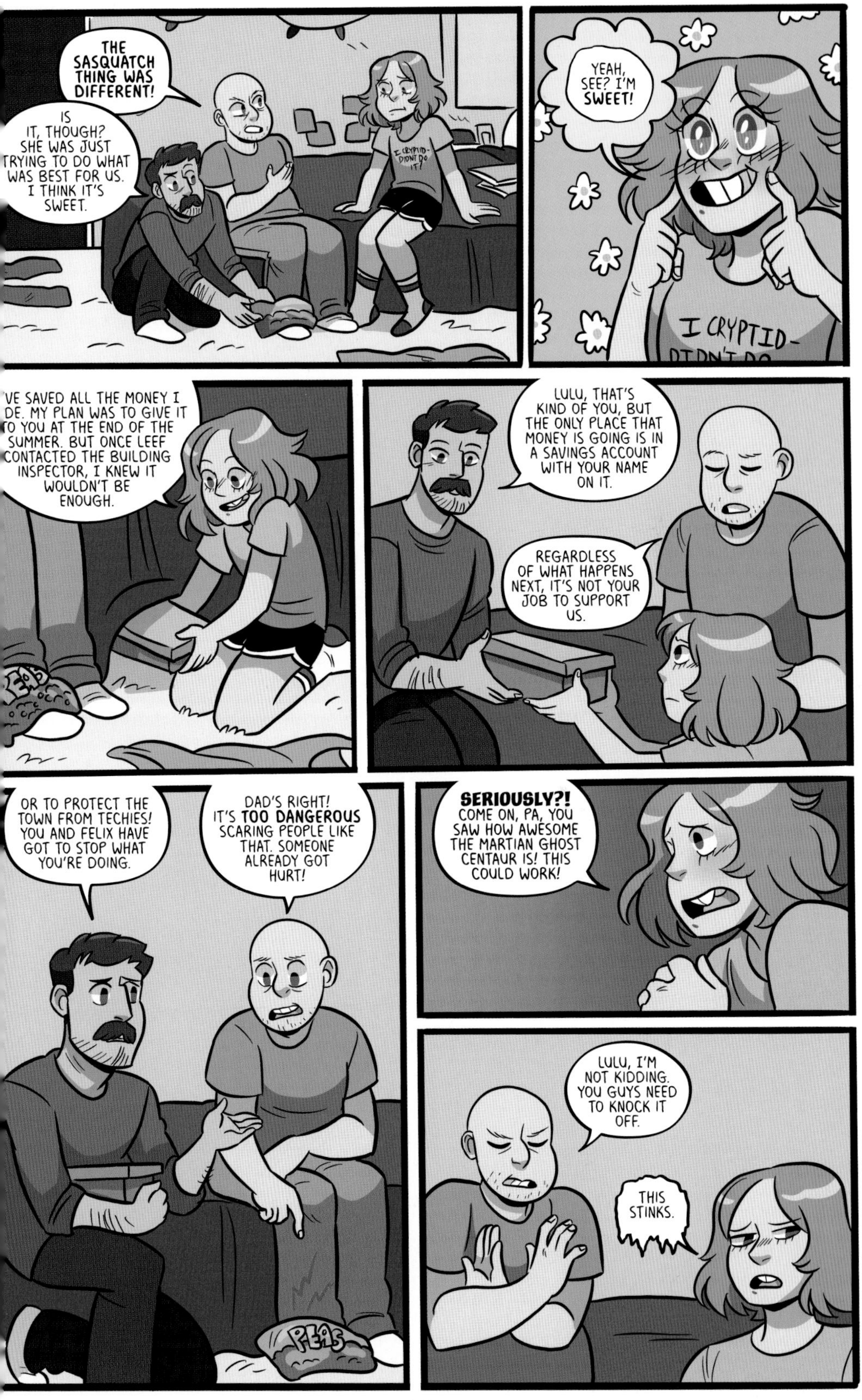
THE SASQUATCH THING WAS DIFFERENT!
IS IT, THOUGH? SHE WAS JUST TRYING TO DO WHAT WAS BEST FOR US. I THINK IT'S SWEET.
I CRYPTID-DIDN'T DO IT!
YEAH, SEE? I'M SWEET!
I CRYPTID-
'VE SAVED ALL THE MONEY I DE. MY PLAN WAS TO GIVE IT TO YOU AT THE END OF THE SUMMER. BUT ONCE LEEF CONTACTED THE BUILDING INSPECTOR, I KNEW IT WOULDN'T BE ENOUGH.
LULU, THAT'S KIND OF YOU, BUT THE ONLY PLACE THAT MONEY IS GOING IS IN A SAVINGS ACCOUNT WITH YOUR NAME ON IT.
REGARDLESS OF WHAT HAPPENS NEXT, IT'S NOT YOUR JOB TO SUPPORT US.
OR TO PROTECT THE TOWN FROM TECHIES! YOU AND FELIX HAVE GOT TO STOP WHAT YOU'RE DOING.
DAD'S RIGHT! IT'S TOO DANGEROUS SCARING PEOPLE LIKE THAT. SOMEONE ALREADY GOT HURT!
PEAS
SERIOUSLY?! COME ON, PA, YOU SAW HOW AWESOME THE MARTIAN GHOST CENTAUR IS! THIS COULD WORK!
LULU, I'M NOT KIDDING. YOU GUYS NEED TO KNOCK IT OFF.
THIS STINKS.

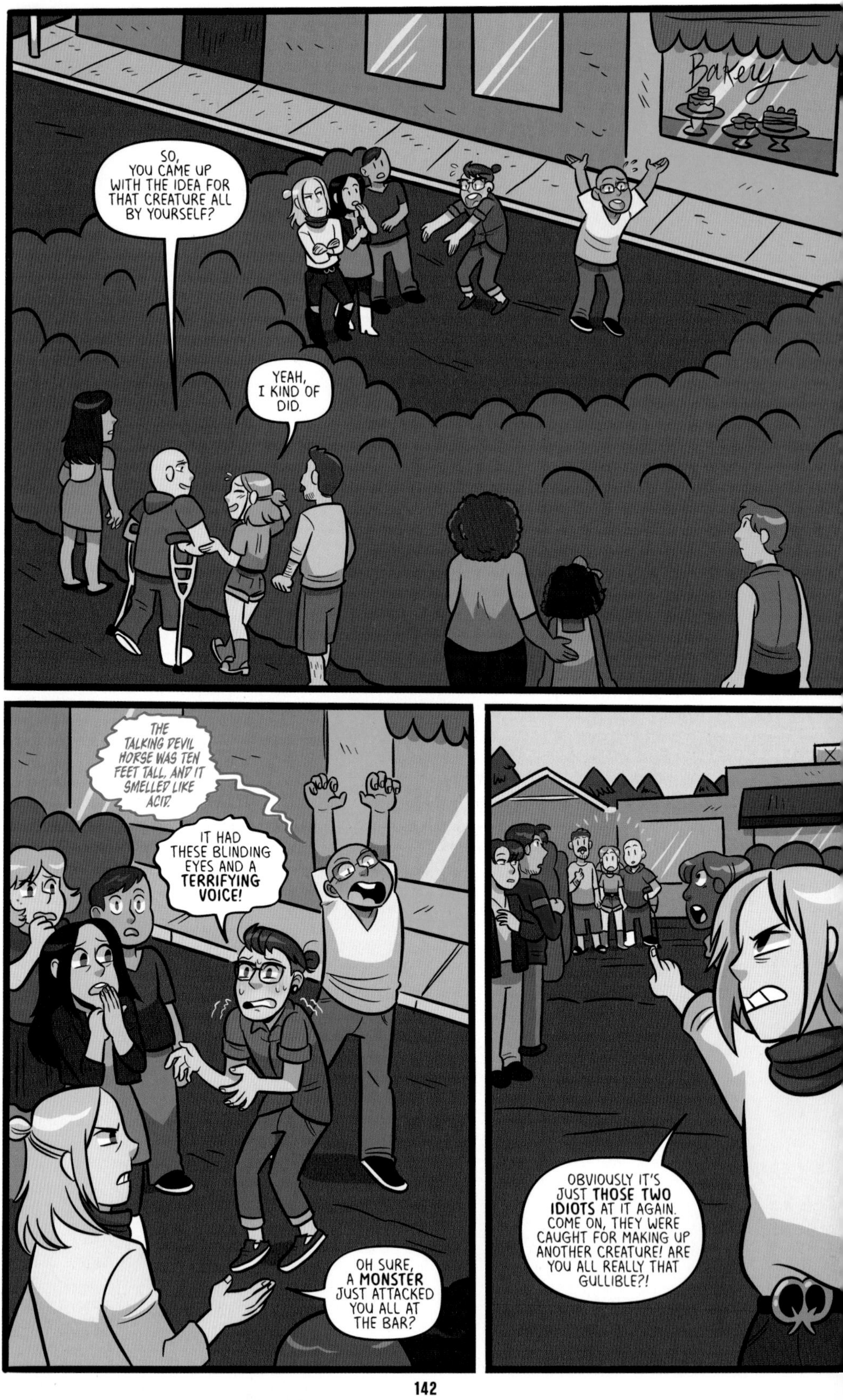
SO, YOU CAME UP WITH THE IDEA FOR THAT CREATURE ALL BY YOURSELF?
YEAH, I KIND OF DID.
Bakery
THE TALKING DEVIL HORSE WAS TEN FEET TALL, AND IT SMELLED LIKE ACID.
IT HAD THESE BLINDING EYES AND A **TERRIFYING VOICE!**
OH SURE, A **MONSTER** JUST ATTACKED YOU ALL AT THE BAR?
OBVIOUSLY IT'S JUST **THOSE TWO IDIOTS** AT IT AGAIN. COME ON, THEY WERE CAUGHT FOR MAKING UP ANOTHER CREATURE! ARE YOU ALL REALLY THAT GULLIBLE?!

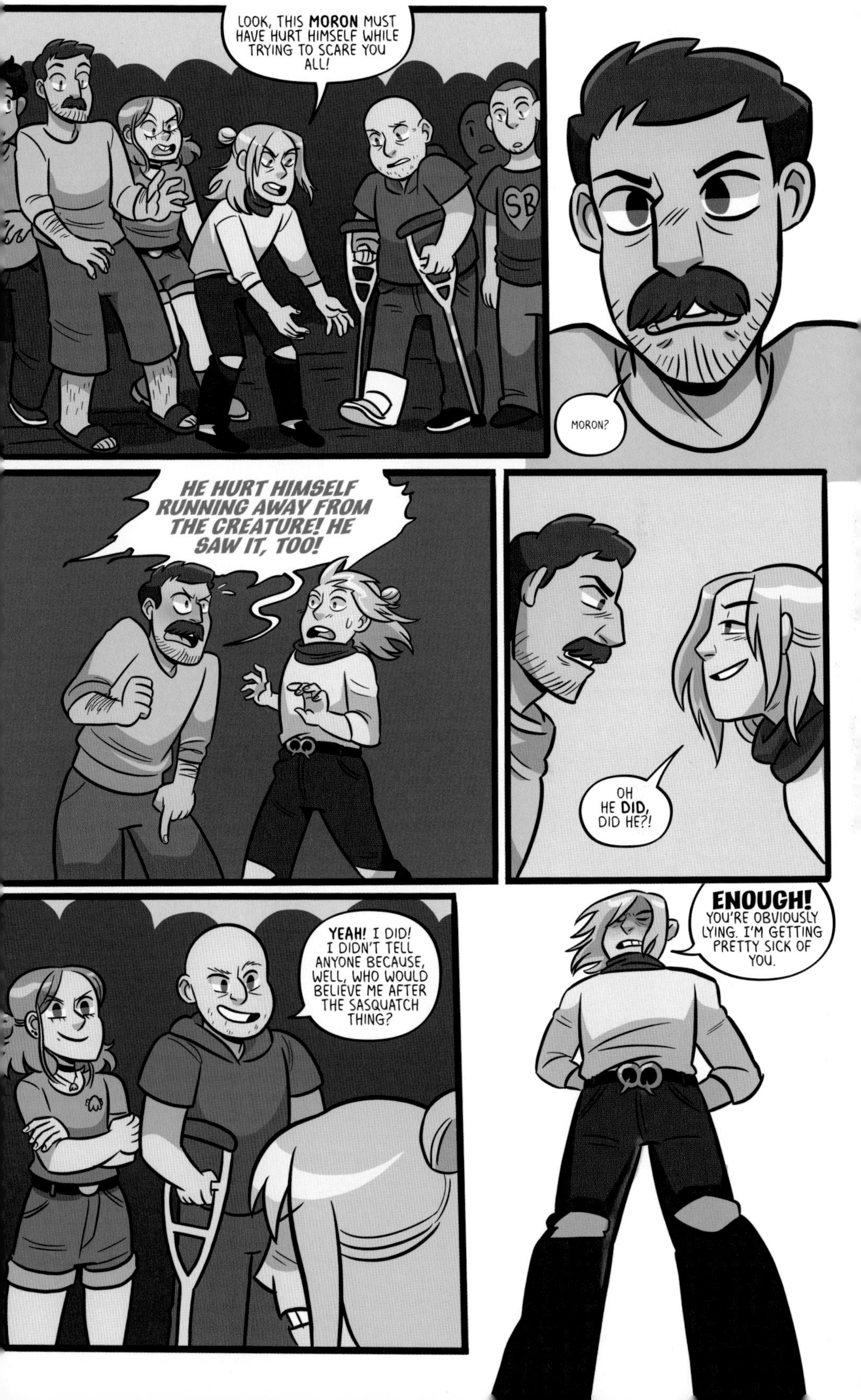

LOOK, THIS MORON MUST HAVE HURT HIMSELF WHILE TRYING TO SCARE YOU ALL!
MORON?
HE HURT HIMSELF RUNNING AWAY FROM THE CREATURE! HE SAW IT, TOO!
OH HE DID, DID HE?!
YEAH! I DID! I DIDN'T TELL ANYONE BECAUSE, WELL, WHO WOULD BELIEVE ME AFTER THE SASQUATCH THING?
ENOUGH! YOU'RE OBVIOUSLY LYING. I'M GETTING PRETTY SICK OF YOU.

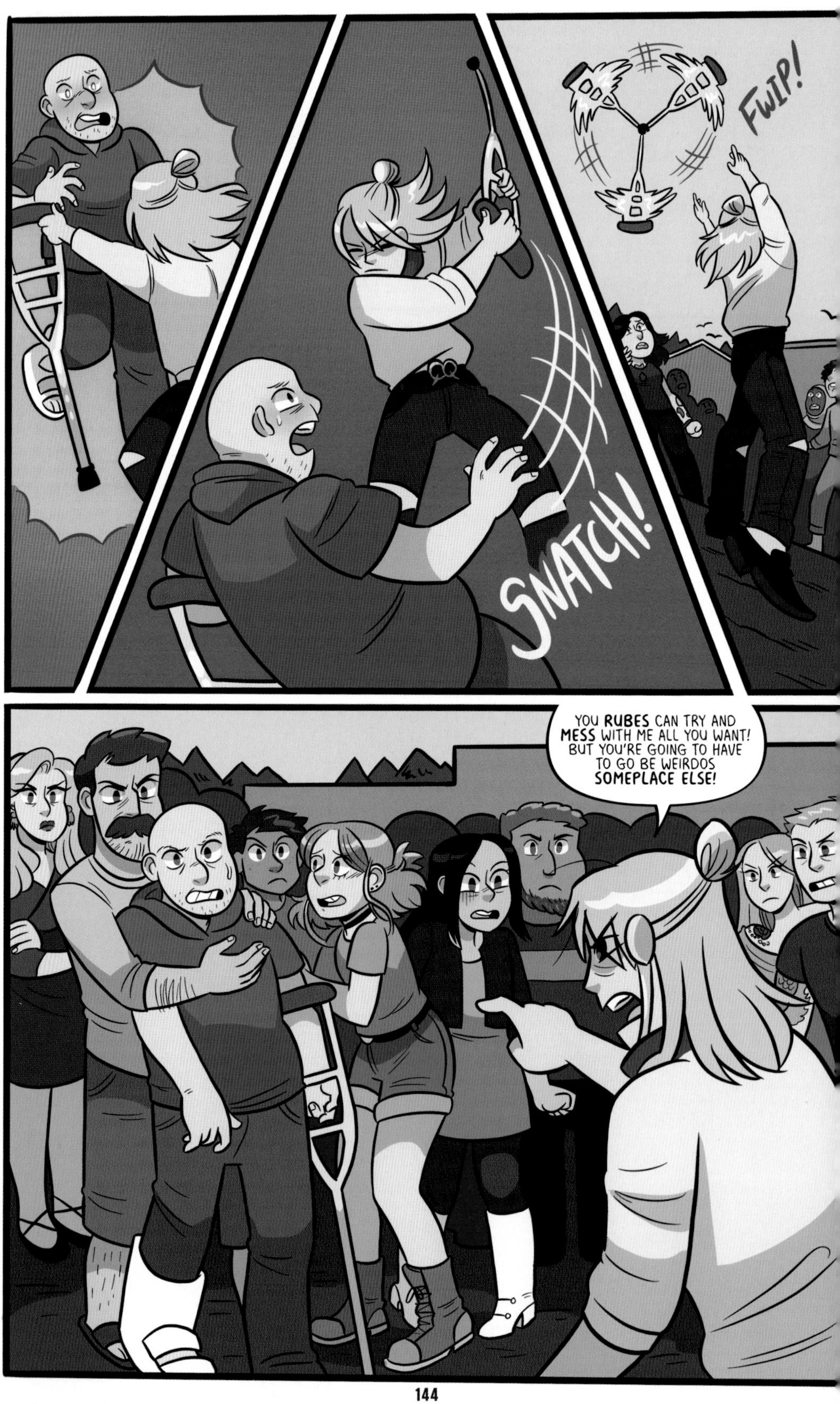
SNATCH!
FWIP!
YOU RUBES CAN TRY AND MESS WITH ME ALL YOU WANT! BUT YOU'RE GOING TO HAVE TO GO BE WEIRDOS SOMEPLACE ELSE!

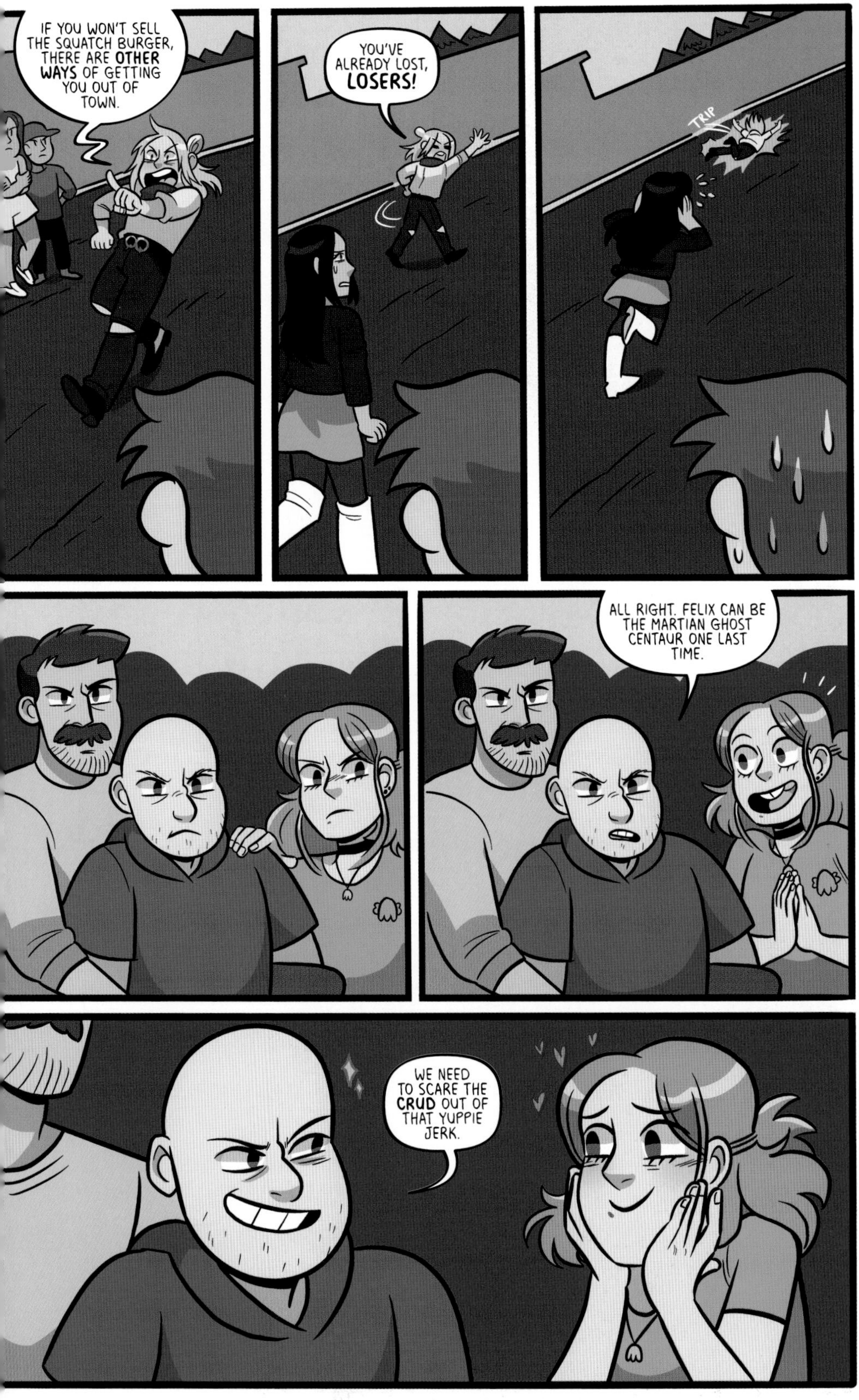
IF YOU WON'T SELL THE SQUATCH BURGER, THERE ARE **OTHER WAYS** OF GETTING YOU OUT OF TOWN.
YOU'VE ALREADY LOST, **LOSERS!**
TRIP
ALL RIGHT. FELIX CAN BE THE MARTIAN GHOST CENTAUR ONE LAST TIME.
WE NEED TO SCARE THE **CRUD** OUT OF THAT YUPPIE JERK.

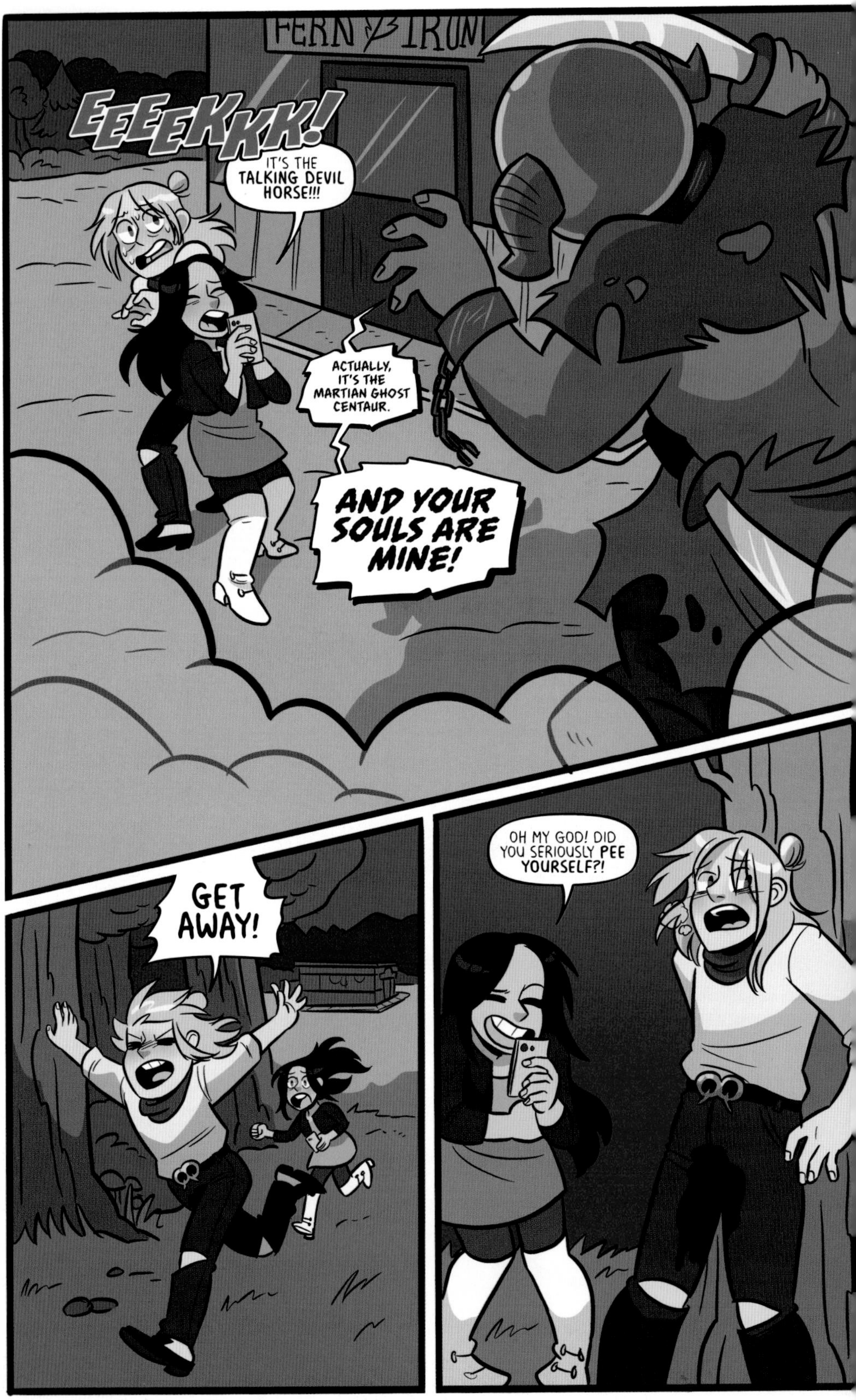
FERN IRON
EEEEKKK!
IT'S THE TALKING DEVIL HORSE!!!
ACTUALLY, IT'S THE MARTIAN GHOST CENTAUR.
AND YOUR SOULS ARE MINE!
GET AWAY!
OH MY GOD! DID YOU SERIOUSLY PEE YOURSELF?!

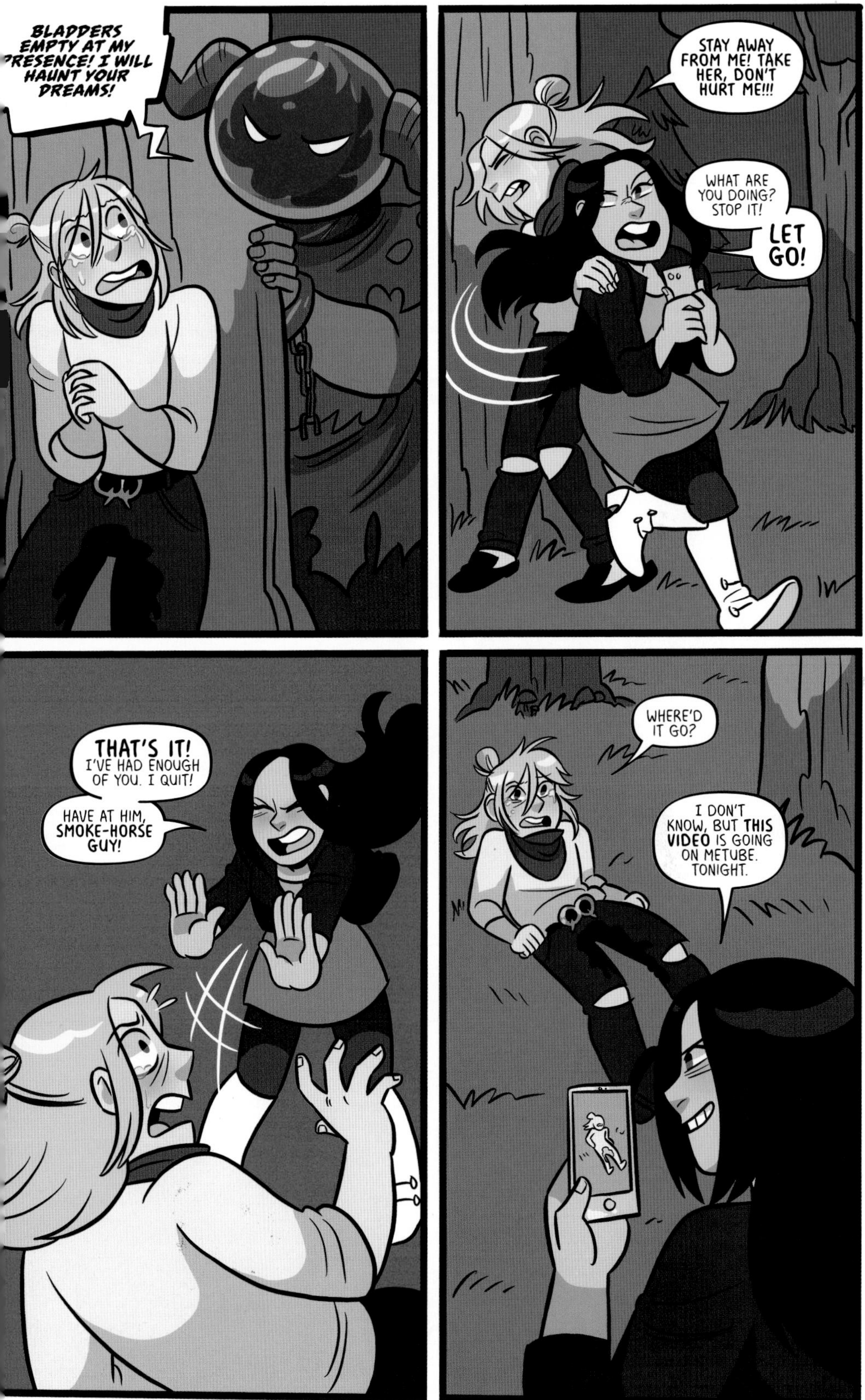
BLADDERS EMPTY AT MY PRESENCE! I WILL HAUNT YOUR DREAMS!
STAY AWAY FROM ME! TAKE HER, DON'T HURT ME!!!
WHAT ARE YOU DOING? STOP IT!
LET GO!
THAT'S IT! I'VE HAD ENOUGH OF YOU. I QUIT!
HAVE AT HIM, SMOKE-HORSE GUY!
WHERE'D IT GO?
I DON'T KNOW, BUT THIS VIDEO IS GOING ON METUBE. TONIGHT.

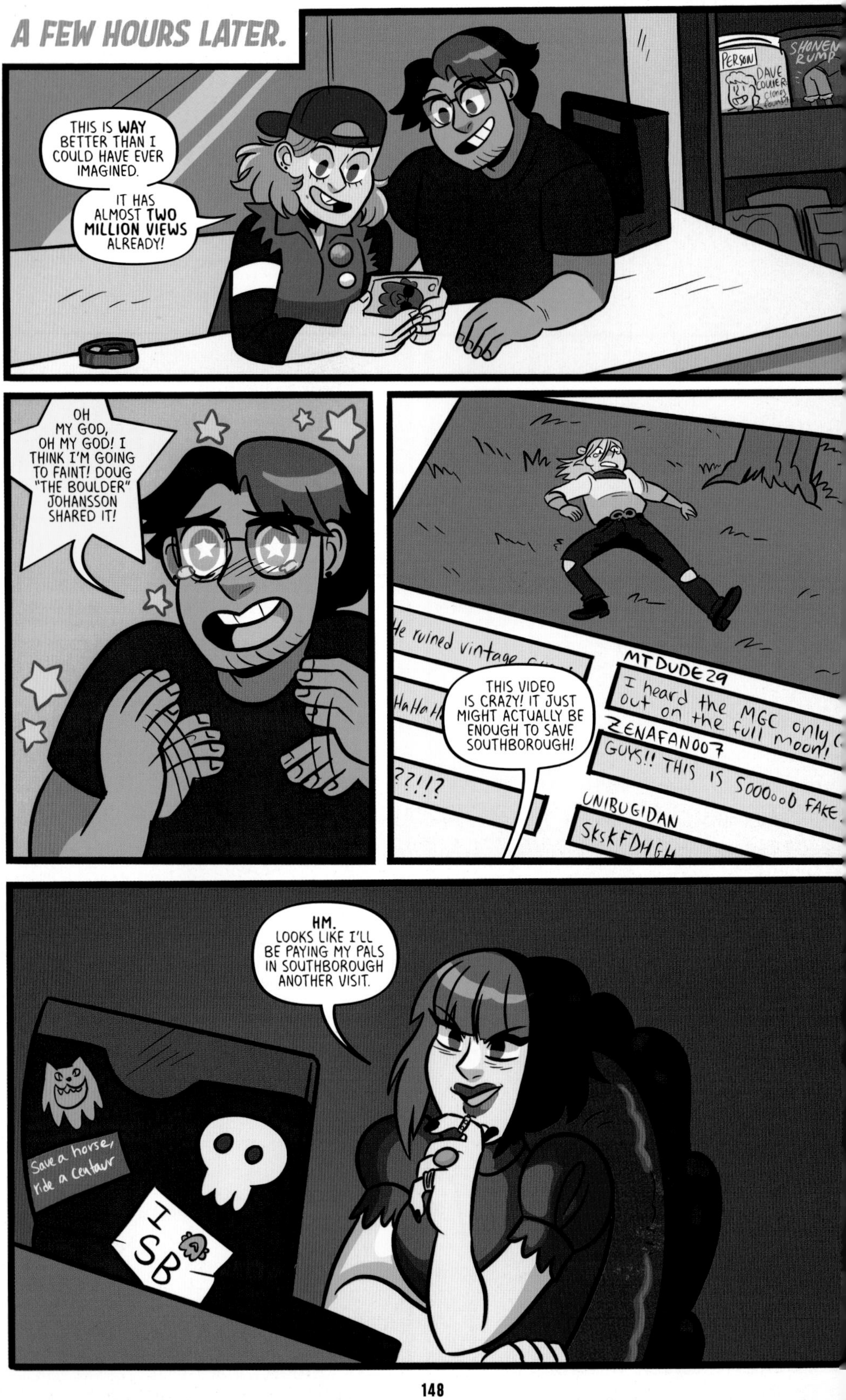
A FEW HOURS LATER.
SHONEN RUMP
PERSON
THIS IS WAY BETTER THAN I COULD HAVE EVER IMAGINED.
IT HAS ALMOST TWO MILLION VIEWS ALREADY!
OH MY GOD, OH MY GOD! I THINK I'M GOING TO FAINT! DOUG "THE BOULDER" JOHANSSON SHARED IT!
MTDUDE29
ZENAFAN007
GUYS!! THIS IS SOOooO FAKE
UNIBUGIDAN
??!!?
THIS VIDEO IS CRAZY! IT JUST MIGHT ACTUALLY BE ENOUGH TO SAVE SOUTHBOROUGH!
HM. LOOKS LIKE I'LL BE PAYING MY PALS IN SOUTHBOROUGH ANOTHER VISIT.
Save a horse, ride a centaur
I SB

CHAPTER 6

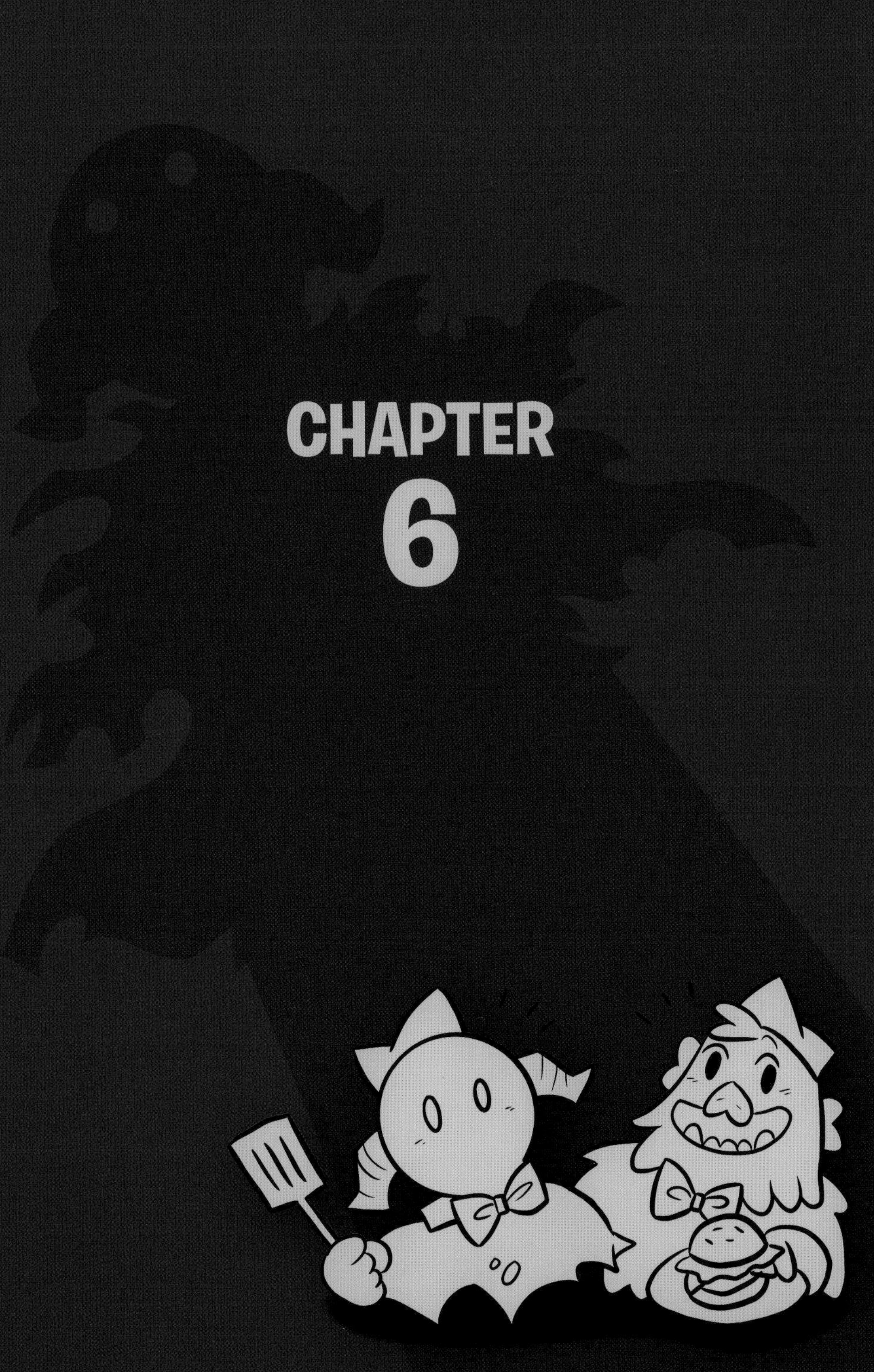

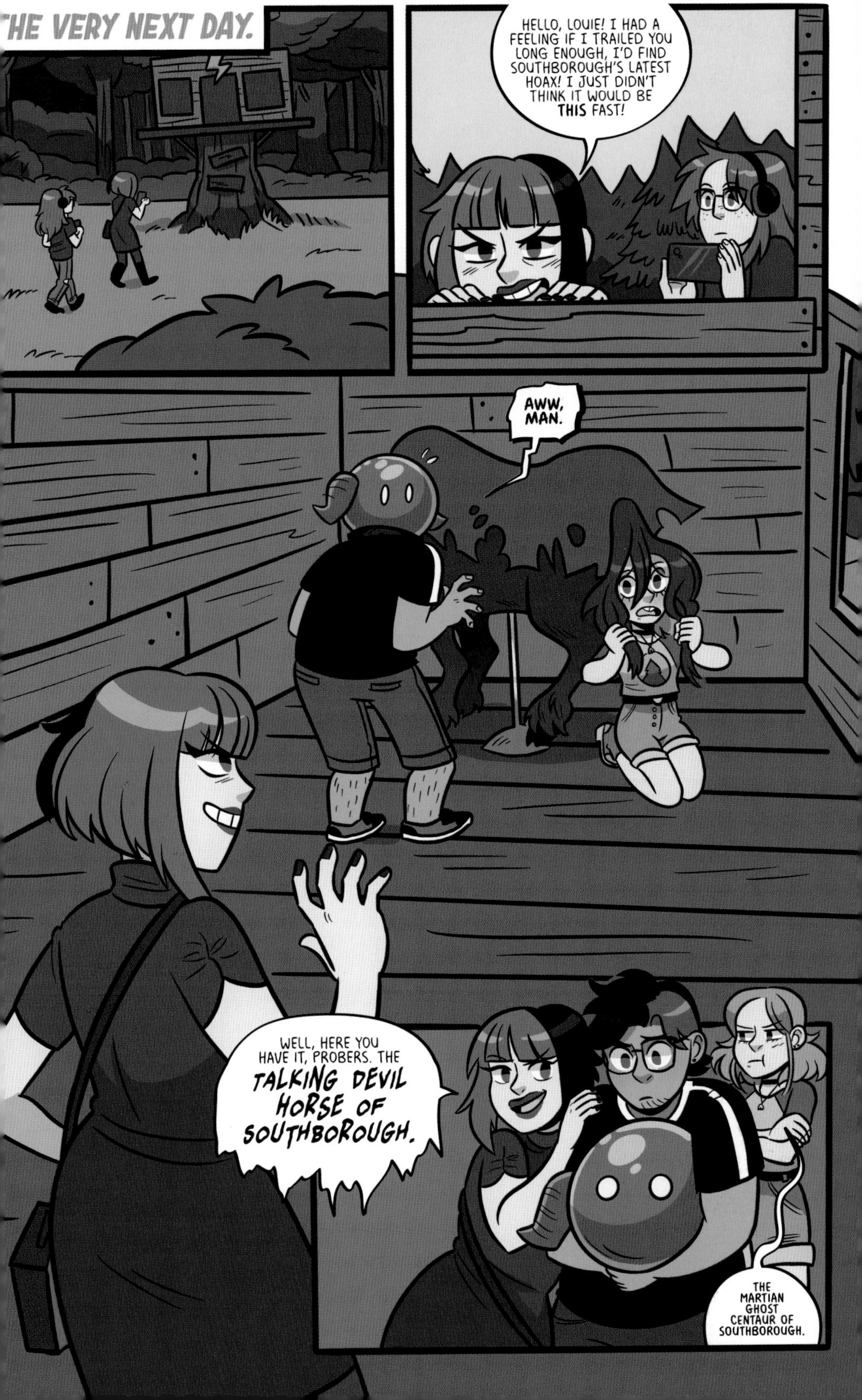
THE VERY NEXT DAY.
HELLO, LOUIE! I HAD A FEELING IF I TRAILED YOU LONG ENOUGH, I'D FIND SOUTHBOROUGH'S LATEST HOAX! I JUST DIDN'T THINK IT WOULD BE **THIS** FAST!
AWW, MAN.
WELL, HERE YOU HAVE IT, PROBERS. THE TALKING DEVIL HORSE OF SOUTHBOROUGH.
THE MARTIAN GHOST CENTAUR OF SOUTHBOROUGH.

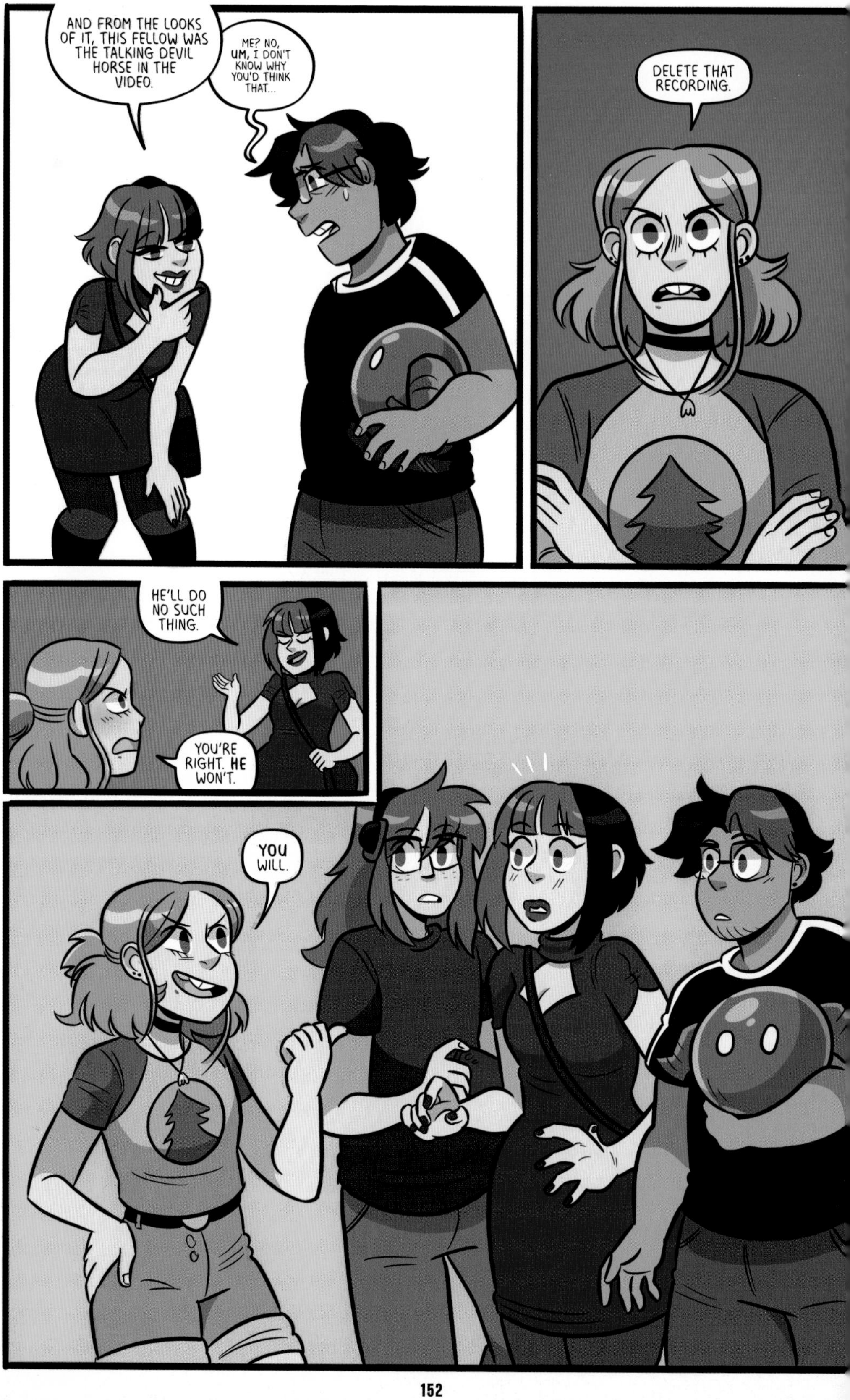

AND FROM THE LOOKS OF IT, THIS FELLOW WAS THE TALKING DEVIL HORSE IN THE VIDEO.
ME? NO, UM, I DON'T KNOW WHY YOU'D THINK THAT...
DELETE THAT RECORDING.
HE'LL DO NO SUCH THING.
YOU'RE RIGHT. HE WON'T.
YOU WILL.

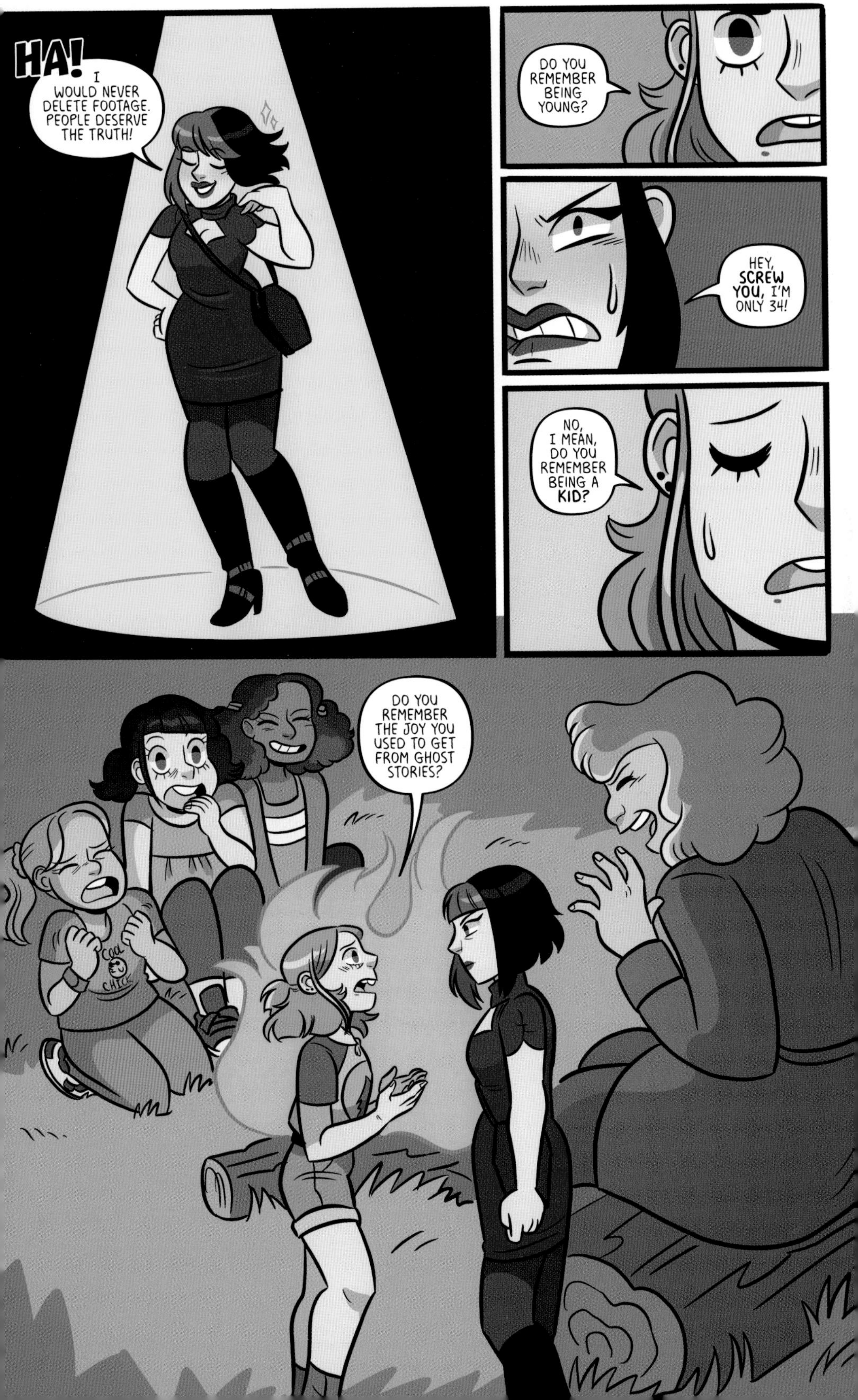
HA!
I WOULD NEVER DELETE FOOTAGE. PEOPLE DESERVE THE TRUTH!
DO YOU REMEMBER BEING YOUNG?
HEY, **SCREW YOU,** I'M ONLY 34!
NO, I MEAN, DO YOU REMEMBER BEING A **KID?**
DO YOU REMEMBER THE JOY YOU USED TO GET FROM GHOST STORIES?
COOL CHICK

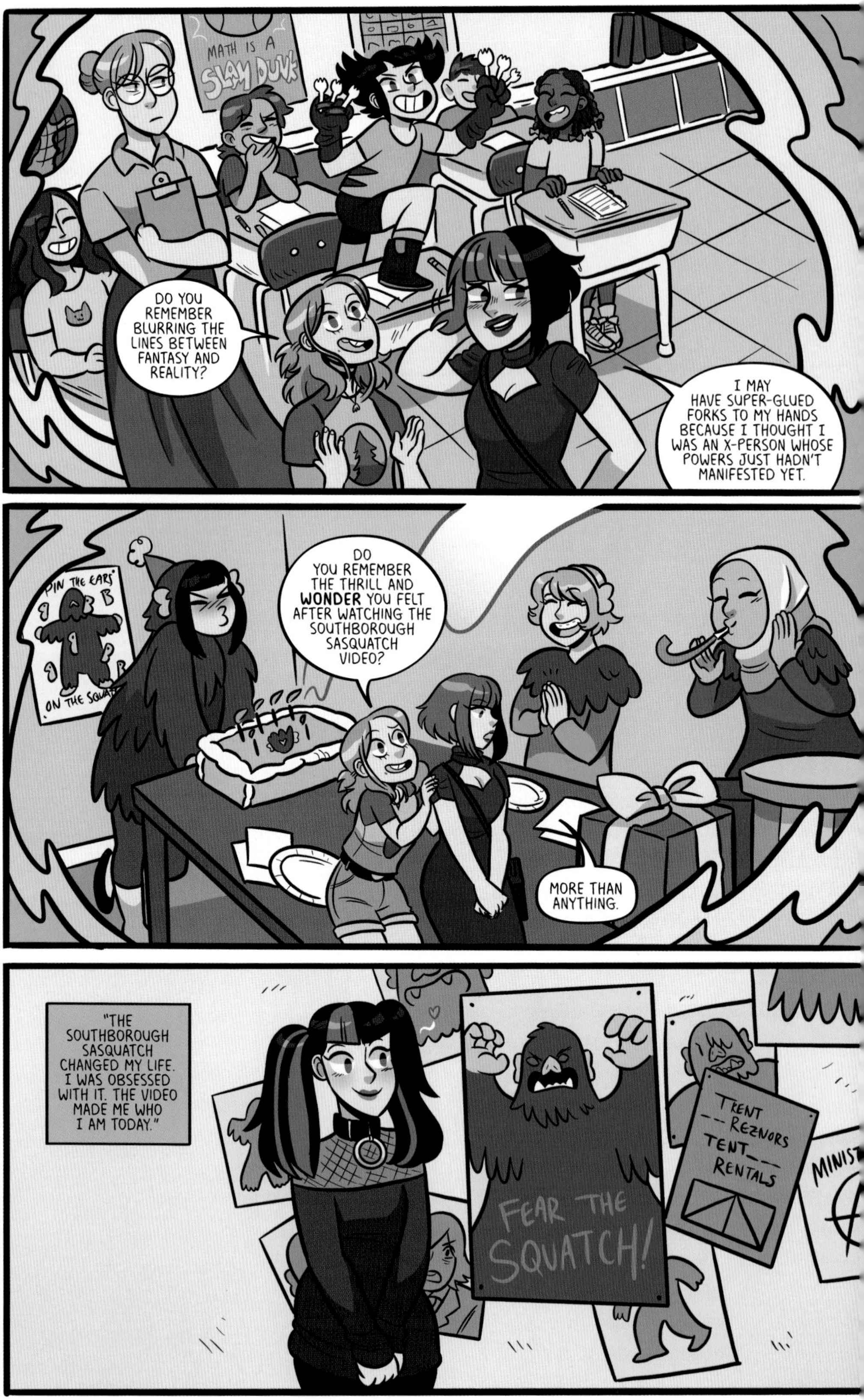
MATH IS A SLAM DUNK
DO YOU REMEMBER BLURRING THE LINES BETWEEN FANTASY AND REALITY?
I MAY HAVE SUPER-GLUED FORKS TO MY HANDS BECAUSE I THOUGHT I WAS AN X-PERSON WHOSE POWERS JUST HADN'T MANIFESTED YET.
PIN THE EARS ON THE SQUATCH
DO YOU REMEMBER THE THRILL AND **WONDER** YOU FELT AFTER WATCHING THE SOUTHBOROUGH SASQUATCH VIDEO?
MORE THAN ANYTHING.
"THE SOUTHBOROUGH SASQUATCH CHANGED MY LIFE. I WAS OBSESSED WITH IT. THE VIDEO MADE ME WHO I AM TODAY."
FEAR THE SQUATCH!
TRENT REZNORS TENT RENTALS
MINIS

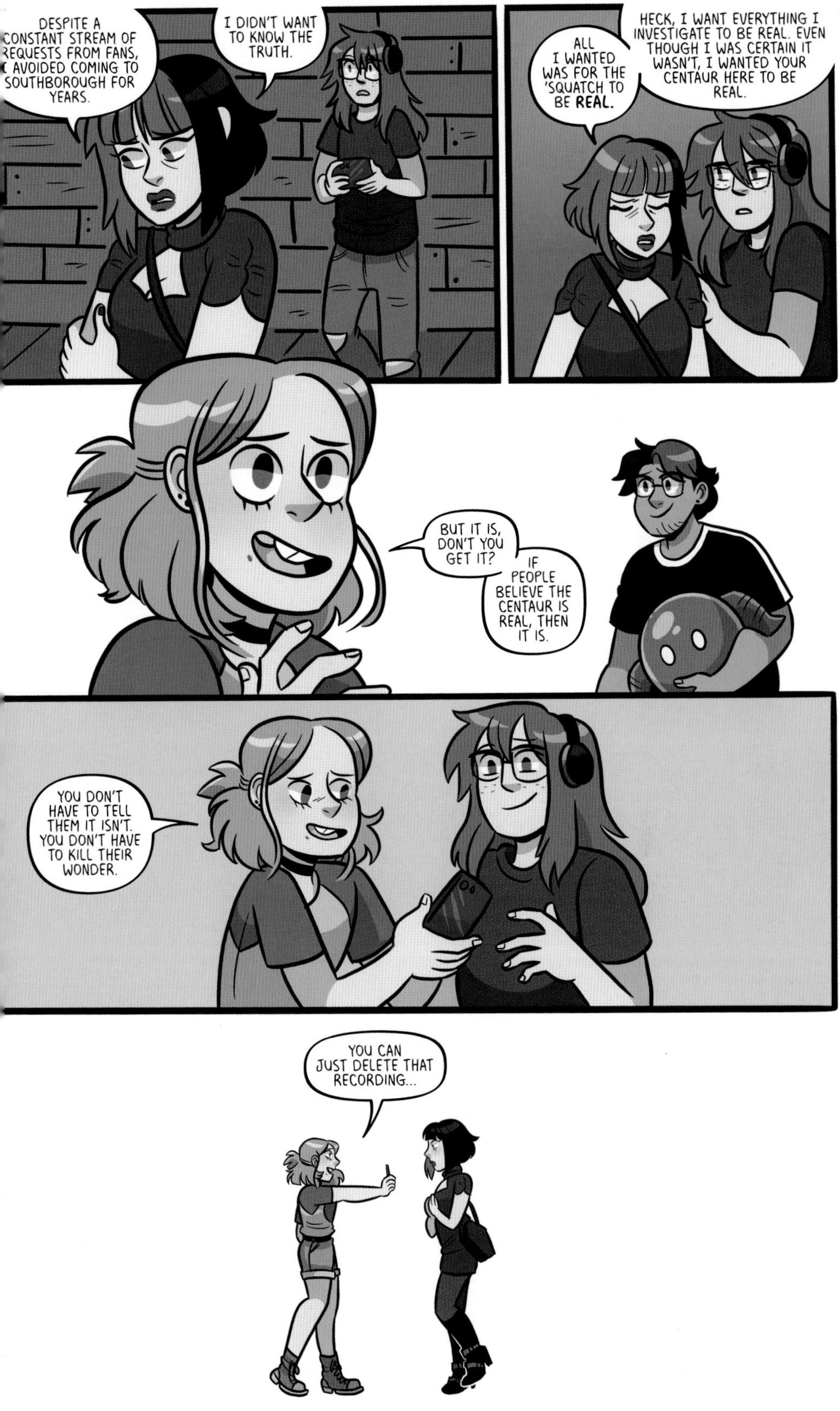

DESPITE A CONSTANT STREAM OF REQUESTS FROM FANS, I AVOIDED COMING TO SOUTHBOROUGH FOR YEARS.
I DIDN'T WANT TO KNOW THE TRUTH.
ALL I WANTED WAS FOR THE 'SQUATCH TO BE **REAL.**
HECK, I WANT EVERYTHING I INVESTIGATE TO BE REAL. EVEN THOUGH I WAS CERTAIN IT WASN'T, I WANTED YOUR CENTAUR HERE TO BE REAL.
BUT IT IS, DON'T YOU GET IT?
IF PEOPLE BELIEVE THE CENTAUR IS REAL, THEN IT IS.
YOU DON'T HAVE TO TELL THEM IT ISN'T. YOU DON'T HAVE TO KILL THEIR WONDER.
YOU CAN JUST DELETE THAT RECORDING...

"I'LL DO YOU ONE BETTER, KID. LET'S MAKE A NEW VIDEO..."

IT'S FLIPPIN' REAL!!!

PROBERS, I CAN'T BELIEVE I'M SAYING THIS, BUT THIS ONE IS **NOT** A MYTH...

YOUR END IS **NOW!**

SO THE VIDEO GETS PRETTY HARD TO SEE AT THIS POINT. BUT WHAT HAPPENS IS MY PRODUCER GARTH ACTUALLY SAVED MY LIFE BY SPRAYING THE CENTAUR WITH **AXE** BODY SPRAY!

PARA-NORMA'S NO DUMMY: EVERY TIME SHE MENTIONS A SPONSOR, SHE GETS PAID.

TROPICAL TRIUMPH SAVED MY LIFE??!

Home

YEAH, UM, SO APPARENTLY TROPICAL TRIUMPH SCENTED AXE BODY SPRAY IS LIKE PEPPER SPRAY TO MARTIAN GHOSTS. SO, IF YOU'RE VISITING SOUTHBOROUGH, MAKE SURE YOU HAVE SOME ON YOU.

THIS IS the real deal !!!

ZENAF

How d

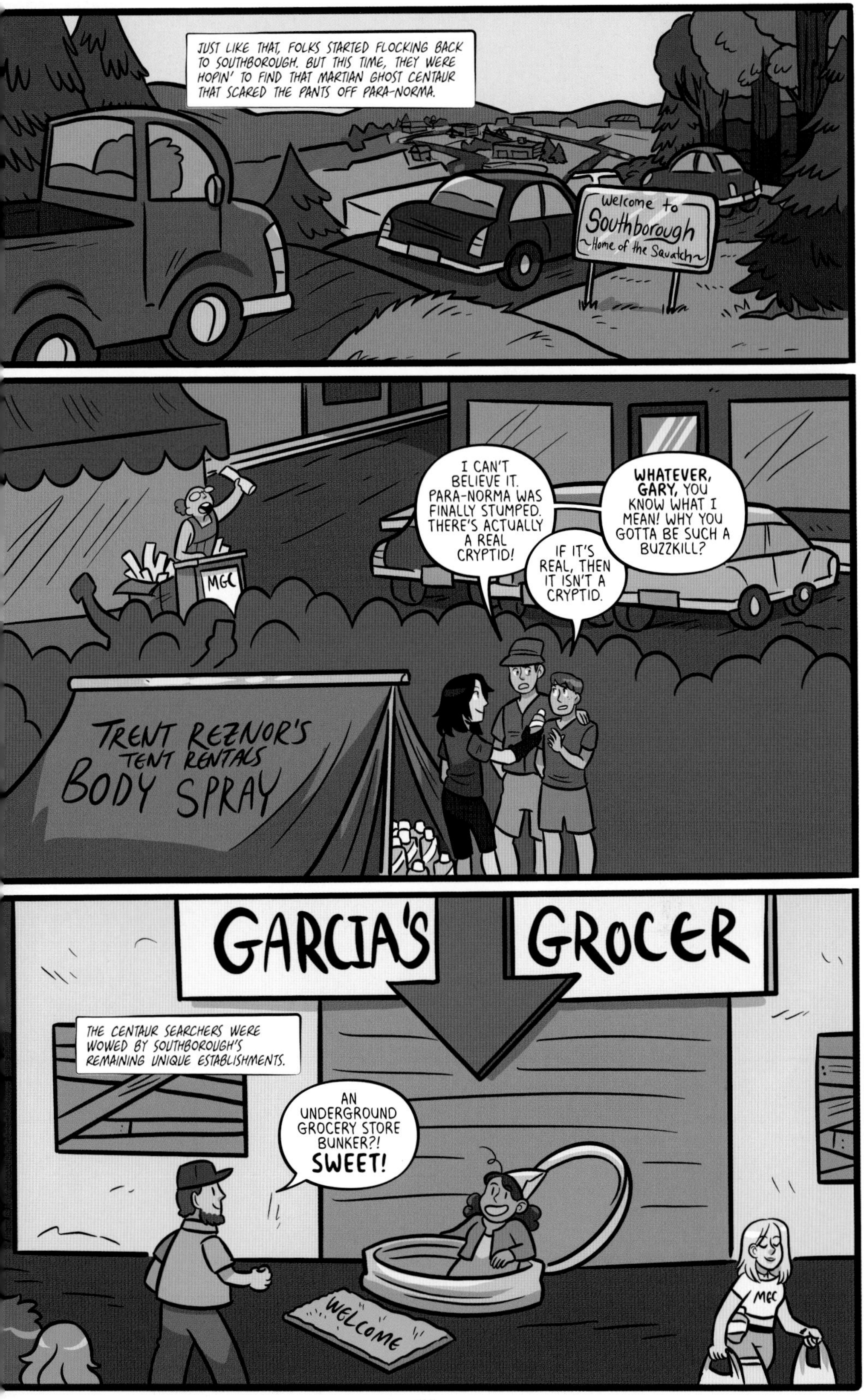
JUST LIKE THAT, FOLKS STARTED FLOCKING BACK TO SOUTHBOROUGH. BUT THIS TIME, THEY WERE HOPIN' TO FIND THAT MARTIAN GHOST CENTAUR THAT SCARED THE PANTS OFF PARA-NORMA.
Welcome to Southborough ~Home of the Squatch~
MGC
I CAN'T BELIEVE IT. PARA-NORMA WAS FINALLY STUMPED. THERE'S ACTUALLY A REAL CRYPTID!
IF IT'S REAL, THEN IT ISN'T A CRYPTID.
WHATEVER, GARY, YOU KNOW WHAT I MEAN! WHY YOU GOTTA BE SUCH A BUZZKILL?
TRENT REZNOR'S TENT RENTALS BODY SPRAY
GARCIA'S GROCER
THE CENTAUR SEARCHERS WERE WOWED BY SOUTHBOROUGH'S REMAINING UNIQUE ESTABLISHMENTS.
AN UNDERGROUND GROCERY STORE BUNKER?! SWEET!
WELCOME
MGC

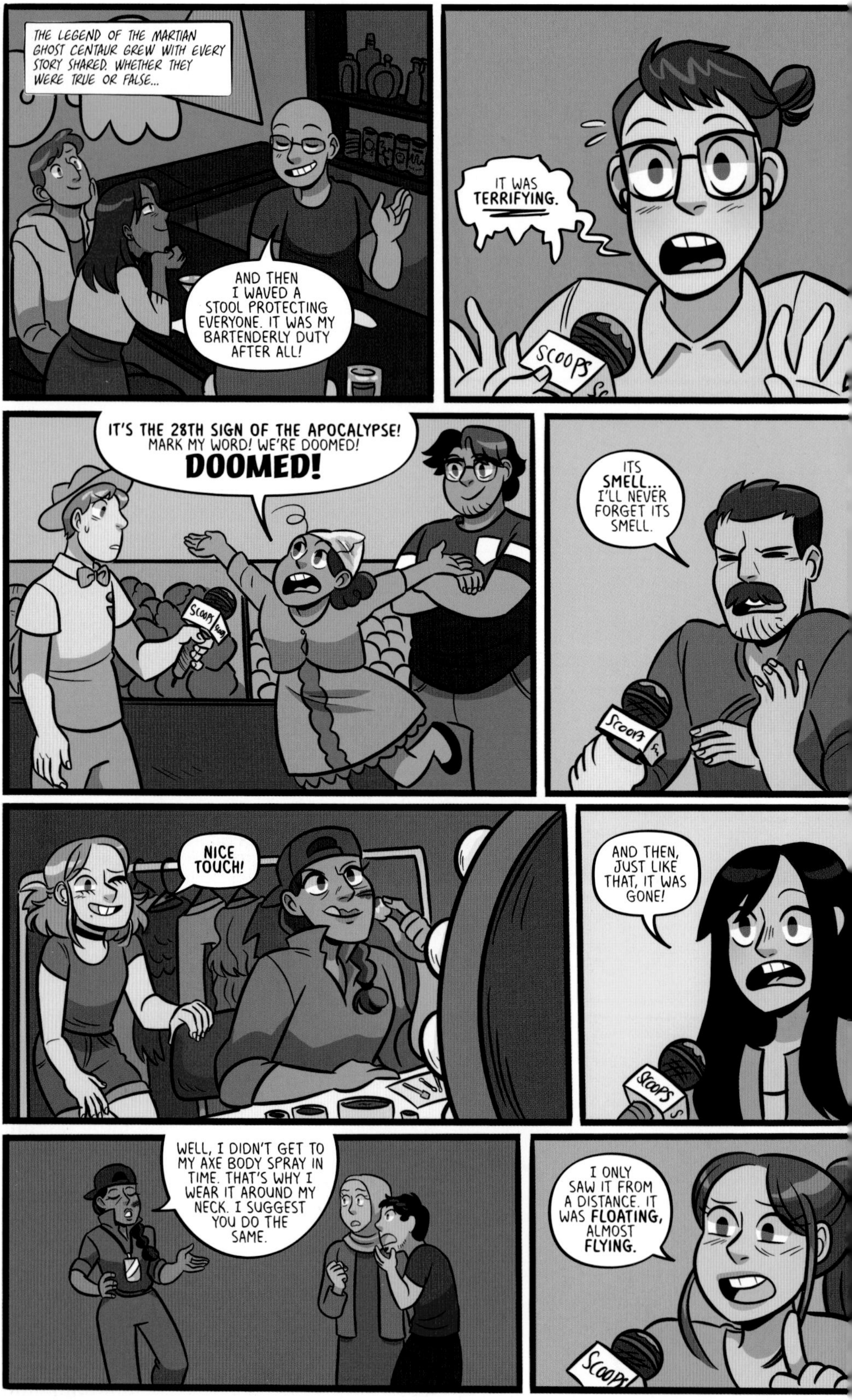
THE LEGEND OF THE MARTIAN GHOST CENTAUR GREW WITH EVERY STORY SHARED. WHETHER THEY WERE TRUE OR FALSE...
AND THEN I WAVED A STOOL PROTECTING EVERYONE. IT WAS MY BARTENDERLY DUTY AFTER ALL!
IT WAS TERRIFYING.
SCOOPS
IT'S THE 28TH SIGN OF THE APOCALYPSE! MARK MY WORD! WE'RE DOOMED! DOOMED!
SCOOPS
ITS SMELL... I'LL NEVER FORGET ITS SMELL.
SCOOPS
NICE TOUCH!
AND THEN, JUST LIKE THAT, IT WAS GONE!
SCOOPS
WELL, I DIDN'T GET TO MY AXE BODY SPRAY IN TIME. THAT'S WHY I WEAR IT AROUND MY NECK. I SUGGEST YOU DO THE SAME.
I ONLY SAW IT FROM A DISTANCE. IT WAS FLOATING, ALMOST FLYING.

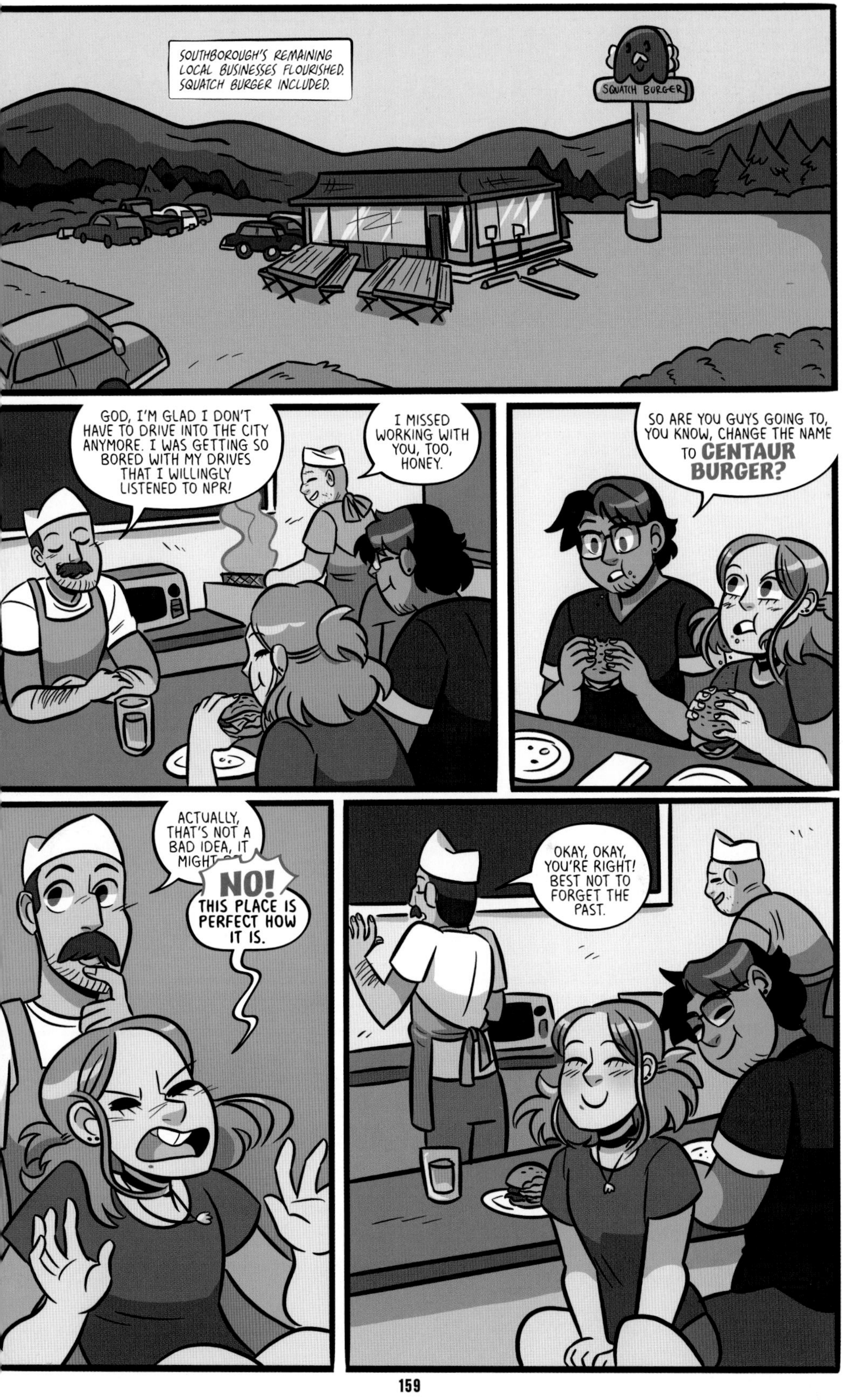
SOUTHBOROUGH'S REMAINING LOCAL BUSINESSES FLOURISHED. SQUATCH BURGER INCLUDED.
SQUATCH BURGER
GOD, I'M GLAD I DON'T HAVE TO DRIVE INTO THE CITY ANYMORE. I WAS GETTING SO BORED WITH MY DRIVES THAT I WILLINGLY LISTENED TO NPR!
I MISSED WORKING WITH YOU, TOO, HONEY.
SO ARE YOU GUYS GOING TO, YOU KNOW, CHANGE THE NAME TO CENTAUR BURGER?
ACTUALLY, THAT'S NOT A BAD IDEA, IT MIGHT—
NO! THIS PLACE IS PERFECT HOW IT IS.
OKAY, OKAY, YOU'RE RIGHT! BEST NOT TO FORGET THE PAST.

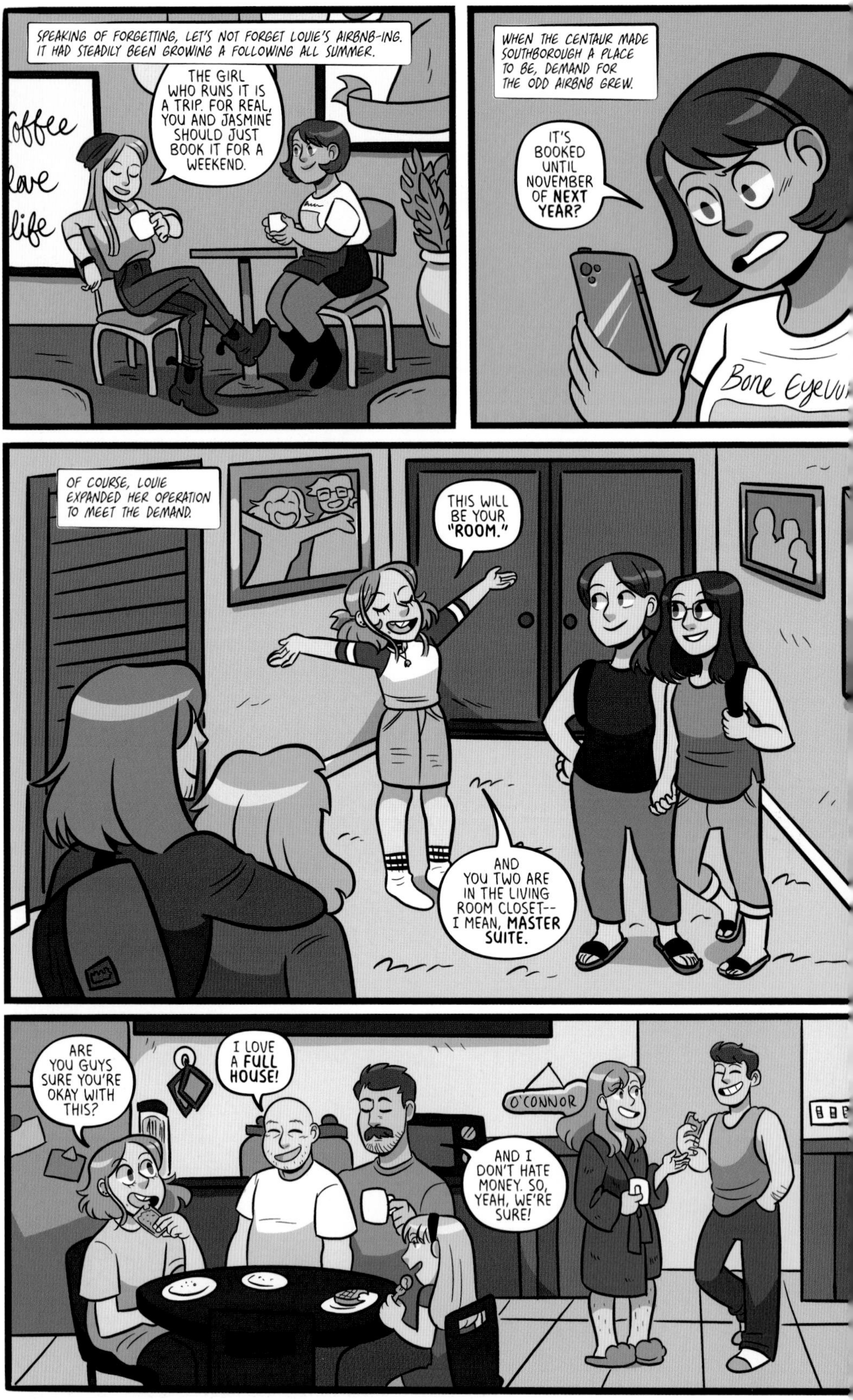
SPEAKING OF FORGETTING, LET'S NOT FORGET LOUIE'S AIRBNB-ING. IT HAD STEADILY BEEN GROWING A FOLLOWING ALL SUMMER.
THE GIRL WHO RUNS IT IS A TRIP. FOR REAL, YOU AND JASMINE SHOULD JUST BOOK IT FOR A WEEKEND.
Coffee love life
WHEN THE CENTAUR MADE SOUTHBOROUGH A PLACE TO BE, DEMAND FOR THE ODD AIRBNB GREW.
IT'S BOOKED UNTIL NOVEMBER OF NEXT YEAR?
OF COURSE, LOUIE EXPANDED HER OPERATION TO MEET THE DEMAND.
THIS WILL BE YOUR "ROOM."
AND YOU TWO ARE IN THE LIVING ROOM CLOSET-- I MEAN, MASTER SUITE.
ARE YOU GUYS SURE YOU'RE OKAY WITH THIS?
I LOVE A FULL HOUSE!
O'CONNOR
AND I DON'T HATE MONEY. SO, YEAH, WE'RE SURE!

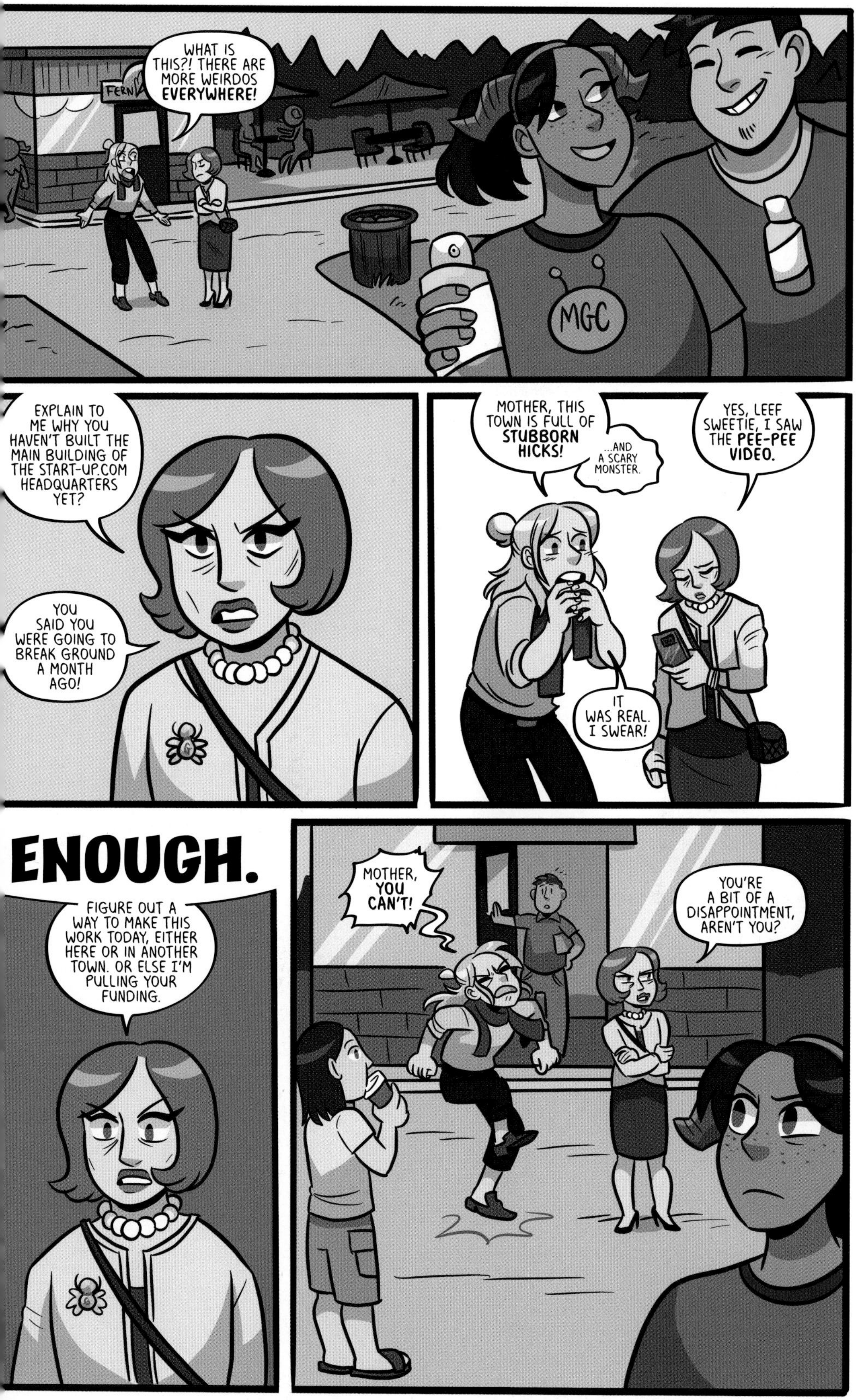

WHAT IS THIS?! THERE ARE MORE WEIRDOS EVERYWHERE!
FERN
MGC
EXPLAIN TO ME WHY YOU HAVEN'T BUILT THE MAIN BUILDING OF THE START-UP.COM HEADQUARTERS YET?
YOU SAID YOU WERE GOING TO BREAK GROUND A MONTH AGO!
MOTHER, THIS TOWN IS FULL OF STUBBORN HICKS!
...AND A SCARY MONSTER.
YES, LEEF SWEETIE, I SAW THE PEE-PEE VIDEO.
IT WAS REAL. I SWEAR!
ENOUGH.
FIGURE OUT A WAY TO MAKE THIS WORK TODAY, EITHER HERE OR IN ANOTHER TOWN. OR ELSE I'M PULLING YOUR FUNDING.
MOTHER, YOU CAN'T!
YOU'RE A BIT OF A DISAPPOINTMENT, AREN'T YOU?

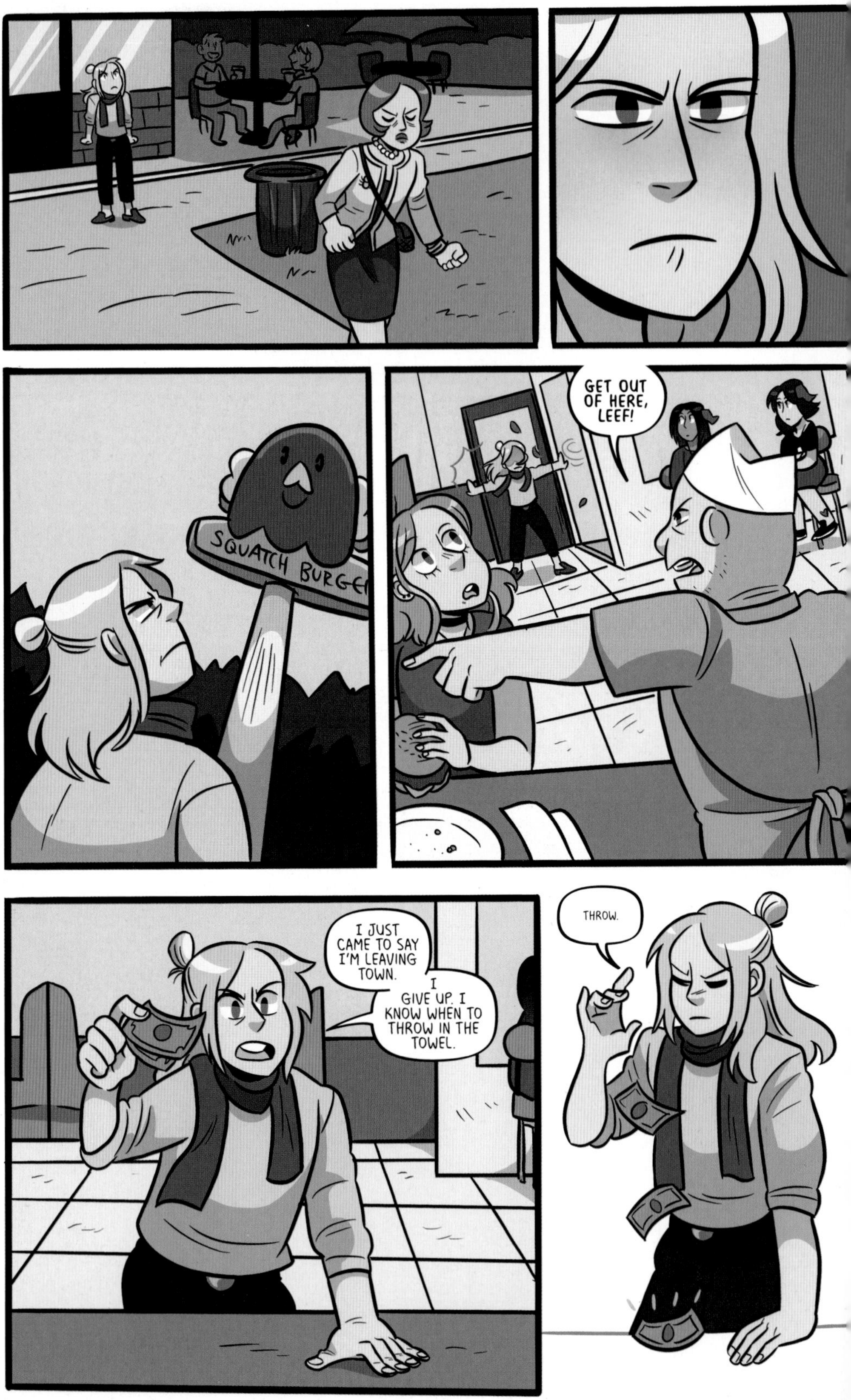
SQUATCH BURGE
GET OUT OF HERE, LEEF!
I JUST CAME TO SAY I'M LEAVING TOWN.
I GIVE UP. I KNOW WHEN TO THROW IN THE TOWEL.
THROW.

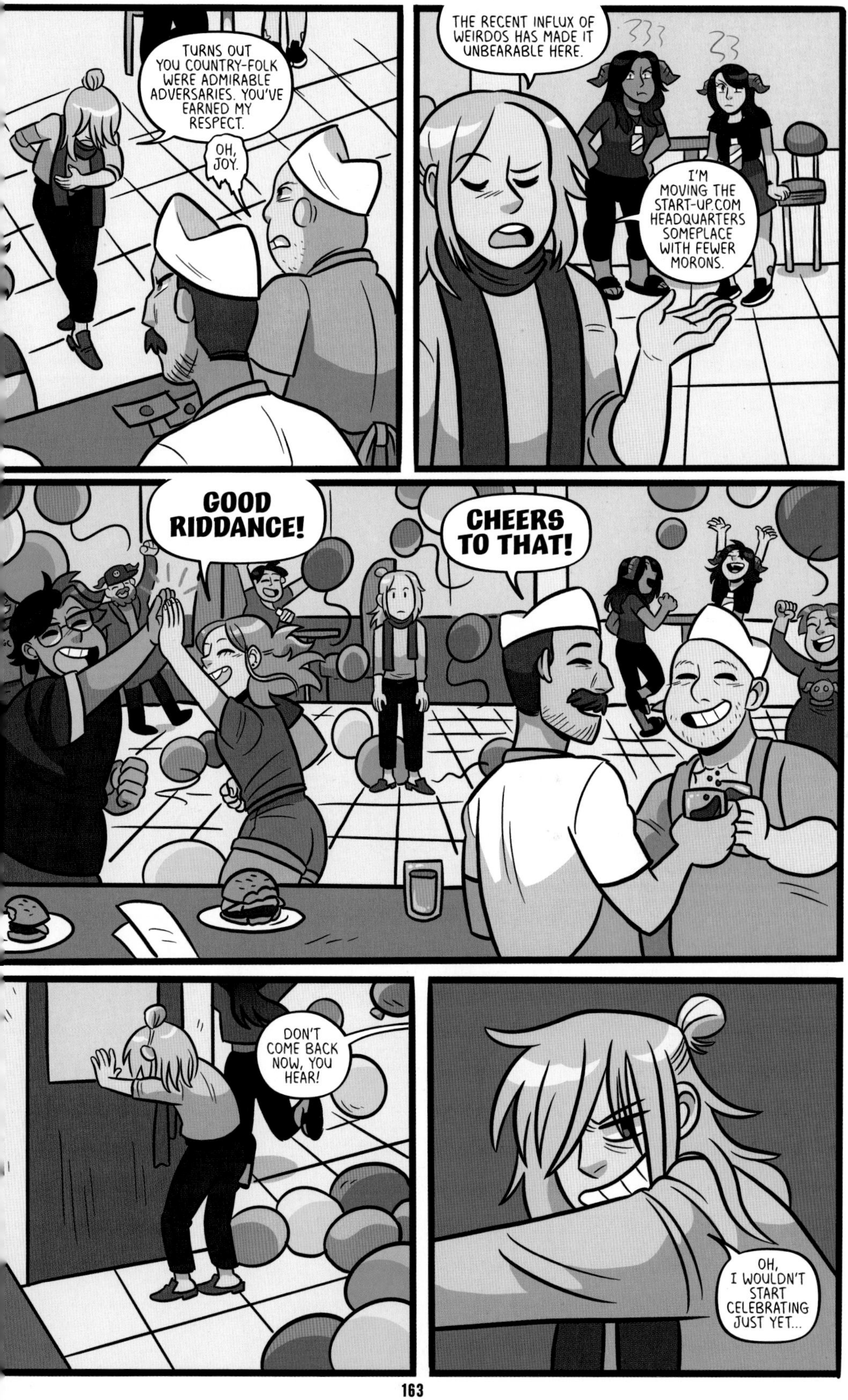
TURNS OUT YOU COUNTRY-FOLK WERE ADMIRABLE ADVERSARIES. YOU'VE EARNED MY RESPECT.
OH, JOY.
THE RECENT INFLUX OF WEIRDOS HAS MADE IT UNBEARABLE HERE.
I'M MOVING THE START-UP.COM HEADQUARTERS SOMEPLACE WITH FEWER MORONS.
GOOD RIDDANCE!
CHEERS TO THAT!
DON'T COME BACK NOW, YOU HEAR!
OH, I WOULDN'T START CELEBRATING JUST YET...

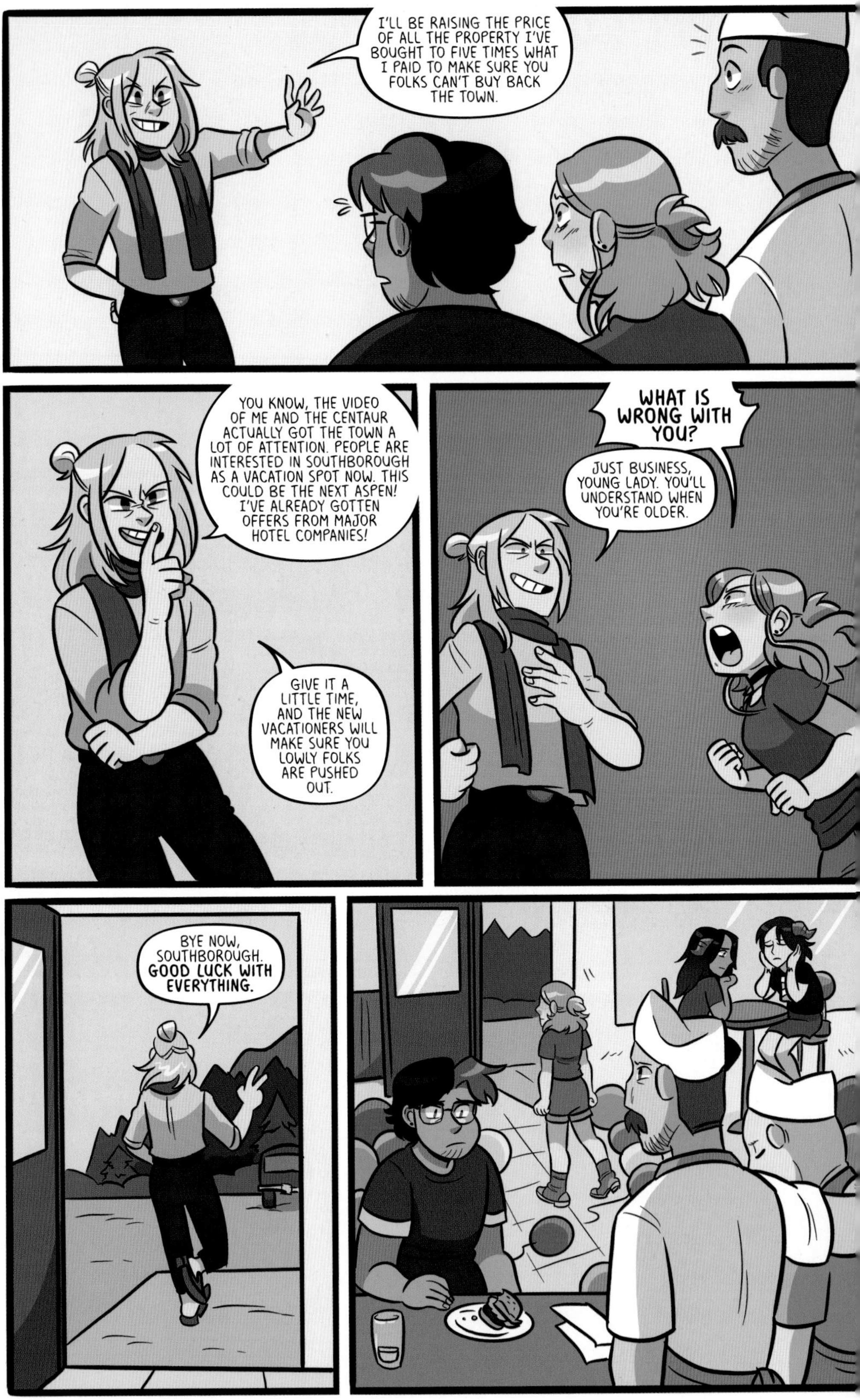
I'LL BE RAISING THE PRICE OF ALL THE PROPERTY I'VE BOUGHT TO FIVE TIMES WHAT I PAID TO MAKE SURE YOU FOLKS CAN'T BUY BACK THE TOWN.
YOU KNOW, THE VIDEO OF ME AND THE CENTAUR ACTUALLY GOT THE TOWN A LOT OF ATTENTION. PEOPLE ARE INTERESTED IN SOUTHBOROUGH AS A VACATION SPOT NOW. THIS COULD BE THE NEXT ASPEN! I'VE ALREADY GOTTEN OFFERS FROM MAJOR HOTEL COMPANIES!
GIVE IT A LITTLE TIME, AND THE NEW VACATIONERS WILL MAKE SURE YOU LOWLY FOLKS ARE PUSHED OUT.
WHAT IS WRONG WITH YOU?
JUST BUSINESS, YOUNG LADY. YOU'LL UNDERSTAND WHEN YOU'RE OLDER.
BYE NOW, SOUTHBOROUGH. GOOD LUCK WITH EVERYTHING.

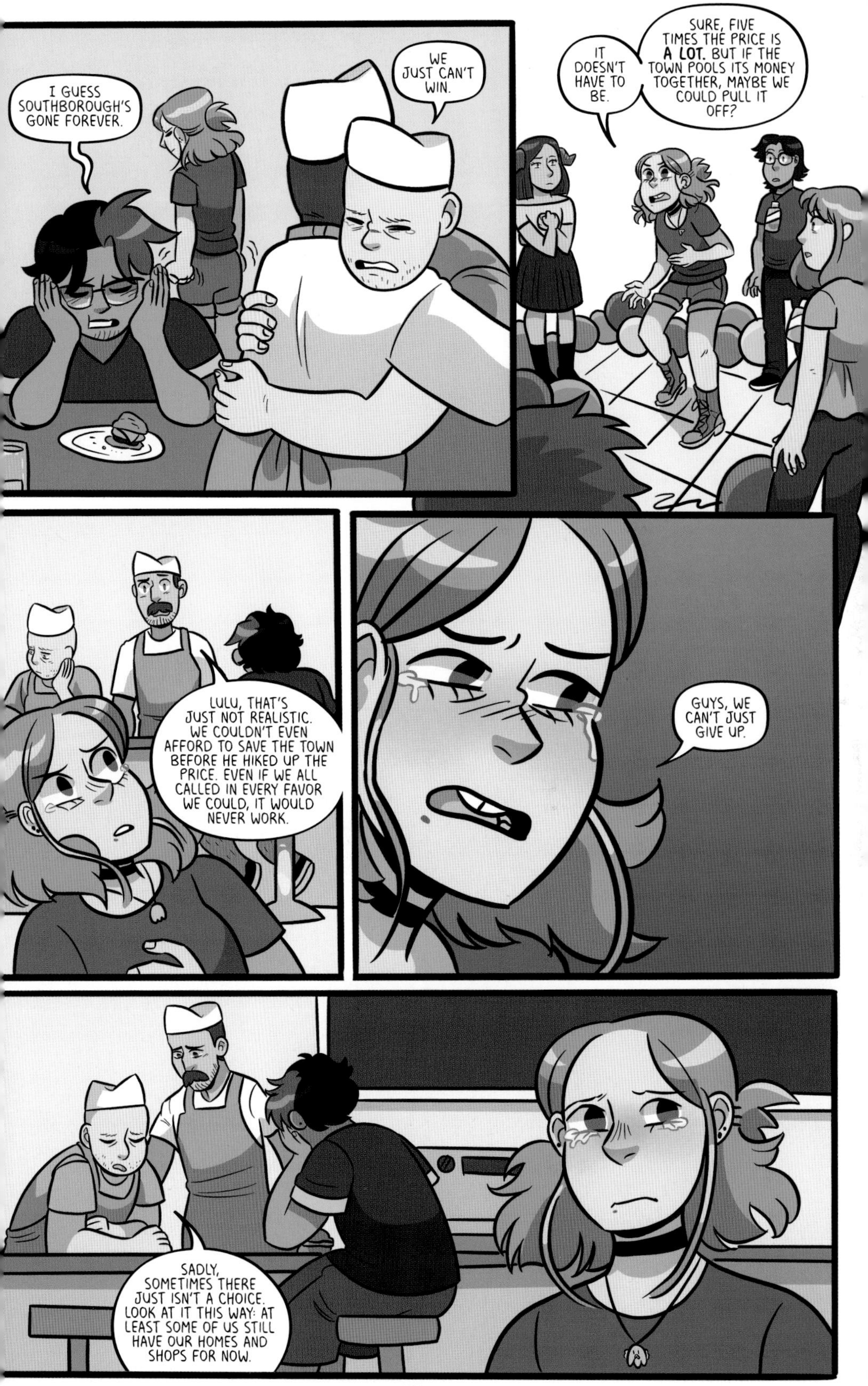

I GUESS SOUTHBOROUGH'S GONE FOREVER.
WE JUST CAN'T WIN.
IT DOESN'T HAVE TO BE.
SURE, FIVE TIMES THE PRICE IS **A LOT.** BUT IF THE TOWN POOLS ITS MONEY TOGETHER, MAYBE WE COULD PULL IT OFF?
LULU, THAT'S JUST NOT REALISTIC. WE COULDN'T EVEN AFFORD TO SAVE THE TOWN BEFORE HE HIKED UP THE PRICE. EVEN IF WE ALL CALLED IN EVERY FAVOR WE COULD, IT WOULD NEVER WORK.
GUYS, WE CAN'T JUST GIVE UP.
SADLY, SOMETIMES THERE JUST ISN'T A CHOICE. LOOK AT IT THIS WAY: AT LEAST SOME OF US STILL HAVE OUR HOMES AND SHOPS FOR NOW.

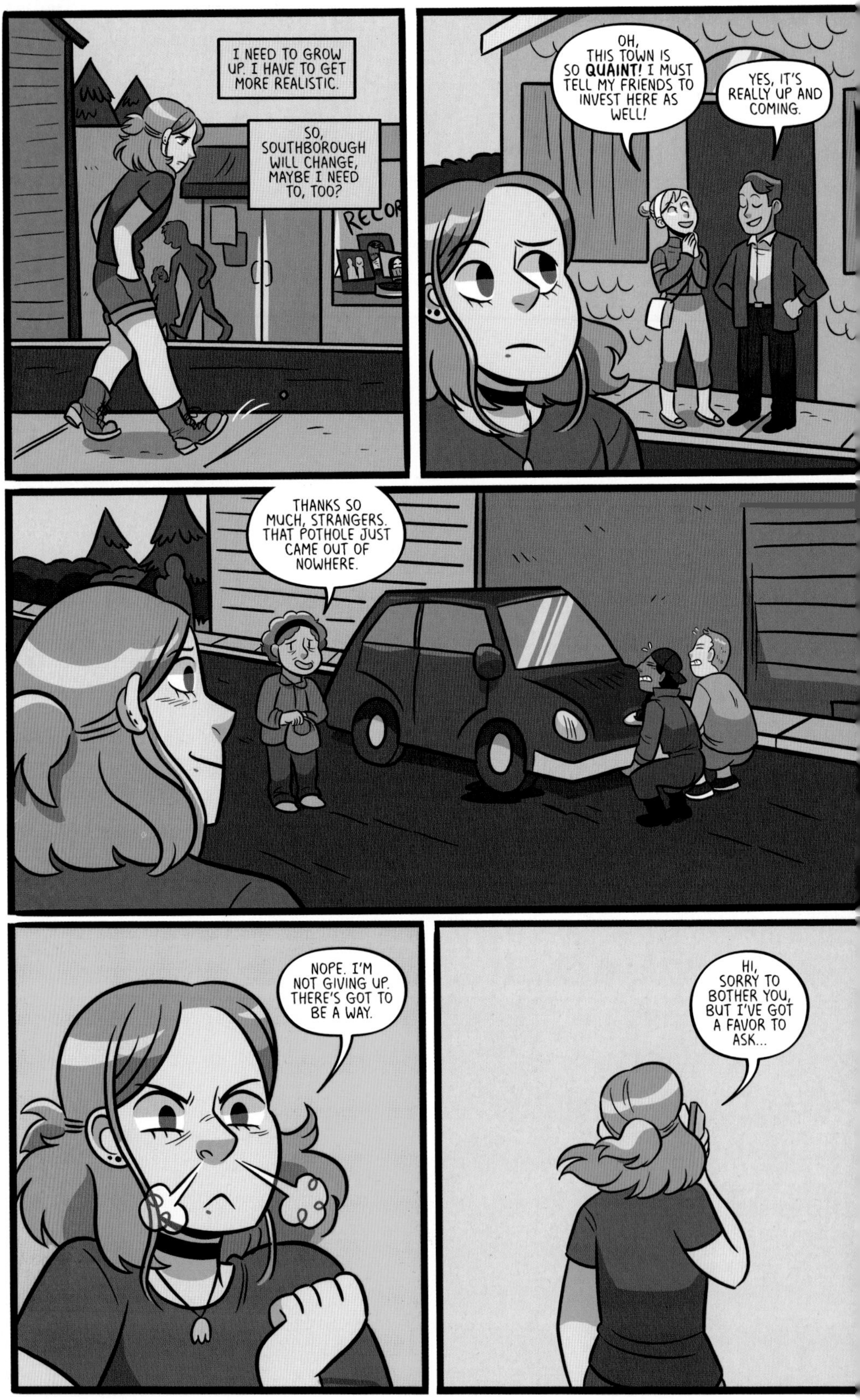
I NEED TO GROW UP. I HAVE TO GET MORE REALISTIC.
SO, SOUTHBOROUGH WILL CHANGE, MAYBE I NEED TO, TOO?
RECOR
OH, THIS TOWN IS SO **QUAINT!** I MUST TELL MY FRIENDS TO INVEST HERE AS WELL!
YES, IT'S REALLY UP AND COMING.
THANKS SO MUCH, STRANGERS. THAT POTHOLE JUST CAME OUT OF NOWHERE.
NOPE. I'M NOT GIVING UP. THERE'S GOT TO BE A WAY.
HI, SORRY TO BOTHER YOU, BUT I'VE GOT A FAVOR TO ASK...

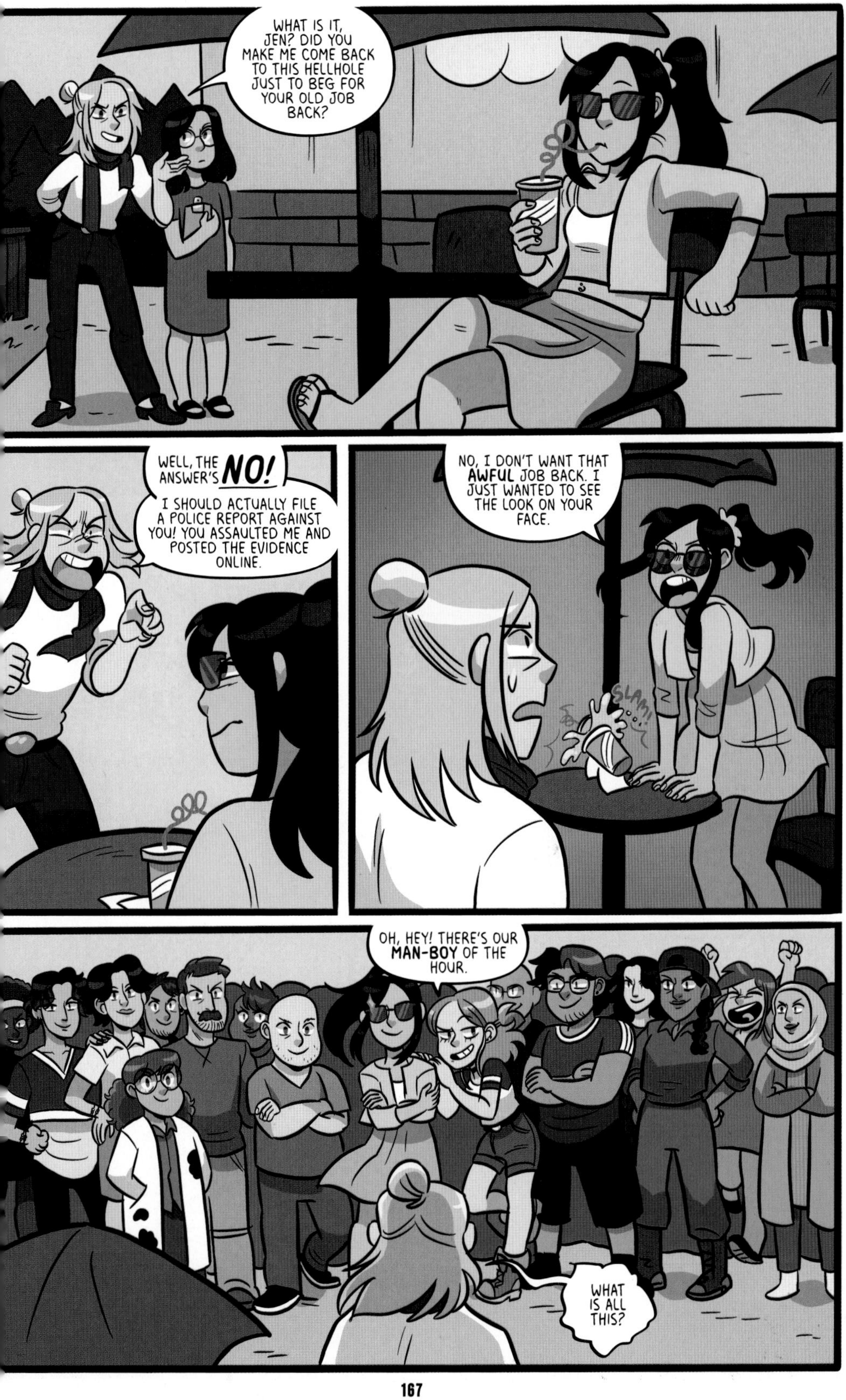
WHAT IS IT, JEN? DID YOU MAKE ME COME BACK TO THIS HELLHOLE JUST TO BEG FOR YOUR OLD JOB BACK?
WELL, THE ANSWER'S NO!
I SHOULD ACTUALLY FILE A POLICE REPORT AGAINST YOU! YOU ASSAULTED ME AND POSTED THE EVIDENCE ONLINE.
NO, I DON'T WANT THAT AWFUL JOB BACK. I JUST WANTED TO SEE THE LOOK ON YOUR FACE.
SLAM!
OH, HEY! THERE'S OUR MAN-BOY OF THE HOUR.
WHAT IS ALL THIS?

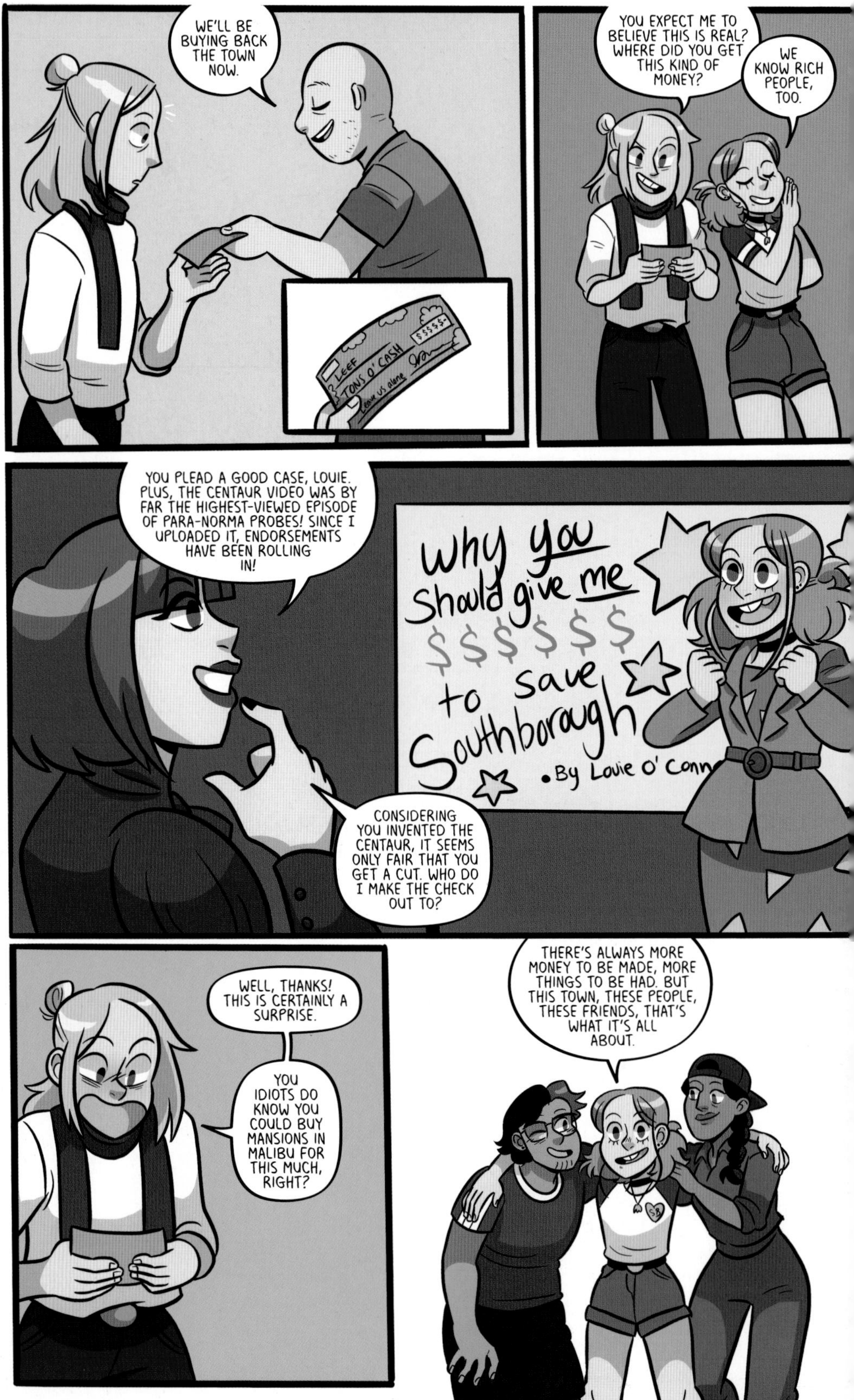
WE'LL BE BUYING BACK THE TOWN NOW.
LEEF
TONS O' CASH
leave us alone
YOU EXPECT ME TO BELIEVE THIS IS REAL? WHERE DID YOU GET THIS KIND OF MONEY?
WE KNOW RICH PEOPLE, TOO.
YOU PLEAD A GOOD CASE, LOUIE. PLUS, THE CENTAUR VIDEO WAS BY FAR THE HIGHEST-VIEWED EPISODE OF PARA-NORMA PROBES! SINCE I UPLOADED IT, ENDORSEMENTS HAVE BEEN ROLLING IN!
Why you Should give me $$$$$$ to save Southborough
•By Louie O' Conn
CONSIDERING YOU INVENTED THE CENTAUR, IT SEEMS ONLY FAIR THAT YOU GET A CUT. WHO DO I MAKE THE CHECK OUT TO?
WELL, THANKS! THIS IS CERTAINLY A SURPRISE.
YOU IDIOTS DO KNOW YOU COULD BUY MANSIONS IN MALIBU FOR THIS MUCH, RIGHT?
THERE'S ALWAYS MORE MONEY TO BE MADE, MORE THINGS TO BE HAD. BUT THIS TOWN, THESE PEOPLE, THESE FRIENDS, THAT'S WHAT IT'S ALL ABOUT.

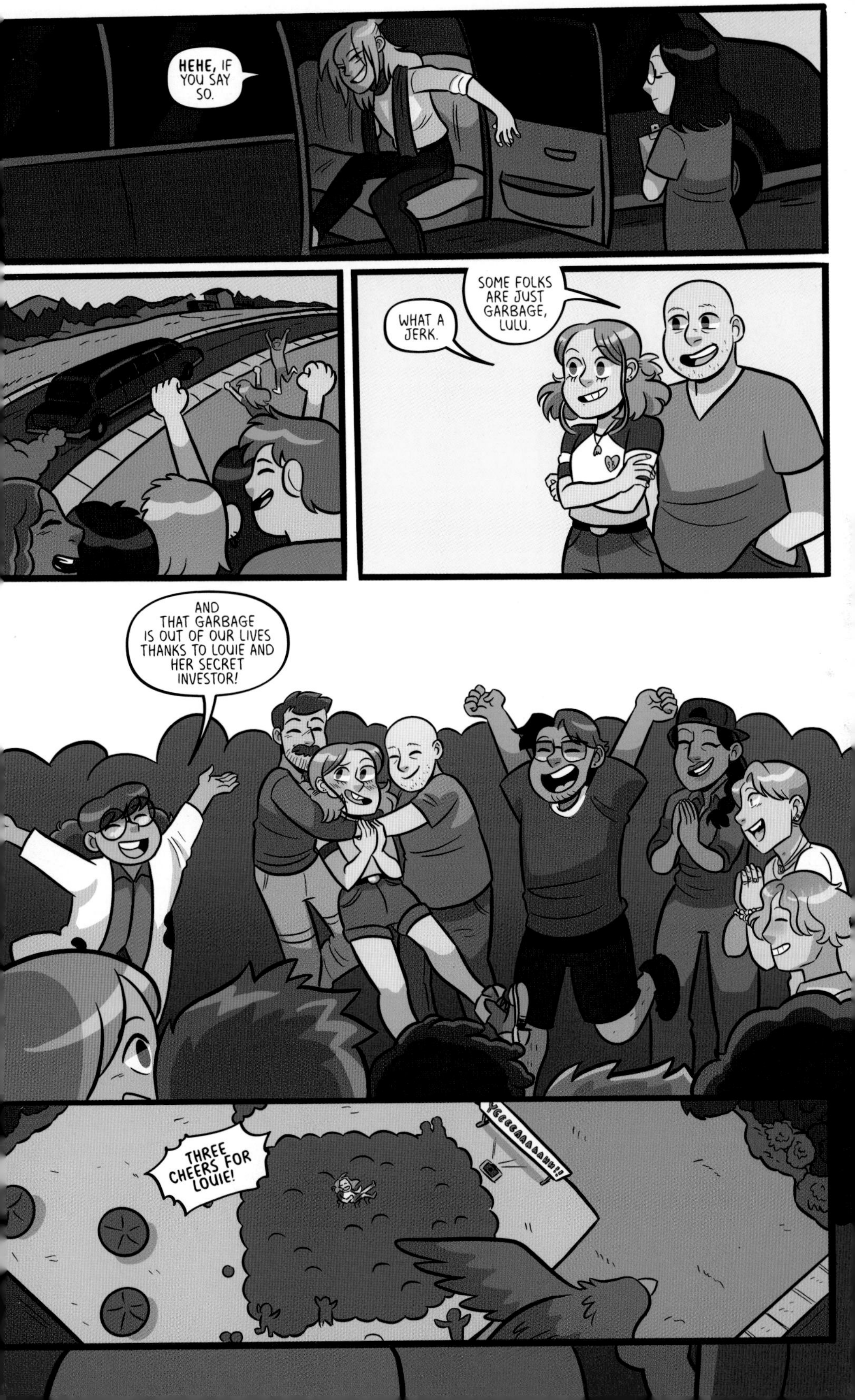
HEHE, IF YOU SAY SO.
WHAT A JERK.
SOME FOLKS ARE JUST GARBAGE, LULU.
AND THAT GARBAGE IS OUT OF OUR LIVES THANKS TO LOUIE AND HER SECRET INVESTOR!
THREE CHEERS FOR LOUIE!
YEEEEAAAAAAHH!!

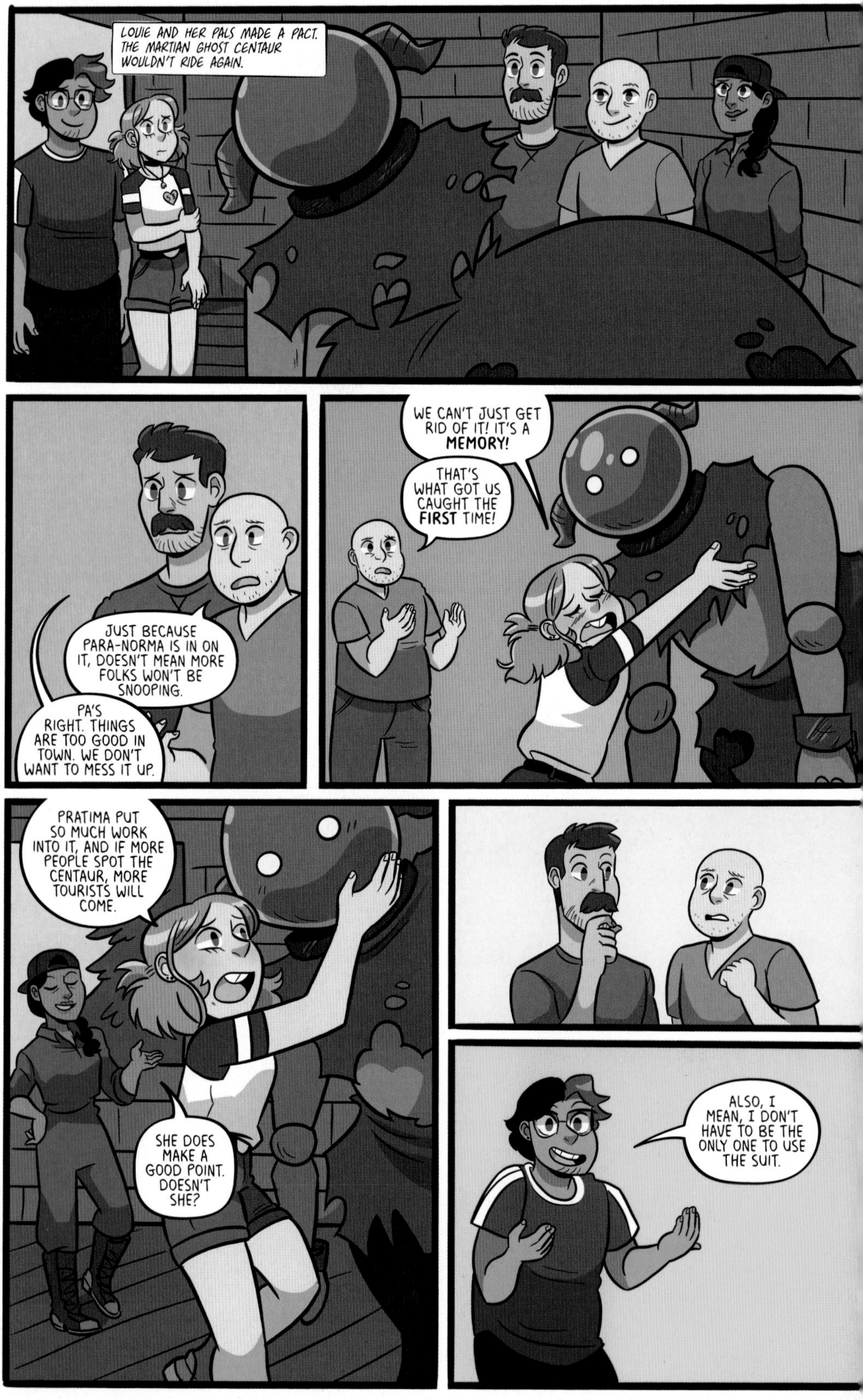
LOUIE AND HER PALS MADE A PACT. THE MARTIAN GHOST CENTAUR WOULDN'T RIDE AGAIN.
JUST BECAUSE PARA-NORMA IS IN ON IT, DOESN'T MEAN MORE FOLKS WON'T BE SNOOPING.
PA'S RIGHT. THINGS ARE TOO GOOD IN TOWN. WE DON'T WANT TO MESS IT UP.
WE CAN'T JUST GET RID OF IT! IT'S A MEMORY!
THAT'S WHAT GOT US CAUGHT THE FIRST TIME!
PRATIMA PUT SO MUCH WORK INTO IT, AND IF MORE PEOPLE SPOT THE CENTAUR, MORE TOURISTS WILL COME.
SHE DOES MAKE A GOOD POINT. DOESN'T SHE?
ALSO, I MEAN, I DON'T HAVE TO BE THE ONLY ONE TO USE THE SUIT.

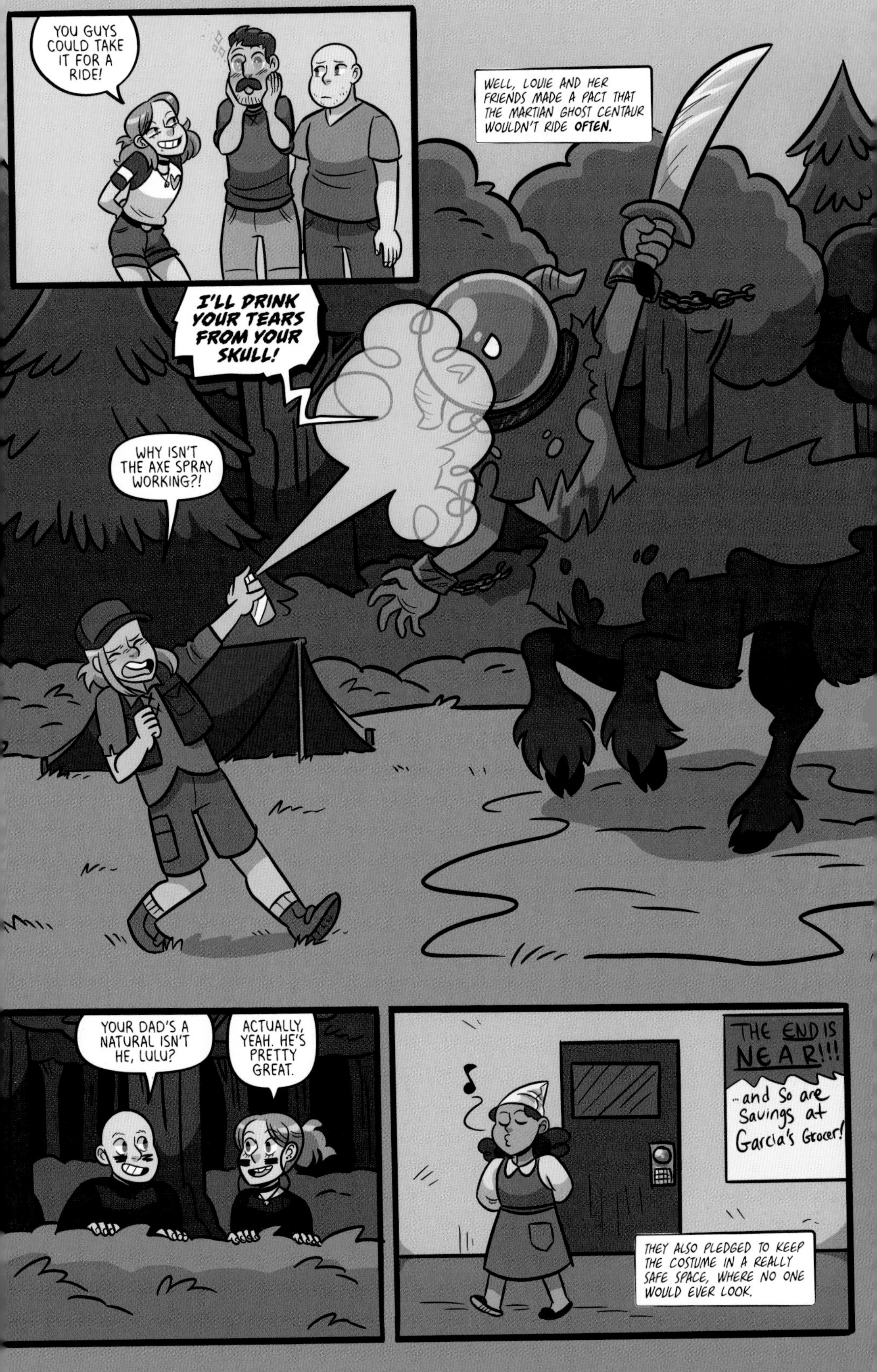
YOU GUYS COULD TAKE IT FOR A RIDE!
WELL, LOUIE AND HER FRIENDS MADE A PACT THAT THE MARTIAN GHOST CENTAUR WOULDN'T RIDE **OFTEN.**
I'LL DRINK YOUR TEARS FROM YOUR SKULL!
WHY ISN'T THE AXE SPRAY WORKING?!
YOUR DAD'S A NATURAL ISN'T HE, LULU?
ACTUALLY, YEAH. HE'S PRETTY GREAT.
THE END IS NEAR!!!
...and So are Savings at Garcia's Grocer!
THEY ALSO PLEDGED TO KEEP THE COSTUME IN A REALLY SAFE SPACE, WHERE NO ONE WOULD EVER LOOK.

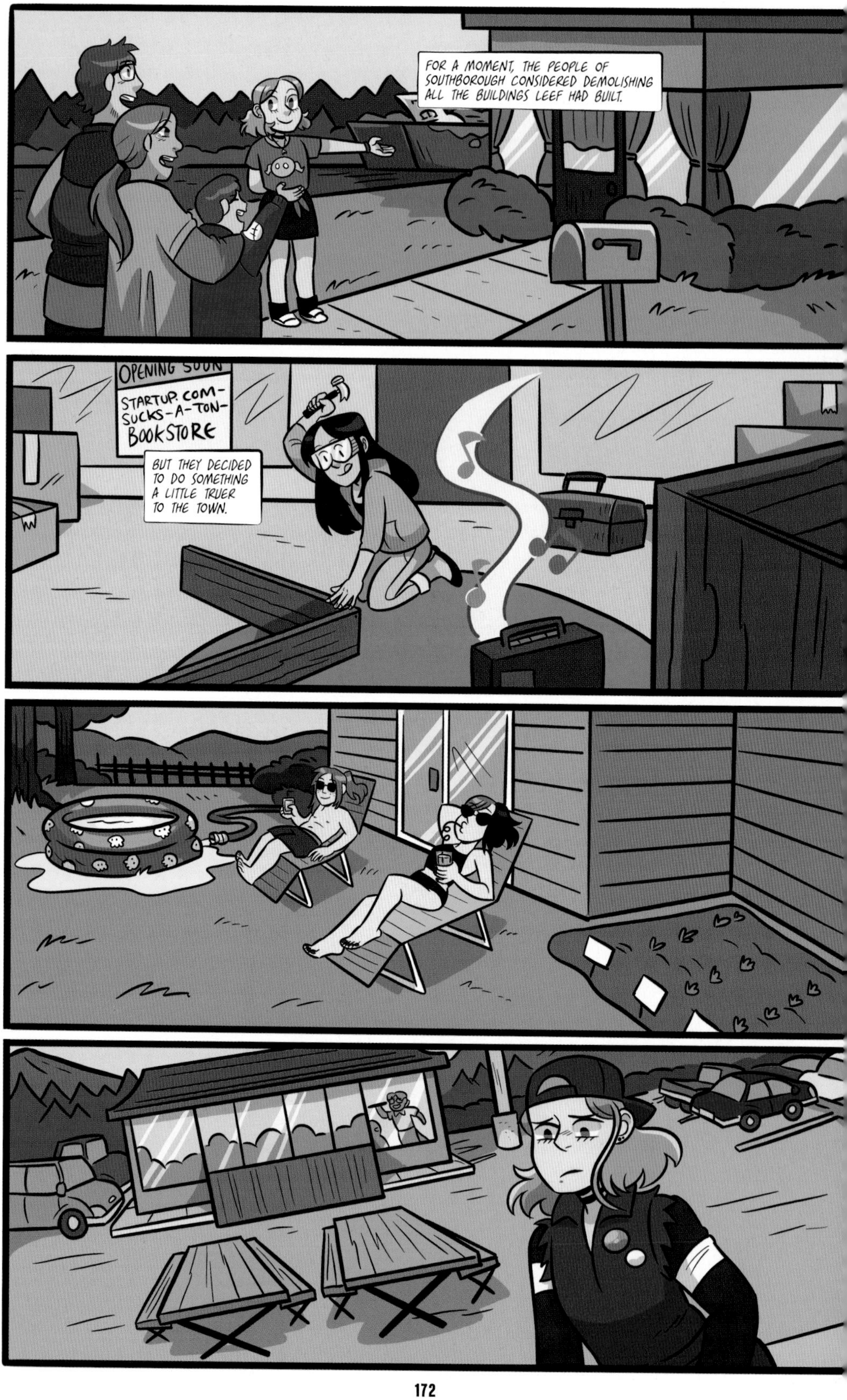
FOR A MOMENT, THE PEOPLE OF SOUTHBOROUGH CONSIDERED DEMOLISHING ALL THE BUILDINGS LEEF HAD BUILT.
OPENING SOON
STARTUP.COM-SUCKS-A-TON-BOOKSTORE
BUT THEY DECIDED TO DO SOMETHING A LITTLE TRUER TO THE TOWN.

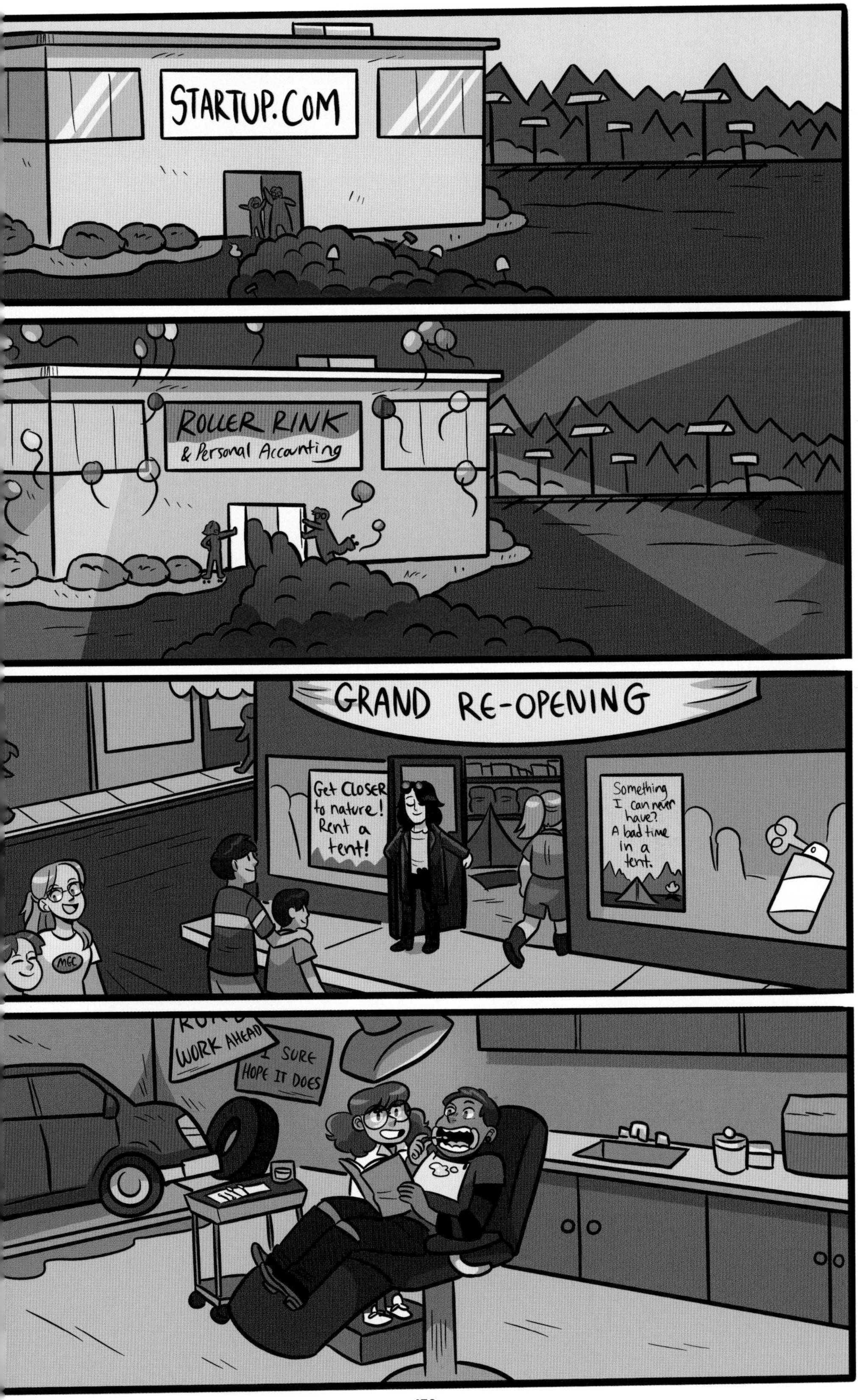
STARTUP.COM
ROLLER RINK
& Personal Accounting
GRAND RE-OPENING
Get CLOSER to nature! Rent a tent!
Something I can never have? A bad time in a tent.
MGC
WORK AHEAD
I SURE HOPE IT DOES

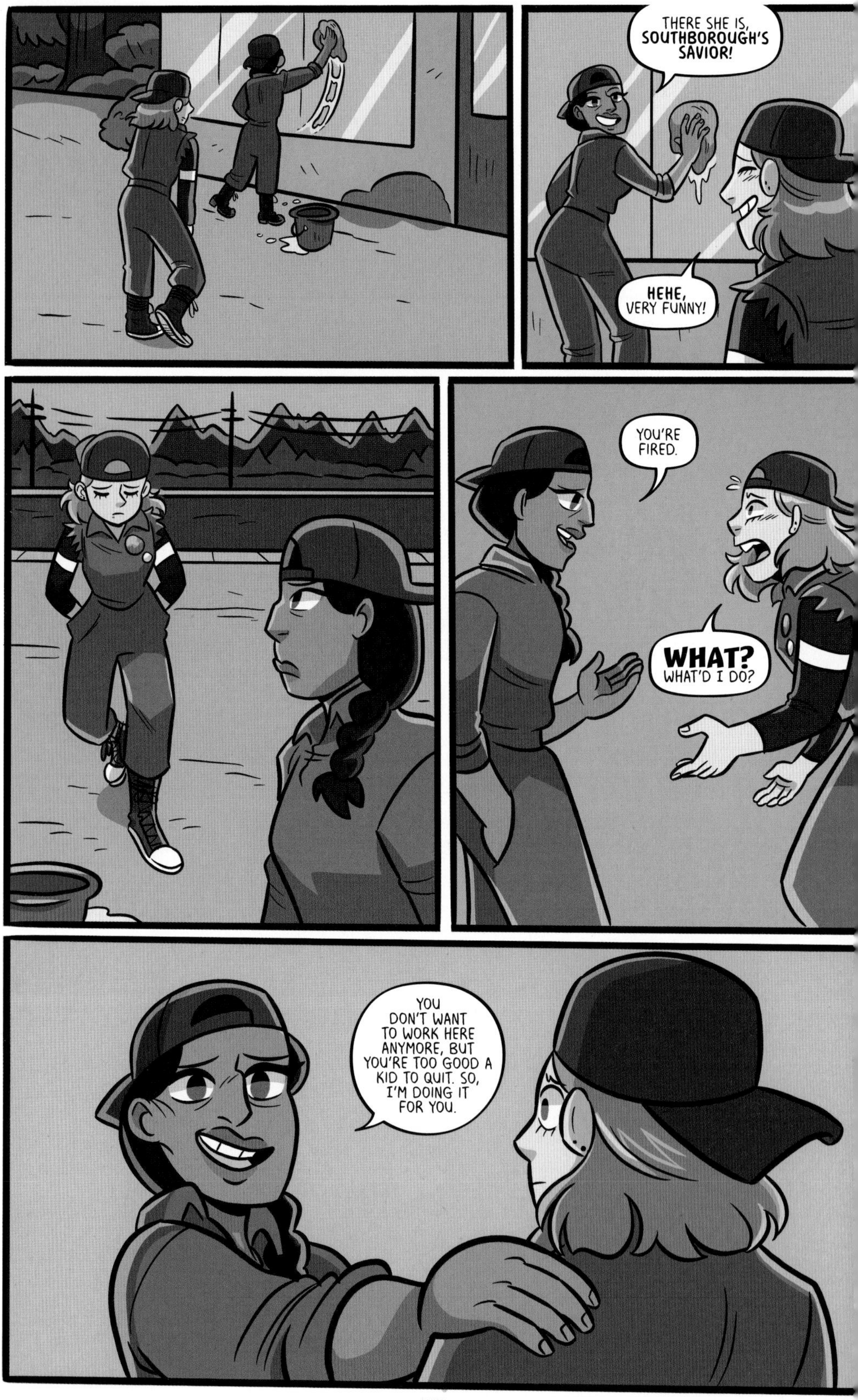
THERE SHE IS, SOUTHBOROUGH'S SAVIOR!
HEHE, VERY FUNNY!
YOU'RE FIRED.
WHAT? WHAT'D I DO?
YOU DON'T WANT TO WORK HERE ANYMORE, BUT YOU'RE TOO GOOD A KID TO QUIT. SO, I'M DOING IT FOR YOU.

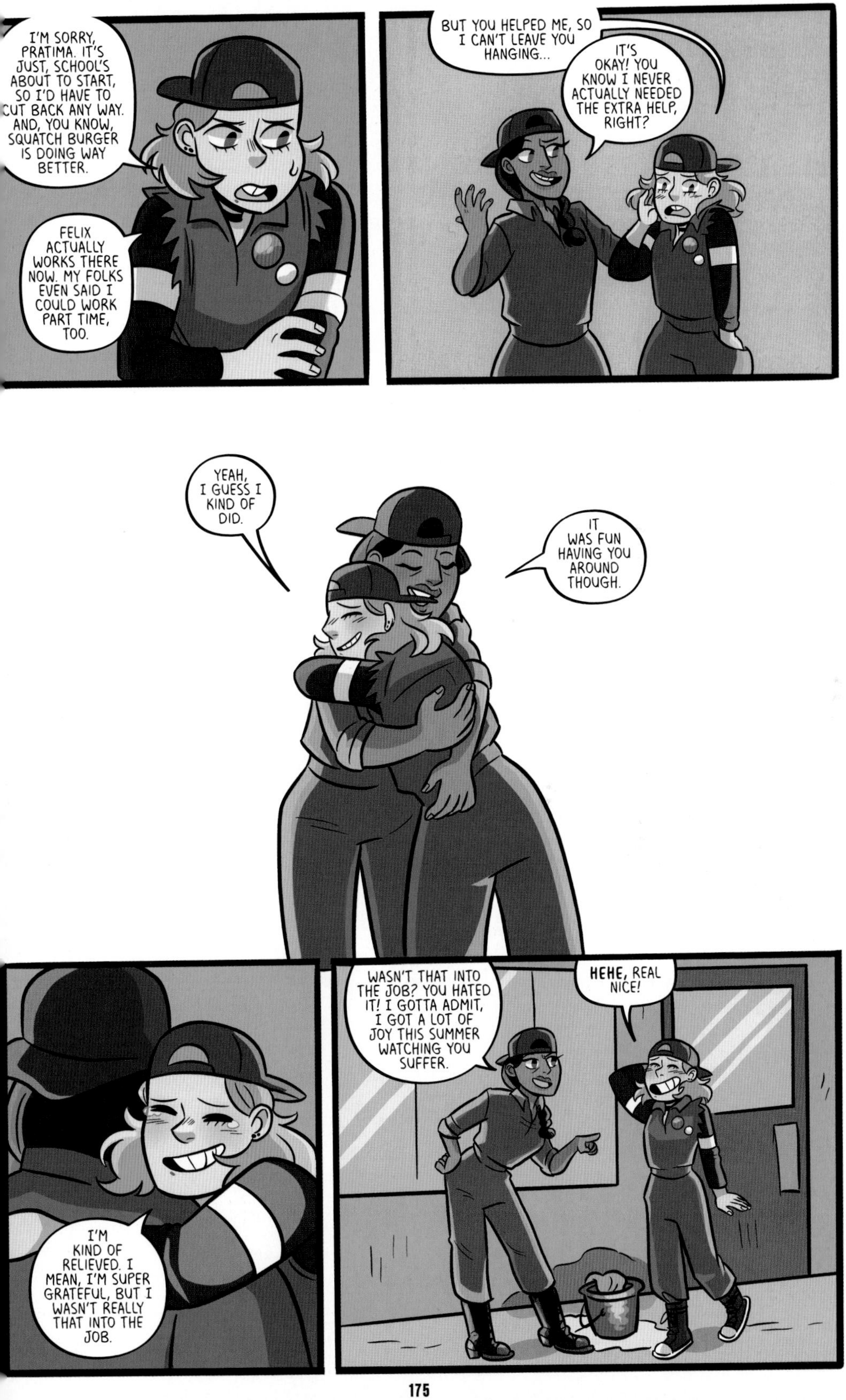
I'M SORRY, PRATIMA. IT'S JUST, SCHOOL'S ABOUT TO START, SO I'D HAVE TO CUT BACK ANY WAY. AND, YOU KNOW, SQUATCH BURGER IS DOING WAY BETTER.
FELIX ACTUALLY WORKS THERE NOW. MY FOLKS EVEN SAID I COULD WORK PART TIME, TOO.
BUT YOU HELPED ME, SO I CAN'T LEAVE YOU HANGING...
IT'S OKAY! YOU KNOW I NEVER ACTUALLY NEEDED THE EXTRA HELP, RIGHT?
YEAH, I GUESS I KIND OF DID.
IT WAS FUN HAVING YOU AROUND THOUGH.
I'M KIND OF RELIEVED. I MEAN, I'M SUPER GRATEFUL, BUT I WASN'T REALLY THAT INTO THE JOB.
WASN'T THAT INTO THE JOB? YOU HATED IT! I GOTTA ADMIT, I GOT A LOT OF JOY THIS SUMMER WATCHING YOU SUFFER.
HEHE, REAL NICE!

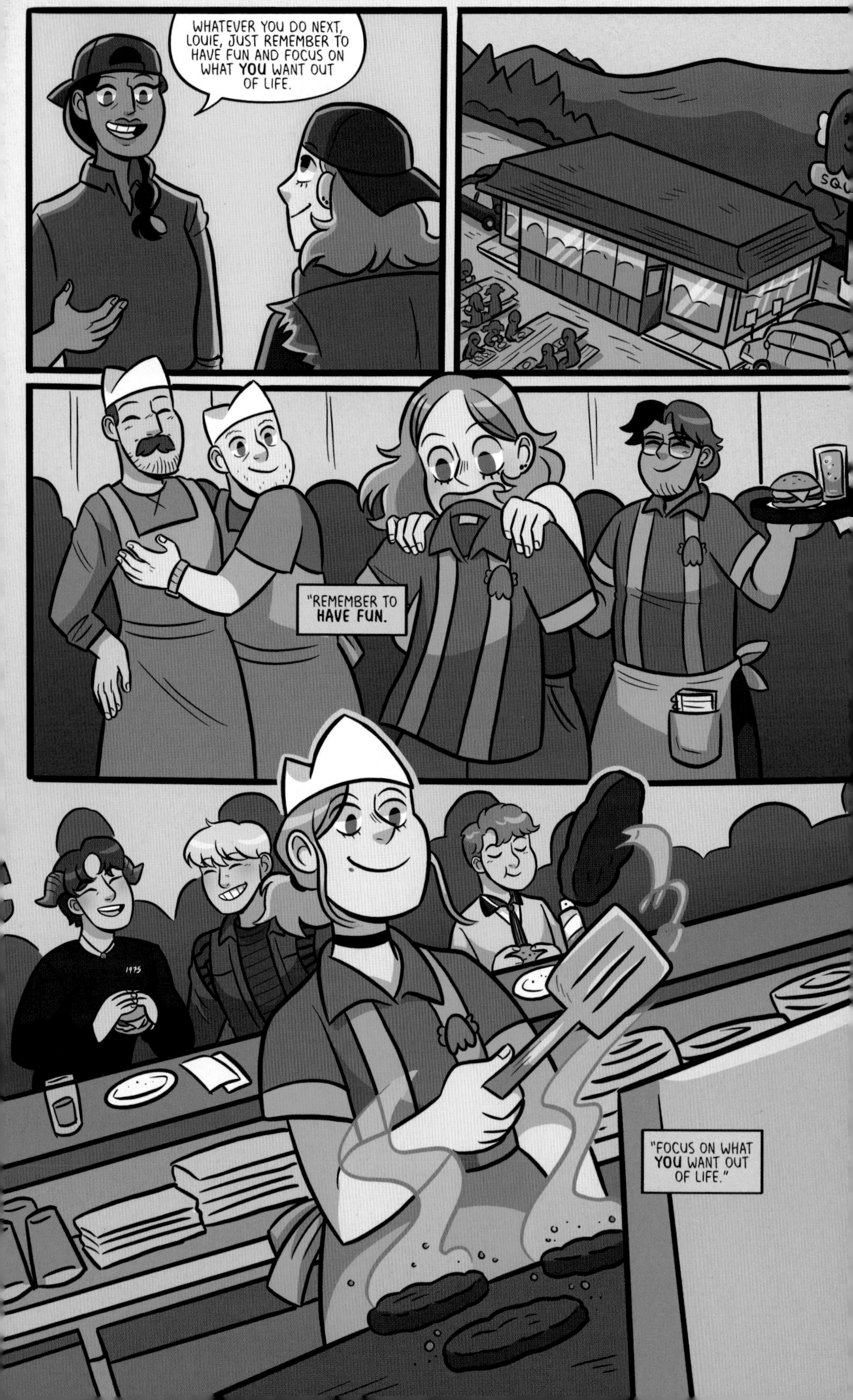
WHATEVER YOU DO NEXT, LOUIE, JUST REMEMBER TO HAVE FUN AND FOCUS ON WHAT YOU WANT OUT OF LIFE.
"REMEMBER TO HAVE FUN.
"FOCUS ON WHAT YOU WANT OUT OF LIFE."

CHAPTER 7

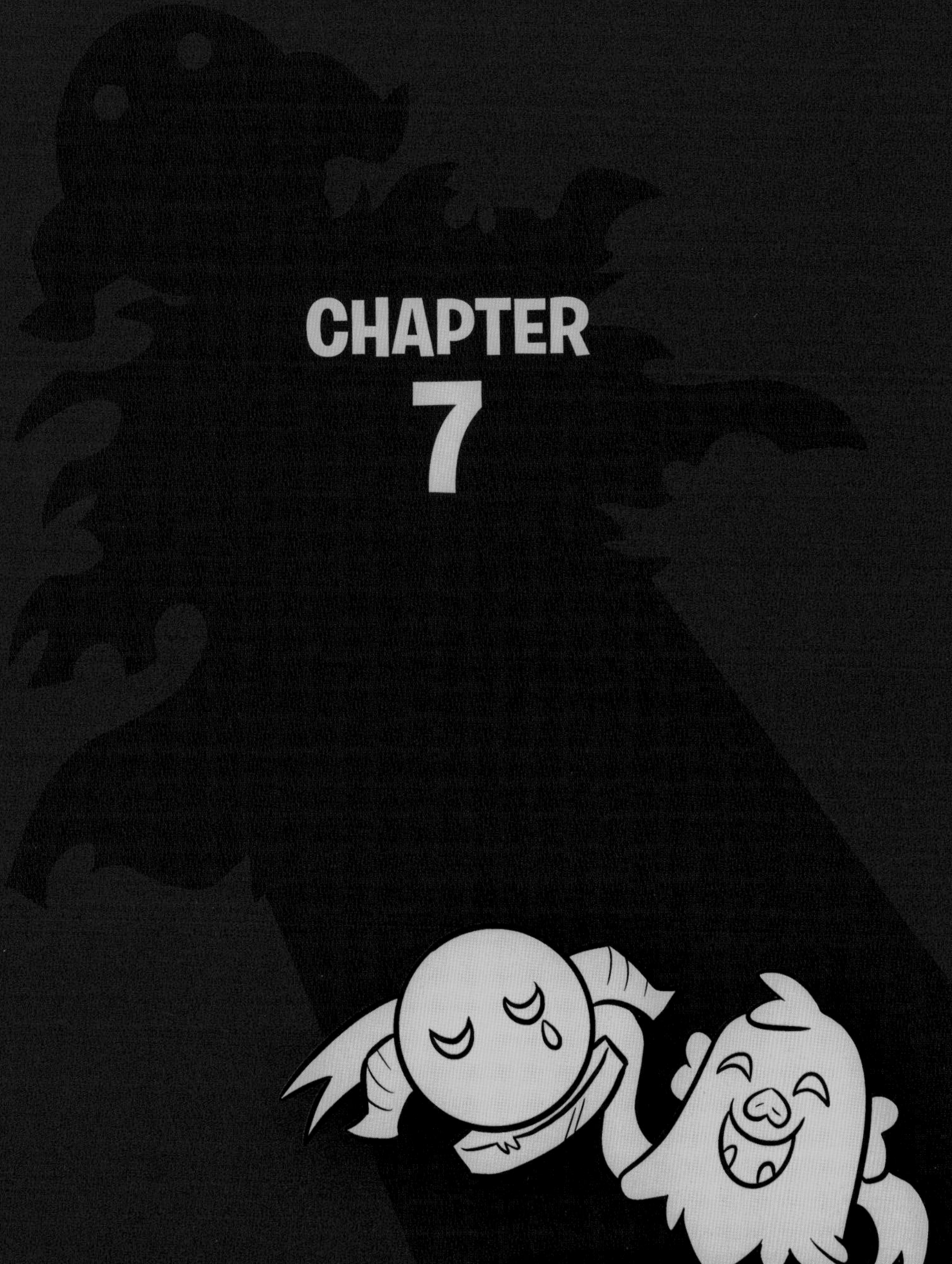

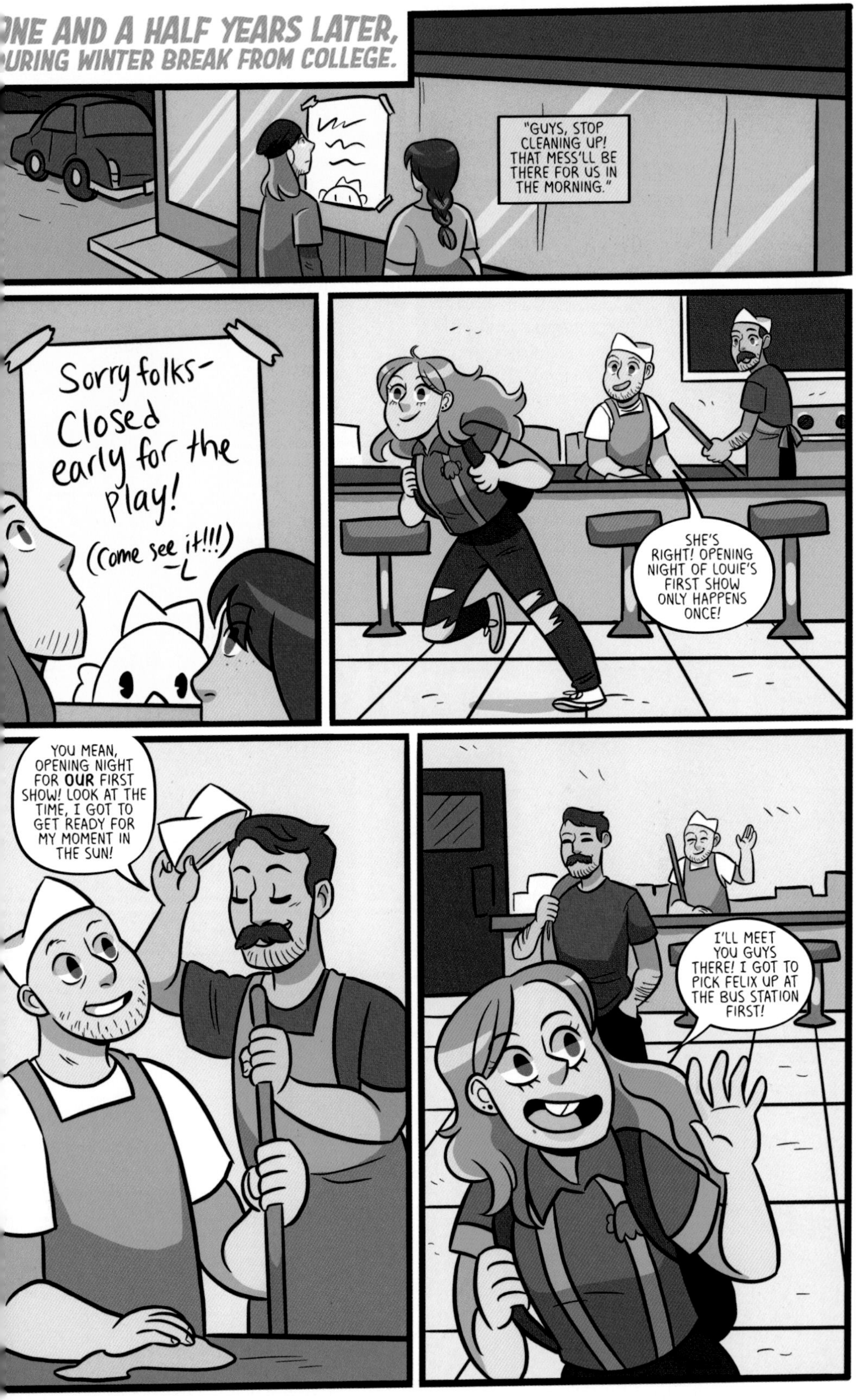
ONE AND A HALF YEARS LATER, DURING WINTER BREAK FROM COLLEGE.
"GUYS, STOP CLEANING UP! THAT MESS'LL BE THERE FOR US IN THE MORNING."
Sorry folks- Closed early for the play! (Come see it!!!) -L
SHE'S RIGHT! OPENING NIGHT OF LOUIE'S FIRST SHOW ONLY HAPPENS ONCE!
YOU MEAN, OPENING NIGHT FOR **OUR** FIRST SHOW! LOOK AT THE TIME, I GOT TO GET READY FOR MY MOMENT IN THE SUN!
I'LL MEET YOU GUYS THERE! I GOT TO PICK FELIX UP AT THE BUS STATION FIRST!

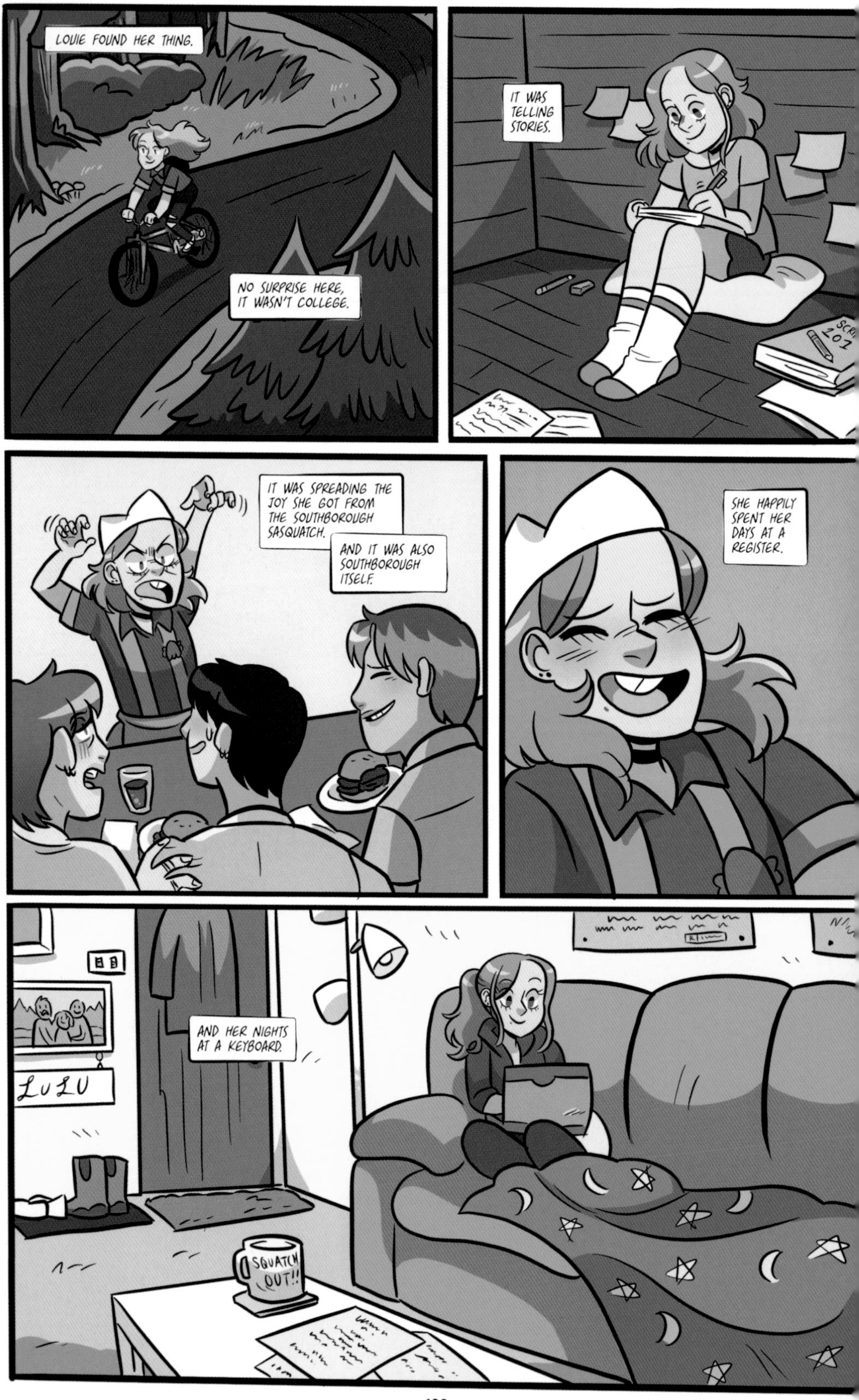

LOUIE FOUND HER THING.
NO SURPRISE HERE, IT WASN'T COLLEGE.
IT WAS TELLING STORIES.
IT WAS SPREADING THE JOY SHE GOT FROM THE SOUTHBOROUGH SASQUATCH.
AND IT WAS ALSO SOUTHBOROUGH ITSELF.
SHE HAPPILY SPENT HER DAYS AT A REGISTER.
AND HER NIGHTS AT A KEYBOARD.
LULU
SQUATCH OUT!!

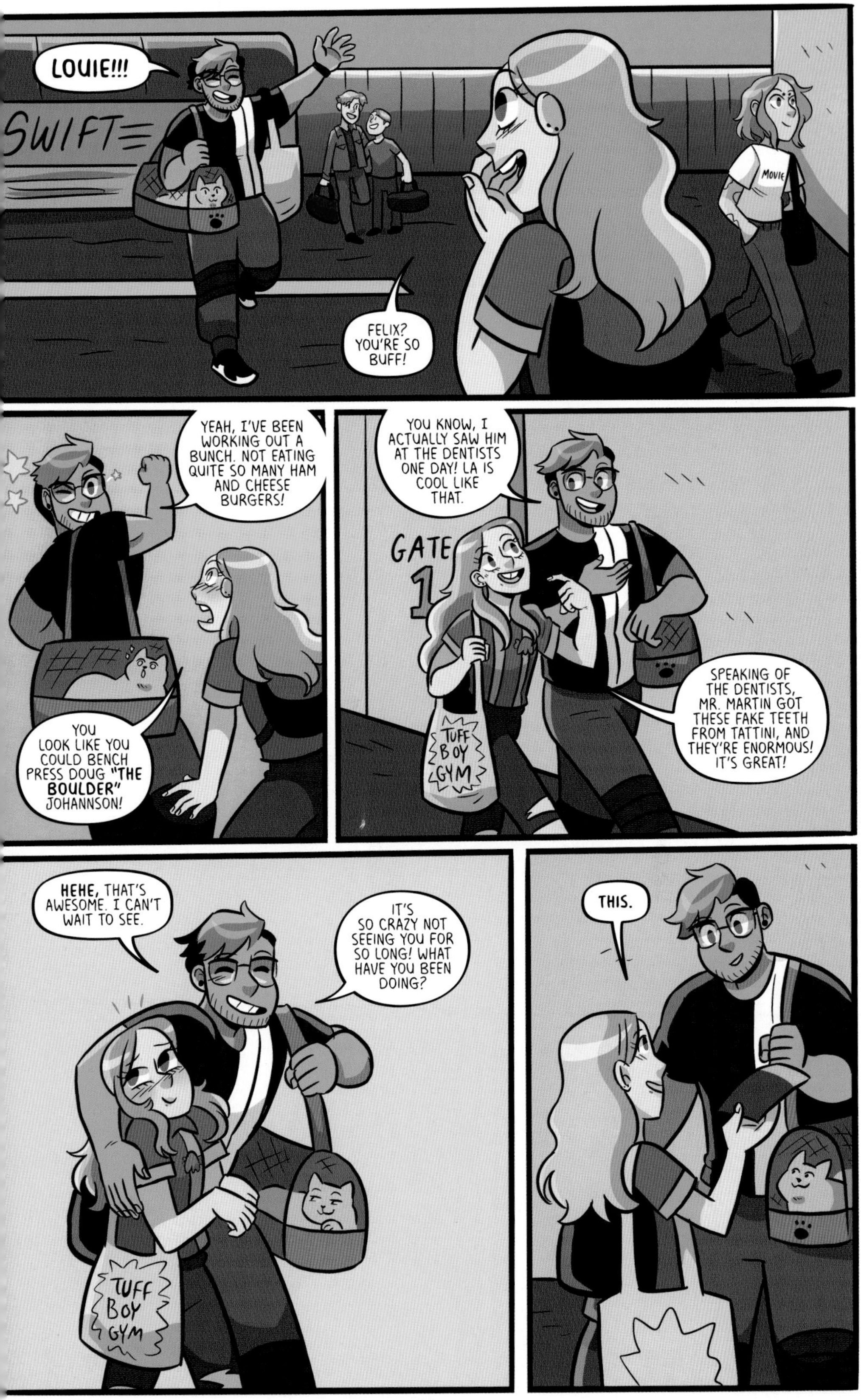
LOUIE!!!
SWIFT
FELIX? YOU'RE SO BUFF!
MOVIE
YEAH, I'VE BEEN WORKING OUT A BUNCH. NOT EATING QUITE SO MANY HAM AND CHEESE BURGERS!
YOU LOOK LIKE YOU COULD BENCH PRESS DOUG "THE BOULDER" JOHANNSON!
YOU KNOW, I ACTUALLY SAW HIM AT THE DENTISTS ONE DAY! LA IS COOL LIKE THAT.
GATE 1
TUFF BOY GYM
SPEAKING OF THE DENTISTS, MR. MARTIN GOT THESE FAKE TEETH FROM TATTINI, AND THEY'RE ENORMOUS! IT'S GREAT!
HEHE, THAT'S AWESOME. I CAN'T WAIT TO SEE.
IT'S SO CRAZY NOT SEEING YOU FOR SO LONG! WHAT HAVE YOU BEEN DOING?
TUFF BOY GYM
THIS.

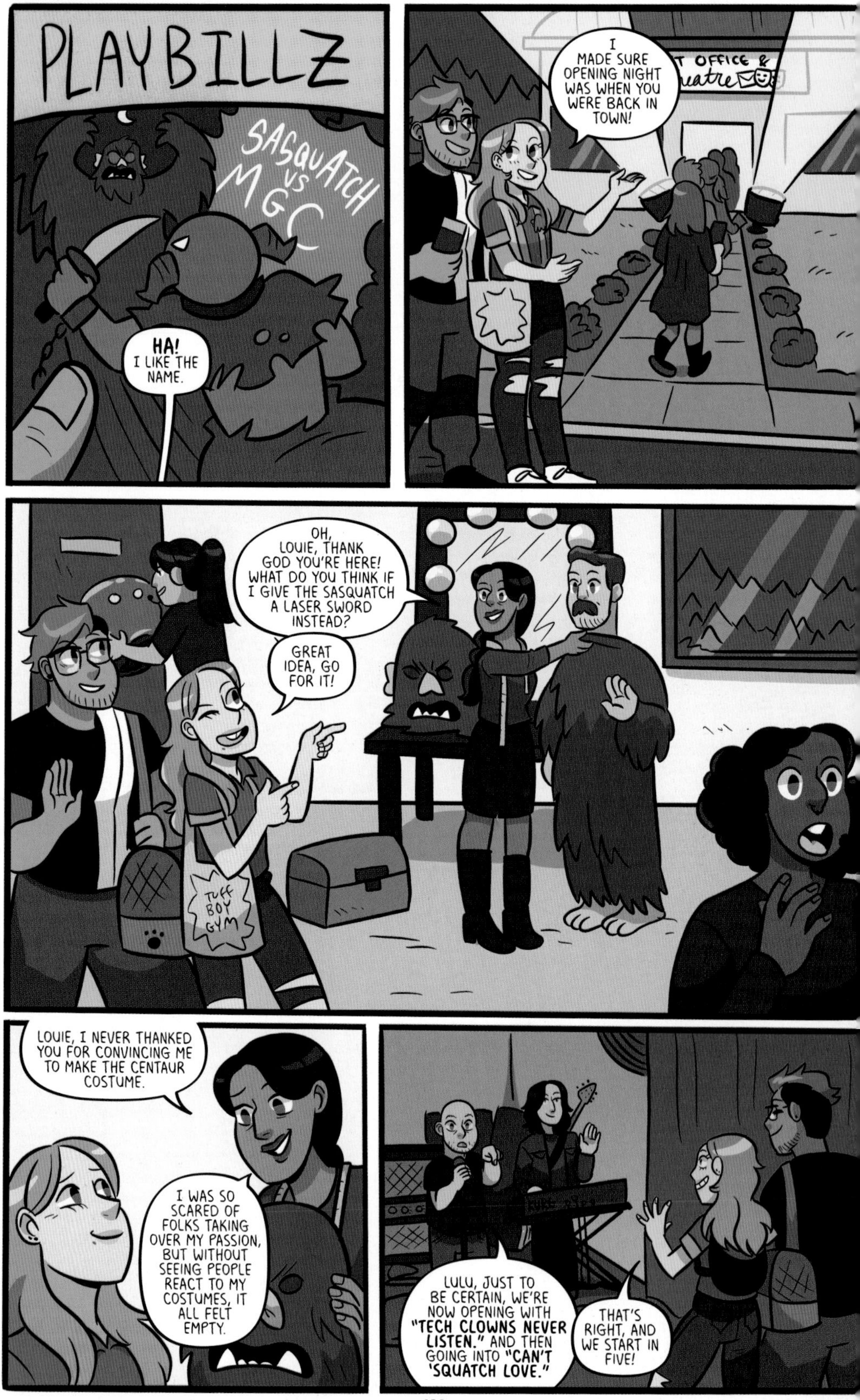
PLAYBILLZ
SASQUATCH VS MGC
HA! I LIKE THE NAME.
I MADE SURE OPENING NIGHT WAS WHEN YOU WERE BACK IN TOWN!
OH, LOUIE, THANK GOD YOU'RE HERE! WHAT DO YOU THINK IF I GIVE THE SASQUATCH A LASER SWORD INSTEAD?
GREAT IDEA, GO FOR IT!
TUFF BOY GYM
LOUIE, I NEVER THANKED YOU FOR CONVINCING ME TO MAKE THE CENTAUR COSTUME.
I WAS SO SCARED OF FOLKS TAKING OVER MY PASSION, BUT WITHOUT SEEING PEOPLE REACT TO MY COSTUMES, IT ALL FELT EMPTY.
LULU, JUST TO BE CERTAIN, WE'RE NOW OPENING WITH "TECH CLOWNS NEVER LISTEN." AND THEN GOING INTO "CAN'T 'SQUATCH LOVE."
THAT'S RIGHT, AND WE START IN FIVE!

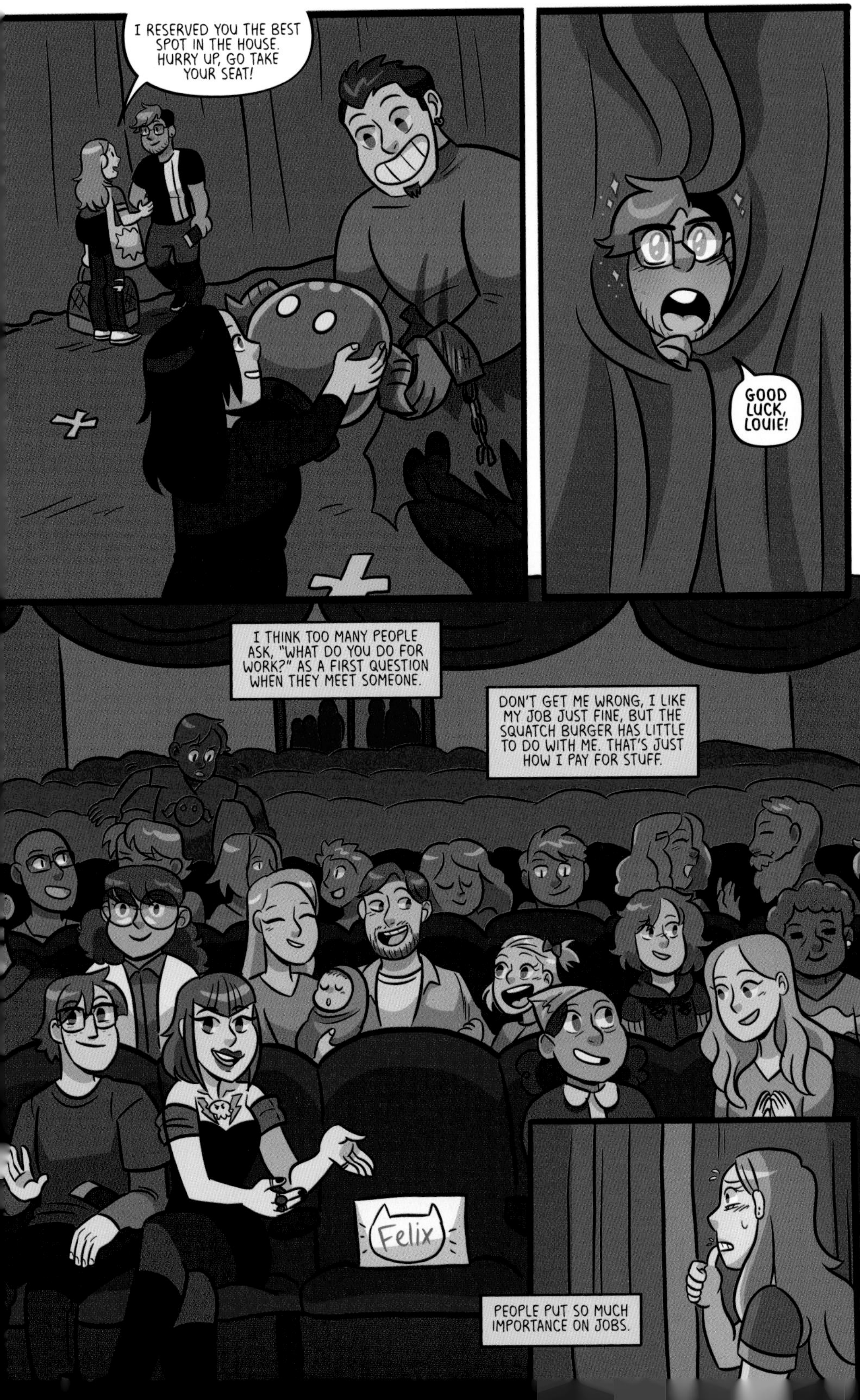

I RESERVED YOU THE BEST SPOT IN THE HOUSE. HURRY UP, GO TAKE YOUR SEAT!
GOOD LUCK, LOUIE!
I THINK TOO MANY PEOPLE ASK, "WHAT DO YOU DO FOR WORK?" AS A FIRST QUESTION WHEN THEY MEET SOMEONE.
DON'T GET ME WRONG, I LIKE MY JOB JUST FINE, BUT THE SQUATCH BURGER HAS LITTLE TO DO WITH ME. THAT'S JUST HOW I PAY FOR STUFF.
Felix
PEOPLE PUT SO MUCH IMPORTANCE ON JOBS.

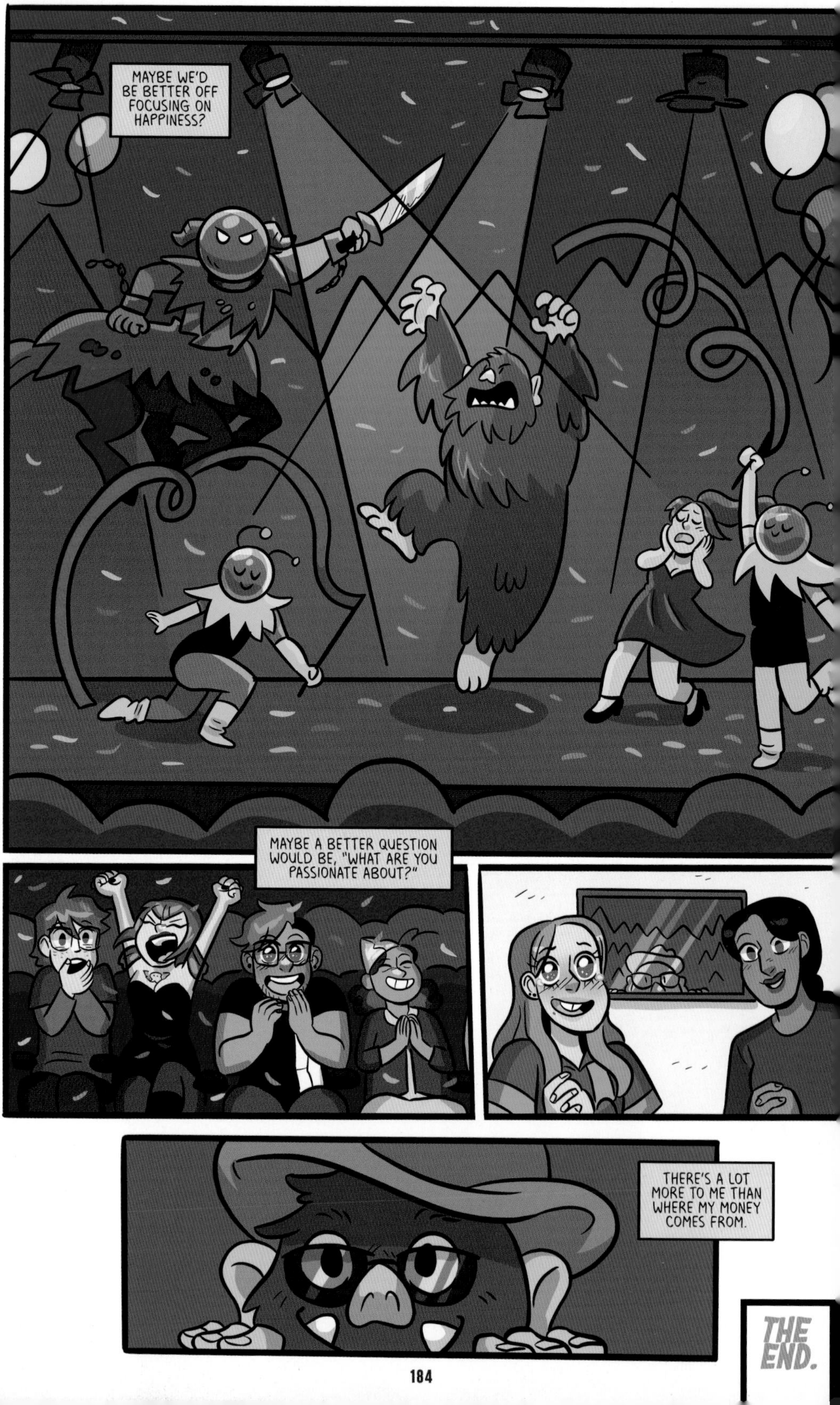
MAYBE WE'D BE BETTER OFF FOCUSING ON HAPPINESS?
MAYBE A BETTER QUESTION WOULD BE, "WHAT ARE YOU PASSIONATE ABOUT?"
THERE'S A LOT MORE TO ME THAN WHERE MY MONEY COMES FROM.
THE END.

CHARACTER SKETCHES

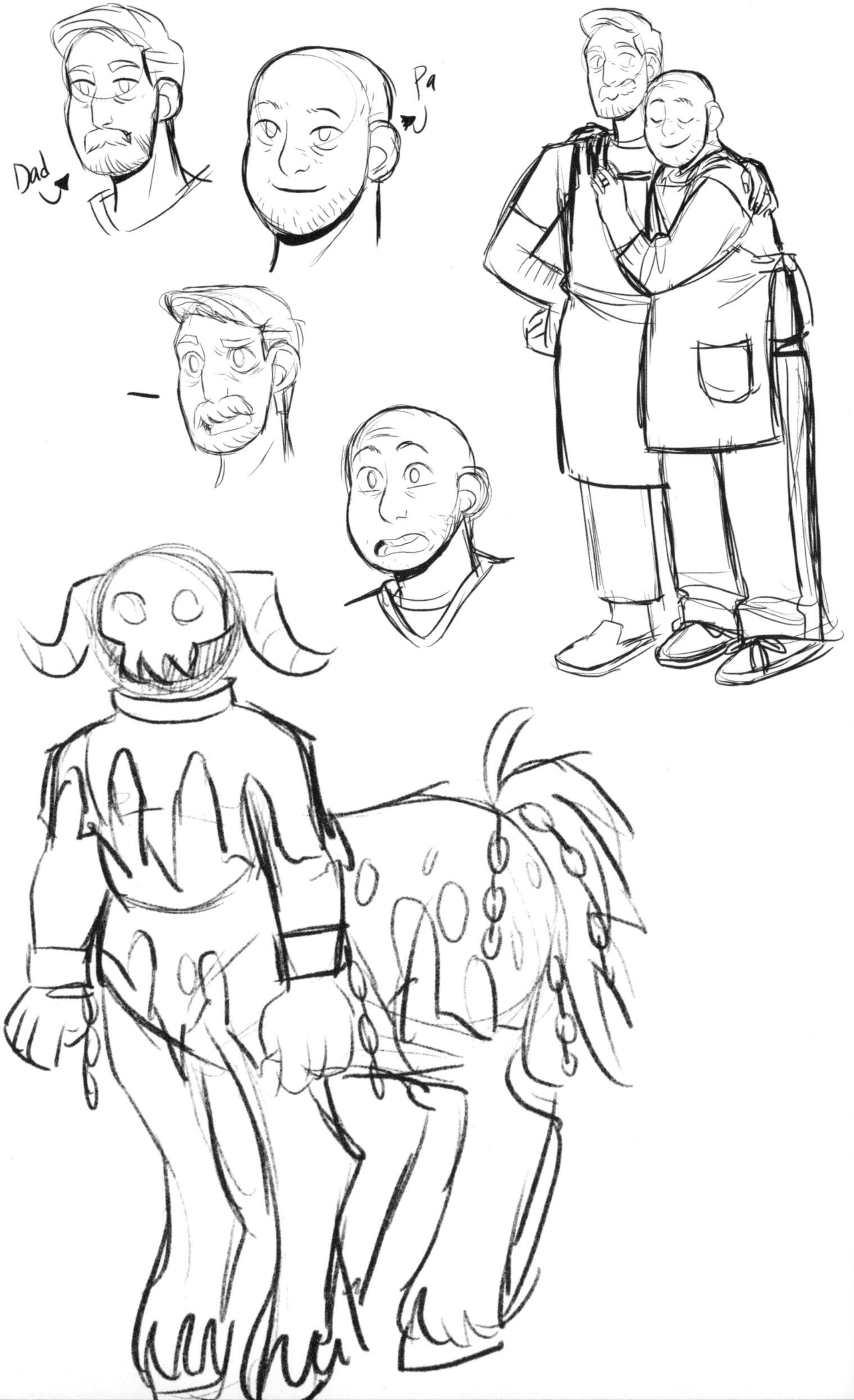
Dad
Pa

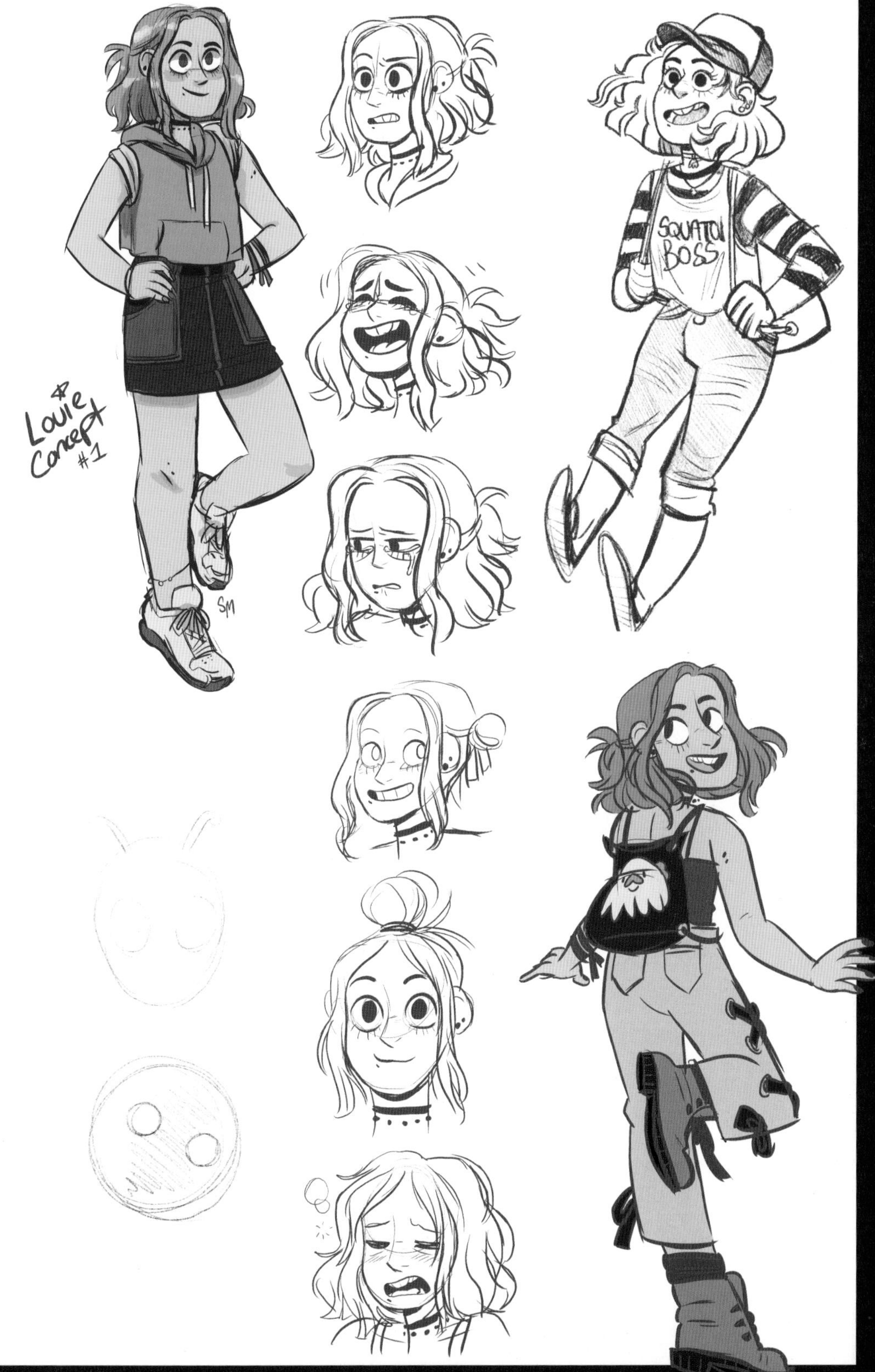

Louie Concept #1
SM
SQUATCH BOSS

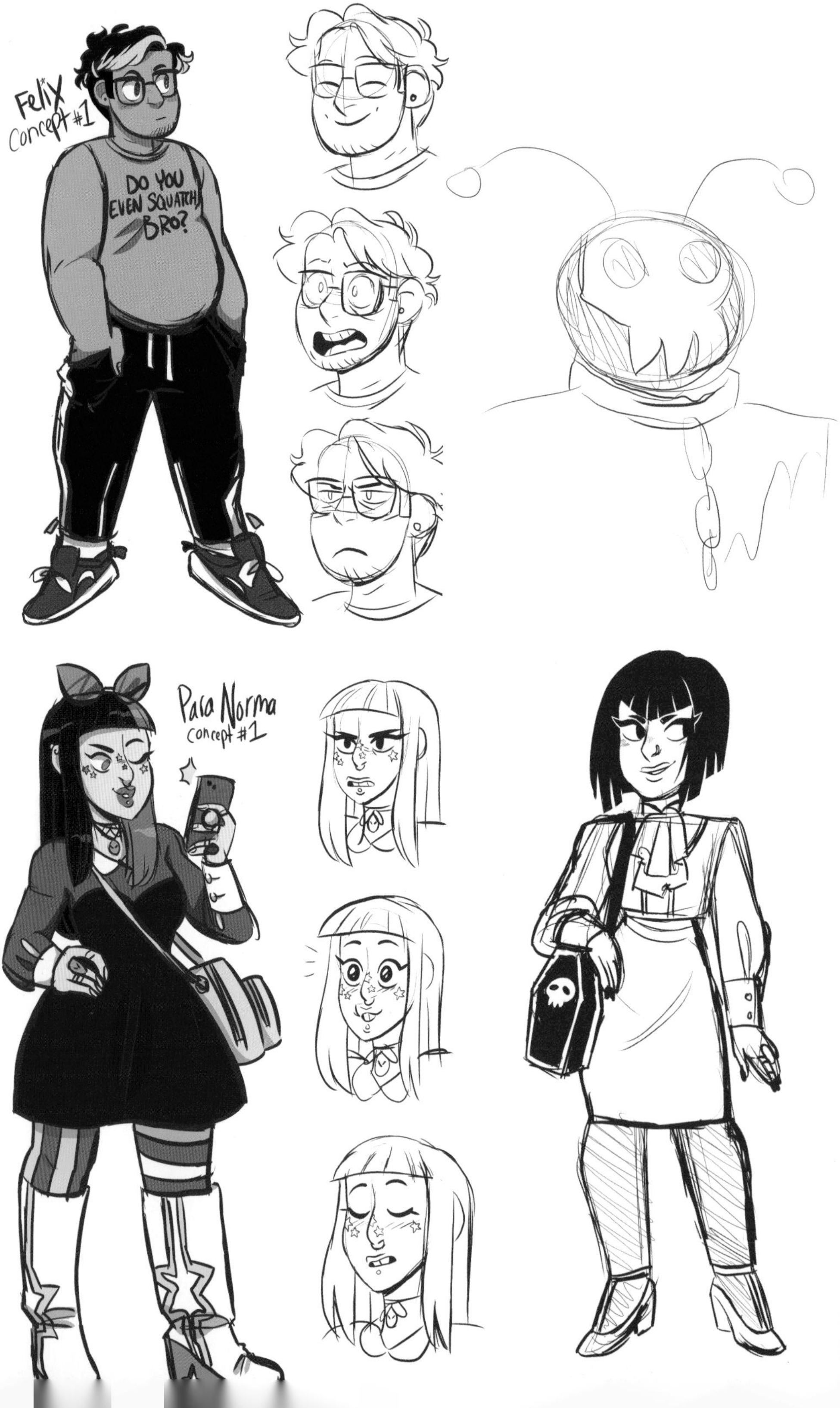
Felix concept #1
DO YOU EVEN SQUATCH BRO?
Para Norma concept #1

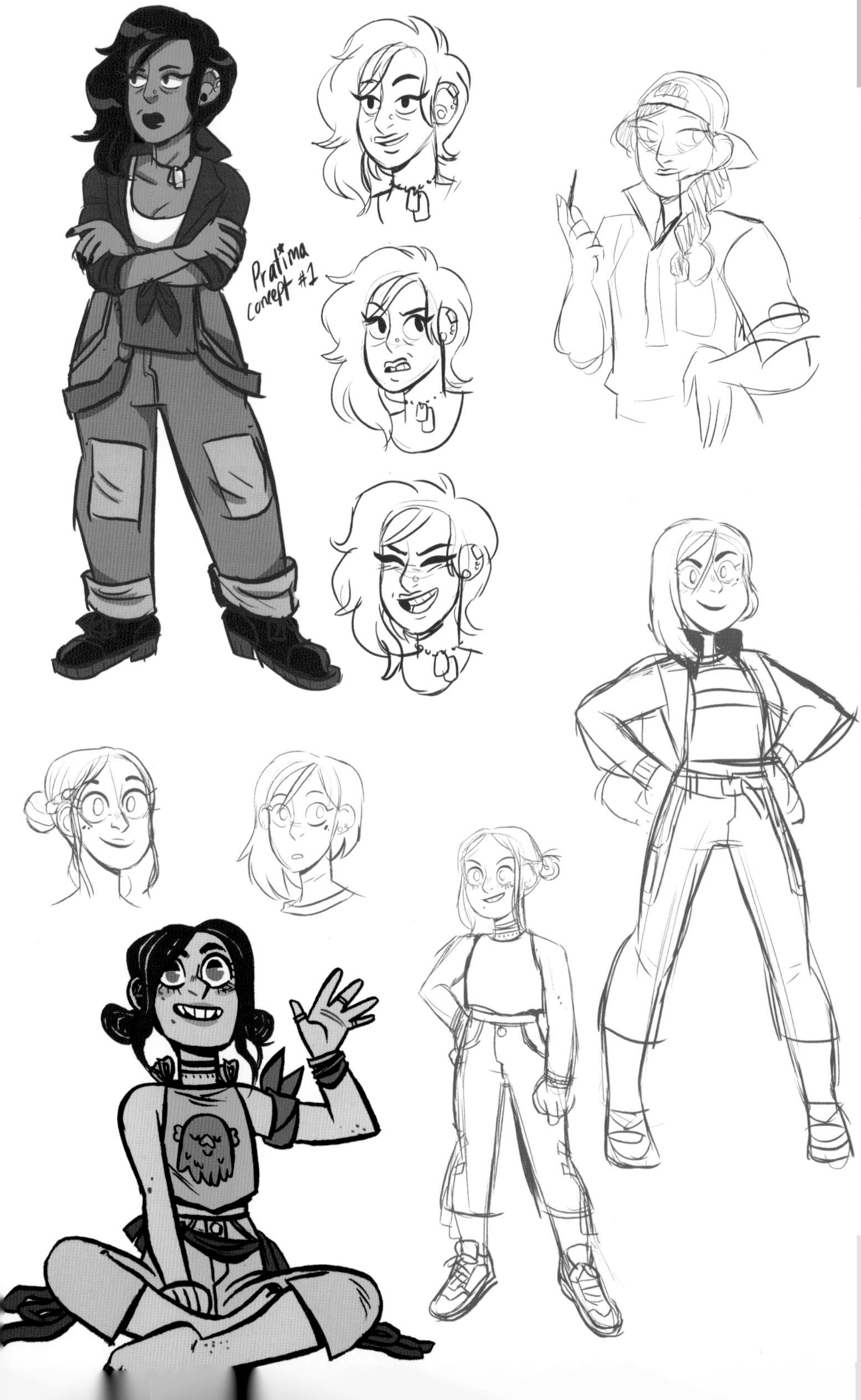
Pratima concept #1

ACKNOWLEDGMENTS

Thanks to Grace Scheipeter for treating Louie's story with such sincere care. To Andrea Colvin and every other person who said "yes." Thanks to El Rio SF for the inspiration. My wife, Blair, for her support. Thanks to my grandma for being Louie's namesake. Maria Vicente at P.S. Literary for being the best agent in the world. And last, but certainly not least, thank you to Steph for agreeing to work with me and for being the best collaborator ever!!

–Mat Heagerty

I'd like to thank my ma and pa for supporting my artistic career since I was a kid, and my brother and sister-in-law for cheering me on no matter the distance. A big thanks to my best friends Sam, Becky, Abe, Mikaila, and Kristen for reminding me to breathe on a daily basis. Thank you to our amazing *Martian Ghost Centaur* team: my editor, Grace, for being so patient and caring during the whole process; our amazing letterer, Hassan, who tied everything together; and all the folks who believed in the book at Oni. But perhaps my biggest thanks goes out to Mat for trusting his amazing story and characters with me; He truly is one of the greatest friends and mentors I've had. (I'd thank my cats again, but they already got top billing in the dedication, and I don't want to inflate their egos further.)

–Steph Mided

Mat Heagerty lives in the Bay Area with his wife, daughter, son, and black lab. For over a decade, he's bartended at a really special bar in San Francisco called El Rio. Mat's dyslexic and struggled a bunch in school, but now he writes rad comics like *Unplugged and Unpopular* and this one!

You can find him on twitter @matheagerty or on his website, matheagerty.com.

Photo by: Blair Heagerty

Steph Mided is a comic artist and illustrator from Chicago, Illinois who loves all things comedic, cute, and colorful. When she isn't working on comics, she spends her time collecting records and stopping her two cats from spilling drinks all over her desk.

For more of her work, visit stephmided.com or find her on twitter @noctart.

MORE GREAT READS BY ONI PRESS

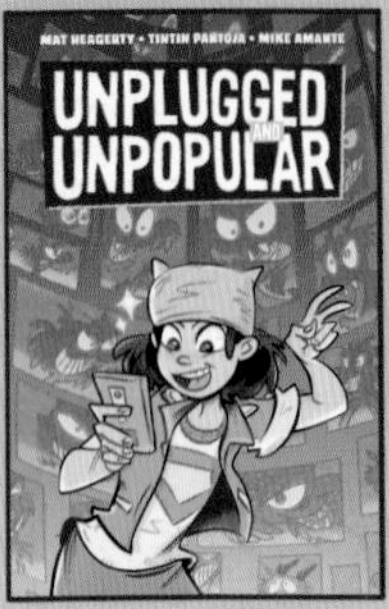
MAT HEAGERTY • TINTIN PANTOJA • MIKE AMANTE
UNPLUGGED AND UNPOPULAR

Unplugged and Unpopular

by Mat Heagerty and Tintin Pantoja

After Erin Song's parents ban her from using her phone, TV, Internet and all her screens, she soon discovers mysterious, strange creatures and must foil their plot to take over Earth in this hilarious sci-fi graphic novel for tweens.

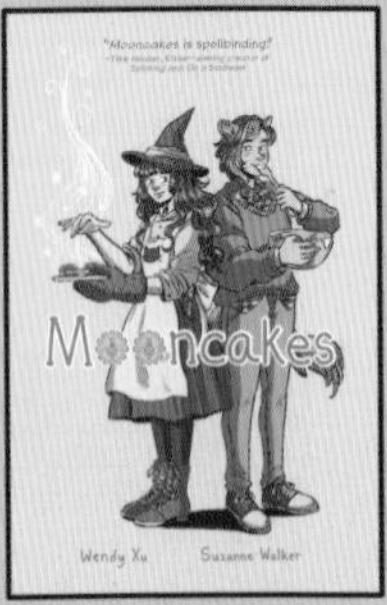
Mooncakes
Wendy Xu
Suzanne Walker

Mooncakes

by Suzanne Walker and Wendy Xu

When teenage witch Nova's childhood friend, Tam, moves back to town, the two discover a sinister group plotting to harness Tam's werewolf powers for their own gain.

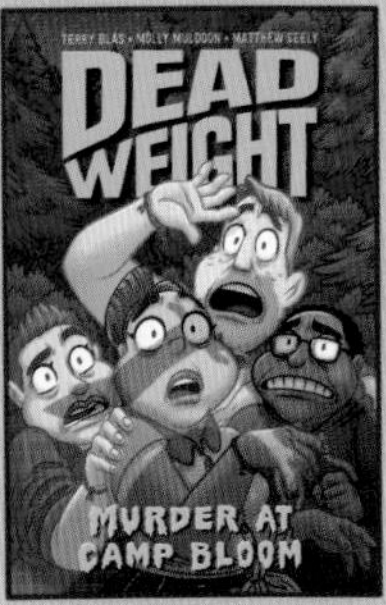
TERRY BLAS • MOLLY MULDOON • MATTHEW SEELY
DEAD WEIGHT
MURDER AT CAMP BLOOM

Dead Weight

by Terry Blas, Molly Muldoon, and Matthew Seely

Dead Weight is a hilarious story of a diverse group of young sleuths who ban together to solve a murder mystery while at a weight-loss camp.

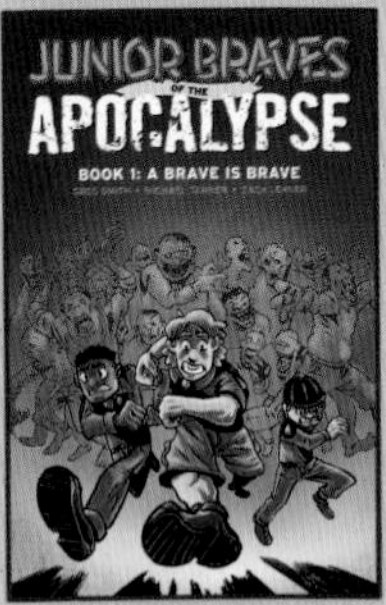
JUNIOR BRAVES OF THE APOCALYPSE
BOOK 1: A BRAVE IS BRAVE

Junior Braves of the Apocalypse

by Greg Smith, Michael Tanner, and Zach Lehner

The Junior Braves of Tribe 65 return from a camping trip to find swarms of bloodthirsty mutants have overrun their town, bringing death and destruction everywhere they go! These plucky kids must use all their scouting talents, combined smarts, and teamwork to survive the end of the world!